# Dark Heart of the Earth

a novel by
Jacob Russell Dring

1

Of course he was grateful for the clear weather, after nearly an entire week of hard rain. Although, most would argue the opposite, relieved about the precipitation in a region of southern California that was one of the driest in the country. As he left the Miramar Base where he worked, he was at least glad that he didn't live in Calipatria. Elevation wise, the lowest city in the western hemisphere, much less the nation. It was hardly a two-hour drive east of his nice community of Tierrasanta, but quite a change in scenery.

Meanwhile, a five-hour drive northbound would land him at the lowest point of elevation on the continent—Badwater Basin, Death Valley.

"The people who used to name things were so cynical," Bastian had said shortly after moving here from Houston, eight years ago.

"Easy for *you* to say, Mr. Thur*good*," his wife had replied. They were in the presence of their daughter, who at the time was only two, and simply chuckled.

Sebastian Thurgood could recall the moment as if it had been yesterday. Little Eliza went from amused to hungry and crying in a matter of seconds. Everything that preceded that, however, had been just shy of sublime. And, not long after, that same joy resumed.

Bastian was never ungrateful for his family, and knew that he would be a lost soul without them.

Work, however, had its moments of monotony that he couldn't ignore. Today had been just another day at the office, although since his promotion three years ago, he was promised less time at his desk and more hands-on experience. The type that utilized his twenty years of military service, from two consecutive tours as a Ranger and just over a decade as a Navy SEAL.

Bastian smiled through his thick, grizzled beard and gave the security guard at the parking lot gate a friendly wave as he drove under the raised barrier.

*I bet you're not as grateful for these clear skies, Benny*, Bastian thought to himself.

Benny Leeman was going on his ninth year as the security guard at Miramar, pushing sixty and somehow seldom complaining. He was a gentle giant kind of guy, not too unlike 6'2" Bastian, at least demeanor wise. Benny was almost as rotund as he was tall, and would say that he blamed the vending machines on the grounds for that.

If Bastian had to stay in that concrete hut of a poorly ventilated security booth for nine years, Monday through Friday, on ten-hour shifts, he imagined he would pack on a few…hundred…pounds, too.

As it were, Bastian was grateful for a high metabolism and the motivation to consistently work out. It had long since become almost as much of a passion as it was a habit, inflicted into his lifestyle through so many years in the military. Being a SEAL for twelve years practically enforced it upon him, infecting Bastian with a rigorous exercise regimen that he couldn't shake even if he wanted to.

Fortunately, in a way, he seldom did. He liked maintaining his healthy, robust figure, especially when he was pushing forty-seven. His birthday was in two months, and knowing that he had the build of a middle-weight champion half his age was extremely satisfying.

Maggie Thurgood would have to agree.

He met her just outside of Houston, sixteen years ago. There was a reason that neither of them believed in love at first sight, or other fairytale clichés. She was the friend of a fellow SEAL's fiancé, and while the physical attraction from both parties was undeniable, the magnetism wasn't complete.

Bastian hated recalling how ignorant and unruly he used to be, and how he used to let alcohol get the better of him. But, six months from now marked fourteen years of sobriety. And, even more importantly—however the two kind of went hand-in-hand—his and Maggie's thirteenth anniversary.

On his drive home, which was usually fifteen minutes around this time, half past four, Bastian tried to focus on the good. No matter how monotonous, disappointing, or even erroneous his day at work was, he wouldn't let it corrupt his mood once he got home.

He owed this much—and more—to Maggie and Eliza. Especially since moving here was based on his job, and while still a family decision, he knew that, ultimately, it was on his shoulders. Maggie was a country girl to the core, but she adapted to the city life rather quickly, once they moved to San Diego upon their fourth year together. He was still a SEAL at the time, but that didn't last long, especially once Eliza was born. He started to reach out to his superiors, demurely seeking a 'safer' position, while yearning not to let his decorated experience go to waste.

*And oh boy, what a change of gears*, he mused in hindsight. There was no regret taking it, but he would be lying if he said that he didn't miss combat, or even training exercises with his comrades. The dedication, the exhilaration, but most of all, the purpose and reward. Helping others, whether directly or indirectly, but always actionably.

It was in his blood.

It definitely made Maggie's fireman fantasy easier to fulfill, whenever they were feeling eccentric.

That notion, paired with a few fond memories, made Bastian chuckle to himself and even blush. His pale cheeks turning pink was difficult to discern with all of his hair, a thick forestation of black and gray and white, the latter gradually becoming more prominent. He wasn't terribly fond of this, but again, counting his blessings, he was thankful to still have his hair at this age, not to mention enough for his scalp *and* his face.

"Oh, and another thing about this promotion," Deputy Director Andrew Bowman had told him, during a meeting in his office following Bastian's pressing requests for more hands-on opportunities, about three years ago, "despite what you might think, shaving isn't necessary."

This had lit up Bastian's brown eyes at the time. He was relieved, and surprised. The majority of personnel with Bravo Clearance were clean-shaven and kept their hair short. Even the women. As relieved as he was to hear this, especially from the Deputy Director himself, Bastian couldn't resist inquiring further.

"I just figured…with a lot of the energy-based testing done in Bravo, and the other ordnance—"

Bowman, a heavyset man with a dark blonde 70's mustache as the last semblance of hair above his neck, was a firm public speaker and despite his satirical appearance was never one to mock. Directly or otherwise. He had a respectable tenure and experience in the CIA before DARPA plucked him to work at Miramar.

With a simple wave of his large hand, the backs of which were hairy, albeit blonde and hard to see, Bowman hushed Bastian who, in spite of his imposing physique and ruggedly handsome appearance, usually emanated a modest demeanor. Sometimes, one might say timid, especially at Miramar, as he wasn't used to having a desk job, even at that point in time, being there for three years.

At least he had not been so diffident when requesting a more proactive opportunity.

"As I said," Bowman reiterated firmly, nonetheless with a microscopic smirk beneath his bushy mustache, "*despite what you might think…*"

"Apologies, sir." Bastian cleared his throat and stood straight up, hands behind his back, his suit feeling particularly snug in this very moment. "If you grant me this opportunity, I'd be grateful, and indebted to you, and to CHERI. You can expect nothing less than every breath of my dedication—"

"You Navy guys sure do know how to talk, huh?" Bowman simpered and this time waved at Bastian more casually. "At ease. Take a seat. Let's discuss some of the details, then I'll let you outta here early, so you can celebrate."

What followed was an eager, strong handshake and then a loosening of Bastian's tie before he sat down. He looked forward to not having to wear a suit anymore, not even a button-down necessarily, as long as it had some air of professionalism. Slacks, though, never cargo pants or shorts. Less pockets the better.

Usually, for Bravo personnel, they changed once they started their shifts, depending on the schedule for the day.

As he drove, Bastian daydreamt about the better times in his current position, a promotion from being a weapons designer and consultant to one who actually tests equipment and offers more intimate analysis. He had overseen major changes to innovative equipment and weapons over the last three years, feeling more purposeful than his first three at Miramar, ordnance anticipating military distribution in the next four years, two at the earliest.

Remembering those days filled him with satisfaction and motivation. However, they had recently become few and far between, instead plagued by the more common experience, which was one of monotony, disinterest, and frustration.

"No more pushing papers, Navy boy," Bastian mumbled to himself as he drove his truck off the highway and onto a more suburban road. He altered his deep, hoarse voice to parody Bowman's. It was cruder than reality, but it satisfied his inner child. "No, you'll only be pushing cartridges into a magazine, or armor onto a carapace. Blah-blah-blah."

Of course, Bastian knew not every day at the facility could be exciting and thorough. Being Delta Clearance, which is where he had been previously, was the top of the bottom, and being Alpha was reserved for superiors like Bowman, who hardly did anything but oversee and approve or disapprove projects as they developed. Alpha Clearance staff answered directly to DARPA executives in Arlington, Virginia, where *their* headquarters were. And those folks answered to the Department of Defense, privy to presidential matters.

It was a long, complex chain of command, but Bastian knew his place, and was grateful to have the spot he had secured. The pay was monumentally better than being a Ranger or even a SEAL, and significantly safer. Virtually devoid of danger, or at least it had been before he took the promotion.

While Maggie only knew the limited amount that she acknowledged was a given considering that her husband worked beneath DARPA, she wasn't bothered by it. Or at least she didn't let on that she was.

"As long as you're not in the line of fire," she had insisted upon him six years ago, when they initially moved to this small community of Tierrasanta, "then

I'm content. And if you're happy with it, then I'm more than content. Then I'm happy, too."

He would do anything to make her happy, so he thanked his Navy superior for making the right calls to get him hired at the CHERI facility in Miramar, and never stopped regularly counting his blessings for how things lined up to this day.

"Just tell me one thing, though," Maggie had demanded, hands on her hips. He sighed gutturally and kneaded his brow, looking up between his fingers to see her grinning, almost maniacally. She tried to ask the question in an austere voice, versus laughing. "What the *fuck* do DARPA and CHERI stand for?"

Bastian's demeanor had loosened up and he threw his arms around his wife, swinging her around like a ragdoll, pumps falling off her feet. She shrieked and giggled, holding on. They landed on their bed, which was quality enough not to enforce a painful impact, and after a few bounces he found himself supine, while she sat up, her knees bent, straddling his pelvis.

He was still in his suit, home from work, three years ago, after discussing the promotion with Bowman, but not yet confirming it. He wouldn't, not without his wife's approval, which was more than reasonable to Bowman, but a given.

"Maybe I don't wanna tell you," Bastian had smirked, feigning a diabolical gesture, as his callused hands rode up Maggie's waist, beneath her blouse. She was not the petite woman she had been when they first met, and there wasn't a single inch of her body that he would alter at that very moment. To this day, he was more attracted to her than he had ever been, to the woman she had become, both physically and psychologically. Spiritually, her youth remained intact, as it had in him, too, and together it was an insoluble union.

Maggie laughed, almost madly, and tilted her head back. Her recently straightened, blonde hair dangled above her shoulders. She then leaned forward, palms pressing into his robust chest, evident even through his suit. The angle of her arms barred his hands from elevating any further up her blouse, unless of course he applied force.

"Nuh-uh," she said, tongue curling up the front of her incisors. "You don't get to play that card. That's mine, dear."

Sebastian grinned and loosened up. He even retracted his arms, elbows out, and cupped his hands under his head. This untucked his dress shirt from his slacks and exposed his darkly haired abdomen.

"So, mister. Are you gonna spill the beans or make me...interrogate you?" Her hands lowered, but her green eyes never left his.

Bastian knew she wasn't alluding to something sexy. No, she of all people knew his gravest weakness—worse than water-boarding, or so he claimed, a joke he made although he knew better, having experienced it once fourteen years ago. Nonetheless, she didn't need to know that.

Before she began tickling him that day on the bed, Bastian forfeited his breath to a panicked laugh, and ultimately wrestled his wife onto her back. Now it was he who hovered over her, petting the strands of stray hair from her face.

"DARPA—Defense Advanced Research Projects Agency."

"Sounds like broken English to me," she whispered.

He smiled but continued, his voice almost robotic, albeit smoother than usual, and his eyes never not tracing the filaments in Maggie's green irises.

"CHERI—Central Hub of Experimental Research and Innovations."

"Where's the O and A?"

Bastian grinned momentarily. "I think the FBI is missing an agent. Are *you* not telling me something, Mrs. Thurgood?"

She shrugged lackadaisically. "It's top secret."

"What if I'm a spy?" Bastian widened his eyes, imitating a surprised child. "Oh, my."

She chuckled and then put on a serious face.

"I don't buy it."

"All the better," he added, and began to work his hands under her crossed arms, unbuttoning her shirt. "Easier for me to discover those...*top secrets*."

She giggled and wrapped her legs around him.

A long, blaring car horn behind Bastian's truck jarred him from his visceral daydream. He cursed under his breath and waved a hand out the window, a casual gesture of fault and apology. He drove through the green light, just before it turned yellow, and he gritted his teeth, mouthing "sorry" into the rearview mirror, as if the other driver—and the line of cars behind them—could understand.

He decided to turn off the main road and take a series of back routes for the sake of those behind him, at least. The people of Tierrasanta were modest seeds, but nobody was flawless. Even the refined Sebastian Thurgood had his baser moments, whether they were vented on the road or at the range.

The important thing was to not let those emotions burden him at home. He wanted to make sure that the Thurgood residence never became a house more than it was a home.

Maggie and Eliza helped with that.

Helped remind him of his humanity, and that the twenty years of his life spent in active combat had its roots in good intentions. And that even now, despite not squeezing a trigger downrange, he was still making a difference, serving and protecting the welfare of his country. It wasn't a pure, incorruptible nation, but it was undeniably one worth fighting for—especially the people occupying its soil, and those hopeful of finding futures within its borders.

These thoughts contributed to the fruition of a calmer, more comforting mindset as he neared home sweet home.

It was a tried and true mental process, especially when leaving work dissatisfied. Today had been particularly disappointing, but again, he knew better than to be so impatient. He and Maggie both had made it almost a motto to Eliza, since she was seven—that "patience is a virtue," as true as that statement had always been.

And no circumstances could change that.

Heeding his own advice, Bastian simply looked forward to the near future. Soon the INFERNO Project would exit the prototype phase and its confidentiality wouldn't exist, letting him gloat about it to Maggie without breaching his NDA. He highly anticipated that day, not just selfishly for himself, as he acted as the lead designer for the concept since before he took up the promotion, and shortly after that was encouraged to become its primary tester. Various volunteers, all retired infantry units, had recorded time in it, but ultimately Bastian had logged the most hours, amounting to entire months, while others allotted days at most.

It was his pride and joy, which made him sensitive to how long it was taking to reach the latter stages of development. As if stuck in a sort of limbo over the last few weeks, part of Bastian feared that the INFERNO Project might never see the light of the public eye, let alone even the next military convention eight months from now.

"It's ready," he mumbled to himself, shaking his head. The base of his fist drummed the arch of the steering wheel, not irately, but meditatively. A pensive gesture of frustration. "It's *been* fucking ready…three weeks now, Bowman. Put it in a live-fire exercise and I'll give you my *word* that it—"

Bastian had grown a little more zealous and vocal about the issue than he would have liked in the moment. In immediate hindsight, he was grateful for the interruption—the monologic rant was detrimental to his previously acquired 'Zen.' And especially so close to home.

However, the nature of the interruption wasn't exactly something he could be openly thankful for. Hopefully just a small quake, or an aftershock of one that didn't cause any damage wherever it originated. The tremor was felt through the road and the thick tires of his pickup truck, briefly vibrating the leather wheel in his hands. After the fleeting deviation in his steering, he braked on the backroad, no cars behind him, and glanced out the window to his left. A parked vehicle shook for an instant and its alarm went off, as did a few in the surrounding suburbia.

Whatever the source of the tremor was, Bastian wondered whether or not it would be on the news. If it was in fact localized, with no linking quake, it wouldn't make any headlines, even in their small community.

*Wouldn't be the first time*, he thought, as this was southern California afterall.

He shook his head and sighed, then proceeded on his drive, eager to get home, and let the clarity of his mind achieve its zenith. He longed to stride into his wife's arms, to kiss his daughter on the forehead, and count his blessings in the flesh.

Numerically, two was a small number.

Spiritually, for lack of a better word, it was more than enough; it was immeasurable—his love for them, and theirs for him.

With this in mind, easing any proverbial weights on his shoulders or in his chest, Bastian breathed easier, and entirely forgot that his day had been disappointing or frustrating. At that point, pulling into his sloped concrete driveway, lush vegetation in the front yard of the two-story house, Bastian didn't even know what those words meant.

All he could feel was gratitude and a certain kind of mortal, modest serenity.

## 2

Bastian entered the house in normal fashion. Announcing his arrival to Maggie, who wasn't far from the foyer when he walked in. After shutting the door behind him, he was relieved to feel the coolness of air-conditioning as opposed to the dry heat outside. He turned to face the bowels of the house, its white walls and stucco ceiling a comforting motif, paintings and photos hung up, moderate decorum to remind him how much of a home it had become over the last few years, especially.

Maggie greeted him with a big smile, but before she could hug him at the edge of the kitchen, ten-year-old Eliza rushed past her and between them. She giggled as she hugged her father, and Bastian gasp-laughed playfully, flashing a playful look to Maggie before hoisting Eliza off her feet and embracing her firmly yet gently, ultimately returning her to the floor, kissing his wife on the cheek in the same motion.

It was almost overwhelming, the welcome he received, and he looked forward to it every day.

What ensued was nothing out of the norm. It had become routine, but not one that bored the mind.

Eliza returned to her room, stomping through the Pergo halls with her slippers on, while Maggie went with Bastian upstairs, after he discarded his Oxfords in the shoe closet. Despite not needing to wear a suit to work anymore, dress shoes were still required, like a residual semblance of professionalism.

Maggie clung to him up the carpeted steps, down the hall and into their bedroom. They hugged and pecked kisses on each other's lips before she plopped down at the foot of their bed and flipped on the TV opposite it.

Meanwhile Bastian wandered into the conjoined bathroom, toggling the light switch and looking at himself in the illuminated mirror. He unfastened his tie, and unbuttoned his shirt.

Neither Maggie nor their surprisingly attentive daughter mentioned anything about an earthquake, so he had entirely forgotten about the tremor until he heard the TV. Maggie was flipping through channels, the local news among them, which reminded him. He decided not to bring it up, not wanting to alarm her.

"Sooooo," she drawled from the bedroom, "how was work?"

"Same old," Bastian replied, dully. He then smiled to himself before leaning around the corner, catching his wife's eyes. His button-down shirt hung open, his hairy chest and abdomen visible. His voice became more lighthearted. "Sorry, I still haven't been able to bring home any souvenirs."

"I'll be patient," she smiled, and gnawed her bottom lip.

He grinned and withdrew into the bathroom. He started to remove his blazer and then shirt, followed by the unbuckling of his belt.

"Oh, wow," Maggie's voice from the bedroom.

"What is it?" Bastian raised an eyebrow.

"An earthquake in Calipatria. It's on the news."

Bastian paused and looked up at the mirror, staring back at himself.

"No shit?"

"Really. They're saying it's a big one. Six-point-six. Wait…" He heard his wife's voice dip a little. "Oh, God…"

"What is it, honey?" Bastian's brow furrowed. He left his belt alone, the metal buckle dangling free, and emerged from the bathroom. He observed Maggie's shocked facial expression as she viewed the TV, its volume low.

"They're…they're saying other earthquakes, smaller ones, but like, a lot more, in Nevada, Arizona, Utah, even *Wyoming*…"

Now Bastian was a little concerned. He mouthed "what" and entered the bedroom, circling around to view the TV. He stood to the left of where Maggie sat, who now leaned forward with her elbows on her knees, feet dangling above the floor.

Bastian barely got a glimpse of the news report when the screen flickered amidst a wave of static, followed by a quake that shook the house. The lamp on their mahogany nightstand toppled and shattered on the floor. Maggie yelped, startled, and Bastian extended his arms for balance, his right hand descending to clutch her shoulder. He then rubbed it in consolation, and the tremor passed.

"Eliza," Maggie said worrisomely, looking up at

Bastian, wide-eyed.

"Go, I'll be down in a sec," Bastian said, pecking a kiss on Maggie's forehead as she rose to her feet. His voice caught her in the doorway. "Honey—try to relax. Don't let her see you panic."

Maggie gulped and nodded, flashing a dubious smile. She then disappeared into the hallway and he could hear her socked footfalls pound the steps. She called out for Eliza on her way downstairs, and Bastian heard their daughter reply "Mommy" sounding frazzled. He rubbed his face with his right palm, eventually dragging his fingers down through his beard and taking a deep breath.

A passing tremor here and there was nothing to be alarmed about, especially in California. Nor even a six-pointer out east, close to the Nevada border. Obviously it was enough to cause concern, but not induce major panic.

Several, however, even as far inland as Wyoming, and big enough to be felt, was disconcerting. The fact that they all seemed to be linked, somehow or another, was no less unnerving.

It was in moments like this that Bastian wished he had a career in something else, say, geology.

A seven-pointer was real bad, this much he knew. So a 6.6 earned some right to be awestruck by.

Part of him immediately regretted not telling Maggie about the tremor he felt earlier, but ultimately it would not have made much difference.

At the moment he just wanted to make sure that his family was safe, and if he could mitigate their worry at all, he would chalk that up as a victory for the time being.

Local earthquake protocol entailed *not* running outside or getting in a vehicle, staying away from windows and light fixtures, and contrary to popular opinion, standing beneath doorways wasn't recommended. Nor was standing or taking shelter next to furniture that could potentially topple, such as dressers and cabinets.

Since they moved here from San Diego, where they never experienced anything more than a few light tremors in passing, they had only endured one quake, a 4.2, and nobody was injured. It was two counties over, too, so they only braved some aftershocks.

The one they just felt did not come close to those they experienced two and a half years ago, but the array of quakes reported on the news was far more demoralizing.

They certainly wouldn't be mentioned to Eliza.

Bastian refastened his belt on his way down the stairs, throwing on a fitted white tanktop in the process, having shed the open button-down before Maggie even reached the last step.

He was at the end of the upstairs hallway, the top step a few inches from his black-socked feet when he heard tires screech outside and a loud metallic crash. That sharp sound of glass shattering was unmistakable. And then a long, drawn-out horn blaring. The kind that usually meant the driver's deadweight had fallen onto the center of the steering wheel. Which would mean that their airbags didn't deploy, and the death was caused by something, likely, not the collision.

Bastian paused instinctively at the top of the steps and raised an eyebrow.

"Mommy's here, sweetie," Maggie's voice was barely audible downstairs, probably at the end of the hallway leading to Eliza's bedroom.

"Mags, go to the rec room! Under the pool table, like last time!" Bastian called down. "I'm right behind ya. Don't worry, Eliza, Daddy's coming! This'll be over before you know it."

He tried to sound consoling, just as he heard more tires squeal outside, and more metallic crashing. This time it was louder, more thunderous, perhaps a larger vehicle, or maybe it tumbled.

On his way down the steps, he dug his smartphone out of a pocket and started to phone the Sheriff, directly.

Another quake shook the house, significantly harder than previously. Bastian cursed under his breath as he lost his footing and tumbled down the steps, the phone falling from his hand. He was able to catch himself halfway down, to keep from hitting his head on the railing. By that time the tremor passed, and he heard a resonant cacophony of screams outside the house.

There were about a dozen houses between their end of the cul-de-sac and the main road.

"What the…hell…is going on?" Bastian grumbled to himself as he struggled back to his feet.

"We're okay!" Maggie called out. "Stumbled and fell but we're okay. Almost to the rec room!"

Amid his panic, Bastian forgot about the phone

and staggered down the remaining steps, until his socks slid across the Pergo floor. He almost stepped on small shards of glass from a broken photo frame that had been hung on the wall, opposite the base of the stairs.

"Watch out for broken glass, some frames have fallen!"

He heard Maggie swear under her breath in frustration, something she would never do in Eliza's company unless experiencing extreme duress.

"Mags, where are you?"

"Rec room door is *stuck*!" she exclaimed.

He made his way through a couple of hallways, a mere five seconds later, before he spotted the two at the far end of one. Eliza was clinging to her mother's legs like a koala bear, though with both feet on the floor. Maggie was still struggling to open the door, but Bastian could see from where he stood eight or nine feet away that it likely wasn't going to open.

"One of the quakes must've caused that," he said, indicating the right corner of the wooden lintel, which had split and jaggedly sunken into the jamb. Like a domino effect, the door knob and lock were consequently damaged.

*More like fucked*, Bastian thought, angered.

They felt another tremor pass beneath their feet, but this one was not as violent as the last, nonetheless alarming.

Eliza yelped and then sobbed into Maggie's sweatpants.

"Here, let me try," Bastian suggested, gathering his breath and moving forward. Maggie stepped aside, taking Eliza a few feet back. Bastian paused and allocated his strength while adjusting his stance, lowering his right shoulder, and wishing in this moment that he was still wearing his button-down. At least it had sleeves.

He charged into the door and its oak frame barely budged, but the knob rattled. The lintel above made a cracking sound, which didn't sound safe.

"Step back, honey, sweetheart," Bastian said, gesturing at his wife and daughter for their own safety.

Maggie tentatively took a few more steps back, and with her eyes still on her husband, shuffled Eliza behind one of her legs—but never let go of her hand.

"Be careful, Bastian."

*Shit, honey—caution is my middle name.*

He took a couple of steps back before going at it again. Just as his shoulder connected with the door, his legs bent more so that the impact was closer to the knob this time, the lock mechanism rattled and sprang free. The door swung in, nearly off its hinges, and Bastian's momentum carried him a few paces into the room.

Immediately, he reoriented himself and turned to face them down the hall. Maggie's face lit up with relief, her eyes wet, and even Eliza was acute enough to acknowledge the small victory here. She giggled and clapped her hands, now in front of Maggie.

The Pergo floor between her and the now open rec room doorway suddenly erupted, splinters flying into the air and something humanoid burst through. Its lanky arms bent at the elbow joints and gaunt hands ending in four fingers that were more claw than digits scraped across the intact floor around the breach. It lifted its body halfway out of the hole in the floor, and despite its emaciation, it was evidently tall, likely seven feet head to toe once upright.

Its emergence instantly startled the three, almost to the point of heart attack. Maggie's hands were immediately upon Eliza, who shrieked, and she impulsively reeled back. Her socks slid on the Pergo and her footing was forfeit. As she fell back, so did Eliza, between her legs.

The humanoid creature wading in the floor swung its grisly face their direction. They were maybe six or seven feet from the edge of the hole.

Bastian, opposite them, was much farther, but he rapidly changed that, charging the creature, only to slide to a halt a few feet away, beneath the unstable lintel. He successfully snatched its attention, but once its eyeless face was directed at him, he felt his heart sink and tasted bile in the back of his throat.

Everything was wrong about this situation, in ways he struggled to comprehend.

The absence of eyes aside, the abominable creature was disturbingly humanoid. It was so gaunt that it appeared to barely have flesh and muscle adorning its bones, just enough to function, although its animation was in itself questionable.

The top half of its skull was missing, as if the creature had been brutally lobotomized, except not fatally, because it was still alive.

'Alive'—or a wretched version of that.

Whatever 'life' flowed through this creature's

veins, supposing it even had veins, was unlike any *life* that Bastian was aware of.

The exposed part of its cranium looked like a honeycomb, but instead of bees infesting the cavities, there were teeming maggots.

Bastian's gut lurched.

The creature hissed and growled all at once, a disturbing sound alone. It tilted its head on a scrawny neck, appearing to observe the immobile Bastian from a mere few feet away, blindly. Its mouth hung open, which was just as humanoid as the rest of it, except for the rows of jagged teeth, like some kind of sharpened rock. Its lean, pointed, sallow tongue emerged from its mouth and danced as a snake would when charmed. As if it was licking the air.

As if it was…savoring the flavor of human fear.

Bastian gulped and flexed his fists.

He couldn't take his eyes off the abomination before him, mostly because he didn't want to hint that it should pay attention to anything else but him. However, he did notice in the background of the creature—which was still a couple of feet lower than him—that Maggie and Eliza had finally gotten back up.

Slowly and cautiously.

Most of all, quietly.

And then Eliza screamed. Maybe she had been turned away or temporarily 'blindfolded' by Maggie. Whatever the case, Eliza now screamed, a piercing sound that rattled Bastian's ears and bones and, frankly, was basically speaking for himself.

Maggie exclaimed something incoherent and

tried to cover Eliza's mouth, while simultaneously careening in the opposite direction.

"Maggie, closet!" Bastian shouted. "Safe!"

He withdrew into the rec room, only to emerge again, quick on his feet, and with his hands. He witnessed the tall, lanky abomination climb out of the hole in the floor and begin crawling—not walking, but *crawling*, like an insect, except on hands and feet, limbs bent inhumanly at the elbows and knees—down the hall. *Away* from Bastian. But he wouldn't have this, no matter how terrified he was of the creature himself.

"*Heeeeeey*!" he suddenly shouted, his face red, spittle flying from his mouth, veins embossed along his neck and forehead.

The creature paused a few feet down the hallway, and skittered around to face Bastian. It then rose into a bipedal, upright stance. It rolled its gaunt shoulders and then its head, as if a fighter stretching in the ring before a match.

Bastian seethed and steamed.

Sure, it was a foot taller than him, and sure, it had teeth and claws of an inhuman nature, and sure, a hundred other bullet-points that could be mentioned to daunt Bastian, but he had weight and military experience on his side, and humanity, for what it was worth, including the rawest emotions of anger and hate...

And love.

He would do whatever it took to protect his family. Unfortunately, with all the screaming outside, he had to assume, fearfully, that this creature was not an isolated nightmare. He had to assume the worst, and prepare for it, which meant he couldn't go into this with even a hint of suicidal madness.

He had to survive and be there for his family.

Bastian spat on the wall to his right and lifted his hands. He had snatched a pool stick from the rack on the rec room wall by the door. He would have grabbed another if he had the time to spare, and while he could theoretically lure the creature into the rec room where he had more obstacles to take advantage of, maybe this was best.

*Head-on. No bullshit.*

Besides, he couldn't toy with time, not with his wife and daughter out of his sight. He told her to go to the closet, the one by the front door, not to hide, but because of the gun safe behind the coats, in a compartment. She knew the combination. It was all three of their birth years—his, hers, and Eliza's, respectively.

73-70-10.

Like a rapid countdown with a .45-caliber reward inside. One that Maggie had gotten comfortable with over the past few years, on her insistence not his, at the range.

There was another upstairs, a simpler variant, including a shotgun for hunting turkey, although he hadn't done so in three years. He still cleaned and took care of it, still used it at the range on occasion.

He stored this in the back of his mind while he stared down his eyeless opponent, no longer keen to waste any more time.

His strategy was a little questionable, but the biggest part of it was to bypass if not kill or at least momentarily incapacitate this freakshow and then reunite with his family.

Earthquake protocol might strongly suggest avoiding the urge to run outside, but he thought the best case scenario might be to get everyone in the truck and haul ass away from here.

Afterall, earthquake protocol didn't exactly address a contingency like *this*.

"You and me, motherfucker," Bastian growled. He glared up at the shockingly patient creature from under his rigid brow, sweaty and shaking hands clutching the pool stick, one at either end, holding it in front of himself in a more defensive manner than offensive.

Finally the creature hissed, and to his surprise turned its back on him. It lurched down the hall, or at least in that direction, but Bastian didn't let it get more than two strides over the hole in the floor. He bounded over it, lunging at the creature. He clutched the pool stick like a baseball bat now, his hands gripping the thinner end. He swung it, hard, and struck the creature's right shoulder. If he was only a few inches taller, or it shorter, he would have landed a blow to its head, and likely had a better effect. As it were, the impact sufficed to break the stick in two, leaving him with the blunt tip in his hands, and a tapered stake where it had split. The creature wobbled trivially, instantly regaining its composure and swiveling to face him, arms wide and jaws hissing.

Bastian had been grateful the hallway was just wide enough for him to get a good swing, but now wished it was narrower. The creature's arm span was intimidating, especially with such claws protruding from each digit.

He looked down at its three-toed feet, which ended in similar claws, grating the floor as it walked. He only lowered his gaze because he also lowered his stance, now gripping the broken pool stick in an under-hand stance, and as the creature sprung toward him, he thrusted the makeshift stake upward with all his strength. The jagged end impaled the gaunt creature's stomach, just below its visible rib cage and sternum. Blood spewed out, some of it dappling Bastian's hands. It was startlingly bright red and hot, to the point that it burned his skin but not acidically.

"Fuck!" he cursed impulsively, and without thinking let go of the pool stick, only to lunge past the creature, simultaneously lowering his shoulder into its chest. Its footing wavered and its body staggered, smacking the wall and shattering a framed photo of Maggie's late parents. Part of the drywall dented and white dust misted the creature like a hazy corona.

Bastian paused at the mouth of the hallway to glance over his shoulder at the creature. It was disoriented but didn't appear to be dead or dying. Only wounded and, if he had to guess, really pissed off.

Supposing the atrocity even had feelings.

Not knowing what else to do except find his family, and wipe his hands off on his white tank, Bastian turned his back. He hated doing that, taking his eyes off the enemy without confirming the kill, but in all his years of combat experience, this couldn't be logistically assessed like any other.

He just had to wing it until he was given more breathing space.

Bastian veered around the corner of another hallway, leading into the crescent kitchen, and bumped into what he anticipated to be Maggie. Instead it was another of those gangly creatures, its back turned. That didn't last. It slowly pivoted to glare down at a fear-stunned Bastian. He gulped and gathered his bearings, best he could in the face of such terror, unarmed.

When the creature suddenly threw open its jaws and shrieked at him, a gurgling cry that made his teeth rattle, he recoiled. His back struck a wall and his hands searched for something, anything, to use as a weapon.

Nothing but empty, smooth drywall.

And then his eyes searched, but not behind him. Around the creature, behind its lanky figure. Tall as it was, it didn't exactly have a muscular build. Between a lean arm and its gaunt torso, Bastian glimpsed movement.

"Duck!" Maggie's voice barked.

Bastian's knees bent, and he squatted in a heartbeat. The ghastly creature had enough time to withdraw its looming attack on Bastian, but wasn't given the chance to even turn around. The pistol in Maggie's hands exclaimed, and bullets walloped her target square in the back, shoulder to shoulder, and eventually higher, as the muzzle climbed and she surrendered to its recoil.

For once Bastian was grateful for this.

The creature was faltered by the .45-caliber bullets it took to the back and shoulders, more than what it would take to neutralize any grown man. Body armor or not. Most of the bullets lodged into flesh—or bone—despite its gauntness. Bastian counted five rounds before finally one ascended and landed in the back of its half-skull. Then its body lurched forward, its face caving in a spot of drywall a foot above Bastian's head, and his hands raised to shield himself.

Its abysmal body, however, didn't go limp as he expected it would, but instead started twitching. A sputtering, guttural sound emanated from its unseen mouth, surrounded by drywall. It was coughing, growling, and spitting all at once.

Catching its breath.

Bastian sprung to his feet, wishing he had shoes on, but only thin black dress socks. Nonetheless, with the power of brute strength fueled by anger and fear, he cranked his right leg high before driving down his heel into the base of the creature's neck. Mere inches from where a bullet had caved in its flesh. There was a sickening *crack* and then the creature's body did go limp, like a ragdoll, for all intents and purposes lifeless, or so it seemed.

Maggie yelped at the sight, but then sighed with a form of shaken relief.

Bastian glanced at her, and down at Eliza, who clung to her left leg. Their poor daughter's face was sapped of color, her eyes awestruck and wide. She visibly shook, and was genuinely scared mute.

When he looked back down at the creature, after half a stumble back from its body, blood on the base of his sock, something happened that made his heart skip. The corpse dissolved inwardly, from the edges of its flesh until nothing remained, not even a skeletal structure, just a mist of embers and scattered ash.

And, ultimately, nothing at all.

Bastian turned away to look at Maggie, his eyes now just as wide as Eliza's. Maggie's brow furrowed, dumbfounded and quizzical.

He didn't have any answers, of course, and he imagined his questions would be expressed the same as hers. A lot of profanity and a lot of exclamation marks.

"Get your shoes on, we're leaving," Bastian said in one breath.

"W-Where?" she stammered.

Clawed footfalls sounded down the hall, behind Bastian. In the direction of the rec room. And then a gurgling growl.

Eliza whimpered softly and held onto Maggie's leg tighter than before.

"I've gotta go back upstairs," Bastian hated to admit.

"What? No. Why?"

"The twelve-gauge," he replied, barely breathing now, his chest heaving nonetheless, as if to give his heart space to pound. His eyes weren't even on her anymore; he stared at the edge of the hallway, anticipating the emergence of the other creature that had survived his previous attack.

"But…" he heard Maggie whimper.

He blindly gestured at her to move. He loathed having to insist she go about without him, especially now that his plural theory was confirmed for these anomalies.

"Keys are on the hook. Get in the truck. There's another SIG under the seat. Same as the one in your hands. *Go.*"

As soon as that last syllable dropped from his mouth, injected with great urgency, she moved. Eliza in tow, just shy of being carried along.

Bastian moved, too. He couldn't waste another second, especially now that his family was mobile and without him.

He trusted Maggie's capabilities, of course, but he would be damned if he couldn't be right there beside her. At all times, ideally.

Instead of directly turning the corner and risking another face-to-face with the creature—monster, alien, or something worse, he didn't know what to call it—Bastian bolted right past the mouth of the hallway without even glancing down it. Out of his left periphery he glimpsed a dark figure of motion, indubitably the wounded creature, and he absentmindedly wondered whether or not they had healing abilities.

Obviously not to the point of invincibility, supposing that whatever he did to the other one was actual death. It gave him the thought of banishment, or completely vanquishing something from this realm.

*Vanquish. Not kill. I kinda like that.*

It was an almost psychotic thought to even have at the moment, considering all the bedlam. And the pressing matter of life or death.

Even then, life as Bastian had come to know it would never be the same.

All of this, and chaotically more, stormed

through his mind as he beelined for the staircase. His socks provided him a sliding ability, especially around corners. Fortunately he didn't have that far to go before he launched himself up the steps, and their carpeting supplied traction.

Until one foot stepped on his phone and he almost slipped. He stooped to pick it up, glad it wasn't broken, and speed-dialed Ray while on the move.

Only once topside did he throw a frantic glance over his shoulder, and down the staircase. There, the lanky creature lumbered, its pace impaired, likely due to the broken pool stick *still* skewering its torso.

This didn't make Bastian pause any longer, however, he did have a passing thought.

The creature was clearly mindless enough not to pull the stick out of its body, which suggested that it had a more feral mentality.

This was neither good nor bad news, as far as Bastian was concerned. It was just as terrifying and alarming as it was comforting. While a methodical enemy was definitely a threat to take seriously, making evasion and tactics more difficult, a wild one without a specific strategy was not to be underestimated.

Some say that a child with a gun is more dangerous than a trained soldier.

Obviously not true in every scenario, but speaking from experience, Bastian would have to agree on the underlying point.

Besides, he harbored more fear dealing with an enemy gunman than he did with a wild animal, especially one prone to aggression.

Whatever was now trudging up the steps behind him, was neither, and in the worst way.

He knew there would be no reasoning with it. While, in hindsight, he had attacked first, its sheer appearance and demeanor was an assault on the senses.

There was nothing that could change Bastian's mind that the creature was a shade of evil. And if it wasn't born of immorality, it certainly had hostile intentions. So, it would be dealt with hostilely, and Bastian saw to it that nothing less would come its way.

Having returned to their bedroom, he hurriedly retrieved the shotgun from his closet, and in that moment dropped the phone to the floor. From the speaker echoed a disconnected dial tone. If he got that trying to call the Sheriff, then he assumed a tower was down or out of commission.

This only debilitated his concern more.

Shakily—yet deftly, with great haste—he loaded three shells from the top shelf, sliding one after the other into the underbarrel, tubular magazine.

And then the sound of the creature's presence ensnared him.

It had finally reached the top floor, its clawed feet tearing up the carpeted floorboards leading down the hall. Its husky and inhuman breathing all the more audible, Bastian didn't hesitate.

He fired the shotgun, buttstock anchored against his shoulder. The 12-gauge buckshot perforated the thin drywall next to the open doorway into his and Maggie's room. He heard, on top of the ringing that swiftly subsided in his experienced ears, an animalistic skirl.

Bastian mostly had 16-gauge shells for turkey shooting, but he liked to use 12's at the range, and some nearby in case of an emergency home-defense situation. Down in San Diego that concept may have been more reasonable, especially on his lesser salary, but up here in Tierrasanta, in such a nice community, it was borderline silly.

"That's just bonkers," the surprisingly reserved, somewhat demure Sheriff Raymond Abbott had told him one evening.

The two were friendly with each other without being actual friends. Sheriff Abbott, or Ray as Bastian had come to know him, served as a Marine for three years before being discharged due to an injury.

*Respectfully, Ray, who the fuck is bonkers now?* Bastian thought to himself as he racked the slide on the pump-action shotgun and fired again, this time a few inches higher. The buckshot shredded the already peppered drywall and another shriek, this one throatier than the last, spewed from the creature's mouth.

Through the drywall, now not so different than Swiss cheese, Bastian witnessed the creature stagger into the platform railing. The banister broke against its momentum and its body cartwheeled off the ledge, crashing into the credenza below.

Bastian racked the slide and briskly darted through the doorway, into the hall. It was now but a platform, as the entire railing opposite the wall was destroyed. He peered over the ledge to observe the 'crash site' of the creature, having not fared well from the twelve-foot drop.

Apparently these *things* did in fact have bones—evident by the multiple compound fractures it now suffered from. Starkly white bones jutted from each wound, one knee and one elbow. Additionally, while the pool stick had dislodged from the fall, another shard of wood, probably a baluster, was now stuck under its ribcage. From its wounds blood flowed profusely, bright red and, if Bastian had to guess based on recent experience, *hot*.

Not enough to burn through any surface, however, so this was a salvageable plus.

Still, the creature had yet to disintegrate like the other. Bastian deduced that this meant that it was still, for lack of a better word, alive.

Instead of wasting another shell on something that was likely raking in its last breaths already, Bastian rushed back into the bedroom. As soon as he passed over the threshold, he almost tripped on himself at the sound of Maggie screaming.

His name, particularly, distorted and drawn out. Riddled with nothing but bad emotion.

"*Maaaags*!?" he howled, reemerging from the bedroom.

"There's one outside the front door! It's trying to get in! There are more outside the windows!"

Which meant those would be making a violent entrance anytime now. Especially after the first had gone so far as using the crawlspace before bursting through the fucking floor.

"Hold tight! On my way!" It was all he could think to say at the moment, his pulse galloping.

He dragged himself back into the room, scrambling for the closet. He stuffed a carton of 12-gauge shells into one pocket, and went for the 16's. But his hands were shaking, something that he never had to deal with in all his years of combat, at least not once he had gotten his feet substantially wet.

This was a new breed of combat, and the immediate presence of his family was not helping.

The tremor in his hand inadvertently dumped the carton of 16-gauge shells onto the floor. He barked the F-word out loud and immediately disregarded them. He didn't have time. Instead he snatched the revolver from the top shelf, requiring that even he go on his tiptoes. The metal, nickel finish scraped against the shelf lining as he frantically pulled it down.

It was always loaded, for emergency purposes. Additional rounds and moon-clips were available, but he didn't have time to pick and choose right now. He dumped a handful of rounds into his other pocket, plastic moon-clips and other cartridges clattering at his feet. He stepped on one as he headed for the door and immediately grimaced.

*Still not as bad as a Lego.*

Frenetically, he rushed down the steps, revolver in his left hand and shotgun in his right. His burly arms and shoulders pulsed, vascular, sweat gleaming his hairy skin. His muscles ached and then some; he had endured worse for longer periods of time, but this whole fiasco had proven more stressful in a myriad of ways than anything else he had ever experienced.

A split-second before his feet smacked the last

step, he heard glass shatter. Not from outside, either, but *within* the house.

The windows.

"They're inside!" Maggie screamed.

"Where are you!?" Bastian hollered. He swung around the base of the staircase to face the wounded creature. The smashed credenza would be its grave.

"Still by the door! Eliza's in the shoe closet!"

*Smart*, he thought. The shoe closet was in the foyer, within arm's reach of the front door. A little cubby of safety for their daughter, as hard as it must've been for Maggie to put her out of sight. It was only a temporary hideout.

"Stay put!" Bastian shouted, raising the .38 revolver in his right hand. He had wanted to purchase a .357 or .44, but instead chose something with more manageable recoil, in case Maggie had to use it. Which was why the semiautomatic pistol currently in her hands was the better fit.

He squeezed the trigger once, aim tight, hand steadied for a fleeting moment. The creature had started to right itself despite the fractured limbs and wounds to its center mass, but Bastian's shot clipped its brow, inches above teardrop cavities that he presumed to be its nostrils. Its half-head whipped back, bright blood and yellow fluid that he guessed was brain matter spraying the wall.

Bastian didn't stick around to watch it disintegrate. He heard glass shards crunch under inhuman feet, and guttural breathing from what he deduced to be two different creatures now inside the house.

Where the one he just slayed had originally come in, he didn't know. Possibly Eliza's room, or another window, without them hearing it. Likely during one of the quakes.

"This door isn't gonna hold!" Maggie shouted.

"Stand clear of it, and the second you see an opening, fire!" Bastian replied. He raised his voice to be exceptionally loud, not only careless of attracting the intruders, but counting on it. "Try to conserve ammo, Mags! On my way!"

It took Maggie less than a month, two years after they were together, to not only grow accustomed to his nickname for her but actually love it. The double entendre was satisfying, considering his role in the military. Every soldier knew how critical bountiful ammunition was, even when not engaging the enemy.

Maggie's love for Bastian was bountiful to say the least, and he cherished her for it. Even when they weren't on the same page about something, or fought, he never stopped loving her, and never would.

"Did you call Ray!?" she called out.

"Line's down!" Bastian hated to admit.

A pause of demoralizing silence.

"Please hurry!" Maggie exclaimed, her voice dry and shaken.

"On my way, babe," Bastian mumbled to himself, resolute.

Naturally, he wished the best for Ray and his three deputies, but felt guilty for assuming the worst.

Instead focusing his mental power on the safety of his immediate loved ones, Bastian proceeded with as much haste as vigilance, if not more of the prior.

He tucked the revolver between his belt and slacks, avoiding the hot muzzle, and put two hands on the shotgun. He started to cautiously navigate the house, knowing that the pace would pick up real fast. It wasn't a particularly large building, and after killing two of these creatures already, he anticipated more urgency from the others.

Arriving at a four-way intersection of hallways, like a plus sign in the floorplans, gave Bastian a gift and a curse. The first was, sight line of his wife in the foyer—her back to him, though, staring intently and aiming at the door. As he had advised. The latter was also sight lines of the two intruders—one creature impending, on either side of him, down the opposing hallways. Judging from the direction, one had come from Eliza's room, to his left, and the other from the sunroom, down his right.

Instead of snagging Maggie's attention, he focused on the immediate threats.

As soon as the creatures saw him, probably perceiving easy prey since he was between their intersecting paths, they sped up. And they made themselves more known than they already were, with bloodcurdlingly high, wet-sounding shrieks.

Which was an odd observation considering how dry and earthlike the creatures appeared.

*The only wet traits about you are your blood and guts,* Bastian thought to himself, spitefully, as if telepathically addressing the creatures.

He pivoted to his right, swinging the shotgun as

if it was attached to him at the hip, and focused on aim only briefly. He expected the creature to anticipate a higher shot, which it did, instinctively ducking while its charging momentum carried it forward. He fired the shotgun in the same instant—tactful timing. The buck-shot was a tight cluster in the narrow hallway, shredding the creature's face and shoulders from less than ten feet away.

It peeled back, both stance and flesh, exposing much of its stark white skull. The dozens of maggots writhing in its brain cavity were discharged instantly via a yellowish mist.

Bastian was a little amused at how dumb the creature had proven, miscalculating his attack and essentially diving right into the path of his gunfire.

*Born yesterday, half-brain?*

"Bastian!" Maggie's voice pervaded the halls and filled his ears, even from twenty feet away.

It immediately reinjected panic into his bloodstream.

Without turning to face what he already knew was coming, aided by Maggie's alert in addition to a high, looming shadow, Bastian ducked low. Just in time, too; the pouncing creature missed him by inches, only to tuck into a tight roll and spring to its feet on the other side of its disintegrating compatriot.

Far too nimble for Bastian's liking.

Scowling, he stood up and emphatically racked the shotgun slide, ejecting the last spent shell. A stream of smoke followed it, clattering against the wall and then rolling across the floor. However, the reload was incomplete—the tubular magazine empty.

"Fuck," he mumbled, and began fumbling for shells in his pocket.

On his left, about twenty feet away, Bastian heard whimpering from a secluded area followed by a loud wooden crack, and then the distinct sound of Maggie exclaiming the F-word. He knew it was impulsive; despite the incomparably stressful circumstances, she would still try to censor herself around her daughter.

Bastian immediately wielded the shotgun as if it was a staff instead of a firearm, just as the creature in front of him collided. Its clawed hands extended, and likely would have grappled his shoulders or biceps had he not parried it with the shotgun. It appeared momentarily confused, as if genuinely dumbfounded that its human opponent—its *prey*—was capable of such improvisation.

It had been a primitive maneuver in Bastian's mind, however effective.

He took advantage of the mindless creature's pause by using the shotgun as a bludgeon. He swung it at the creature's head, like a baseball bat, both hands gripping the tapered waist of the buttstock. The solid steel end of the weapon—the business end—struck the creature in its gaunt left cheek. It was thrown into the side of the hall, its head crashing through drywall. Its neck got caught on a jagged edge of plaster but it was quick to dislodge itself.

In this time, Bastian heard more wood splitting from the front door, brass hinges rattling, and Eliza whimpering in the shoe closet.

Deftly, hands nonetheless shaking, just less than when he was upstairs—perhaps thanks to what his superiors have called a soldier's second wind—he reloaded the shotgun. He was able to rack the slide before the creature was in his face again, screeching, spittle bridging the gaps between its sharp teeth.

Wordlessly, Bastian yelled in response, and then squeezed the trigger. He was unable to shoulder the shotgun with so little space between them, but from the hip it had the desired effect...

And then some.

The point-blank range intensified the lethality of the 12-gauge buckshot. The creature's torso was thrown backwards, leaving its legs to stand by themselves for a couple of seconds before toppling limply. A ring of bright red blood had sprayed outward, splashing the walls and dappling the floor.

Bastian scowled at the stench of the mess, and the fleshy debris itself, even though it was a sign of victory, no matter how small of one.

He looked down at the rapidly disintegrating creature—both halves—including every bit of blasted meat and viscera. He also noticed that the warm, viscous blood that had misted his white tanktop now dissolved, too. The fabric itself was relieved of any stain or even moisture, leaving behind a heated sensation on his underlying skin, and a rankness in the air.

The sheer shock and awe aspect of this whole debacle sunk its claws into him and for a moment he genuinely felt nauseous.

If anyone or anything was able to quite easily

lasso himself out of such disorientation, it would be his wife's terrified voice. Until now he had never heard her voice shake so awfully, never actually tasted fear and panic from every sound she uttered. It was dizzying in its own right, but he had been trained to master at least some form of that 'weakness.'

Bastian Thurgood remembered all of his years of training, and two whole decades' worth of combat experience.

Men with guns, even women and children with bomb vests, still somehow paled in comparison to whatever new evil this was.

All of these things warped through Bastian's head and heart as he recalled himself into action. He reloaded on his way to the front door, hands only minutely trembling now. Yet he didn't drop a single shell in the process.

On the other hand, Maggie was palpably dismantled by panic. Not even a century spent at any gun range could have prepared her for a fraction of this kind of fear and anxiety. Tears glistened her cheeks and her bottom lip never seemed to hold its ground. Her usually pale complexion was now flushed—but she wasn't a statue of cowardice. She had stayed here the entire time, as he instructed earlier, eyeballing the door even as it was slowly beaten down by the creature on the other side. Their daughter's whimpering in the closed shoe closet to her right certainly didn't mitigate her anxiety.

Bastian had arrived now, though.

Maybe not a knight in shining armor, no matter how much the sweat made his tanned skin gleam or his teary eyes glint, but the best helping hand she could pray for.

"Oh, God, baby, you're okay!?" she exclaimed, embracing him with her free arm, the other blindly aiming her pistol at the door still. It continued to rattle and gradually crack, its condition worsening quickly.

"That's a word for it, Mags," he breathed hoarsely, and briefly glared at the door over her head, which was tucked under his chin. Heavy oak as it was, he knew the front door wouldn't stand for much longer. Part of him was surprised the creature remained so persistent, when the house offered a plethora of other weaker entry points, but he couldn't complain.

"I never thought I'd say this, Bastian, but please, can we *please*—" her voice shook through whimpered syllables until she quieted enough to whisper, aggressively: "—get the *fuck* out of this *hell-hole*!?"

"Your wish," Bastian said low, through a forced simper, and gently yet firmly scooted his wife aside, "is my command."

He cradled the shotgun in both hands, its buttstock anchored against his right hip, and racked the slide. A pause that lasted a heartbeat, and the creature on the other side squalled, as if it knew. In the next nanosecond, Bastian squeezed the trigger. The doorknob and a chunk of the connecting jamb exploded in a spray of splinters, as buckshot tore through it and perforated the creature on the other side. Its abominable cry took on a guttural sound as it recoiled, gurgling its own blood.

Bastian racked the slide and like a man on a mission marched forward, through the now gaping doorway, to where the creature struggled to regain its footing. He didn't offer it the chance to rise higher than a three-point stance, whereupon he shoved the muzzle of the shotgun into its face—and fired another shell. The creature, despite only having half a skull to begin with, made quite a mess. The point-blank headshot produced a plume of yellow and red gore, ending the source's miserable existence.

Or so Bastian hoped—that by killing these things, it was a permanent death, not some sort of recycling. As far as he was concerned, they deserved no second chance, not even a purgatory. There was something particularly foul about these abominations—something genuinely evil. The miasma was one hint, if even trivial, but the palpable corruption in the air from their presence was something fiercely different.

Not to mention the earthquakes preceding their manifestation.

Whether it was an extraterrestrial *arrival*, a subterranean *emergence*, or even an interdimensional *materialization*, he couldn't be sure. He couldn't even begin to imagine.

*And, frankly*, he thought with a morsel of disgust, *I don't even* want *to.*

The repulsion was paired with bewilderment, and without any certain answers he didn't care to waste another second of brainpower on the matter.

Emotionally, he felt too close to drained, and now that he stood outside, he knew that it was too early for that.

His head pivoted.

The end of their cul-de-sac was facing its proverbial extinction. End of an end.

Not remotely strong enough of an irony to make him smirk.

The air was thick with smoke from fires that poured out of car hoods, house windows, and jagged cavities in the planet itself. Middle of the road, a sinkhole wide enough to fit a city bus with space to spare. The Thurgood residence's nearest neighbor's front lawn was replaced by another sinkhole that appeared to have already devoured their entire driveway.

Some people ran amok, screaming.

There weren't many.

The creatures outnumbered them and, unlike their wretched corpses, the humans' didn't dissipate upon death. The bloodshed that Bastian now witnessed in horror was nauseatingly gruesome. Blood and viscera everywhere; dismembered torsos, severed heads, and the like.

Bastian's stomach turned and he heard Maggie's voice behind him, finally reaching through a ringing in his ears to lasso his attention.

"Is it dead!?" she all but screamed.

He turned on his heel to see his wife holding their daughter close at her side, a few feet from the threshold. Tears painted both of their terrified faces.

Bastian gulped and struggled to repress his own. He nodded sternly.

Finally, a voice gathered past his dry lips.

"Absolutely, honey." He took a deep breath and then glanced around at the rest of the cul-de-sac. The humanoid creatures were beginning to look his way. He even noticed some that looked a little shorter than the half-skulls, but with a webbed feature between their wrists and hips. The thought of any of these atrocities being capable of flight sent an additional shiver down Bastian's spine.

He shot his gaze back toward the house, which he knew he may never be able to return to again. At least not anytime soon.

This, he could live with, so long as his family was by his side, and if not, so long as they were safe.

"Come on, get in the truck," he gestured. "Fast. Don't look around."

Maggie nodded and looked down at Eliza, who was torn between whimpering and sobbing up a storm.

"*Now*, Mags!" Bastian barked, making Eliza flinch. He scowled at himself for startling her, and hated to have to shout at Maggie that way, but urgency was now more key than ever before.

Without even looking back at the road, he could *feel* the enemy's collective attention focus on him.

With her daughter's hand in hers, and her face pressed against her waist, Maggie rushed out of the house. Though she veiled Eliza's eyes, it was difficult not to lose herself at the surrounding mayhem.

Bastian noticed that Maggie had tucked the pistol into the taut waistband of her gray sweatpants. He immediately escorted them to the truck.

He suddenly paused outside the passenger side

door and cursed under his breath.

"The keys, I forgot the—"

Maggie let go of Eliza's hand and briskly unearthed the truck's remote-key from a pocket.

Bastian smiled falteringly and snatched the keyring, which was home to other items that jingled. He then planted a probably-too-long kiss on Maggie's lips before unlocking the truck. He rushed them in, and while ten-year-old Eliza wasn't as tiny as she had been a few years ago, she still sufficed to sit in her mother's lap, given the circumstances.

"Sorry, sweetie," Bastian said, standing outside the door, brushing Eliza's tear-stained cheek. "Patience isn't the virtue it used to be."

### <u>3</u>

Horde. For some reason that word stuck to his mind more aptly, and disturbingly, than any other. In describing the amount of creatures that now stormed their way toward the Thurgood residence, as he climbed into the large pickup truck, "horde" found a home.

This wasn't exactly comforting, of course.

Part of Bastian wanted to keep his mind occupied as he focused on not panicking. At least there was no fear in inadvertently breaking the key off in the ignition, as it was a push-start vehicle.

The only requirement was anchoring the magnetic side of the remote to a pad under the ignition button on the steering column. The dashboard lit up with a cheery chime that didn't resonate the same with Bastian as it usually would.

The only remotely comforting fact at the moment was that, in addition to his wife and daughter being in the truck with him, they weren't entirely helpless. He had set the shotgun above the dashboard, against the windshield, where it seemed to fit as if it belonged there. The shells in his pocket were a consoling weight, and the revolver cartridges in his other, not to mention the handgun itself presently stuffed between his legs, against the seat.

It was at no risk of going off on its own, so he could drive without that fear.

Unfortunately, there was a surfeit of other things to fear at present.

A glance at his rearview mirror, which offered a straight and wide view out the rectangular window behind the backseat, revealed a harrowing sight. The *horde* of anomalous creatures closed in on their driveway in record time, their nimbleness terrifying in its own right.

"Hold on, babe," Bastian said in a low, hoarse voice as he looked over at Maggie. She had already put on her seatbelt, but let it cross over Eliza, too. Though not ideally safe, it was better—in her mind at least—than leaving her daughter to sit on her lap without any safety measure.

There wasn't a lot of time for proper thought processes right now.

Bastian threw the truck into reverse and accelerated. The heavy frame lurched on its chassis, which was neither stiff nor loose, ideal for rough terrain. Nothing extreme, like rocky cliff-climbing. Although, with the proper adjustments, the three-ton pickup could easily be capable of such feats.

*Hold onto your hats, assholes,* Bastian thought madly, and then chuckled subconsciously as the truck's tailgate struck the first unsuspecting half-skull. *Oh, wait, that's right—you don't have heads for hats.*

The truck didn't even budge when it backed up over the first creature. Even though it stood seven feet tall, its gaunt body was sucked under the heavy truck's chassis and what the impact didn't finish, the enormous tires did.

A few went down and were chewed up under the wheels by the time Bastian reversed out into the road. He swung the wheel, leather gliding under his callused palms, and the truck hopped the curb before striking his own mailbox. The wooden post snapped against the front left fender and the green-painted, aluminum box noisily tumbled over the truck's hood.

Eliza scream-cried out of panic and shock, clinging to her mother's arms, which embraced her.

Bastian mumbled an apology as he righted the truck, all four tires on pavement, and shifted into drive. One of the winged creatures propelled itself at his side of the cabin, clinging to the door and making the chassis shake. Its hot breath fogged up the window to the left of his face, and as much as he wanted to shoot the creature, he didn't want to shatter the window.

With the truck in gear, he accelerated, hard, making it lurch and the creature—likely seconds from head-butting through the window—was thrown off. It rolled across the blacktop, drawing Bastian's gaze as he drove around the jagged edge of the nearest sinkhole. There, asphalt had been torn as if construction paper. As he put some distance behind them, he lifted his eyes to the side-view mirror, and witnessed a red-orange glow emit from the cavity in the middle of the road. The glow seemed to billow, as if the pit was breathing.

He scowled and focused on the road ahead.

A creature suddenly launched itself onto the truck's hood, skittering briefly before its claws hooked steel and it rose to all fours, its lanky limbs adjusted like an arachnid. Its half-skull head caterwauled, saliva dappling the windshield.

Eliza screamed again, or maybe it was Maggie. Bastian couldn't tell. Maybe it was himself. All he knew was that it scared the hell out of him, and them, and he had to get it off.

He began veering the truck left and right, so long as he could see around the creature enough to know he wasn't going to crash or, worse, drive into another sinkhole.

"Get it *off*, Bastian!" Maggie howled.

He gritted his teeth and drew the revolver from between his legs, brandishing it.

At the mere sight of the raised gun, the half-skull shrieked again and scampered off the hood.

*It actually recognized the threat*, Bastian thought worriedly. Which meant the creatures were already learning. *Not good.*

Nothing about any of this catastrophe was good, of course.

Unfortunately, the creature had not just leapt off the truck, instead, it scurried *up* the windshield and onto the roof of the cabin.

Bastian was doing his best not to fire the gun inside the car, less than two feet from his wife and daughter's faces. So he stuffed the .38 revolver into a cup-holder and returned his hand to the wheel.

"Hold on, girls," he reiterated, and all but floored it. The truck jerked forward and the diesel V8 roared.

Jagged gaps formed in the roof above their heads, through metal and fabric, as the creature clawed for traction. Almost immediately, it lost purchase and was flung into the bed of the truck.

Ahead, Bastian saw obstacles.

And not the kinds he could just risk running over. He slowed down, Maggie shouted something incoherent, and he felt his adrenaline rush unlike ever before.

Behind them, with only the backseat as a 'moat,' was the half-skull that had previously mounted itself to the truck's hood. Now it gained traction in the bed and shattered the rear window with its own head, screeching and growling simultaneously.

Bastian stomped the brakes on impulse, forced to with the obstacles ahead. Consequently the half-skull was propelled through the rear window frame and directly into the backseat. It flopped around like a fish out of water, making a discordant mess of noises. Eliza screaming on top of that didn't dizzy Bastian any less, but it did motivate him.

He spun in his seat, the truck in park, and snatched the revolver from the cup-holder. Using it, he struck the flailing creature in its head and shoulders until it stopped, just enough to glare up into the front of the cabin and snap its jaws. Narrowly missing his hand, but not the revolver. He squeezed the trigger twice in quick succession and the creature's half-skull was obliterated through a temple. Maggot-infested gore sprayed the backseat and the creature disintegrated seconds later.

With a deep, rugged breath, Bastian returned to his seat, and looked down at the revolver. The creature's bite force had proved more dangerous than he anticipated. He was lucky it had not backfired, but alas, the cylinder was irreparably damaged.

He dropped it onto the floormat and tiredly looked over at his family. Eliza was whimpering into her mother's hand, who, meanwhile, was gawking at the situation before them, speechless.

It was utter chaos.

Not forty feet in front of them was an overturned metro bus and two abandoned cars, one of them on fire. Creatures roamed the street between and around the vehicles, as well as the front lawns of houses on either side of the road. They had reached the mouth of the cul-de-sac, and thus the main road, just on the other side of the flipped bus.

More importantly, to Bastian in the moment at least, were the neighbors scrambling fearfully between their lawns and the road. The few survivors from the bus were either trying to crawl out of the windows facing skyward, or running from it altogether.

Men and women.

Unarmed, defenseless, terrified civilians.

Bastian had distorted flashbacks to combat overseas. Still, no amount of those experiences compared to this…

*This clusterfuck.*

He finally abandoned indecision and acted on his gut impulse. Which was to help.

He reached under the seat and briskly dug out the pistol that he kept there, the same one he had told Maggie to get earlier. Of course, none of that had panned out as he saw it in his head.

None of this could have been fathomed.

He popped open his door and emerged, one foot inside the cabin and the other down on the raised step. Using the open door's upper frame for support, he extended his arms, elbows locked and both hands on the pistol. He began firing immediately, making his superiors of past proud. He had always been a master marksman, even when shit hit the fan.

The first creature he clipped in the shoulder had been about to pounce on a woman fleeing the wrecked bus. It shrieked and turned to face him, then he put two more rounds dead above its nostrils, where its eyes might have been, if it had any. The creature's head whipped back and he moved onto the next target before it disintegrated into ash and ember.

In less than twenty seconds, he had killed three creatures, two half-skulls and one of the smaller winged abominations.

And then the pistol's slide locked back, its twelve-round magazine spent.

"Mag, I need a mag," he mumbled fast, ducking back into the truck.

"Honey, go," Maggie whimpered as she forced the words out. Her hand squeezed his right forearm, which was swollen with strain and madly perspiring.

He looked up, frantic-faced and befuddled. His gaze swept from his wife's to the windshield, and the scene of mayhem before them.

One of the women he had just saved was suddenly tackled by a winged creature that tore her throat out in its beak-like jaws in the next second.

Bastian's stomach knotted and his hands blindly searched the cabin for ammunition. It was in the glovebox, but he had forgotten in the heat of the moment.

His eyes locked onto another man, who reached his front door only to be grabbed from behind by a half-skull, its claws sunk into the meat and bone of his shoulders. And then it released one shoulder to grab his forehead and yank his head back, splitting open his jugular in the same instant.

All of this and more in mere seconds.

Bastian's pulse raced, boiling, and he didn't know what to do. He didn't know what—

"Just *go*," Maggie insisted again, the pain in her voice tangible. She squeezed his arm again, while her right hand clutched and rubbed Eliza's, somehow managing to placate her. If even transiently.

"Please, Daddy, can we go?" Eliza mustered.

Bastian's heart sank. He slammed the door shut and set the pistol down so that he could shift the truck back into drive.

He glanced over his shoulder, into the now empty backseat. A few motes of ash shifted across the fabric as he accelerated. His gaze returned to the path ahead, and at first he barely even touched the pedal, unsure of which route to take. The bus was practically blockading the mouth of the road, and the other vehicles made it difficult to circumvent.

"Mount the curb," Maggie suggested, indicating the right side of the road. For whatever reason, most of the bloodshed and mayhem was being conducted on the left side of the road, so there were more people and creatures over there.

The numbers were starting to dwindle, though, and fast—less people, more creatures. There seemed to be five to every one person, it appeared. And soon no prey for them to attack.

Bastian repressed his thoughts, forcing himself *not* to overanalyze the situation.

Instead, he focused on the basics.

Getting his family to safety. And the truck didn't count, not like this at least.

"Hang tight," he said, and drove up onto the sidewalk to the right of the blazing car. Its triangular column of flame and black smoke scorched the afternoon sky.

The large pickup barely bounced as it mounted the curb and crashed through another mailbox. The windshield splintered a little and the wooden post somehow wound up in the bed. Before reaching the main road, Bastian cursed under his breath as he drove beside of another sinkhole that had swallowed part of someone's front lawn and an entire turn lane leading out of the cul-de-sac. The truck's front left tire vibrated against the jagged asphalt at the edge of the cavity, and for a fleeting second he peered into its fiery abyss.

*Fiery. So close to the surface.*
*What the fuck?*

Bastian could only try, now, and try hard, to suppress his paranoid thoughts.

"Oh my God…" Maggie muttered quietly.

Bastian refocused as he drove the truck onto the main road, and immediately veered to avoid hitting two cars that had collided into each other. He slowed down just enough to observe the surrounding chaos, but this didn't last long, as the population of creatures running amok was too overwhelming to not go faster.

*Mobility is life.*

A common idiom in combat, or survival in general, for most situations anyway.

This hardly counted as 'most,' as far as he was concerned it was utterly unprecedented in the history of mankind.

Nonetheless, he trusted the saying even now.

"*Where* are we going, Bastian?" Maggie demanded, her voice shaking a little less than it had been before.

Moreover, he noticed upon glancing over at her, that she had unearthed a small carton of .45-caliber rounds from the glovebox. She even had Eliza hold it while she slowly reloaded the ejected magazine, as her husband had taught her over the years. It could be frustrating for someone inexperienced, much less under these circumstances, but somehow she held it together in this moment.

He couldn't be prouder, couldn't be more grateful, and couldn't be more enamored. It was like his soldier's second wind: her maternal instinct, and the superpowers associated with it. Or at least that was how he saw it, proven over the last decade.

The turmoil through which he drove was unavoidable by their eyes and ears. Even with the windows up, the back was shattered and the disorder was audible. Whether this included screams, both human and not, or the sound of cars colliding and glass breaking. Every few seconds a gunshot echoed, but its range and direction couldn't be pinpointed.

It had quickly become evident to Maggie that her husband was concentrating on a new resolve. Advancing through this nauseating chaos to reach some kind of objective, one that took utmost priority, above even trying to help others along the way. Perhaps a cruel manner of thinking, but the truth was raw and inescapable: even with their tiny arsenal available, even with Bastian's military experience, they wouldn't be able to help anyone without gravely risking their own lives.

Bastian had to prioritize his loved ones amidst all this, as hard to swallow as that was, especially for him, of all people.

So he drove, and occasionally dodged an inanimate obstacle, but never a person. The human casualties were apparent by the bloodshed, most of it already wrought, and left to paint the urban environment various shades of red.

For minutes he drove, staying on the main road, favoring the broader space to maneuver. Occasionally he would glimpse another vehicle on the move, doing what he did, but in a different direction. All he could do was subconsciously wish upon them the best, and hope they found shelter somewhere.

The amount of sinkholes on the main road were few and far between.

Since they started heading this way, they stopped feeling tremors of any kind. And the radio in the truck was fruitless; every channel drowned in static. Not even as much as a hint of a voice or garbled frequency.

White noise.

Like a sea of blank faces and severed tongues.

*This feels like hell*, Bastian couldn't help but think, as cliché as a statement as it seemed, it felt unnervingly genuine.

"Locked and loaded," Maggie finally said, snapping the slide of the pistol, making Eliza flinch. She apologized to her quietly and kissed her head. She then put the pistol muzzle-down into the cup-holder before looking over at her husband again, who appeared disturbingly pensive, but not aloof. "I'll ask one more time, Bastian. *Where* are we going?"

He realized that, while he was lost in thought, she had actually given him space to think. He knew she was an incredible woman, one of his dreams, and that not many people ever had the chance of finding someone like that in their lifetime.

"Sorry, love," he sighed, glancing over at her and then shaking his head before returning his eyes to the road. He dodged, almost too casually it seemed, an abandoned car before flexing his hands on the steering wheel and driving stably again. "Been trying to work out a lot of shit in the old noggin'."

Maggie smirked briefly, infinitesimally.

"I can only begin to imagine what this is like for you. But please…give me *something*."

"Of course, Mags." He took a deep breath and wished he could pull onto the shoulder and talk to her face-to-face, while doing his best to comfort their daughter.

Instead, he had to keep driving.

The sustained 'traffic' of empty or wrecked cars was enough to slow him down here and there, but so far the four-lane road wasn't entirely obstructed, so he was thankful for that. He also harbored some gratitude that none of the creatures moseying around the sides of the road were paying much attention to him or any other occasionally spotted moving vehicles.

*Thanks, I guess,* he mused bitterly.

He also knew that the closer he got to Miramar, he imagined, the more clogged the roads would become. It was late afternoon, night would be upon them in a couple of hours, and a lot of people were still leaving work or transitioning into graveyard shifts.

"CHERI," Bastian finally said, still focusing on the road ahead. "I'm driving to work, Maggie. It's the safest location I could think of. For various reasons. I just hope…"

He sighed and glanced over at her.

"I just hope they haven't initiated full lockdown yet." He diverted his eyes back to the road. "I don't even know how bad it is up there. Could be worse than here, or less. The compound property is on a dense concrete slab, in every direction. I *doubt* there have been any sinkholes within its perimeter. Outside, maybe, but not on the grounds."

Maggie took all of this in. She had visited the compound at the Miramar base once, but even as the wife of someone with Bravo Clearance she wasn't permitted access inside the building. So the farthest she got was the parking lot, and she exchanged some friendly words with Benny, too.

"Does that include the parking lot?"

"What's 'cherry,' Daddy?" Eliza asked.

Bastian and Maggie smiled.

"It's where Daddy works," she said, petting Eliza's hair. "It's an acronym, sweetie. Like *DARE* and *NASA*."

"Ohh, that's smart," she said, sounding light-hearted in lieu of everything that had transpired and was still happening.

"Daddy's a smart man, sweetie," Maggie said. She looked up at Bastian. "Aren't you, dear?"

"Sometimes," he said.

She scoffed playfully and just as playfully smacked his arm.

He grinned, but it didn't last long. As soon as he took his eyes off her, the broad sight of the world around them was instantly demoralizing. It was a hard pill to swallow.

"And yes, that *does* include the parking lot. Impenetrable from below, and most of the compound itself, from the outside, too."

"That's pretty comforting," Maggie admitted.

"Most of where I work, the testing facilities, are below ground, though. Should still be safe." Bastian's words were quick and to the point; some might analyze this as uncertainty or skepticism, but not Maggie. She knew how to read her husband, from body language to speech patterns, and currently he was very much 'in the zone.'

She trusted him, and moreover, trusted his confidence in this endeavor.

"CHERI has taken into consideration a lot of earthquake protocols, and even worked hand-in-hand with FEMA during the construction of their underground facilities. CHERI, much less DARPA, has never been one to underestimate a worst-case scenario."

"I must admit, that *is* comforting to know."

"It is. Trust me, baby, this is the absolute best place we could go. Better than any police or fire station, or hospital." As he said this, it pained him to think of Sheriff Abbott—Ray—but tried to keep him in his positive thoughts, for what it was worth. "If we're able, once we reach the property, I'll try to bring in any other survivors in the area."

"Good," was all Maggie could say right now, doing her best to ease her own mind and heart.

"Furthermore," he added, confidence growing once he really worked it over in his head, "there's a sufficient arsenal in the facility. Whether at the security armory or in the Bravo Vault."

"It's nice to hear you sound so reassured, for once, I mean, genuinely…I can tell, babe."

Bastian grunted and sighed, unable to hide his fervor for reaching CHERI and arming themselves to the teeth against these wretches.

"Sorry for seeming so glum otherwise, it's just…overwhelming…"

He spoke drearily, as they drove by another empty car with human remains adorning the roof and smoky flames pouring out from under the hood. A half-skull creature crawled out from inside the car with entrails dripping from its jaws. And on the other side of their truck, as it drove by, they glimpsed one of those winged creatures twist a severed human arm in its bird-like feet talons.

"You obviously don't have to explain," Maggie groaned, rubbing her chest, beside Eliza's head. The girl was half-asleep, or unconscious, waning in and out like a weak flame in a hurricane.

"I suppose this means I'm not bound by my NDA anymore. At least, not explicitly."

"Have you even *read* the small text, Sebastian?" Maggie asked snidely. It made him smile, made him want to kiss the sarcasm right out of her mouth.

"I meeeaaan…" he drawled, and then they both chuckled wearily. It was short-lived, as his eyes caught a sign and he abruptly veered left at an intersection. They both pitched in their seats, and tires squealed against asphalt. The truck hopped the corner of a sidewalk, running over a dead body in the process.

Bastian grimaced and mouthed "sorry" as if the poor man's soul was still in his disemboweled body.

It occurred to him that so many corpses remained fairly intact, or at least, not in as many pieces as one might expect—supposing the creatures ate them. Instead, they appeared to mutilate as if solely intent on inflicting pain and causing as much harm as possible. Even once the person was dead, they still occasionally crawled by and picked at it. Slowly dismantling the body, piece by piece, flesh and artery, sinew and organ, leaving only marrow in bone.

If that.

For all he knew, they eventually lapped that up, too. He was only observing things in passing, with a cautious eye, his acutely trained knack for details.

A trait he as of today wished he didn't have.

Of course, he knew it would now serve as a gift as much as a curse. A burden, to notice the grimmest details, but also an advantage, to dissect the 'battlefield' and assess combat situations before they unfolded, or in the heat of it.

"Sorry, almost missed my exit," he finally let out, looking around more vigilantly now. "Won't be long, Mags. Five to ten, I dunno, never had to face this kind of…traffic."

He gulped before that last word.

"Just get us there in one piece and I'll call it even," she said, trying to stay lighthearted, the challenge of the century.

"*Even*? For what?" he scoffed playfully. His puzzlement, however, was authentic.

"In the hall, back home. Admit it. I saved your butt. Literally, I might add."

Bastian looked over at her smiling. Now he *really* wanted to kiss her. No amount of dirt and dust, sweat and soot, tears and fears could sully or detract his love for her.

A tremor passed under the pavement, sizable enough to not only jerk the wheel out of Bastian's hands but also shake the concrete foundation of an overpass a hundred yards down the two-lane road. A tree nearby, on the side of the road, cracked and fell, its bushy canopy shuddering and loosing natural debris across the asphalt. Birds scattered, fluttering into the sky, a sight that may have been some kind of wonder, but was now despondent due to the soot in the air and the despair just as thick.

The asphalt split quite audibly beneath the truck, and Bastian witnessed the blacktop cleave just as they drove over it. He reacquired control of the vehicle, and the tremor passed, but the tree blocked the road. He would have to circumvent it, carefully but aggressively in the end.

For the time being, he stomped the brakes to keep them from colliding with the tree trunk or its ruffled canopy, the length of it all about three minivans.

He extended his right hand to make sure that Eliza was okay, and clear of the dashboard. Maggie caught her breath through a whimper and managed to mitigate Eliza's panic enough to quell any crying.

"Bastian?" Maggie croaked, looking around.

"I know," he said, and reached for the pistol in the cup-holder. It was freshly loaded, thanks to Maggie.

He racked the slide to chamber a round, and his eyes darted left to right.

Creatures were slowly, methodically closing in.

There were no buildings nearby, not until well past the bridge ahead. This side street curved uphill after that, and far behind them it wound down, back to the main road. No sidewalks on both sides, either, and only two other vehicles in the immediate vicinity.

Bastian felt especially cut-off right about now.

"It's gonna get a little loud, sweetie, okay? I want you to cover your ears for Daddy."

Eliza whimpered and firmly cupped her hands over her ears.

"Honey, please, just drive. Can't we go around that? It looks doable on the left."

He noticed, on the left side of the road, that it would be feasible to circumvent the fallen canopy. It would require driving at the edge of a vegetated ditch and the bordering greenbelt there. They were close to the edge of Tierrasanta, and where the town's limits dropped off, so did the foliage. Its scarceness was inevitable and prominent the closer they got to Miramar. A few hours farther north and they would be in Death Valley territory. Dry deserts and rare rainfall.

Not far southeast of their home was Calipatria, too, which shared a similar climate. And to Bastian's memory, from the TV earlier, that was the source of the 6.6 quake.

"We can and we will," Bastian said through a gulp, tasting fear and bile in the back of his throat.

Instead of setting the pistol down, however, he held it in his left hand, against the steering wheel. He let up off the brakes and began to accelerate.

The creatures closing in around them were taking their time, which in a way worried him further. It was as if *they* had adopted patience as a virtue—troubling in itself.

The truck suddenly stalled. The front tires spun madly against the asphalt, spewing smoke around the bulky front end of the three-ton vehicle. The back tires, however, snagged something and would hardly budge. One began to spin, but was quickly stopped with a loud pop and hiss, followed by another.

"The back tires just blew out," he muttered under his breath in dismay.

"*What*!?" Maggie gasped. She threw her head over her shoulder, her hands covering Eliza's face, and then her eyes widened.

Bastian's did, too, when he looked into his side-view mirror.

A sinkhole had formed directly behind the pickup, close enough to have likely caught the back wheels between torn 'teeth' of asphalt. As soon as he witnessed a glowing flame emanate from the cavity behind them, he was newly invigorated.

"Abandon ship, Mags," he said to his wife, leaning over the center console and unfastening 'their' seatbelt. It whipped back, clear of Eliza, and Maggie reached for the handle. He briskly shook his head and brandished a palm, demanding "Wait!"

"What?" she asked, her voice a croak.

"Let me be a gentleman," he said, his voice rugged but somehow smooth, and he whispered: "For once."

He then winked and pecked a kiss on her lips. When he withdrew, he exited the truck and slung the shotgun onto the hood before taking himself the opposite way. He swung around into the bed, more nimbly than he even expected himself to be. It was invigorating in itself, and without even glancing back at the sinkhole which now seemed to slowly devour the truck foot by foot, making it tilt back, he hurdled out of the bed and alighted on his feet. The tattered dress socks were a microscopic barrier against the hot blacktop, and his soles smacked it hard, but it was a pain he ignored.

Vigorously, Bastian opened the door to escort Eliza and Maggie out of the truck.

Eliza was first, transferred from Maggie's lap into Bastian's hands. He kissed her quickly on the forehead and eased her down.

"Hold onto Daddy, sweetheart," he said.

She clung to his leg not unlike she had to Maggie earlier. The frantic embrace was unyielding, and comforting for once to Bastian.

He then reached out to take Maggie's hand.

The truck lurched backwards a few feet, the rear wheels bending against broken asphalt, through punctured tires. The front two wheels lifted off the road, just high enough, and adequately a surprise, to disconnect Maggie's hand from Bastian's. The shotgun previously on the hood bounced off and clattered to the road a few feet from Bastian.

Maggie barely contained a panicked scream, taken aback by the suddenness, and gripped the dashboard for traction. She looked over her shoulder, through the broken rear window, down the bed and over the tailgate—into the gaping sinkhole behind the truck.

Bastian was trying to get Eliza to calm down, while creatures formed a patient circle around them on all sides, when Maggie Thurgood all of a sudden screamed. It was the loudest, most piercing and thick-with-fear sound Bastian had ever heard from his wife. It chilled his bones to the marrow and made his heart leap into his throat. He gawked up at the truck and his eyes followed it as the front wheels touched back down.

Maggie's face was dumbstruck as she pivoted her head to look at Bastian, less than eight feet away. The passenger side door had swung shut in the time that the truck rocked like a see-saw.

She popped the door open and Bastian moved forward to help her out. Eliza no longer clung to his leg, but her hands seized fistfuls of his shirt.

An immense shadow briefly obstructed the sun as it poured over the truck. Its source emerged from the sinkhole, leaping into the air and landing on top of the truck's cabin. Glass blew out, tiny splinters misting the air. The chassis gave way, crushed under the weight of the beast, its giant black hooves severing the bed from the cabin, its clawed fists grinding the front two wheels into the asphalt. Its brown-orange knees, as if made of impervious clay, straddled the edges of the cabin, which practically pancaked beneath itself.

The abrupt impact shook the ground and staggered Bastian in the opposite direction. Eliza was knocked onto her back, crying.

As soon as the reality struck Bastian, almost immediately, he screamed a discordant sound that tore at his throat and reddened his face. His lungs dried out in the exodus of air before his breath gave way. He stumbled forward a few steps, his legs wobbling but somehow still afoot. Phlegm dripped from his flaring nostrils, saliva from his mouth, tears from his eyes. A blood vessel in his left eye had popped during the strain of the scream, and the hot gallop of his pulse, resulting in a red blotch amid the white.

His bearded jaw now hung agape, no breath to howl or curse or bawl, just stare in disbelief. His eyes focused on the flattened cabin of the pickup truck, the hints of blood on the surrounding asphalt and some parts of the metal itself, trying his damnedest not to imagine Maggie's utterly crushed body inside.

He was about to lose his wobbling knees to the ground, had he not lifted his gaze higher.

The beast responsible for this remained on top of the truck as if it had found a throne. Even squatting as it now did, straddling the crushed vehicle, it was easily ten feet from hoof to horn. Its appearance immediately made Bastian associate the creature with Hell, and he didn't care about the clichés. If anything, the beast itself was pure stereotype, in all of its impurities. The bipedal legs, hocked like a goat's, and the cloven hooves, black as obsidian and quite possibly just that, not to mention the two gnarled horns protruding from its temples, crescently curving outward before pointing in. They were just as black as its hooves, and the tips appeared fatally sharp. The rest of the beast, save for its legs and hindquarters, was a dark red—like fire at its angriest, engulfed by the night and stained with blood.

In other words, not quite right—almost impossible. The beast was all of this and then some. Its vaguely humanoid skull had very little flesh or fat on it, just red skin pulled taut over the bone, including a domed brow and prominently cleft chin. The lipless mouth and slightly crocodilian teeth, sharp and misarranged, were just as disturbing. Tiny, neon-green eyes beneath its heavy brow were soullessly unnerving.

It tilted its massive, horned head to the side, the way a dog would if confused.

Through its idling growl of a breath, husky and uneven, certainly inhuman, thick ropes of saliva dribbled down its chin.

Bastian now started to growl himself, his chest heaving and his breath husky to say the least. He felt Eliza's hands clutch at his left pantleg. He couldn't hear her crying, or screaming, he couldn't hear anything really. Just Maggie's scream resonate in his skull, a memory all too recent and seemingly too permanent.

Unlike the unfazed beast responsible for her death, Bastian could hardly keep still. His hands fidgeted like a gunslinger anticipating his enemy to draw first. Except that Bastian's pistols were in the truck, both of them, and the shotgun was about seven feet to his right.

Part of him wanted to lunge at the beast, suicidal, and rip it apart with his bare hands. He knew that was beyond impossible, it was a sick fantasy he would have every passing second of his life, supposing he even survived this encounter.

Eliza's voice started to crack and make its way back into his world.

He turned away from the foul, infernal abomination on top of the truck to see his daughter be taken from him. Her handfuls of his shirt loosened as a half-skull pulled her by the shoulders, until she staggered into its gaunt, clawed embrace. She already bled from the shoulders and Bastian's eyes were wider than before, pouring tears as if blood from an arterial wound.

He reached out and grabbed her flailing hand to pull her back into his arms. Something tore and Bastian came away with only part of his daughter. His stomach jolted and he rolled like a barrel, across the road, until he came over his shotgun. He vomited onto the road and shouldered the weapon almost in the same motion. His head spun and he tasted more than tears in the back of his throat, he tasted something resemblant of death.

As he rose to one knee, he aimed high and fired. The blast spread buckshot high above wherever Eliza might be, as short as she was. As his eyes batted away globs of tears, stinging in the process, he saw a half-skull staggering away from her, holes in the side of its face and part of its shoulder missing.

Bastian's eyes readjusted. He spotted Eliza lying on the road, unconscious, missing an arm. The dark red stream gushing from the wound was incessant.

He felt dizzy as he tried to stand, and wobbled forward several paces.

When he racked the slide, ejecting a shell and loading a fresh one, he heard metal and glass crunch behind him. Ignoring it, he fired at chest level, into the crowd of winged creatures hunkering around Eliza's body, their beak-like jaws snipping.

Bastian yelled something incoherent as he fired a third shell, and obliterated the head of one creature. And then another filled its place.

The circle of atrocious creatures around him started to tighten. Either their patience had run thin, or they were given a signal.

From their superior.

Impulsively, Bastian turned to face the enormous, horned beast that had just now disembarked from the truck wreckage. Standing upright on its hooved feet, the bipedal, grossly humanoid monstrosity was about eleven feet tall.

He racked the slide and aimed at its knees. The trigger responded with a hollow click.

His free hand went to dig shells out of a pocket. Instead, .45 cartridges clinked to the asphalt. He was too disarrayed to focus.

As he fumbled his hand into the other pocket, he heard sounds that made him want to vomit again. His feet pivoted and he looked to where Eliza was. He could hardly see her small white sneakers amid the throng of creatures huddled around her.

So much blood, so many limbs.

He led himself to believe that he couldn't see what he saw all too clearly.

His knees buckled but he somehow kept one foot on the asphalt. The three-point stance he dropped into was going to be his liberty before death, he felt certain.

*I deserve it. I couldn't protect you.*

His mouth started to move, lips fumbling words. His organs ached fiercely, a harbinger of surrender.

Gunfire barraged the beast as it started to double over Bastian, likely to scoop him up or worse. It back-pedaled, teetering briefly before raising a burly arm to shield its face from bullets. The gunfire came in two different volleys, one from a semi-automatic weapon and the other from a shotgun. Judging by the sound and lack of delay between shots, it too was semi-automatic.

These were kind of reassuring to Bastian's ears, but as he forfeited his grip on reality, he started to care less. Part of him yearned for the abyss.

Other creatures in the area began to caterwaul as the gunfire persisted, steady enough to push the large beast back even farther. The last things Bastian perceived before darkness seized him were flashing red and blue lights, illuminating the backs of his eyes until nothing could penetrate the chasm of unconsciousness.

Except for the overlapping screams of Maggie and Eliza Thurgood.

Those felt eternal.

# 4

Layered voices, incoherency plaguing them. Bastian's eyelids fluttered as consciousness returned like a wave crashing ashore. Numbness retreated from his body and he could feel the pain resurface, first no more than a soreness, then something much stronger. However, it was the incorporeal pain that hurt the most. The loss, the grief, and the sheer disbelief infecting it.

The fact that he had survived, moreover, seemed to exacerbate the pain.

Otherwise, it was quite possible, if even theoretical and outside his personal beliefs, that he might be able to see them again. Hug them. Kiss them. Love them and be forgiven by them.

As it was, Bastian couldn't be consoled by any of these things.

Instead, he was forced to live with it.

Indefinitely.

Meanwhile, the overlapping voices—although a little hushed from what would be normal speaking volume—continued. They did so until Bastian's vision cleared through the muddiness and he blinked his way back into the light. He imagined it must be close to dusk by now, but still a relic of daylight seeped through the windows.

Windows. He looked around, and slowly—sorely—lifted himself up. He had been lying on his side, in what appeared to be the backseat of a car. Once he sat upright, he groaned sorely, and the intersecting voices in front of him stopped. Heads turned. Faces came into view.

Not quite slowly-but-surely, instead rather briskly, Bastian reeled himself back to reality. Fully awake. His body felt groggier than his perception, and his mind, the deep recesses of it, remained mired by the pain of his loss. And the memories, all too fresh, like gunshot wounds that refused to heal even the slightest, nipped at his focus.

Distant echoes, as if buried in a cave somewhere in his subconscious. Water on the floor, and dripping off stalactites.

Different voices; Maggie and Eliza.

"He looks rough," the man in the passenger seat said, looking across the bulky center console, at the driver.

"Reasonably," the driver said. He was pale-skinned with a stubble beard, buzz-cut, and blue eyes. He had bags under them, as if he hadn't slept for days.

Like his passenger, and probably partner as far as Bastian deduced, he wore a San Diego Police uniform. Both of their collars were unfastened, as were the top few buttons, exposing their sweaty undershirts.

The passenger was darker-skinned, Hispanic if Bastian had to guess, his accent making it more obvious. He had brown eyes against the receding sunlight that flowed into the car, a slightly round face and a tuft of black hair on his chin, stubble on his upper lip. The fatigue on his face suggested he had seen better days, by far.

Bastian imagined these were the faces of men everywhere right now, especially those in law enforcement, bearing the burden of serving and protecting civilians in need, while struggling to survive themselves.

It had taken Bastian mere seconds to realize he was in a squad car, well before he even noticed the men's uniforms. The mesh divider between the backseat and cabin was the dead giveaway.

"Please tell me," Bastian dug up his voice from the grave, croaking the syllables at first. "That I got drunk and imagined this whole wretched thing. Please tell me..." He grimaced and groaned briefly, as he brought his hands into his lap and looked down at them. He then mumbled, so fast it was hardly coherent: "That I'm in cuffs for public intoxication."

"Sorry, buddy," the Hispanic man said, clicking his tongue and sighing. "For once, I wish that was the case."

"Drunk and disorderlies are the worst," the driver said, scoffing and smirking wryly, shaking his head, looking over at his partner.

"Until now," the other said, his voice monotonous, as he stared back at Bastian.

"Officers..." Bastian mumbled, slowly looking up from his hands, which were certainly not in cuffs, and then sweeping his gaze over to the window at his left. His voice trailed off as he realized where they were.

On top of a parking garage somewhere, in the middle of the lot, at the top of the concrete ramp leading up to whatever level this was. There were scarce trees around, as he swiveled his head, trying to discern their location, at least in correlation to where he had been, before their truck got...

Bastian's stomach turned and he tasted filth in the back of his throat. He couldn't remember what he had for lunch at work earlier today, in fact, he couldn't remember anything except for Maggie's scream before the truck's front wheels touched back down, and the sound of metal crushing under a monstrous weight, glass shattering, flesh tearing, and a little girl crying as she—

"Names, let's do names," the driver abruptly said, rather loudly, as if trying to snag Bastian's attention. He even snapped his fingers, not at Bastian but at his partner, who then said "oh" and nodded briskly.

"Mister, hey mister," the officer in the passenger seat said, lightly tapping on the mesh divider.

Bastian drearily jerked his head to the right, no longer staring out the window but instead at the brown-skinned man. He found himself getting lost in the fatigue sullying an otherwise handsome face.

"Eduardo Zavala, mister, you listening?"

Bastian kept his mouth shut as he coughed a couple of times, battling the urge to vomit from a bilious sensation a moment ago. He then nodded, acknowledging the man. He sat up straighter and did his best to not only stay conscious, but fight for clarity. He even used his hands, which trembled a little, to rake his hair and brush any strands from sticking to his sweaty forehead.

"Only my Ma and the Cap call me Eddie, I dunno why Cap does it, probably just to be an asshole, but anyway," the passenger talked like automatic gunfire, only with a softer voice, "my friends call me Z. For all intents and purposes, mister, you can call me Z, too."

The driver nodded and kneaded his chin.

"You're a real charmer, Z," he said, poorly repressing a chuckle.

"What?" Z shrugged, shooting his partner a sarcastically critical look.

The driver shook his head and held onto his open collar with both hands, his shoulders and arms drooping. He turned in his seat enough to look directly through the mesh at the man in the backseat.

"Jake Taylor. Nobody calls me 'T' except for *this* doofus." He used his head to indicate his partner, and then shrugged, still holding his open collar. "But, considering the circumstances, I think you can, too."

Bastian nodded repeatedly, albeit slowly, and let his eyes fall back to his lap. He brushed his hands against his tarnished slacks, and then looked back up at the two officers, who he guessed to be in their low to the mid-thirties, and took a deep breath.

"I'll admit," he said, his voice scratchy, "y'all seem like a couple of clowns. But…T and Z, better than T and A, name-wise, at least…plus, makes it easier on me. Like call-signs."

"Call-signs, hell yeah," was all Z got from that, smirking and lightly slapping his partner on the arm. It was a fleeting moment of amusement.

"You military?" T asked, letting go of his collar and narrowing his eyes on Bastian. Despite his body language, the question wasn't asked bitterly, but curiously.

"Ex," Bastian sighed. He shook his head and looked over his shoulders, both of them, and then back forward. "Clearly not worth a damn anymore."

"You can't put that on yourself, man," T said, glum but stern. "When we got there, a quarter of the bogeys were dead. Besides...you were way outnumbered. And the circumstances were...just plain bad. FUBAR, really."

Bastian raised an eyebrow. "Let me guess, *T*...you've served. In...the Corps."

"One tour," T raised his index finger. Something wet made his eyes redden and then gleam. "Then I got the boot."

"Friendly fire?"

T's forehead creased and he nodded. "Unintentional."

"Almost always is."

"And you? The Corps, too?" T asked.

Meanwhile Z just watched them go back and forth, likely wishing he had a bucket of popcorn.

Bastian shook his head. "Ranger. Then Navy."

"Navy...as in..." T paused and his eyes widened. "Were you a *SEAL*?"

Bastian nodded. "Half a lifetime ago, seems."

"Oh, shit, let me guess," Z butted in. "Either you're retired, and you live in Tierrasanta—or you're deployed at Miramar? Like an instructor or consultant?"

Bastian shrugged and combated tears. "Yes and no. But let's cut the intros. You can call me Bastian. Keep it simple."

"Bastion," T said, brandishing a tiny smile. "Like the word?"

Bastian sighed. "Short for *Se*bastian. Smartass."

"Was just a joke," T recoiled, palms up.

"Only my wife can make that joke," he replied, lightheartedly at first. Her voice resurfaced from the depths of his subconscious, unable to remain banished. And it wasn't a pleasant version. Bastian's own voice started to distort and trail off. "And she's...not here..."

Unable to repress it anymore, Bastian caved and planted his face into his hands, his fingers rising into his thick dark hair. He began to sob quietly.

T and Z exchanged slightly confused expressions before frowning and then trying to word themselves appropriately. They stumbled through various attempts before finally T got his voice straight.

"Look, man—Bastian—we're awfully sorry about your little girl. I've got, a uh, I've got one on the way. My fiancé is with her family right now. They're wealthy. Got a fucking *fortress* up in Anaheim. I'm...I'm trying to do my best to *believe* they're okay. But you...your daughter, I presume...I mean..."

T paused, realized he was rambling, and started to sniffle. He mumbled "sorry" and withdrew, planting his back to the seat, facing forward. He kneaded his face and Z leaned over the console, not to comfort his partner but to look at Bastian through the mesh.

"We've all lost someone or are on the verge of

losing someone," Z said through a shaky voice, though it didn't last. "My *whole* family is in Oceanside right now, boarding up. Ma, Pops, cousins, even my little niece. Lost comms with them an hour ago. But me? I'm a fucking *castle*, bro. Ain't *nothing* tearing me down. T, here, is my main man. Freshmen besties. All the way through the academy. Look…I might not have military experience, I might be a nerd from the ghetto, growing up with no dad, but I am SD*PD*, baby. We don't lay down for *shit*. So how 'bout we cut the waterworks and hit the road, Jack?"

Bastian sniffled until he was congested and lifted his head. He looked over at T, who was now staring across at his partner.

"Where'd you find this guy, T?" Bastian asked.

"Dude found *me*," T said quietly.

Z just shrugged, a matter-of-fact expression on his almost comical face.

"You must be grateful," Bastian said.

"More than you know."

"I used to be grateful. Now, for two people in my life, the only ones I genuinely cared about, that are no longer with me. But…I *am* grateful for you two, coming when you did, however late, but you saved my life. I can't say I'm relieved-to-be-alive right now, but, I also can't deny that I'm glad it was you two who saved my sorry ass."

T nodded, clearly still fighting some tears, and Z nodded, too, and the pair of them exchanged nods, evidently a little at a loss for words.

"Where were—" Bastian started, wanting to

avoid stagnancy or wallowing, but was interrupted by T. His voice broke through a little louder than Bastian expected, and it was obvious that he was working through something emotional, too.

"It was too late, ya know, by the time we got there," T said, talking fast, his voice somewhat tremulous, "and rest assured, we weren't cruising around real slow. We saw the horned bastard from the bottom of the turn-off and sped up, even more. Was no debate between us, I just floored it and we got out the hardware. Heard gunfire before we even arrived, and any potential hesitation was abandoned."

A few tears streaked T's cheeks.

"Y'all are literally the few and should be proud, too," Bastian said, raising his eyebrows before they sunk down, along with his gaze. "And like I said, I *am* grateful you came, with such aggression, too, but I can't...I *can't*—" he vehemently balled up his fists and gritted his teeth as that word pushed through his system "—force myself to *not* be angry that you didn't come sooner, if even a few seconds, a minute, anything."

Slowly, Bastian slackened, and his fists unfurled. He shook his head and smirked for a moment, maniacally even, but only transiently. When he looked back up from his hands, which had turned pale, he regarded the two officers with glassy eyes that expressed something kinder than spite.

It was a mutation of compassion.

"But I also can't put that on you guys," he said. "No matter what, know that, and believe it. I *am*...grateful."

He mumbled the last word, hardly audible, and the officers knew why, for good reason.

Bastian hated that he even voiced that, having aired it out to sink into their thoughts when they weren't busy thinking about something else heavy.

A part of him, however, felt infinitesimally lighter than before, for heaving that off his chest, if even his veins remained burdened by life.

"We, uh, we appreciate that, Bastian, we really do," T said, nodding and kneading his lips.

Z was speechless, save for some vague body language and facial expressions that suggested the same sentiment as his partner.

"I hate to sound cold, but we oughtta wrap this shit up and get on the move again," Bastian said. "Hell, I can't believe we're just sitting still right now. Shit is surreal. How'd you guys find this spot?"

"Used to light-up here, on duty," Z blurted.

T scoffed, as if they were going to get in trouble for confessing their transgressions.

Z shrugged. "Fuck it, man. This is Revelations shit. I'm just being honest."

"Revelations?" Bastian actually chuckled. "Are you serious?"

Z shrugged nonchalantly. "I mean…you saw that goat-legged, horned motherfucker. And the vulture-like things with the beaks and wings. Coming outta the *ground*. They're demons, right? I thought that was obvious by now."

T scoffed, simpered, and shook his head. "Oh, boy. The cauldron has been stirred."

Z's brow furrowed. "What?"

Bastian waved his hands. "Let's not get wrapped up in the terminology and theories, all that bullshit. Whatever. Call 'em demons, call 'em aliens, call 'em Canadians, I don't care. They're *evil*, that's for fucking sure. Can't change my mind about that. Let's focus on something else, here."

"Ain't no disagreement there, mister," Z said. "Bastian, I mean. Uh, yeah. Evil as fuck. Soulless ass-holes. Has a ring to it. Fucking vermin from down-under. Dissolve into fire and ash when they die. I mean, hell…literally…"

"Does he ever shut up?" Bastian asked, leaning forward and looking at T.

"Sometimes. And that's when you know shit's *really* hit the fan. He's like a dog when the weather changes. Or a cat when there's a monster in the house."

"Did you just call me a *dog*—?" Z scoffed, but stopped himself.

"*Anyway*," T said emphatically, rolling his eyes. He shook his head at Z and then looked back at Bastian. "Before we roll out, I gotta ask a question."

"Oh, same!" Z blurted, rather excitedly, which made T's brow furrow.

"Can I go first? This shit's heavy. I just gotta ask it," his eyes transferred from Z to Bastian and he sighed. "Regretfully."

"How 'bout we go, same time?" Z said, as if it was a game.

It was clear to Bastian, as a blind man could see, that Eduardo Zavala was one of those people who masked despair with comedy. When things got heavy, he acted light, or else he would be crushed under the weight of the doom and gloom.

Bastian had met men like him before, older men even, when he was a Ranger. He couldn't judge them for this strategy, as it usually wasn't intentional, but a part of their personality.

If anything, Bastian envied them.

Meanwhile, T just sighed and rolled his eyes, then faced Bastian again and started to pose his question. As the words rolled out, his partner asked another question, too, their voices overlapping.

"Where is your wife?" T asked, solemnly.

"Where were you headed?" Z asked, and immediately regretted being so casual. He even cringed, at himself, as their words breached the atmosphere, and Bastian kneaded his brow, while T shook his head and jostled his partner.

Stifling another fit of crying, Bastian sighed and mustered a lowly voice for replying to the heartfelt question. Afterall, when the officers had arrived, there were no humans in sight, except for Bastian and…whatever remained of Eliza at that time.

"She was in the truck," he said, barely audible.

Slowly but surely the two officers did the math and their deduction reduced them both to rubble. Z sunk in his seat, facing forward, shaking his head. T kneaded his temples and tried to get a grip before he made a fool of himself.

It became evident to both young men that Bastian

had to be composed of something exceptional, considering how well he held himself together in lieu of such a tragedy. As if losing his daughter so brutally wasn't enough to drive any father insane, whether maniacally or depressively, a wife lost in such a manner seemed unbearably overwhelming.

"We're sorry, Bastian, really," Z finally said, sooner than T expected. Not even he had garnered the voice and composure to say it himself.

Bastian effortlessly detected the genuineness in Z's voice and carriage that it actually touched him.

Instead of continuing to dredge up the all-too-fresh wound of a memory, Bastian diverted his focus. It was not a far redirection, but it sufficed to allay his sadness, not completely, just bearably.

"Did you guys manage to kill the big one?" Bastian asked, hope on the tip of his tongue, and producing a glint in his eyes.

"Psh, nah," Z said, shaking his head. Disappointment on his face. "Fucker was way too big. Bullet sponge. Supposing our rounds even penetrated. *Maybe* T's Remington, but at that range, I dunno."

"How far were you when you rolled up?"

T lifted his eyes, thinking. "Twenty feet, maybe. Fifteen or so from you. It was right above you, too. Didn't see any blood on you, so…I'd guess we didn't hurt it much. Not for lack of trying, though."

"Yeah, I remember…hearing quite a volley."

It was evident by Bastian's pause and disposition that he would rather not recall anything about that whole incident, despite himself asking.

"Emptied a whole Glock mag into it before re-loading and switching to the Crawlers."

"The *what*?" Bastian asked, eyebrow raised.

"Oh, that's just what we've started to call them, the skinny ones with half a head," T chimed in, rather casually.

"Oh, gotcha."

"I'm not taking credit for that one, though," Z said. "*Zero* creativity."

T rolled his eyes. "It's a *call-sign*, Z, not the name of an abstract painting."

Z just shrugged, wearing an expression that said 'whatever' in the manner that a teenager might.

"It's straight to the point, I dig it," Bastian said rather casually. "Give 'em names, makes it easier to assess the threat and call-out targets."

"Exactly," T said, full of relief that he wasn't alone on the concept.

Z appeared unfazed. He just stared through the windshield.

"So, I assume you named the others, too?" Bastian asked after clearing his throat.

"Yes and no," T said, following a brief pause. "The winged ones we call Vultures, for obvious reasons. Z insisted on gargoyles, but I couldn't. Loved the TV show too much."

Z rolled his eyes.

"If you were *five years older*, Z, you'd have known it, too, and loved it just the same."

Bastian actually smiled. He could relate to T on this note, but didn't bring it up. And T was too busy playfully berating his partner to even notice the light expression on Bastian's face. By the time he looked back again, it was gone.

However, it was nonetheless noticeable that Bastian had since loosened up a little. Perhaps by preoccupying his mind with things like this, little details about the enemy, and treating his new acquaintances more like comrades rather than adolescent uniforms, he could focus on moving forward instead of wallowing in the past.

The all-too-immediate past.

A history nipping at his heels…

Buried directly beneath the surface, clawing through the soil…

"'Vulture' works," Bastian blurted. "Gargoyles sounds like a stretch. The purpose of call-signs is succinctness, not creativity."

"Couldn't agree more," T said, and then looked at his partner and grinned. Z glanced at him briefly before shaking his head and resuming his detached gaze through the windshield.

"Have you engaged with them much? More, or the same as Crawlers?"

T shook his head. "A lot less, actually. They didn't seem to start sprouting 'til about a half-hour after the first Crawlers did. And they act differently, too; scavenge and cower much more than Crawlers. Makes their name even more appropriate."

Bastian nodded, appearing somewhat pensive. He tried to avoid drawing from memory, his limited encounters with them.

"We still haven't named the big one yet, though," T said. He sighed and looked at his partner, but continued to speak to Bastian. "Maybe we should give this one to Z."

"Oh, how generous," Z said, facing T.

Bastian rolled his eyes and tried to stretch out his feet. He wasn't made to be crammed into the backseat of a police cruiser.

"How about 'ugly motherfucker'?" Bastian offered, his voice monotonous and devoid of satire.

The two officers smirked nevertheless.

"Fitting, for sure," T said. "But too many syllables, unfortunately."

"Damn. Okay, then I'm all out. T?" Bastian was already assimilating into this unusual camaraderie of sorts.

It was only remotely odd because they were strangers to him and the circumstances couldn't be more unprecedented. Everyone in the San Diego area, and possibly elsewhere, were thrust into this unpredictable, terrifying situation with no time to plan or catch a breath.

Bastian was beyond lucky, as much as he would never admit it given recent enormities, to be an exception to that. To have been found by these two men, and offered adequate time to evaluate their predicament.

At least, much more adequately than most.

T shrugged. "I was thinking…something to denote its place among the others. Like a commander. I dunno, but they clearly have a higher rank than Crawlers and Vultures. Not as much as a king, but—"

"A vicar," Z said simply. "Or a baron."

"The fuck is a vicar?" T's brow furrowed.

"Like a substitute or representative, usually in the church. The Pope, technically, is given the title Vicar of Christ."

Bastian pointed at Z. "Catholic?"

"Raised," Z shrugged nonchalantly.

"His family is *very* Catholic," T said, smirking. He then nodded at Bastian. "What about you?"

"I…I'd rather not get into it."

"Why not?" Z pressed.

T sighed.

"I don't know," Bastian shrugged.

"There's gotta be a reason—" Z started, but Bastian interrupted, actually smirking.

"No, that's my stance. I don't know. So, uh, agnostic, I guess?" He shrugged. "I believe in many things. Monotheism isn't one of them. But hey—who knows?"

T and Z looked at each other.

"Can we get back on track, fellas?" Bastian looked around, brow furrowing. "It'll be dark soon. Half an hour, my bet."

"Well," T took a deep breath, "I'm passing on 'vicar.' Sounds cool, to be honest, but these things are the polar opposite of anything religious. Demonic or not, Z."

"What about baron?"

T smirked. "You're gonna hate me."

"You don't know what a baron is?"

T shrugged dramatically, protruding his lower lip

and raising his eyebrows.

Z sighed and kneaded his brow. He started to talk before lowering his hand, but was interrupted by Bastian, who by now spoke so freely and firmly it was as if a metallic mesh divider wasn't between them.

"A political or feudal position, low, but with a direct responsibility to whoever's at the top."

Bastian shrugged while the two men stared blankly at him, although Z's forehead creased as he nodded, seemingly in approval.

"More or less," Bastian added.

"Fuck it. That works." T seemed happy with it. As if he came up with the moniker himself. "I bet that asshole answers directly to whoever is masterminding this bullshit. Devil or otherwise."

Bastian sighed and rolled his eyes.

The car shook as a tremor passed under the parking garage. It went as soon as it had come.

"How many levels is this thing?" Bastian asked.

"Four," T said, resituating himself and gunning the engine.

Z put on his seatbelt and snatched his pistol from the dashboard. He racked the slide to confirm that a round was chambered, and then looked back at Bastian.

"When we were hauling you into the car," he said, "we noticed that you've got some ammo in your pockets. Saw a shotgun but wasn't able to grab it in time. Feared big-baddy would swing back around. Didn't really repel him 'til we were leaving, T on the trigger."

"So what can you offer me?" Bastian asked. "Or

am I expected to fend them off with insults and profanity?"

"Your sarcasm bites just as hard, worst-case scenario," T said, rather snidely, and not caring about backlash as he spun the car around and drove up to the edge of the top level. He idled parallel to the concrete barrier, which came up to the side-view mirror, and rolled his window down. He peered out, looking around.

Bastian ignored his remark and scooted to that side of the car, in the backseat. He pressed his left brow against the glass to look out.

They were at the top of a parking garage that appeared to be under construction—more or less. The building it was technically connected to was being torn down and rebuilt, but aside from some signs and scaffolding, neither personnel nor equipment were on site. Bastian thought that maybe it was a weekend endeavor.

He was silently grateful that they had such a secluded spot for a momentary getaway.

The main street was visible from up here, but only reachable via a series of winding backroads. Hardly any foliage between here and there—they were just a couple hours south of Death valley, here.

Once Bastian recognized a few landmarks, such as particular gas stations in the near distance and a Bank of America, he discerned that they were less than ten minutes from Miramar.

Aside from these details, there wasn't much to take in from the sight up here. Damage assessment or otherwise. Much to Bastian's surprise, two studious sweeps of his gaze through the window lent him a better view than he expected, but moreover, not much in way of danger. No roaming threats or visible devastation.

A few pillars of smoke scarring the horizon in the distance, and a handful of scattered cars that appeared wrecked or otherwise abandoned.

He tried to ignore the images in his head, the likelihood that most of the vehicles' inhabitants had been forcibly pulled—or literally torn—from inside, by creatures beyond their comprehension.

Bastian was still trying to come to grips with the reality of all this, moreover each creature he saw, individually. From one 'Crawler' to the next, it was like each one was a newly discovered species of horror. Of unreality. Nightmare incarnate. Evil materialized.

His skin crawled.

He stifled, angrily even as he sat still, the memory of Maggie's death, and Eliza's. Not to mention their palpable fear preceding—

"Looks clear," T finally said. He sighed and leaned forward, chin against the steering wheel, as he dug under his seat. When he withdrew, he was holding a semiautomatic pistol. It had a black grip and receiver but a chrome slide. He brandished it over his shoulder, and looked back through the mesh divider. "This is my baby, Bastian. But I don't wanna forfeit the shotgun, so you can have her. I trust if anyone could put 'er to good use, it'd be you."

"H and K, USP forty-five," Bastian nodded. "Slick. I appreciate it."

T nodded.

"Loaded?"

"Yeah."

"Any extra mags lying around here?"

"Just one," Z said, fishing one out of the glovebox. He waved it in the air.

"This thing kosher?" Bastian asked.

"Just…don't tell our chief."

"What he don't know won't hurt him."

T flashed a smile. He shifted into park and popped open his door. He got out and gestured to Z, who tossed the spare magazine. Bastian tried the handle and the door opened, since there were no window controls. He started to climb out but T interrupted him.

"Here ya go," he said, handing Bastian the pistol and extra magazine. "We noticed the rounds in your pocket were mostly .45, and some shells. I took the liberty of robbing the shells, since they're compatible with my Remington. You can keep the .45's, obviously, now that you have *her*."

Bastian nodded. "Appreciated."

"We should get moving. Like you said…dark soon." T started to shut Bastian's door but was prohibited from doing so.

Bastian had extended his right foot just enough to keep the door open. He wiggled his toes in the dirty, thin, black dress sock which had already ripped in several places. It had *certainly* seen better days.

"Any chance you have an extra pair lying around? My father used to be a cop, in Baltimore. Where I was born. Anyway, he and the other boys in uniform would often carry spare shoes under their seats, in case theirs got wet."

T just smirked and Z laughed, drawing Bastian's attention.

"Sorry," Z said, shrugging. "But hey, you're not that far off."

"Only a little," T said, pinching his finger and thumb together, save for a tiny gap between them. He then nodded at Bastian, and spoke to Z. "Pop the trunk, Z. And don't worry, I won't give him yours."

"Better not," Z mumbled, leaning over the bulky center console to push the trunk button on the steering column.

"They wouldn't fit," T whispered at Bastian, simpering and winking.

Bastian couldn't help but smile, and shake his head once. While T tended to the trunk, Bastian scooted to the end of the seat until his long legs dangled outside the door.

"Hey, Z, keep an eye out, will ya?" T asked with his head still in the trunk, followed by a mostly inaudible mumble. "For fuck's sake."

"Yeah, yeah," Z said casually, his head nonetheless on a swivel. Despite his sarcasm, he appeared ever vigilant. "Coast is clear, skipper."

T sighed gutturally as he withdrew from the trunk, one of his hands full. He shut it with the other, and the sound practically echoed down into the parking garage, travelling farther than expected. He cringed at this, but with his eyes constantly sweeping and still spotting nothing, he felt somewhat comforted.

When T returned to Bastian, he offered him a

pair of black and red Pumas.

"Sometimes me and Z will stop at a park and shoot some hoops to pass time on slow days when our quotas are done. I'm an eleven, hope they fit."

Bastian was a twelve, and could usually squeeze into an 11.5, but kept this to himself.

"Solid. Thank you."

T nodded. "Sure thing."

As Bastian pulled them on, which was a little bit of a struggle but easier considering the thin socks, T ducked back into the car, behind the wheel. He shut his door and secured his seatbelt, by which time Bastian had both sneakers on.

"Good to go?" T asked.

"Just a sec." Bastian grunted and finished knotting the lace on the left shoe, then he pulled the door shut. "Alright."

T nodded and shifted into drive, slowly pulling away from the concrete barrier.

"Where were you two originally heading?" Bastian asked, finally finishing his other shoe and planting both feet down on the floormats, the rear of the center console between his knees. The shoes were definitely a snug, uncomfortable fit, but better than just socks, especially if—*when*—they had to get out.

"Hard to say, Bastian," T said. "We were on our patrol, and got sidetracked by the tremors, and our operator went nuts with various calls. Then radio silence. A few towers must've gotten hit, whether by quakes or the enemy themselves. Phones are just as useless, now. After that, we roamed northeast. Before radio silence, we'd heard the original quake's epicenter was Cali-patria. More in that direction we went, the more chaotic shit got. Not just the quakes, either, but the…yeah."

"Demons," Z muttered, staring out his window.

Neither T nor Bastian said anything.

At this point T had driven down two levels in the garage, which was vacant save for a parked, empty car here and there.

"Mighty brave of y'all to just venture deeper into the shit," Bastian finally said.

"Well," T sighed gutturally, "I hate to sound cli-ché, but…we're cops. Sometimes we act less like it, but in cases like this, you gotta hope some uniforms take it seriously. Realize that now more than ever, everyday folk need our help. Or *some* help. Whether they trust cops or not."

"Nothing unites people more than tragedy," Bastian mumbled, barely audible.

It was the raw, undeniable truth that everyone wanted to deny, or at least not say out loud.

Bastian especially, given the circumstances.

"Forgive me for bringing it up, but, what about your families?"

"Like I said, my girl's safe, I mean, her parents' place in Anaheim is fucking medieval." T smirked briefly and widened his eyes. "In the best way."

"They're loaded?"

T nodded. "Oh, yeah."

"Lucky," Z muttered.

"And yours, Z? You said Oceanside, right?"

Z nodded. "No fortress, but two years ago one of

my cousins and his friends took up building this real nice basement for Ma. I mean *nice*. I trust that'll keep 'em safe for now. I…I try not to think about it."

Z coughed and shifted in his seat. He went from staring out his window to scrutinizing his pistol.

"I understand. Well, I'm sure they're safe. Y'all seem confident in that."

"What about you, Bastian?" T asked, stopping the car about ten feet from the high-clearance entrance of the parking garage's bottom level. "Where were *you* headed?"

"Miramar," he said simply.

"I could've guessed," T said. "Care to elaborate, though?"

"Do you know the way?"

"Generally. But there are several buildings."

"I'll fill you in, en route." Bastian peered out of the window. "It'll be dark soon…and I have a feeling that our enemy is eager for that."

## 5

Reaching the main road didn't take long. T wasn't adhering to traffic laws, and whenever he could, he would hop a curb or traverse a median to bypass unnecessary turns. Neither Z nor Bastian ever protested his whimsical decisions to make these maneuvers. However, when he bounced the car over the first median, it took Bastian by surprise. Z was unfazed, and probably accustomed to it by now.

It had even interrupted Bastian midsentence.

Since then, he waited until they reached the main road to resume his explanation of CHERI. He took the abridged route, as he didn't want to inundate them with gratuitous information.

"It isn't just about reaching safety. But better means of defending ourselves. And taking the fight to them."

"So, what, arm ourselves to the teeth with cutting-edge tech and wander aimlessly throughout Cali, wiping out this scourge?" T chuckled, off-beat. "I mean, shit, don't get me wrong, it *sounds* like a plan—but looks fishy on paper."

"Not aimlessly, for one," Bastian retorted. "We make a beeline for Calipatria, figure out what's causing this shit. Ground Zero. Hopefully by then we'll have proper military support, supposing D.C. isn't getting hit with some form of this, too."

"If it isn't just local, the country's in for a shit-storm," Z said, sounding exhausted just admitting it. He rubbed his brow and shook his head.

"Before our house got hit," Bastian said, spite tickling his tone, "the news mentioned quakes as far inland as Wyoming. And that was, I dunno, two hours ago? Do the math."

"This isn't exactly something that seems to be going by the numbers."

"Sure, T, but some deductions can't be ignored."

T sighed and his hands gripped the wheel tighter than before. Bastian could even hear the leather wrench under his grip. The car's suspension bumped and rattled as T drove it over another median with a low curb.

Bastian was the only one without his seatbelt on. He bounced in the backseat, but simply wished he had more legroom. He didn't want to buckle in, he preferred to be ready for anything at any moment.

*Mobility is life.*

"How 'bout we focus on the here and now, fellas," Z insisted. He looked intently over his shoulder, through the mesh divider. "Exactly what *type* of weapons are being developed where you work? We talking lasers and shit?"

Bastian sighed and shook his head. Now it was he who stared out his window, as if trying to pinpoint a dust mote of hope on the darkening horizon.

"Not quite," he finally said. "Energy-based weapons are in what we call Development Hell. Most of the 'finished models' are too unstable to carry in the field, and require a lot more testing. The Arbalest, however, has aced all recent tests, but is still likely a year away from approval due to recoil and heat expulsion."

"The what-now?" Z asked, barely blinking.

"Arbalest. Named after an innovative crossbow design from the Middle Ages. Except CHERI's Arbalest is a handheld railgun."

"A *railgun*?" T said, laughing wildly. "I thought the smallest railguns presently available were fitted to tanks and battleships?"

"True. Until now. Or…in a year or two." Bastian emphatically looked around. "Make that a few years, at best."

"Gravy," T shook his head, grimly smirking.

"But like I said…virtually unusable, due to extreme recoil and heat. Same with the Sevin."

"Speak English, doc," Z said.

Bastian smirked. "The Sevin. S-e-v-i-n. It's a seven-barrel minigun, modeled after the six-barrel M61 Vulcan. Belt-fed, disintegrating-link, Gatling-style, gas-operated, rotary *handheld* chaingun. Same issues, though—weight, too, on top of the recoil and heat."

"Wonderful," T said with a burst of borderline maniacal laughter. He clapped the steering wheel and then threw Bastian a glance over his shoulder before returning his attention to the road. "How about what we *can* use, without melting our hands or throwing us into another dimension?"

They reached the main road, and the squad car's

tires squealed against pavement before finding purchase.

"The ROT-20," Bastian said, as if a child reminiscing about his crush. "A *rotary*-barrel automatic shotgun capable of a hundred-and-fifty rounds-per-minute; theoretically, of course. Ammunition is loaded and stored integrally, as you might a revolver, except that each eighteen-inch barrel holds six shells."

"How many barrels?" Z asked.

"Three."

"Why the 'twenty'?"

"It's twenty-gauge, not your traditional twelve. You'd hardly notice, damage wise. A soft target certainly wouldn't. Smaller shells mean tighter buckshot spread, higher rate-of-fire and less recoil, even with the rotary barrels spinning. The other plus is that it's also configured to use twenty-gauge slug rounds, for increased range and damage output."

"Sounds enticing," T said. "And that shit's ready to hit the market?"

"Not quite. It's in its final stages. Nothing we're currently working on, conceptually, is officially ready for distribution. But a few, including the ROT-20, have been confirmed combat-ready."

"That's relieving."

"I'd especially have to agree. Being the lead designer and all."

"So, wait, you *designed* these guns yourself?" T asked, a little dumbfounded but also impressed.

"Not really. Just the aesthetics, and the ideas.

Then guys with real talent, the engineers, put it all together, making magic out of my 2-and-3D designs."

"Psh, so you're an artist," Z said, rather matter-of-factly.

Bastian's brow furrowed and he tilted his head in skepticism.

"I'd hardly go that far," he finally said.

"Agree to disagree," T added. "Jump onto the next one."

Bastian sighed and looked around, trying to be vigilant during all of this talk. His mind did the wandering while his body sat still. When he wasn't patting or rubbing his pantlegs, he was fiddling with the pistol in his hands, safety on, trying to keep his thoughts from wallowing into the deep-end.

"Well, there's the, uh…the Supe."

"As in the meal?" T asked.

"Uh, yes and no," Bastian said with a little smirk. "It's actually one of the designs that *isn't* mine, but the idea is, something I pitched when given the theme of breaching and close-quarters engagements with enemies wearing body armor."

"Do tell," T said, briefly eyeballing the tactical shotgun firmly set between the windshield and dashboard.

"So, the Supe is essentially a sawed-off, double-barrel shotgun. Technically, the term is short-barrel, but at sixteen inches that makes it—"

"Illegal," Z said simply.

"Exactly. It's not quite a traditional type of gun

for tactical scenarios, the sawed-off, that is. Like the Lupara. But Imagine a Lupara made of steel, polymer plastics, and capable of not only obliterating a target five feet away but also one well across the room."

"*How*?" Z asked, emphasizing the H.

Bastian leaned forward, feeling somewhat rejuvenated, as if doing a sales pitch for something that made his blood itch—in a good way.

"A barrel extension," he said, using hand gestures that were essentially useless to T, who focused on driving, but occasionally glanced in the rearview, while Z twisted in his seat to pay more attention. "Now, the Supe's standard orientation is a sawed-off format, like the Lupara, with a sixteen-inch double-barrel, side-by-side. Imagine a sawed-off with the same stopping power as your run-of-the-mill elephant rifle. When engaging in CQC, the extension is folded down, and a tactical foregrip protrudes for better recoil control."

"Needed for a sawed-off," T thought out loud. "Shorter the barrel, harder the kick, higher the muzzle climb."

"Yep. Now, say your target leapt out the window and is hauling ass on foot, increasing the distance. Or say you exit the hallway or room and are in the parking lot. Target's a good thirty feet away. You're outta pistol ammo or whatever. No worries." Bastian's voice kicked into a state of zeal. "*Grip and flip*—swing that barrel extension *up*, and boom, it's gone from sixteen to twenty-two inches. The foregrip is now facing up; take it and *twist it*, until you hear a *click*, and bam, barrels are locked, secure and ready for action. Grip is facing down again, for recoil control, and range has been sufficiently increased."

"Goddamn, color me impressed," T said. "I dunno what you just said, but I like it. Where's mine?"

"Get us to Miramar in one piece and I'll slap one in your hands."

"Whew," Z said. "I'm impressed. Not gonna lie, Bastian, sounded like a stretch. But I guess, in this day and age, with government tech, there's no telling."

Bastian just nodded, and the INFERNO Suit not crossing his mind until now. It lit him up from the inside, and gave him a plethora of ideas, including a version of hope that he hadn't thought feasible before this moment. However, its prototype condition beckoned many questions of an incredulous nature. As confident as Bastian had been about it earlier today, now he wasn't terribly certain.

"What is the Supe, twelve-gauge?" T asked.

"Oh, yeah," Bastian said, reeled back to reality. He cleared his throat and wiped off the concerned look on his face, which neither of them had noticed, fortunately. "But not buckshot."

"Slugs?"

"Kinda. Bolo rounds."

"Oh, shit," Z said. "Aren't those illegal, too?"

"In three states, yeah. Not Cali, although it doesn't really matter, since the Supe isn't and will likely never be for civilian purchase or use."

"Bolo rounds," Z raised an eyebrow. "Aren't those the barbell things?"

"Yep," Bastian nodded. "Steel barbell slugs.

They've been heavily improved upon at CHERI, we have manufactured a double-ought variant for use in the Supe."

Z whistled low.

"So why's it called the 'Supe'?" T asked.

"Double entendre. 'Supe,' short for 'super,' 'cause that's what you're getting, a super fucking shotgun. And 'soup,' as in, it'll turn your enemy to red soup."

The two officers scoffed, scowling, but in an impressed manner.

"That is, of course, if they're not wearing body armor," Bastian added. He then pointed. "Oh, take this exit."

"But Miramar is the other—"

"Trust me, T," Bastian insisted. "Remember what I said, CHERI isn't exactly front-page. Even the NSA is more publicized than CHERI."

"No shit," T mumbled, and slowly changed lanes to take the westbound exit.

Darkness was just about upon them, dusk on its way out the door so to speak, and their lack of engagement with the enemy—or spotting any survivors for that matter—was kind of unsettling.

Then again, the closer they got to the Miramar military base, the farther from 'civilization' they ventured. Miramar included an airfield that required a broader perimeter than most other military bases, due to its restricted airspace. Hence the seclusion, despite being surrounded on all sides by suburbia.

"So, what else?" T asked after a deep breath.

"Please, keep my mind off all this doom and gloom. Surprised how little activity there is on the road. I've seen some bogeys meandering in the distance, but they don't seem interested in us."

"Might be following, spying, scheming," Z said, paranoia evident in his voice and body language.

Bastian clicked his tongue. "That would suggest that they're sharper than the mindless beasts I've taken them to be."

He of course knew this wasn't entirely true. There had already been times where the creatures showcased some form of methodical intelligence. However, their callous hostility made it easier to accept them as feral killing machines.

Perhaps the two officers felt the same way, or shared a similar mentality, because their reaction was mute. They even exchanged a brief glance between themselves, which Bastian inferred as a tacit agreement, before finally T said something neutral.

"Regardless, I gotta be shamefully *grateful* they aren't on us like white on rice." He sighed, theatrically. "Now, *please*, Bastian, give me more good tidings from this heaven-on-Earth place you call CHERI."

Bastian couldn't help but don a transient smile. He empathized with T, as he himself felt pleasantly detached from emotional burdens when talking about CHERI. From the first mention of the Arbalest to the Sevin, and then the ROT-20.

And yet, as his tiny smirk fled, he realized that that was where things fell off the map.

"Unfortunately, guys," he said through a rough

exhalation, "that's about it. I mean…there are a few other WIP projects that have tantalizing futures, but they're not even remotely close to being combat-ready."

"Whip?" Z asked, eyebrow raised.

"W-I-P," Bastian said. "Work-in-progress."

"Jesus, Z, get with the program," T said.

"Sorry I'm not *acclimated* yet to your nerd-slang."

Bastian's brow furrowed and he let loose a little chuckle.

"'Acclimated,' whew, that's a biggie for you, Z," T blithely scoffed. "How are your lungs holding up after that?"

"I'll show you a *biggie*, ass-hat," Z gritted his teeth and clutched the groin of his uniform pants.

"Gentlemen, please, can we try to focus, here?" Bastian said from the backseat. "Or would you like *me* to drive?"

"Shit, not gonna lie, I'd love to take a cop-car-backseat-nap right about—" T's sarcasm was fluid but short-lived. They had been approaching an underpass to a small bridge that appeared to be in stable condition, with sizable concrete abutments. With dusk upon them and the disappearance of sunlight altogether in a matter of minutes, Bastian reckoning ten or fifteen, distinguishing shadows from potential threats became more challenging.

In hindsight, Bastian wished they had been paying more attention to their surroundings, and less dismissive of the enemy slinking in the distance.

When the two 'Vultures' descended from the beams below the bridge above them, T impulsively hit the brakes. The car's frame lurched and Bastian's face struck the mesh divider.

*Should've buckled in*, he thought regrettably, and his nose and forehead ached. When his body withdrew from the recoiling momentum of the car, he felt a sting on his brow followed by a wet warmth.

Looking up bore witness to the two Vultures landing on the car. The first alighted on the hood, denting it but not crushing the engine beneath, thanks to the creature's winged deceleration. Same with the other, which landed on the roof of the car, and while the ceiling inside barely dented, the exterior light-bar instantly shattered. The siren itself made a dying sound, and sparks illuminated the creature outside as it shrieked.

Streaks tore through the ceiling above Z's head as the Vulture's foot talons scored the roof.

Meanwhile the one on the hood leaned forward on hook-like arms, its wings folded between its 'elbows' and hips. Though not as tall and gangly as a Crawler, this breed of creature was nonetheless an upsetting sight. Its eyes glowed like bright embers, and its oddly beaked mouth, lined with hundreds of tiny, sharp teeth like broken crystals, released a terribly grating sound.

"Fuck, why'd you stop, T!?" Z exclaimed, lifting his pistol. "Punch it! Throw these motherfuckers off!"

"Fuck!" T snapped, and changed pedals with a lead foot. The car jerked forward, its chassis lurching back, and Bastian sank in his seat. He involuntarily swallowed a lump in his throat, whether fear or nausea he couldn't be certain.

The Vulture on the roof was thrown off, and the one on the hood caught off-balance.

Unfortunately, neither creature was entirely removed from the vehicle. Both stubbornly held onto the now accelerating squad car.

The Vulture on the hood was driven headlong into the windshield, its beak actually penetrating the Plexiglas, only to have its head lodged there like a stick in solidifying concrete. The small hole that its beak and head had bored through wasn't tight enough to shear its long, thin neck, however, as T deliberately slalomed, it did suffer cuts. Blood striped the windshield in long, winding red streaks as the creature struggled to hold on, its winged arms and stubby legs skittering across the hood. Meanwhile, its shrieking beak-jaws snapped inside the car, and T maddeningly demanded that Z "shut it the fuck up."

Despite his seatbelt, Z was having trouble sitting still, thanks to T's jerky steering, which he knew, too, was necessary to keep the Vulture from reaching either of them. Just the same, the seatbelt prohibited much movement from Z, as he struggled to aim at the creature without the risk of including T in his line-of-fire.

In the same moments of this madness, behind the two officers sat Bastian, but not for long. He ultimately clambered onto his knees to face the rear window, through which he saw the other Vulture. It hung onto the trunk of the car with not one but both of its hook-like arms, while wailing crazily and probably dragging or 'running' its legs across the road. Simultaneously its wings flapped in a frenzy, whether trying to gain flight or simply reorient itself, Bastian wasn't sure.

He knew, though, that if these things were actually capable of full-fledged flight, then humanity might have to call it quits.

He immediately abandoned that kind of mindset and kicked into third gear, two-handing the pistol that T had gifted him. His elbows locked and as he kneeled in the seat, his back against the mesh divider, Bastian all but pressed the muzzle to the sloped rear window. He squeezed the trigger twice in rapid succession, aiming slightly down. The bullets tore through the glass, the second shot from the muzzle energy alone shattering it altogether. Both rounds struck the creature as it was pulling itself forward, trying to mount the trunk.

Where exactly the bullets hit, Bastian didn't know, but the creature bled the same as a Crawler, and was immediately flung off the car. He victoriously watched it roll down the road behind them like a fleshy tumbleweed.

Z was less triumphant about the gunshots, as they startled and disoriented him inside the car.

Even T exclaimed from them, but wasn't taken out of the action. Instead, he actually noted where Bastian was, with his head and back to the barrier, and it gave him an idea.

Knowing that Bastian wouldn't be harmed in this maneuver, T abruptly slammed on his breaks once the car was linear again.

Bastian felt the momentum shift and was glad he

was positioned like this when the tires screeched.

T was even more pleased by the consequence of his decision. The Vulture flailing on the hood was thrown from the car, and the violent deceleration caused the sharp hole in the windshield to sever its neck in the process. The decapitated body struck the asphalt and—along with the head on the dashboard—disintegrated into embers seconds later.

They looked like fireflies in the night.

The sun had just about submitted to darkness.

"Everyone…everyone okay?" T asked through jagged breaths.

Ashen tire-smoke obscured the base of the car on all sides. It glowed red from the tail-lights at the rear, where Bastian found himself staring.

"Affirmative," Z muttered, his voice thin.

"Not hurt," Bastian replied, sounding distracted but present nonetheless. "Sorry about the shots. Was necessary."

"Any action taken with my baby is necessary," T said.

"Yeah, she handles tight," Bastian nodded, his clammy mitts still firmly gripping the .45-caliber pistol.

"Do you know where we are?" T asked. "How far to Miramar? I can't…I can't tell…"

Bastian took a few deep breaths, and finally gave up half-expecting the Vulture he shot to reemerge through the red-lit smokescreen behind the car.

"Yeah. Less than five. Take the left at the end of this road. You'll hit a circle. It can be confusing even in daylight, so hopefully the signs are still up. Look for a reflective red 'one-way, do not enter' sign."

"And let me guess," T added, "enter there?"

"You got it," Bastian nodded firmly, and adjusted himself in the backseat, ready to peel out of the car as soon as needed. "There'll be a long, narrow road, like a driveway with a high curb on either side—take that around a bend. Employee lot is just yonder."

"Any gates or security I should expect?"

Bastian blanked for a moment as he thought of Benny, and wondered if the man was still on duty. Or acting it. Knowing how stubborn he could be, and his genuine nature to help others despite caring for his bedridden father at home, Bastian would bet Benny was there. Whether inside the building, as Bastian hoped for his sake, or at his security booth.

*Too exposed, if they realize he's there.*

Supposing, of course, that Benny was even still alive. As much as Bastian hated to consider otherwise, it was foolish and even dangerous to not accept that possibility.

T got to driving more seriously and urgently, the closer they got to the base. There were still signs up indicating the 'only authorized personnel beyond this point' nature of the property, as well as the penalties for trespassing.

Taking the circle without getting turned around, T dodged some wreckage of a car and motorcycle, including two mutilated bodies that made him grimace, before sighting the red one-way sign. He took it without hesitation, clipping the curb in the process, which wasn't a quiet error, and they lost a hubcap.

"Sorry, sorry," T mumbled, worked up but keeping himself locked down.

"Easy on the gas, T, narrow route, and yes, there's a steel gate at the lot entrance. One of those yellow bars, but it's unyielding. Concrete barriers on the sides. So take it easy. Worst-case, we hop out."

"Shit," T mumbled.

"How busy is this place at nightfall?" Z asked, almost as on-edge as T, but trying to keep his cool for both of them.

"Not very. Most of the work is done during the day. No major night crew, just janitorial personnel and some security with low-level access."

"So, lot should be pretty empty?"

"Theoretically. Unless..." Bastian trailed off as the cynical thoughts crept into his skull. With T driving them closer and closer, it was only a matter of seconds before they rounded the bend and the parking lot came into view.

The anticipation was torture for Bastian.

"Unless *what*?" Z asked.

"Unless the late-shift personnel couldn't get out in time."

"W-Well, m-maybe this shirt-storm hasn't even reached 'em yet," Z stammered. He was starting to sweat profusely.

"Maybe," Bastian's voice was small. He was trying to convince himself.

Once T turned that corner and their route opened up into two available lanes, there were no more doubts to harbor. Everything was certain, to an extent.

Bastian gulped, speechless, as light from the few parking lot lamps reached out to splash the squad car. The flickering glow from scattered fires added an orange luminance, and combined, they turned Bastian's face into a distorted palette of trepidation.

# 6

It was undeniable, now—not only had their enemy reached the Miramar base, particularly CHERI's compound, but they had not relented. Bastian's first impression was all he needed to construe that the creatures weren't just focusing on civilian areas. They likely aimed to seek out every form of life, able to somehow detect even those within fortified buildings.

He was unnerved and then some, but most of all, he was angry. Bastian had not felt an iota of this kind of rage for over an hour.

He was able to bottle it up then, though he knew in his heart of hearts that it was merely a temporary fix. A soppy Band-Aid over a fresh wound that refused to stop bleeding. The adhesive had finally given up, and the pain returned twofold.

Along with it, however, the ache for a more permanent remedy. Which, in Bastian's tormented mind, was a very long route. A very long and likely implausible one, but that which he couldn't ignore now.

*No matter what,* he thought bitterly, teeth gritting. *Must reach—*

"You see any survivors?" T asked, his voice low. The car idled about forty feet from the gate. One of the yellow bars was down and secure. The other was down for the count, all but dislodged from its mount, which would have taken great force—more than most cars.

"Just…bodies…" Z said through a sniffle. "So many bodies."

Corpses littered the parking lot, which was the size of an airport's. It featured numbered clusters, making it easier to remember where one parked. At each cluster was a tall lamp post with an LED light that shone directly down. Most of them were either shattered or broken, several had cars wrapped around their concrete bases. One of them, a large pickup truck, appeared to have rolled into the pole itself, cleaving it and totaling the vehicle.

Most of the bodies, at first glance from this distance, with only the surviving lamp posts and the scattered fires to provide illumination, were fatally mutilated. Decapitated, eviscerated, or otherwise dismembered.

To Bastian, they weren't just bodies of nameless civilians. They were colleagues. Even if he did not know all of his peers' names, they were nonetheless all part of the same team.

The sight was nauseating to say the least, no matter who witnessed it.

The only slightly comforting aspect of this was that no creatures could be discerned amid the ruination.

"What about the demons?"

T and Z slowly turned their heads to face the backseat. The last person either of them expected to have used that term so nonchalantly yet resolutely, was

Bastian. Yet there he sat, like a cemetery statue, a wingless gargoyle, his face warped with vindictiveness.

He didn't elaborate to them, mostly because he didn't feel like it and part of him literally could not throw together a coherent explanation. However, his reason was more or less brutally simple—

*What else could they be?*

Bastian's thoughts throbbed with hatred.

*This kind of indiscriminate barbarism. Merciless? Yeah. And fucking soulless.*

"Uhhh," Z drawled, sluggishly pivoting his head away from Bastian to instead observe the parking lot.

"Drive, T," Bastian all but growled. "Drive or open my goddamn door."

"Slowly, though," T said, meticulously letting off the gas pedal. "Don't wanna draw too much attention. I'm sure they're still here, lurking somewhere."

"Probably," Bastian huffed. "Kill your lights. Stop at the gate. Might have to get out unless I can open the one that's still operable."

"Deal." T switched off his headlights and their view of the security gate was plunged into relative darkness. The nearest fire from the belly of an overturned car on the other side of the broken gate splashed the immediate area with a yellow glow.

At night there were usually spotlights operable from the roof of the security booth, to profusely illuminate cars on approach. However, these were apparently not active tonight, likely having been destroyed. They were on a timer, to Bastian's recollection, which meant that this havoc had to have been caused very recently.

"They're still around, I'm sure of it," Bastian said, growing impatient as he sat like a brick in the backseat. His hands gripped the pistol audibly, making its metal and plastic parts creak under the pressure. "This mess is fresh. I can sense it."

As they slowly approached the gate, less than twenty feet now and closing, the tires crunched on broken glass and metallic debris. Probably from a car that had somehow gotten away.

*Good for you. I hope you made it home safe.*

It was a far-fetched thought but right now Bastian had to acknowledge *some* fragment of hope or else he would find himself waist-deep in despair.

"What's that sound?" Z asked. "Shh! You hear it? Stop the car, T. Rolling the windows down."

From Z's door controls, he automatically lowered the driver and passenger side windows. The back two were fixed shut for security purposes.

T stopped the car only then.

Someone was yelling into the dark night. The voice clearly came from nearby, although it sounded strained and anguished.

Bastian's brow furrowed.

Slowly, his eyes glazed with tears.

The shouting voice took on coherency.

"Stay away! Go! Get outta here! Stay away!"

"Benny," Bastian mumbled, scowling. The grimace turned into something desperate and irate. He scooted and slammed his body weight into the door behind the driver's side. "Open the fucking door!"

T parked the car and got out.

"Open the fucking door!" Bastian yelled.

As T opened the door, Bastian poured from the backseat like a rush of water through a broken levee.

"Wait, Bastian, *wait*!" T started calm, but then had to growl the last word and managed to grab Bastian's arm, restraining him for a moment. The man's body was shaking, T could tell just by holding his exposed right arm. T's brow furrowed and his expression was nothing shy of dumbfounded. He kept his voice quiet, but assertive. "I get it. You know the guy. But *listen* to what he's saying, for fuck's sake. We gotta be smart about—"

"*Goooooo*!" Benny shouted, his voice scratching and wavering in the fire-scarred night.

"No, *you two* gotta be smart," Bastian growled. "*I* gotta be *me*. Now if that means being mad and stupid and crazy, then so be it."

He forcibly pulled his arm away from T, who was not a short or small guy, but Bastian had him beat in the muscle department. And the anger department. And everything that was attached to that kind of traumatized, chaotic energy in a man.

Bastian eventually dragged his stern eyes off of T and swung himself to face the compound. It was a massive building with multiple wings, the third of which was facing the opposite direction and couldn't be seen from here. The entrance on the other side of the parking lot was about a hundred yards.

Considering all of the cars and wreckage, and bodies, and possible lurking threats, that football-field's length felt more like three or four of them.

In that moment, as Bastian picked up speed in his march toward the security booth, he realized it might as well be the entire state of Delaware he would be crossing.

He was more grateful now than before, for the shoes he had borrowed from T, especially as small crumbs of glass crunched under the soles.

"It's not safe for you here," Benny continued to say, his voice on the verge of a whimper.

"Nowhere is safe right now, big guy," Bastian said, trying to summon hope from the bones of his own despair. He finally reached the concrete hut of a security booth and stood in the arched doorway. Benny was sitting down, his legs sprawled before him, with his back and head against the wall.

Benny croaked through a gasp as he looked up at Bastian and his eyes widened. A thick stream of coagulated blood ran down his forehead, from a gash on his scalp. He had also suffered some kind of sharp contact to his stomach, which bled from a slit in his navy uniform, and beneath that, a wider opening in his dark skin.

Immediately, Bastian dropped to a knee and solemnly shook his head, trying to assess Benny's wounds without touching him too much. Without causing him more pain as it were.

"Goddammit, Benny, you and your ten-hour shifts. What happened to you? Hell, can you at least *walk?*"

"No use tryna walk," Benny grumbled, exhausted from the shouting and, clearly, the tribulation.

"Let me and the guys haul you with us. We're

headed inside."

"Who's with ya? Maggie with ya?" Benny strained to sit up more, to pull himself out of a slouch, and call out Maggie's name. He ended up coughing through it.

A light tremor shook the ground momentarily, and dust from a split in the concrete ceiling drifted down. It exacerbated Benny's cough, while Bastian scowled and stood up, leaning out of the security booth to fervently beckon the squad car closer.

T parked it directly outside the booth, as close to the lowered barrier as possible.

"That's…that's more of 'em, Bastian," Benny wheezed. "They…they come up through the ground…killing at random. Sometimes even…even eating…more will…more will be here shortly. Some are…some already are. In the lot. Staying low…staying quiet. You gotta…"

Bastian shook his head as he kneeled back down beside Benny.

"Six years, I've been working here. Six years we've been friends; before anyone else at this installation said a word, *you* welcomed me. I'm not about to leave you here to—"

"Die? Too late, friend." Benny took his eyes off Bastian to stare straight ahead. "Please. Go, be with your family."

Tears dappled Bastian's cheek and seeped into his bearded jawline. He hardly even blinked as he stared at the left side of Benny's face.

"What about yours, Benny? What about your

Pops?"

"I'll see him in a few minutes," Benny said, his voice running thin.

Bastian's brow furrowed and he wanted to refuse to accept these things, but the last thing he was going to do was tell Benny that Maggie and Eliza were also dead.

He could not resist it, though.

"I'm here with two cops, Benny. Help us get inside. We can pull you into the infirmary."

"I wouldn't make it halfway," Benny wheezed, still staring forward. "Take my gun. Ammo in the bottom drawer. Keys…"

Blood spurted from his lips and he coughed violently for a few seconds.

A shadow fell over Bastian and he looked up to see T standing in the doorway, his eyes down.

"Keys on my belt," Benny continued. His body began slackening all over. He was forfeiting the fight, at last. "Emergency entrance code…lockdown in effect…'good cause.'"

It only took Bastian a second or two to realize that Benny was referring to the alphabetical traits of the keypad at the compound's entrance, other side of the lot. As for the meaning, that was fairly simple—Benny had always stated that he worked here because he believed CHERI's intentions were genuine, not just to profit from weaponry and war, but to protect the country and to defeat any enemy that threatened the way of life. That of America, or any nation.

The way of life was universal. And any threat to that deserved elimination.

This was how Benny put it, in more or less words, and always more cordially than anyone else could.

"If we hurry, and are careful," T suggested, clearly with grave hesitance, "we can maybe—"

Bastian raised a hand over his shoulder to gesture for silence among them.

"Benny," he said quietly, sensing the life leave the man, like a wave of cold air, "I know they know this, but please tell them that I love them. And that I'm sorry. I'm so sorry…I couldn't be strong enough…"

Whether or not Benny heard Bastian before he took his last breath was uncertain, but it didn't matter to him. He just had to speak it.

"Uh, T?" Z said, standing by the car. His voice quivered. "We got company."

"Bastian, I'm really sorry, but—"

"I heard him, T. Just give me a fucking second."

Hurriedly, and ignoring the briny stinging to his eyes, Bastian unearthed Benny's wallet, and then pocketed his driver's license, as well as his security access card. He then snatched the keys from his belt, and as he did so, Benny's heavy torso slumped to the right, against a filing cabinet.

While Bastian searched the bottom drawers of the desk, T leaned in.

"Anything I can help with?"

"No. Go outside. We need to reach the compound entrance. It's closest to parking cluster G. Look for G. I'm right behind you."

T stammered.

"Go!" Bastian snapped, and T removed himself from the security booth.

Through several deep breaths, Bastian finished inside. He found a small carton of 9mm cartridges for Benny's semiautomatic pistol. He pocketed the carton and kept the gun in his right hand. On his way out of the booth, he wiped the tears from his eyes and cheeks with his sweaty arm, and drew T's lent .45 with his free hand.

He spotted T and Z advancing into the parking lot, slowly and constantly looking behind themselves. Likely waiting for Bastian. Eventually they spotted him, and he stuck out like a sore thumb in the erratically lit night, with his white tanktop and exposed arms. Unlike T and Z, who both still wore their dark blue uniforms, sans their hats.

Once they made eye contact with him, they proceeded with greater haste, but no less alert.

A brief quake faltered the men, and the sound of the earth splitting was not terribly far off.

However, Bastian was relieved the slightest in that he'd been right about one thing—CHERI's thick concrete foundation seemed impenetrable. No sinkholes spotted in the parking lot, and if what they had just felt and heard was one itself, it sounded distant enough to not be on the property.

"The hell was that?" T asked, dumbfounded, stopping midstride.

"Another sinkhole, probably," Z muttered. "Same as earlier. They're trying to converge on us."

"'Cause they can't get under our feet," Bastian said, still striding forward. His voice was husky, pushed through a series of panting. "CHERI's foundation won't allow it."

"Well…that's relieving," T admitted, and started moving again.

"Just keep your head on a swivel, shoot anything that moves," Bastian insisted, doing the same. "Don't think there are any survivors here. Maybe inside."

"Y-You think they can smell us?" T stammered, his composure starting to dwindle.

"Doesn't concern us right now," Bastian lied. "Just focus on that 'G' sign, and cover my back while I enter the code. Building's on lockdown."

The parking cluster signs were almost all lit up, as they were connected to one of the two backup power grids linked with the CHERI facility.

"There's still power inside?" T asked.

They were all jogging now, grateful to have gotten halfway across the lot at this point without spotting any threats.

"Oughtta be," Bastian said, taking the lead. He noticed, as he passed between the two officers, that Z was not in the best shape and T, while taller and fitter, appeared remarkably shaken.

"That's comforting," Z said, panting.

A loud, shrill screech pierced the otherwise still night. It immediately drew their attention, inadvertently slowing them down, and to their far right they saw a car on its roof slide across the pavement. That was the source of the screech, the metal grating, sparks flying around it.

"*That's* not," Z added, in reference to his last

statement.

T and Z found themselves standing still, staring in that direction, as the car was pushed across the lot.

Meanwhile, Bastian had continued. He didn't notice that they had even stopped until he was about thirty feet from the G cluster. His shoes—T's rather—which he had since almost literally broken into, scuffed the pavement as he came to a stop. He looked back, hands and pistols dangling at his sides. At first he stared at the two policemen who were in awe of what they witnessed, and then Bastian's own eyes redirected.

He began to call out to them, a reminder of urgency, but his voice caught in his throat.

The cause of the sliding car had risen up from behind it, and stood about eight or nine feet tall. How it had even hidden behind the vehicle was beyond them, unless merely masked by the night, no lights or fires in the immediate area, and it must have been hunched on all fours. Now, however, it was bipedal and humanoid, inexplicably burly with thick arms and legs, a broad chest and shoulders, a condensed abdomen and imposing claws at the end of each digit.

In the darkness it was difficult to discern specific features and coloration, but something about the monstrosity made Bastian think that it was in fact 'of this Earth.' Contrary to the opposite statement that most people made when referring to alien life.

*But this isn't alien*, Bastian was convinced. *This is something far worse.*

The large beast roared, a sound torn between rolling thunder and a bloodcurdling howl. From the abyss between its disturbingly humanoid jaws—similar to a Crawler's—flared a bright orange glow. As if the beast's insides were composed of flame.

And then its veins, if they could be called that, illuminated this same color. All over its bulky body, giving it a fiery glow.

The features of its face became clearer, although Bastian wished they hadn't. For it had small, beady yellow eyes that glowed, too, a bulbous forehead and a smooth, pale dome of a skull, but no nasal or ear holes.

For five long seconds since it roared, the beast just stood there, glaring at the petrified men.

Bastian snapped out of his own daze and shouted one word that reanimated the officers' muscles.

"*Moooove!*"

T and Z spun in Bastian's direction and bolted. T moved faster off the bat, but Z was close at his heels.

The large beast snarled and hunkered forward before loping after them. Its gait was sluggish in comparison, the weight of its body a burden, but five seconds into the pursuit and Bastian realized the creature was picking up speed.

"Come on! Go, go!" Bastian yelled, beckoning the men and waiting to move himself until they had reached his position. As soon as he did, however, he only backpedaled, mindful of his feet, while raising the two pistols and firing as fast as he could squeeze the triggers. He knew that the 9mm he had taken from Benny would hardly do any damage, but hoped that with T's .45 it would suffice to at least delay the beast.

"Watch your back!" T shouted, and Bastian

turned just in time to bounce off a parked car. He staggered into a stumble, facing the building and taking his aim off the creature in order to balance himself.

"What's the code!?" Z shouted, having gone ahead and reached the keypad by the double-doors.

"Not that one!" Bastian yelled, pointing with a pistol to indicate a lone door ten feet to the left. "Side entrance. Flip the guard. Enter 'good cause.'"

Z moved over to the single door and flipped the metallic casing off the keypad mounted to the wall. His fingers shook something fierce as he typed in the code.

Bastian glanced over his shoulder to see the beast close the distance between them. He could feel its heavy footfalls shake the pavement and his knees wobbled. He almost fell as the momentum carried him closer to the building.

All of a sudden T strode past him and stood his ground, shotgun shouldered. He began firing the pump-action weapon up at the approaching creature.

"Fall back, T!" Bastian yelled, stopping ten feet behind Z and about the same from T. He turned to face T as the shotgun blasted. His eyes lifted from T to the creature as it lumbered forward, beginning to slow down. T's shotgun was a semiautomatic Remington, so there was hardly any delay between shots.

The beast took the rounds to its chest and mouth, to the point that it had to raise an arm to shield its face.

*How many rounds in that thing? Six or seven?*

The seventh shell ejected and gunsmoke curled out of every hole in the weapon. It then clicked and T cursed under his breath. He extracted shells from loops on his belt and began loading them into the shotgun's underbelly.

"I got you covered, T, meet Z by the door!"

As if on cue, Z shouted: "Door's open, let's fuck-ing *go!*"

Bastian stepped forward, but stuffed Benny's 9mm into the tail of his slacks. He then double-handed the USP and locked his elbows, aiming high, one eye shut, the other focused on the pistol's foresight.

The beast had all but stopped midstride from T's shotgun blasts, which had chewed through its pale clay-like flesh in several spots, but not enough to drop it. Nonetheless, it bled the same bright red that the others did. And with its arm raised to shield its face, it couldn't see where it was going. As soon as it lowered the arm, no more than fifteen feet from where Bastian stood like a rock, he began squeezing the trigger.

Bullets struck the creature in its face and no-where else. The bulbous skull was a big target, its glowing yellow eyes making this easier in the darkness. The .45 rounds penetrated bone whether on first impact or second, fragmenting the beast's skull and forcing it into a backwards stagger.

The pistol's chrome slide locked back and smoke rose from the vacant breech. Bastian's training didn't just kick in, it flowed like the blood in his veins. With-out a hitch, he ejected the spent magazine and loaded the other after unearthing it from his pocket. His thumb nudged the release latch and the slide locked forward. He resumed firing, getting off only two more rounds un-til the beast turned its back on them and fled.

At that point Bastian waited a few seconds and fired one into its fleeing back before it vanished into the night. It passed a car on fire that splashed light onto its pale body before it disappeared for good.

Or at least, for now.

A firm hand gripped Bastian's bare shoulder and he turned with a jerk, his body shaking. T looked him in the eye and nodded sternly.

"Great shooting, man," T said, his own voice like a sputtering engine. His body language, however, was more or less composed. "Door's open. Let's go."

Bastian coughed and caught his breath before nodding, then followed T toward the building. Z stood inside the door, halfway leaning out, waving them in.

"It's all clear," Z said quietly as they neared.

T went first, and then Bastian paused in the threshold. He surveyed the parking lot, his eyes darting back and forth, noting the flames that danced on cars and the lamp posts whose lights still flickered.

He spotted movement against these sources of light, but they were obscure in the night and at this range. They mostly appeared smaller, however, like Crawlers or Vultures.

Or something else.

At this point Bastian didn't know what to expect from these wretched creatures. But at least he knew they were mortal and capable of being injured, which was some caliber of relief. Unfortunately, he also knew they were more or less sentient, according to how that big one had acted. Almost fatally wounded, it retreated. He wanted to know why, but then again, he had bigger questions that he feared might never be answered.

"C'mon, Bastian," Z insisted.

Bastian glanced over his shoulder. Z was standing a couple of feet away, his arms extended to hold the heavy metal door open.

T was moseying inside the room, gazing up at the high ceiling, his eyes scrupulous and his hands clutching the shotgun tightly.

With a sigh, Bastian nodded at Z and then looked out into the parking lot once more.

"I'm sorry, Benny," he whispered. His insides were much louder.

He turned away and let Z pull the door shut, not caring about the echoing slam. There was an electronic beep that indicated the door had not only resealed but the lockdown measure was in place again.

This reprieve came to Bastian lightly.

Although consoled by the fact that they had managed to make it into the building successfully, and in one piece, unscathed as it were, something still itched Bastian's nerves. Like termites under his skin.

"What is this room?" T's voice was hoarse. They were all terribly dehydrated and exhausted.

The room was about thirty by sixty feet, rectangular, with a high ceiling and white metal beams crossing below it, from which hung fluorescent fixtures. At least, in comparison to outside, every corner of the room was bathed in light. Mostly filing cabinets and desks, many of which were toppled, but otherwise no sign of life.

Bastian imagined that was because of the quakes.

No matter the foundation of the property, it wasn't immune to aftershocks.

"Small deliveries. UPS, Fed-Ex, vending machine refills, shit like that. Main deliveries are out back. Opposite side of the facility. Big roll-up doors. Secure as fuck. All main entrances, like those double-doors…" Bastian pointed over his shoulder, and then coughed, and caught his breath eventually through a rugged exhalation. "They won't budge 'til the lockdown is lifted, which can only be authorized by the Deputy Director or DARPA headquarters in Arlington."

"Upscale shit," T muttered.

Bastian nodded. He couldn't help but think of Maggie in that moment, and tears welled up in his eyes.

"I knew this would be a safe place to go. Secure. I told her. I assured her. I promised…"

Bastian trailed off mumbling things that were entirely unintelligible, to T or Z, to himself even.

He could not recall if he had actually promised her anything, or swore upon it, but he thrust into his mind that he had done both, and thus blamed himself all the more.

As if anyone's promise in this kind of unprecedented ordeal was expected to be shatterproof.

"Hey, hey, hey," T said, walking up to him with the shotgun dangling in one hand. He gripped Bastian's right shoulder with his left hand and tried to shake him. Bastian, normally a tower of steadfast resolve, was in that moment a wobbling game of Jenga.

T damn near toppled him.

And yet Bastian wasn't listening; he kept rambling, tears streaking his cheeks, his eyes aimless.

Briskly, and without saying anything, T shoved the shotgun into Z's empty hands, and then placed both hands on Bastian's shoulders. He gripped him firmly, and gave one solid shake, but applied a lifting motion the best he could, to assist Bastian on his feet. At the same time, T spoke, not necessarily loudly, but commandingly.

"Get it together, man. *We need you.*" T looked up and around, then back at Bastian. "Now more than ever. So *shape the fuck up*! What's done is done. Let's work together on the next step, and wipe this *evil* off the face of our planet."

Whether it was T's first statement or his second, or his last, that worked its way beneath Bastian's skin and shifted him into the right gear, nobody knew. Not even Bastian himself.

But, like a machine cleared of an obstruction, Bastian got a hold of himself and restarted.

He even apologized under his breath and kneaded his brow.

"I feel dizzy," he added, mumbling.

"It's the dehydration," T said, "among other things. You mentioned vending machines a minute ago. Where are the nearest ones?"

"Out...outside this room. In the corner of the main lobby. Two for food, two for drinks. Water fountains, too, on...on the other side of the lobby, closer to the elevators, outside the bathrooms."

"Great. Would you mind leading the way?"

Bastian nodded and finally lifted his face from his hand to look around. His eyes rested on T, or more precisely, the weapon in his clutches.
"On one condition, though."

# 7

Bastian proceeded through the push-bar exit door of the deliveries room. There was no quiet way of doing it, even if he took it slow, from experience, he knew how creaky the door was. Additionally, its push-bar made a loud, metallic sound that was unavoidable. So he led with a lowered shoulder, his bicep pushing the door open. He passed over the threshold and swept the lobby with the aim of T's shotgun. The loaded Remington was about nine pounds, which to Bastian in the fervent moment was hardly nothing.

He hardly even noticed the added, or returned, bulging weight to his slacks, from all the 12-gauge shells T had given him.

Behind him, Z immediately emerged from the room, extending his right foot to hold the door open. T exited and fanned right, sweeping the aim of his .45 pistol—Bastian had returned it with gratitude—to cover the front of the lobby. Including the secured double-doors, and the roll-up gate that was lowered in front of them.

Although there was no sign of life, the presence of death was tangible.

"I'm gonna go out on a limb here," T said, his sarcasm misplaced, but his voice and expression acutely tense, "and say that this can't be a good sign."

"Please, can the sarcasm while you're here. These are…" Bastian held back bile. "These are people I've worked with for over six years. Some. I may not know their names, but…I also might, if…if they had faces to recognize."

Most of the bodies littering the lobby were beyond mortally wounded and mutilated. Faces torn from the skulls, exposing the shockingly white bone beneath, albeit usually plastered with blood and sinew, strips of flesh and nerve tissue. In a few cases, there was no blood left on the bone, suggesting that it had been licked or *drank* from the body.

T apologized quietly, and started to retch but contained it. His eyes watered and eventually he turned away from the front of the lobby, where most of the carnage was. He noticed a gap in the ceiling above and his eyes narrowed on the missing panel.

"Guys, look," he said, pointing with his pistol, both hands gripping it. "I…I think they came in through the ceiling. Probably the ventilation ducts."

"So much for impenetrable," Bastian mumbled, and turned away from the lobby. He meandered toward the water fountains on the far side of where the lobby opened up into a wider space, before bottlenecking between elevators.

He didn't quite reach it before vomiting abruptly. It was mostly dry-heaving after the first projection, and he repressed the involuntary urge to sob simultaneously.

Z let the door shut as quietly as he could, as if it

mattered at this point, and jogged over to Bastian, who was doubled over, propped up by the shotgun as if a crutch. He holstered his pistol and tried to console Bastian, but the brokenhearted man shrugged him off before standing up and exhaling gutturally. He then stepped right over the pool of vomit on the floor, which was composed of alternating white and black tile squares.

When Bastian reached the water fountains, he stooped over them, leaning the shotgun against the wall. The motion-activated sensor directed a low arc of clean, crisp water that he lapped up like a parched dog. When he finally stood up and took a deep breath of relief, retrieving the shotgun simultaneously, Z was right there behind him.

"Earlier, you said 'demons.' Why'd you cave in to that idea?"

Bastian sighed and blinked slowly. He looked around. When he did, he arced his gaze so as to avoid fully gleaning the bloody lobby.

And then he realized that T had also walked close, enough to hear Z's question. There was a disturbed look on his face, and while it had struck Bastian that T wasn't an easily shaken man, he now had proof of his humanity.

The expression was more than skin-deep, and the aversion currently among them spread like a sort of disease. It was inescapable at this point, and undeniably palpable.

Bastian could not fault either man for feeling this way, of course. It was a given, under the circumstances.

It seemed to Bastian or certainly felt like it anyway, that each new setting he found himself in was more discomfiting than the last.

"Bastian?" Z asked, motioning to shake his shoulder, but restraining from actually making contact.

Bastian blinked rapidly and then widened his eyes before answering. They were borderline bloodshot, and one burst vessel from earlier remained.

"They're soulless, that's why. Isn't it obvious?" He shook his head and adjusted his eyes. "I beg either of you to say otherwise."

"When they die, they are reduced to embers and, at the very most ash." Z shook his head. "Sounds sketchy to me."

"Fine, fuck it," T said, approaching the two. "I give up. You're probably right. Especially with how they look and where they came up from.

"So it's settled. They're pure fucking evil," Bastian said, nonchalant but no less solemn. He held the shotgun at port-arms, both hands clutching it in the right spots. "Now we can get on with it, less questions."

Z and T looked at each other concernedly while Bastian pushed between them and made a beeline for the elevators.

"Hold up, man," Z called, keeping his voice down at least.

He and T briskly visited the vending machines. Meanwhile, Bastian lingered in front of the elevator buttons, keeping an eye out. His patience, what little remained on the surface, hardly at all, was marching on thin ice.

At least the two officers weren't so casual with their time. They quickly returned to stand on either side of Bastian, carrying in each hand bottled beverages and protein bars. They apparently had a little more than they needed for themselves.

"I'll be a gentleman," Z said to him, "and not charge you a convenience fee for these."

"Did you guys actually pay for them?" Bastian mustered a smirk. It was like a rainbow above a smoggy battlefield.

T shrugged. "We always carry a few bucks in our back pockets."

Bastian couldn't help but let the smirk mutate into a grin, and then his head bowed and he shook it a few times until the expression faded. However, when he looked back up at them, his eyes were a little wet and he nodded.

"I appreciate the gesture," he said, leaning the shotgun in the corner between the button panel and closed elevator door, thus freeing his hands. They had certainly seen better days. "I'll take the Dasani."

"Sure you don't want a Fanta?" Z said, double-fisting two Fanta's.

Bastian's brow furrowed and he shook his head once, firmly.

"You *do* know that a soda will dehydrate you worse, right? Much better off with a water. Especially amidst all this shit."

"Yeah, but, fuck, man," Z said, guilt in his voice. His eyes narrowed. "There's just something so refreshing about a cold orange soda when you're all hot and worked up and *pissed off.* Ya know?"

"I guess I missed that memo."

"You're missing out, for sure," Z said, as T smirked and shook his head, handing Bastian one of two bottled waters in his left hand. In his right, and Z's left, were protein bars.

"Good luck downing that dry-ass Cliff Bar with a *Fanta.* Ugh." Bastian accepted the white chocolate protein bar from T's hand, which he also scowled at, but scarfed half of it down in a matter of seconds. He then chugged most of the water bottle before exhaling loudly.

"Fuck, these things taste like cardboard," T said as he devoured his peanut butter and chocolate Cliff Bar. He occasionally swigged his Dasani between big bites. Halfway through the bar, his expression lightened. "Peanut butter and *chocolate* cardboard. Mmm."

Bastian smirked wryly and shook his head.

"Nothing's quite as bad as it normally might be, under these kinds of circumstances. As undocumented as they might be."

"Combat is combat, I know what you mean," T nodded, speaking through a mouthful. "That said…yeah…all this shit exceeds experience."

"As shaken as *we* are to it," Z said, grimacing as he struggled to stomach the protein bar under swigs of Fanta, but refusing to admit his error, "imagine how the common civvy feels. I can't fathom."

"I can," Bastian said, having finished his protein bar and leaving only a sip's worth of water in his bottle. He zoned out briefly, the tattered skin under his eyes puffy, and the tone in them sullen.

It didn't take a psychologist to deduce that he was referring to his wife and daughter. How they acted and felt when the first creatures attacked them, much less just before they died.

While anyone who wasn't actually there couldn't be privy with a certainty, the observation sufficed. And the way Bastian acted when he let the tragedy creep back from the depths of his psyche, served as a sort of conduit for their last moments.

A vicarious experience for his family's fear and, ultimately, death.

Only a hint, though, at the true horror they suffered. As Z suggested, too, it was far worse for them than it could be for people like Bastian and T. While they were no less human than regular civilians, they had extensive military experience and training that made them accustomed to cruel scenarios. Many of them were capable of flipping a switch and detaching themselves from emotion, in order to achieve missions.

Bastian definitely had this hardwired into him, however, it was only a temporary fix. And the more he mulled over it, the more he sided with the idea that it wasn't a solution but instead a problem.

He didn't snap out of his traumatized delirium until Z reached in front of him to hit the elevator button. The motion blurred his already watery vision but at least reinjected life into it, reminding him he wasn't entirely alone. And then the *ping* sound was the alarm that pulled him from an upright stasis.

Part of him wanted to apologize to the men for

zoning out again, for walking that line of completely losing it, but instead he just snatched the shotgun and got himself ready. He took a step forward, so that the two officers were no longer at his side but directly behind him, although they were at least mindful enough to give him some space. He cleared his throat a few times and even double-checked the shotgun to confirm that it was operational.

As the elevator descended from whatever level it had previously been on, T and Z wiped crumbs off their uniforms and checked their weapons.

"Wait, I thought the whole building was on lockdown?" Z mentioned.

"It is," Bastian said. "This is the freight elevator. The others are currently inoperable. Believe it or not, but this beats the stairs. The level access doors tend to auto-lock at this facility. Nothing protocol related. Just annoying."

"Good to know," Z nodded.

"Besides," Bastian said with a shrug, "where we're going, the stairs won't take us. Sublevels are only accessible by elevator."

"No shit? So…we're going *underground*?" Z asked, suddenly intrigued.

"Most of CHERI's work is conducted in the subterranean levels. It isn't as deep as the building is tall, but much more expansive. Can be like a maze of corridors if you don't know the floorplan, so, stay close."

T and Z both appeared a little befuddled by this, perhaps more so than they expected themselves to be. The concept seemed genuinely overwhelming, on top of everything they had already experienced.

When the freight elevator ground to a halt at their level and the doors peeled open, another sound snagged their attention. It cut the silence in a burst of static, followed by a human voice and other muffled sounds.

"The hell is that?" T raised an eyebrow, looking around. His gaze focused on the lobby, which remained an undisturbed scene of bloodshed. However, it sounded evident that the noise was coming from that direction.

"Wait," Bastian's eyes widened, an expression of surprise touched by hope. He carried the shotgun with him as he shuffled past the men and toward the lobby. His borrowed sneakers slipped through a puddle of blood but he caught his balance and continued his path as if it was nothing. He was like a dog following its nose. And then he skidded to a stop at one of the front desks. His right palm slapped the white countertop, which was misted with blood, however, his attention was fixated elsewhere.

Behind the desk, on a forty-inch flatscreen TV mounted to the wall.

"Get over here," he called out, not terribly loud, just audible enough for the men to hear. Additionally he beckoned with the shotgun, urgency in his body language and voice.

T and Z quickly assembled, more mindful of their step though, but once they stood in front of the counter, it was like the world around them ceased to exist.

The TV screen sputtered with static, but a few

things were clear: the CNN logo and the disheveled anchorwoman. An emergency broadcast alert scrolled across the banner along the bottom of the screen, but was too awash in static to read.

Her voice, however, was generally coherent.

"Why'd this come on now?" Z couldn't help but ask out of curiosity.

"The elevators. Even the freight one," Bastian said with a touch of relief that bordered on dumb joy, "they're wired into the PA and emergency broadcasts. Must've triggered the TV."

"Turn it up, can you turn it up?" T asked.

Bastian nodded and bypassed the counter via a gap in the center, and then reached up, his hand gliding behind the monitor. There wasn't much space between it and the wall, but finally his fingers found the volume control and he tapped it up a few intervals. Then he backpedaled until he stood beside T.

Slowly but surely, all three pairs of eyes widened. And so did the atria in their hearts as their pulses raced to accompany this new realization.

*"...the source of the earthquakes that have been ravishing southern California and other parts of the western United States, appearing to slowly reach other parts of the* continent, *is believed to be this unidentified structure in the desert outside of Calipatria..."*

The CNN broadcast displayed a basic map of Calipatria in southeastern California, and its measured distance from San Diego. It also included a red dot for the aforementioned 'structure,' and rings pulsing around it, indicating shockwaves from the epicenter.

Aerial footage of the structure during daylight then re-placed the map on the screen, and while suffering from bouts of static, it was clear enough for the three men watching.

"What the fuck *is* that?" T asked under his breath, scowling.

As if she heard him, the anchorwoman's voice returned, talking over the aerial videography.

*"This footage was taken above the structure, dubbed the* Monolith *by our military correspondents, who have already coordinated several attacks. All of them have been futile. More on that in a little bit."*

"Motherfucker," Z muttered, and then covered his mouth with his hand.

*"You'll have to excuse the poor quality of our footage…"*

Bastian scoffed to himself.

*Quality enough,* he thought as a chill ran down his spine.

*"By allocated calculations, the Monolith is roughly four-hundred feet tall at its highest corner, or just a little taller than the Statue of Liberty. It is the width of two football fields with a thickness of about half that. It is solid black, with no visible markings, except for a* glowing *red line from its center down to the ground. According to our military correspondent, all initial attempts at communication have failed."*

"Fuck talking, kill it," T sneered.

Footage of the massive structure changed, with a highlighted timestamp. It was still during the day but a little darker than the last one.

"Six-twenty-nine," Bastian said. Without taking his eyes off the screen, which to his surprise didn't feature a clock, he asked: "What time is it now?"

"Seven-thirty-six," T said after checking his wristwatch.

"I think the first footage they showed was even earlier."

"It was," Bastian said. "Timestamp said six-forty. Maybe an hour after I felt the first quake."

"Well, good to know they're not totally oblivious, right?" Z said, sounding relieved.

It didn't last long.

Under their voices, the anchorwoman continued to speak. They had caught most of it in one ear, but nothing really drew their attention again until the next statement.

*"As you can see here, a variety of attacks have been strategized and executed, all yielding no effect on the target. The first attempts were made by fighter jets and attack helicopters following failed efforts of communication."*

The footage, still aerial and clearly from far away, then zoomed in, depicted various unarmed air-craft—and ground vehicles—approach the Monolith, each instance with different timestamps. Once they reached a certain distance, represented on the screen as roughly half a mile, they exploded. The aircraft didn't just lose control and crash into the ground, they detonated en route.

*"According to our military correspondent,"* the anchorwoman's voice resumed in the background,

while the footage continued to show various armed craft attempt firing outside of a mile, only for their missiles to detonate while airborne, *"this suggests that the Monolith possesses some kind of EMP field around it. That would be a form of defense in the style of what we know as an* electromagnetic-pulse. *This would normally cause anything electronically powered to shut off and, in extreme cases, explode. However, as you can see, when the explosions occur, the flames do* not *course over an invisible surface, suggesting that no physical shield is present, but instead, the Monolith has its own electromagnetic atmosphere."*

"Good God," Bastian muttered, rubbing his mouth with his tattered knuckles.

*"As such, all attempts of attacking the Monolith have ceased as-of seven o'clock, PDT,"* the anchor-woman continued, the screen returning to her and the dumbstruck expression on her tired face. *"As you could tell, the high concentration of ground threats surrounding the Monolith within a quarter-mile radius, currently deters any kind of infantry assault. These...uh, these* bi-ological anomalies...*have not yet been named by our military correspondent...but we will have more news on—"*

The broadcast abruptly plunged into static before the television shut off completely.

"What was *that*?" T asked, upset.

Bastian withdrew from the counter to peer through the messy lobby and at the elevator area.

"Elevator must've returned to its previous level," he said nonchalantly, straightening up. "Freight ones do that anyway, if they're called but not boarded after a period of time."

"Should we try to call it again and—"

Bastian shook his head. "No, Z, I think we got what we needed. Not that any of us really asked for it…fucking shit."

He mumbled the last two words and shook his head before heading out of the lobby, shotgun carried in both arms.

Behind him, T and Z shot some words back and forth, inaudible, before they caught up to him by the elevators.

He leaned forward and hit the call button.

"So," Z cleared his throat, evidently reluctant to speak his mind. "It's pretty obvious now, right?"

"What is?" Bastian said without turning around, his body a statue.

"This thing. The Monolith…the creatures…it's, uh, it's gotta be alien, right?"

Bastian sighed deeply. "Can't say I agree."

"How, though? I mean…ain't it obvious?" Z was resolute now.

"I gotta agree. That structure…what, it just appeared outta thin air?" T sounded just as obstinate on the matter all of a sudden. "Shit *had* to come from space."

"I don't care." Bastian was banal, but anyone in his company could tell that he wasn't emotionless.

"You just want 'em dead, huh?" T said, trying to put himself in Bastian's shoes. However casually. "I can dig it. Fuck 'em."

"Well, *I'm* calling 'em aliens," Z said.

"Even if that *thing* came from space, these *abominations* are coming from *under us*." Bastian continued staring forward. The sound of the elevator arriving made him redefine his stance more actionably. "So, they're demons in name. Alien in nature. Evil in manner. They're *mortal*—all I care about right now."

The elevator doors peeled open.

Bloody handprints arrayed the stark steel walls above the handrails on all three sides. But no bodies, or parts. One of the two LED fixtures in the corners flickered incessantly.

Bastian peered inside with a hint of caution, though not as patiently as one might expect, before stepping in. He stood at the center of the spacious freight elevator, instead of backing up to give the others room to enter.

T and Z exchanged skeptical expressions before filing inside, scuffling around to stand behind him, occupying the corners. Then the doors closed, and he robotically pressed the S1 button. The elevator did not have the smoothness of operation that its non-freight counterparts were gifted with, so it prominently lurched as it began its descent.

Bastian's legs were like divided columns, while T and Z staggered briefly.

"So, Bastian, where exactly are we headed?"

"First, T, the security armory."

"And *where*, exactly, in the facility is it?"

"Sublevel 1. Roughly a hundred feet below the lobby. In the east wing. Typically a two-minute stroll from the elevator. I predict it might take us longer, for obvious reasons. I just hope…they didn't make it below. Not sure how they would've, unless they managed to board an elevator, or they attacked underground, from the surrounding earth."

Bastian took a deep breath and sighed. He shook his head and then kneaded his brow with the muzzle of the shotgun, making the other two men cringe nervously. When he lifted his head again, he glared up at the elevator level indicator. It was far less garish than any other elevator, but the raw aesthetic of the interior in general was something Bastian could relate to in the moment.

As tarnished and regretful as it were.

"If they did, we'll kill 'em all," T said firmly. He emphatically racked the slide of his pistol.

Bastian glanced over his right shoulder at T, who did not appear like he was joking the slightest.

"Hell yeah. 'Cause we're a team." Z no longer sounded so hung up on names or purpose. Bastian glanced over his left shoulder at Z, who, despite being significantly shorter than him, now carried himself in a tall manner. He looked ready for anything, and whether that was a brave trait or a reckless one, given the circumstances, Bastian couldn't be sure.

However, his cohorts' gusto did enliven his spirits. It also made him feel all the more responsible for bringing them here, and he couldn't go on without telling them what really occupied his mind.

He reached out to stop the elevator in-transit, which he predicted was mere seconds from arriving at

Sublevel 1.

"What the hell?" Z asked, really to nobody in particular at first, raising his eyebrow.

"First off, I just want to say," Bastian turned his back to the doors and faced the two men. "Thanks for saving my ass back on the road. And for tagging along."

They fumbled with their words, but he continued talking in his peremptory manner that kept them silent.

"I couldn't have made it this far without your help. Both physically and psychologically, no doubt."

Although his voice was as deep and husky as usual, it was at least now hydrated and fed. He sounded a small step closer to being the healthy Sebastian Thurgood he once was on a daily basis.

A microscopic step, as it were.

"And on a lighter note," he added through a gossamer smirk, "thanks for the grub."

"Our pleasure," T said, as if forcing his way into the airspace. He even materialized a big grin, appearing almost comical. "Stuff really goes a long way, huh?"

"It'll have to," Bastian replied grimly. "Can't afford another pause after this."

It was a cold hard fact that Bastian needed to emphasize. Now that they were closer to their objective, tantalizingly so, it was more important than ever before that they not let up.

Especially with their new knowledge sinking in. And all of the questions it raised, but most of all, the new fears that it manifested.

As if the three men weren't distressed enough, already.

The bizarre aloofness to eat snacks and drinks while they waited for an elevator less than thirty feet from the nearest mutilated human corpse had been something they each tried to ignore. It was an impossible feat, however. Their humanity was intact, and being gravely tested. Mocked, even, or so it felt.

Whatever was at work here, whether extraterrestrial or demonic, or something else incomprehensible, Bastian had accepted that it lacked a moral compass.

Which, ironically, made it an easier threat to engage. Because it meant that he, too, could combat it just as cruelly.

This was a dilemma in his soul that was beginning to dissolve. The moral devolution of his spirits, when he fantasized about killing this enemy, was a callous descent that he no longer resisted.

As honest as he was being with his comrades now, however, he couldn't expose them to these cold feelings. It was hard enough to accept them himself.

"After we access the standard armory on Sublevel 1," Bastian said, "we'll be better equipped to handle these bastards. But what we *really* want is the Bravo Vault, located on Sublevel 4."

"*Four*?" T exclaimed under his breath.

"Don't worry. After we stock up on 1, we make a beeline back to the elevator, and take it straight down to 4. No pussyfooting."

T cleared his throat and straightened himself.

"Sounds…like a plan."

"Trust me, T," Bastian said, for once in a while sounding optimistically reassuring, "the second you step through the door at the security armory, all your worries will evaporate."

"Oh, yeah? That juicy?"

This was a new term under the circumstances for Bastian, but he just nodded and raised his eyebrows.

"And the whatever-Vault?" Z added.

"Bravo Vault, and yes," Bastian nodded. "Even *juicier*."

"The Supe in there? And the, uh, what was it…ROT something."

"The ROT-20, and yes, T, the Supe, too. The Arbalest and Sevin as well." Bastian cleared his throat and took a deep breath. "Also, my pride and joy. The INFERNO Suit."

"The what-now?" Z asked, eyebrows high.

"I'll keep this brief, gentlemen, for all we know there might still be survivors in the Sublevels…"

T and Z exchanged apprehensive looks.

"The INFERNO Suit is my meal ticket, proverbially speaking. I've been assigned to the project for the last three years, as the lead designer and tester. It's aced with flying colors but has been stuck in the prototype phase for too long; me and a few colleagues have high faith in it."

"Back up a tick," Z said, brow furrowed. You said prototype…so, I'm gonna guess…there's only one."

Bastian nodded, and then shrugged. "But when has a beacon of hope ever come in two's or three's? Besides, the Bravo Vault as a whole is just as promising as the Suit itself."

"Now when you say 'suit,'" T said, "I assume you don't mean a three-piece."

Bastian smirked briefly, already fueled by that excitement he felt whenever speaking about anything under his care at work.

"Think bomb disposal type of stuff, except with a hard case, and yet with high mobility. I'm not talking acrobatics, but, it won't be like wearing an ADS."

"A what?" T asked, his face blank.

"Atmospheric diving suit."

"Oh, those clunky things," Z said.

"Exactly. The INFERNO Suit might look clunky, but its interior is form-fitting, and the armor plating fits like mesh."

"Why's it called Inferno?" Z asked. "Flame-retardant? Or does it have a flamethrower attached to the shoulder or some shit?"

"That's just kind of ridiculous," Bastian said matter-of-factly before continuing. "INFERNO is an acronym. It stands for INFantry Exoskeletal Resistant Neo-Ordnance."

Z counted on his fingers as if tracking syllables in a long word, and his face warped with incredulity. T's expression was no different, as he worked it out in his head.

"It's obviously a stretch in nomenclature," Bastian admitted, "but the acronym doubles as the word 'inferno,' in reference to the Suit's fire-retardancy, and its initial design to withstand explosive blasts such as IED's."

"An operator can survive an IED in this Suit?" Z

asked skeptically. "At what range?"

"Point-blank," Bastian said, pride lighting up his features. "Of course…given, he or she would be very disoriented and sore, but tests have been conducted, and as I said earlier, not adversely."

Bastian withdrew from the men to hit the button on the panel to make the elevator resume its course.

"I think we've discussed this enough. As I've already mentioned," Bastian was back to sounding radically adamant, "we can't afford to take anymore pauses. Patience…is no longer a virtue."

His stomach turned and immediately his sinuses swelled up. He stifled tears.

"So…what's the plan after we stock up and you, I assume only you," T said, "zip up the Suit? We still going to Calipatria?"

Even with Bastian's back turned to them again, he could *feel* Z's bodyweight shift as he shot T a hard look at his last question.

"I know *I* am," Bastian said simply, but firmly.

"You can't be serious," Z scoffed. "Did you *see* the ground surrounding the Monolith? It was *teeming* with those creatures! There's no way we'd make it a hundred feet, much less a *quarter-mile*."

"Maybe not. But I gotta try."

"Look, we don't know this Suit thing like you do, hell, you make it seem like a tank with legs."

"Accurate."

Z sighed, disgruntled. "That's all well and good, man, but that's just you. What about *us*?"

Bastian turned his back on the doors again to

stare down at Z.

"Look, I'm not asking you to join me. If this all of a sudden makes us not a team, I get it. But I *am* going. With or without help. Some of the guns in Bravo Labs aren't even operable without the Suit. I'll need a vehicle to carry them, and to take me to Calipatria in the first place. Hell, it's at least a—"

The freight elevator lurched to a stop and the doors peeled open without a chime, but instead a gritty, grinding sound.

Bastian spun on his heels to face the elevator foyer, shotgun shouldered. Opposite them were three other elevators, non-freight. Their brushed-nickel doors were shut. Slowly, Bastian emerged from the elevator, his head and feet on a swivel, his firm hands sweeping the aim of the shotgun everywhere he looked. There were two elevators beside the freight one he had just exited. One of them was shut but the other's doors opened and closed, though only ajar, hung up on something in the threshold. Bastian's eyes lowered and he spotted a severed leg that made his eyes roll.

"What is it?" Z asked, quiet.

Bastian gestured them to assemble. They emerged from the elevator and regrouped where he stood between the six elevators. As soon as they saw what he did, they grimaced and looked away.

"Hold," Bastian whispered, and inched closer to the elevator. He prodded the interior with the shotgun's barrel, and then interrupted the door's path with his right shoulder. It locked open as he investigated the elevator. Except for bloody handprints and crimson smears on the mirrored walls, in addition to the severed, clothed leg between the doors, it was empty.

His stomach knotted and the stench of death was tangible. He briskly exited the elevator, nudging the leg into the foyer so that the doors could shut all the way.

"On me," he said, his voice smooth despite the professional order.

As if their little dispute hadn't happened in the elevator two minutes ago, the three men now moved like a squad. They slinked through the foyer, across blood-stained white tile, and into a T-intersection. Both ways offered the same view—postmortem scenes of barbarism. Disturbingly well-lit, thanks to LED ceiling fixtures every ten feet. Bodies strewed the hallways, mutilated and disemboweled. Many of them were missing parts altogether, suggesting they had been eaten.

"H-How many are there?" Z asked, all of a sudden feeling cotton-mouthed.

"Does it matter? This is *fucked*." T shook his head, grimacing.

"Six west," Bastian computed, almost robotically, clearly repressing his emotions. He swung the shotgun down the hallway to their left when he said that, and then aimed it down the one to their right. "Eleven east."

Z gulped. "And we're going east, right?"

Bastian nodded. He seethed.

"They never had a chance to get out," he said under his breath, just shy of growling. It was palpable in his voice, that he suffocated the grief. "These are all late-shift employees. The quakes must've put 'em under lockdown early, then they were just…fish in a barrel. Somehow…the demons broke in, and fucking…slaughtered…everyone…"

Bastian shook his head and proceeded down the hallway to their right. His gaze noted the doors on both sides, at fifteen-foot intervals.

"Don't bother with any of the doors," he mentioned, his voice sullen. "This lockdown is no joke."

The two officers nodded as if he had eyes in the back of his head, but it was a given that they heard him.

Besides, they were too busy focusing on their own path and their own handling of the bloodshed.

Bastian, though slow in his advancement, was steadfast. Despite the carnage that he navigated and the bodies of his colleagues, some whose faces had been torn or chewed off, his pace never faltered. Not once, for even a second, did he pause to catch his breath or concrete his footing. Ostensibly he was collected, and this translated to a stable carriage. Meanwhile, inside, the battles for composure waged invisibly.

Conversely, behind him, the two officers struggled in every facet to maintain this same level of calm. T had a version of it down, walking through the bloodshed without looking at the floor, which saved him from the urge to vomit, however, occasionally his rubber soles squeaked in a pool of blood and he had to catch himself from slipping. Z, on the other hand, was just the opposite; he kept looking down, not wanting to risk stepping in blood or, worse, an actual body, and it slowed him down greatly.

"This isn't too fresh," Bastian noted out loud, albeit in a hushed voice. As much as he hated to admit, after passing a pile of entrails several feet from a corpse, not steaming the least. The fetor, however, had not mitigated. "There's nothing we could've done, rationally speaking. But I have…"

Bastian felt lightheaded and threw up in his mouth a little, then swallowed it and his eyelids fluttered as he combated himself to regain his bearings.

"I have a feeling," he continued, clearing his throat quietly, "that the *perpetrators* are still in the facility. Possibly even this level. Stay sharp."

T and Z were the opposite of sharp.

"I'm feeling quite blunt right about now, to be frank," T admitted. "I don't think—"

T's gaze swept from the back of Bastian's head to his feet, and immediately regretted this inadvertent motion. He saw a dead man's face, where the skin was torn and missing around the nose, leaving the underlying bone of the cheek and mouth exposed through a saucy layer of raw tissue and slack muscle.

After failing to resume his statement, and fumbling with his words as his thought process disassembled, T braced the wall and vomited onto the floor. A previously unsullied portion of tile.

"Fuck, T, now I'm gonna—" Z staggered and doubled over, regurgitating what he had last ingested onto the floor, and whatever corpse was beneath him. He sealed his eyes so tight that they hurt, especially with the briny tears flooding their ducts.

Bastian did not fault them the least, except that

the sound of their repulsion weakened him almost naturally, as it had Z.

He would have given in to it had the ceiling tiles above him not suddenly collapsed. The LED lighting fixture also came down, shattering in a spray of sparks, and the Crawler that had been above it shrieked and tumbled across the floor. Fortunately, in the opposite direction of Bastian, but its manifestation was audible enough to snatch T and Z's unsettled attention, too.

Without a lick of hesitation, Bastian solidified his stance, shotgun shouldered, and fired. The creature had just alighted to all fours when the muzzle flashed, and a tight spread of buckshot caught it in the face. The sheer momentum threw it back into a roll across the floor. Its clawed hands and feet scratched the tile as it struggled up, slipping in its own blood when its leathery palms made contact.

This proved to Bastian that it was *not* a flawless killing machine.

This, of course, still produced zero sympathy for the creature.

Bastian closed the distance between himself and the creature, which gurgled its own blood and finally regained its footing. It was on the floor with more space around it, at the inception of a corner where the hallway took a right turn.

He fired the shotgun again, aiming low as the creature still skulked, except this time his marksmanship was more precise. And the 12-gauge excelled at its duty. The Crawler's half-skull was obliterated, along with its neck and the top portion of its shoulders. Despite appearing earthen, the creature bled its bright red blood profusely, and its flesh fragmented not unlike a human's.

Bastian couldn't help but wonder if the creatures were either teleported from the Monolith or summoned by them, from cavities within the planet, or from the Earth itself. And if the latter, he now contemplated, maybe they gradually became more human as time passed, and less earthly.

Nonetheless, the creature still dissolved into ash and embers upon death, leaving behind no trace of the blood it had spilled from itself. Only that which it had spilled from its victims.

An undeserved legacy for the monsters.

"You guys good?" Bastian asked, his voice hoarse and demanding. He didn't even look over his shoulder when he said it, nor did he try to keep quiet.

"Uh, yeah, and you?" T asked worrisomely.

"Peachy," Bastian growled. "We're maybe a quarter way there. Let's go."

"What was it?" Z asked, his footfalls sounding behind Bastian, quickly catching up, as if he was playing hopscotch. "A Crawler or Vulture?"

"Does it matter?" Bastian said simply, not looking at Z, instead his eyes were glued down the hallway they now faced.

"Not really. Just curious what we might be up against down here."

"It was a Crawler. I think it thought it had the drop on us. Turns out even *they* can be clumsy, too."

"Clumsy and mortal, these are good tidings," T said, now the slower walker, but finally catching up. Once he did, he exhaled with a sign of respite. "Well…this is kinda relieving."

The hallway before them was quite unlike the one they just navigated, except for the layout of doors on either side. It was almost unsullied, aside from a few smears of blood on the floor and walls. Only one body, presumably a woman, about halfway down the sixty-foot stretch. Both of her arms were missing, likely torn straight from the jagged shoulder stumps left behind, their current whereabouts unknown.

"Poor lady," Z murmured.

"How do you know it's a woman?" T asked.

Z indicated the decapitated head that T had somehow not noticed, less than ten feet from where they stood. There was a sparsely dotted trail of blood from the corpse to the head, which had long auburn hair, disheveled and with pieces of flesh in it.

"Oh, fuck me," T said, and he pivoted to face away. He dry-heaved once before coughing wetly and spitting, then he faced the hallway again. "Sorry."

"Get it together. We gotta move faster."

Bastian hated sounding so aloof, but he was growing gravely impatient.

He proceeded down the hallway, silently grateful that it was remarkably less tarnished than the last, his feet nimble and his eyes darting.

"How's this possible?" Z asked, trying to stay close behind Bastian. "So many in the other hallway, but here…"

They passed by the woman's decapitated corpse and successfully resisted looking at it in the process.

"Herded," Bastian thought out loud.

"Say again," T said, gulping, and Bastian sensed that he already understood.

"They were probably herded," Bastian continued. "The demons took advantage of the panic they caused, and the lockdown, herding as many people as they could into one hallway. Then they…culled."

"Motherfuckers," T said, anger now boiling its way past his crippling disgust.

"In due time, we'll be able to do the same to them." Bastian sounded certain, but it didn't detract from the unease in his voice.

He spearheaded their progress to reach the end of this hallway.

His heart skipped a beat. "Hold."

They heard him, and paused about ten feet from the corner, where he stood, facing down the next hall.

T frowned, seeing Bastian's body language and expression deteriorate.

"I have a bad feeling about this," he mumbled to Z, without taking his eyes off Bastian.

"I do, too," Bastian said, somehow having heard him. Given, there was a sickly silence that infected the air of the underground facility, and the word eerie was an understatement.

"What the hell *is* it?" Z demanded under his breath.

"A gang of 'em," Bastian said, trying to gather his breath and fortitude. He continued staring straight ahead. "They must've heard the gunfire, and-or their buddy screaming before I blew its head off."

At that moment, T and Z heard an inhuman roar from around the corner and down another hall. They winced and scowled in apprehension.

"I think they heard you, man," T said.

"Nah, they're just confused. They must think they somehow missed us when they were slaughtering people."

The two men detected as clear as day how Bastian's tone devolved into something unstable and vehement.

"How many, Bastian?" T asked.

"Manageable."

"*How many?*" T insisted.

Bastian gulped.

# 8

Gang, perhaps, was not the right word. Considering the close-quarters environment of the hallway, about eight feet across and ten from floor to ceiling, even a few could feel like a throng. Especially this kind of enemy. Bastian was immediately juggling things in his head, from words to strategies to the dissection of his own fears, and the analysis of their extremely limited arsenal at present.

He was willing to replace 'gang' with 'horde,' although there were 'only' six of the creatures he could see, their various sizes and ferocities made them seem like a legion.

"Six," Bastian finally answered.

And at first they were about fifty feet down the sixty-foot hallway, but now they were slowly closing that distance. Quite slowly, despite their previous vocalization. He imagined that they probably saw him as 'just one man,' and thus dwarfed him in number alone. So, they were patient and methodical in their approach.

"What, all Crawlers?" Z said, trying to pump himself up. "That's not so—"

"Three Crawlers, two Vultures, and one of those big bald motherfuckers from the parking lot."

"Oh, Christ," T lifted a hand to his head, rubbing

169

over his scalp as his face turned pale.

"The Crawlers are using the walls and ceiling," Bastian observed out loud. "They're taking the lead, about thirty or forty feet away. Behind them, the Vultures are…taking flight…and the big fucker is hanging back."

He shouldered the shotgun and dropped to a knee. The elbow to the arm that supported the full-size semiautomatic shotgun planted on his raised knee, acting as a monopod.

"What do we do?" T asked, his voice shaking.

"Hang back 'til I retreat behind you guys, then blast whatever comes around the corner 'til you're low, then drop behind me."

Z nodded. "Take 'em in waves."

"Something like that. Shit…" Bastian watched as the nearest Crawler gave its nickname terrifying meaning, darting across the ceiling toward him. It navigated the ceiling fixtures as if they weren't there, and starting shriek-growling as it got closer. Behind it, two more advanced down the hallway toward Bastian just as rapidly, except clinging to opposite walls.

"How many rounds you got left?" T asked.

Bastian, not looking directly at him, assumed he was asking about the shotgun.

"Full mag, so what, seven or eight?" Bastian announced, while his eyes remained a homing reticle on the ceiling-bound Crawler. "Plus the four on the bandolier, and I dunno, six in my pocket."

"Seven, yeah," T said, nodding and shrugging all in one motion, one breath, "and I was talking to Z, but that's good."

"Z, how about you?" Bastian said, gritting his teeth. Before Z could reply, the shotgun in Bastian's hands fired, and the Crawler on the ceiling dropped, along with a panel. The LED fixture it had just circumvented burst into sparks.

The creature hit the floor wailing and bleeding, but immediately bounded toward Bastian. He lowered his aim and fired two more subsequent shots, his target hardly ten feet away. The first shot blew out its legs from under it, literally, and the second walloped its chest before it could try to adjust.

"Say again," Bastian said, raising his aim above the now disintegrating Crawler to the two on the walls. They gained speed at the sight of their slain compatriot, more vocally, too. Bastian could see the wall being chewed up by claws in their wake.

"Uh…" Z lost his voice. He ejected the Glock's magazine and looked at the holes in it to deduce how many rounds he had left. "Almost full mag. Fifteen, sixteen. And…half a carton in my pocket."

"That's solid," Bastian said, and swept his aim from the Crawler on the right wall to the left, last-second, startling it, especially when the shotgun roared. Buckshot pelted it in the back, and some shore away the top half of its already partial skull. Yellow goop and slaughtered maggots misted the air as its body collapsed off the wall. The other creature bounded from the right wall to the left, and Bastian's next shot missed it midair. He cursed under his breath and rose to his feet, backpedaling.

The creature had gotten too close for comfort.

It now leapt from the left wall onto the floor, coming down to all fours before bounding up to lunge at Bastian on its own two legs. He managed to get off a shot before it made contact, but the creature swiped the weapon out of his hands just as it went off. Bastian could smell the reek of death on the creature's wet jaws, standing a foot taller than him, and anticipated its claws to sink into his flesh at any second. He tried to kick out its gangly legs by striking the knees, but it was unyielding despite its gaunt figure.

"Take the shot!" Bastian yelled, barely able to keep the creature at bay by pushing into its chest with his left forearm, while his right fist punched its high ribs.

"You're too close!" Z shouted, aiming.

"For fuck's sake," T mumbled, and marched closer, standing about seven or eight feet from Bastian and his attacker. The brazen approach alone caught the creature's attention. It whipped its abhorrent face to the left, giving T a nasty look that was met with the muzzle of his .45-caliber pistol. Without hesitation, T squeezed the trigger and the bullet penetrated the Crawler's half-skull between where its eyes would be. Its head jerked back and it staggered away from Bastian, whose ears rang but besides that, he was grateful.

The creature somehow managed to regain its bearings despite its nearly cleaved brain cavity, and screeched at T, its gangly arms thrown open. As if it was going to pounce and tackle T, however, it was hardly given the chance to even contemplate this. T put two more rounds into its face, and a third into its neck. The creature dropped, through the mist of blood that had spewed through the exit wounds behind it.

T faced Bastian, whose eyebrows raised.

"Much obliged," he said, and then retrieved the shotgun from the floor.

"My pleasure," T added. He looked to his right and saw the rest of the creatures Bastian had mentioned now surging down the long hallway.

Bastian froze for a second, not unlike T, realizing something that changed in the enemy's disposition. The dome-headed beast no longer trudged in the background, it now charged forward, a lumbering giant of an abomination. The two Vultures tried to get out of its way and the beast knocked one into a wall as it passed. It was almost comical to see, but the sight of the beast on fast approach was anything but amusing.

"Now what?" T gulped.

"Same strategy applies. Get behind the corner, T. Ready your guns but back up a bit."

"What about—"

"Me? I'll manage. Now go!"

The beast was less than twenty feet away now. Each of its strides wasn't exactly long, due to its stout legs and top-heavy form, but at nine feet tall, they were still longer than a man's.

T retreated behind the corner, guiding Z back even farther, giving themselves cushion-space in case the beast made the turn without slowing down.

Bastian knew the Remington was effective even at medium range, but he wanted to hit the beast low and spare no momentum. He waited until it was about twelve feet away before he squeezed the trigger, and the buckshot started to spread just before impact. Double-ought pellets battered the beast's knees and it faltered a hitch, however, it kept moving. Bastian, grateful for the shotgun's semiautomatic action, fired two more in quick succession, controlling the recoil and keeping the rounds concentrated. Bright red blood splashed the floor and walls as the beast's legs suffered the shots with little to spare.

It let out a hurt growl as it stumbled forward. Even still, the beast did not let up. Though decelerated, it still charged forward, indubitably more irate than be-fore. A hint that these creatures were not devoid of emotion, but not to the point that they warranted—or deserved—any kind of pity.

The ejector bolt snapped back and smoke poured out of the shotgun. It was empty. Bastian immediately began reloading, via the shells in the Velcro bandolier on the buttstock. It was swifter than digging them out of his pocket, especially with his deftly trained hands. Given the circumstances, of course, even a veteran like Bastian was not immune to the shakes.

His breaths cut in and out, rugged, but he was nowhere near fainting. The adrenaline rush was so ludi-crous, it felt like it might be fatal.

"Bastian!" T shouted, inching forward.

Not once did he look to his right where the two men waited, but in his peripheral vision he could see the tall officer take a couple of steps.

"Hold!" Bastian barked, and was forced to raise

the shotgun again before it was fully reloaded. The beast had closed the distance in that time, and Bastian needed to give himself some cushion to move.

He did so with a hip-fired blast from the shotgun, two successive shots that again tore into the beast's legs. Chunks of flesh tore away, blood splattering the walls and floor. This time it did not gasp or yelp, but it roared thunderously, and stumbled forward like a bag of anvils.

Bastian retreated around the corner, instinctually ducking at the same time, as the large creature's shadow loomed over him. The floor even vibrated under his feet, from its heavy footfalls. When its bulky left shoulder collided with the corner, the wall exploded into chunks of debris with a loud crash.

On impulse alone at first, and then panic, the two officers retreated several paces. The three of them cursed under their breaths, Bastian's lungs exhausted as they were, and he half-expected to be crushed by the beast's falling body in the next few seconds.

Instead, when he stumbled, he fell to his knees, and slid across the tile a good six or seven feet. He let the momentum carry him into a spin, and he landed on his back, swinging the shotgun up to aim.

The beast appeared larger in that moment than it had earlier down the hallway, or even in the parking lot outside. He knew it wasn't the same beast, for its horrid face and shoulders were devoid of bullet holes, not to mention that kind of navigation in such a short time would be impossible.

'*Impossible,*' Bastian thought. *No…* this *is fucking impossible.*

The sheer existence of this abomination—and its cohorts—was easily the most nonviable reality he could think of. And yet here it was, towering over him, doubled forward, heaving blood and saliva from its disturbingly humanoid jaws, the hot waves of breath moistening Bastian's face.

Nausea came over him.

Its glowing yellow eyes were still lit up, deathly life occupying the beast.

Bastian's forefinger snaked around the trigger. He realized in that instant that the large creature was only momentarily suspended above him, its left arm caught in the wall it had just crashed through, flesh torn at the shoulder. Whatever bone and sinew survived, were now like unraveling bands on a rope bridge, with too much weight on one end.

"Get outta there, man!" Z shouted.

The creature started to growl, its vitality resurging through aberrant veins. They began glowing, too, as they had in its kin back in the parking lot. It took a sluggish step forward, dragging the clawed foot, while chunks of buckshot-battered flesh fell from its legs.

Bastian heard sounds of the other creatures approach behind it. They weren't far now, nor were they holding back anymore.

He shook his head and elevated his aim, briskly, knowing that any sign of movement from him would cue the beast into acting out of its idle state. And sure enough, as soon as he raised the shotgun a good two feet, its buttstock now planted against the floor under his right arm instead of his shoulder, the beast lunged at him. It snapped its jaws, which chomped the air inches from Bastian's face, and he felt its gory breath mist his skin. Simultaneously, he squeezed the trigger—not once, nor twice, but three times in rapid succession. The shotgun rattled against the floor and in his sweaty hands. The three blasts slammed into the beast's sternum, below its throat. The third perforated bone and flesh to form a messy exit wound out the center of its back, between its large shoulder blades. Blood sprayed the air above it, and the impacts sufficed to push its body backward.

He didn't waste any time once the large creature—in his mind, *demon*—teetered in the opposite direction. He exerted his legs to push himself into a roll over his head, then used the shotgun as a crutch to spring himself back to his feet. It felt far more acrobatic than anything he had done in his life, and the adrenaline was teeming in him fiercely.

Now standing on either side of him were the two police officers, their faces awash with shock. The good kind.

Meanwhile, the buckshot-riddled beast toppled backward, and actually crushed one of the Vultures before it could flutter out from its shadow.

The massive creature took longer to disintegrate than its smaller brethren, but it sure enough did in the end. As did the Vulture it had inadvertently crushed moments before its weight became no more than embers and ash.

"Two birds, one stone," Z smirked.

"Well, quite a few stones, actually," Bastian smirked wildly, digging shells out of his pocket and reloading the shotgun. He also loaded the bandolier loops, until two of the six were left empty, as was his pocket. "Speaking of which, looks like I'm out."

The sound of two Crawlers and a Vulture shrieking from around the corner became more prominent. They were not daunted, however, if they were in fact capable of feeling emotion, Bastian was willing to bet that anger was now their go-to.

"How many?" T asked, nodding at Bastian.

"Uh…" Bastian was quick to count, although he didn't care for the numbers. "Nine total."

"Behind us," T said firmly. "Gotta conserve the 12-gauge 'til we reach this armory. How far? I see signs."

There were in fact small signs adhered to the walls at intersections. But no calculation of distance, only arrow-indicative direction.

"End of the next hallway," Bastian said, reluctantly retreating behind T and Z.

"Fucking hell," T mumbled, raising his pistol.

"Told ya it could be a maze. Gets simpler farther down you go, believe it or not."

"That's relieving," Z muttered.

T gulped audibly. "How many are left?"

"Uh…two Crawlers and one—"

A Vulture didn't just careen around the demolished corner, it *flew*. Shrieking at the same time, and flapping its bat-like wings.

Startled, T fired at the airborne creature. His aim wasn't high enough at first, so the initial two shots missed, but then he adjusted, and the flapping, screaming creature took a few rounds to the torso. It was knocked out of the air, flopping onto the ground.

"Vulture," Bastian resumed his breath.

Through the thin mist of blood in the air emerged one of the two other Crawlers, this one leaping around the corner, from the destroyed wall to the opposite one, intact and more capable of being traversed. It managed to dodge the first of T's next shots, and then a third clipped it in the shoulder and it screeched at him from seven or eight feet away, in that crevice between wall and ceiling.

Z shifted behind T, emerging to his left, in the same instant that he tried tracking the nimble creature. Z popped it twice in the half-skull head and once in the shoulder, rapidly. The Crawler dropped to the floor, growling and snapping its jaws. A clawed hand lashed out, narrowly missing T's left shin. He acted on a dime and slammed the heel of his right boot into its inner elbow, pinning the lanky arm to the tile. Z moved forward to substitute for T's brief unbalance and put one round into the bowels of the creature's maggot-infested brain. Its head ruptured below its chin, yellow goop splattering the floor.

As the body went limp, disintegrating in the next few seconds, they heard the last Crawler vocalize around the corner.

All three men composed themselves, ready to blast it out of the air or off the ceiling if need be.

However, several seconds passed and the creature never made an appearance.

"Where the hell is it?" Z demanded quietly. He caught his breath and wiped sweat off his brow with the back of a hand.

"Maybe it wised-up," T suggested.

"Can't fathom these things having an ounce of wisdom in their half-heads," Bastian said, embittered. He marched not around but through the dissolving Crawler, embers floating beside his legs. His boots scuffed ash against tile, and it was beyond clear that he no longer gave a damn. Not in the least. About the enemy, or himself to that extent, his bravery could be argued to occupy the same space as recklessness.

He acknowledged this in the back of his mind, if only fleetingly.

And then, just like the *demons* he had slain, the thought evaporated.

When Bastian turned the corner, stepping over chunks of the wall, he witnessed the tail end of the last Crawler disappear into the ceiling, behind a light fixture, twenty feet down the hall. He shouldered the shotgun just in time to see it pull its clawed feet into whatever crawlspace was above the ceiling panels.

"All clear," Bastian said out loud, just audible enough. Once he heard the two guys arrive behind him, he added: "More or less."

"Where'd it go?" Z asked.

"Ceiling. Outta sight. My guess is a crawlspace."

"How fitting."

"Would you happen to be familiar with the blue-prints of the facility?"

Bastian shook his head. "Not to that extent. Just the basic floorplan."

"So what now?" T asked.

"Fuck it. Keep hauling ass to the main armory, for all we know the fucker is going to get reinforcements. We don't have the firepower to afford waiting around to find out."

"Good call. Care to keep leading the way?"

"As long as I got your Remy here, I'm down."

"How's it compare to that ROT-12?"

"ROT-20," Bastian corrected, "and no, it doesn't compare. At all."

T smirked. "Well, shit, color me excited. Let's fucking *go.*"

The corner of Bastian's mouth curled up in a little smile and he proceeded to lead them down the hall. Unlike the previous one, and especially different from the first that they navigated, this corridor was completely untarnished. Not so much as a speck of human blood, much less a body or even a hint that any corpse once occupied the floor. The only signs of distress were the claw marks on both walls, floor and the ceiling panels still in place.

Some of the floor tiles were even crushed or shaken from their foundation, thanks to the large beast's lumbering steps earlier. It may have 'only' been eight or nine feet tall but it must have weighed close to half a ton, and shoulder to shoulder it was damn near too wide to fit in this hall.

Seeing how ravaged the floor was from the beast's passage definitely gave Bastian immediate flashbacks to facing its kind in the parking lot earlier, how much of a bullet-sponge to pistol shots it had been. Small calibers didn't seem to do much except annoy it, and even this time in such close-quarters, it took a dumbfounding amount of 12-gauge shells to stagger it.

This reminded Bastian of what it was like to shoot a solid tree, or even the ground. It was damaging, but to what extent? For a tree, depending on its width, the amount of ammunition needed to topple it was shocking.

*Maybe these things really* are *part Earth...*

It seemed evident that the enigmatic Monolith, as seen on the TV screen earlier, was not terrestrial. Unless some kind of secret government project, the likes of which Bastian clearly wasn't privy to, but he doubted this greatly. The sheer nature of these creatures was un-fathomable, and while not necessarily unimaginable, their reality was ultimately implausible.

And yet...here they were, wreaking havoc across the west coast, slowly spreading through the country. Bastian wouldn't be terribly shocked—just bilious—if he learned that sinkholes were starting to pop up even overseas.

Afterall, earth was earth—everything's connected. Distance be damned. Seasons and climates might vary, but beneath, as big as the planet may be, he wouldn't be surprised if the Monolith was somehow able to influence everywhere.

As if it was using Earth as a host for its evil.

Unable to infect humanity as a whole, it instead corrupted the planet's composition and from its subterranean depths produced these wretched creations.

It was about as wild a theory as the next, but it was at least one that Bastian was able to put faith in, however disturbing. It helped drive him toward a direction of understanding, because if he could grasp even the faintest concept of his enemy's conception, then he was more likely able to conquer his fear.

Or face it with greater confidence.

"Y'all give any more thought to this whole aliens or demon shit?" Bastian couldn't help but ask, feeling helplessly alone in his own world if he didn't share his theories. Maybe then he wouldn't believe he had gone entirely mad.

"I mean, the more atrocities they commit," Z admitted, "the more I lean towards something…demonic. Or evil, plain and simple."

"There's hardly anything plain or simple about these fucking things," T said. "Besides, what's new? It was obvious *an hour ago*, or more, that they're just going around butchering and sometimes even *eating* people."

"Yeah, I know, I just…this, down here…I dunno, T, it just feels more…intimate. More fucked."

"Up close and personal," Bastian grumbled, still leading them. He kept his focus on the ceiling as he approached the spot where he had seen the Crawler vanish into. "I know what you mean, Z. I agree with T, of course, though. And more than either of you two can imagine or begin to empathize."

Bastian paused and again was forced to repress a fit of tears that would choke him up and impair his perception. He could not risk that right now.

"You good, man?" T asked, his voice soft and caring. He stepped in front of Z to hover behind Bastian's right shoulder. He started to reach out but instead stayed his hand. "Want me to take the lead?"

Bastian sniffled and took a deep breath, whipping his head back. He shook his head and lifted the nine-pound shotgun, cradling it in his inner elbow, the barrel pointing up.

"They're, uh, they're not aliens, guys," he said, at first taking T and Z by surprise. Not with the statement itself but his unflinching shift of gears, back to what they were talking about. Of course, the reason was a given—Bastian fared better when he focused on anything that even remotely took his mind off Maggie and Eliza.

Their deaths or their lives.

Both, at this point, were equally detrimental to his mental state.

T cleared his throat. "Why, though?"

"I know, the possibility is there, of course." Bastian spoke between deep, rugged breaths. He stayed standing where he was, not wanting to chance walking any farther while his mind wandered and his mouth ran. "The Monolith might very well be extraterrestrial. But rest assured...and no, I can't give you hard evidence, but...the creatures themselves, demonic they may not be, not traditionally at least, but for fuck's sake...they come *from under the ground*. Think about it...they started off as less fleshy, but some time has passed, they've occupied our atmosphere, *feasted* on us, and now they're breaking away as chunks of meat. But still…still mortal as ever before. Destroy the brain, destroy them. And what kind of Little Green Men *disintegrate* into fucking ash and *fire* when they die?"

T and Z entertained the notion, but obviously there was as much room for doubt as there was on any side of any theory at this point.

"One more thing I'll throw out there, before we continue," Bastian said, feeling like he finally caught his breath and straightened his head enough to not let himself be 'distracted' so easily again. "Remember the Monolith on the screen. The shape alone, the clipped corner, this might sound crazy but it's like…it's just *off*, ya know? Not uniform. And the red line going down the center? C'mon."

Bastian scoffed, as if the big picture, the point he was trying to make, was clear as day.

He continued with barely a breath between rants. But he never became unintelligible, never fumbled his words, and always held the two men captive. More so as he went on than when he started.

"What if it was *boring* into the Earth itself, and, I know this is gonna sound nuts, but…what if…whatever is controlling the Monolith, whatever its origins are, has been *corrupting* the planet, using it as some kind of host for its wretched influence? And these creatures…they're just extensions of that corruption. Parasites, culling humans, maybe even trying to take the planet over? I dunno. Never really thought that far ahead.”

“I’d say you’ve got my vote,” T said, circling around to stand a few feet in front of Bastian.

Z came around the other way, drawing Bastian’s eyes to his left. He shrugged prominently and a genuine smile lit up his dark face, more than the light fixture a few feet away, above them.

“Can’t say I’m head-over-heels onboard, but, shit, you got me thinking.”

Bastian shrugged. “I just figured…the more we try to understand them, the better we can face them. Nothing strategic, it’s all mental.”

“Mentality in combat is critical,” T said. “Remember that, Bastian. You’re a smart guy, it seems. Hell…I’m sure of it. Just don’t lose yourself to mindlessness, or else the world will lose you, too, and I think it’s safe to say that we need you.”

“Damn, T,” Z said, brow furrowed. “Where’d you pull that out of? I know *I’ve* never gotten that kind of commemoration from you.”

T knew he was joking, and Bastian, too, if it wasn’t evident enough by the slowly materializing smirk on Z’s face.

“Doesn’t matter,” T said, mustering a little smile himself, “Bastian needed to hear it. Hell, the world’s ending; it’s no time for shortness or biting your tongue.”

“I can second that, my friend,” Bastian said, nodding. His expression, although solemn, was genuine and not without a heartfelt aura. He even offered his left hand, burly arm glistening with sweat, and T took it, fists clasped. Not a handshake between gentlemen, but a gesture of camaraderie.

When their hands parted, as if on cue, a skittering sound caught all three men's attention, above them and down the hallway. Presumably in the hidden crawlspace.

"As much as I wanna get in on what you guys were having," Z said, "I think we oughtta push forward with a little more—"

A discordant scream ruptured the stillness, and farther down the long stretch of hallway ran a man in a white lab coat. He had not screamed until he was about eighty feet away, quickly passing through the T-intersection without even glancing down the route to his left.

"Haste," Z mumbled, finishing his sentence.

The man rapidly drew closer, with no shortness of energy, although clearly strung out. His white lab coat, which now trailed behind him like a cape, while untarnished, was torn in places. The man's incoherent screams tapered off as he panted and scrambled down the hall toward them. His eyes lit up with something resemblant of hope, however distorted, once he closed the distance.

"Well, glad there are in fact survivors," T said, sounding relieved. He moved ahead of Bastian, eager to help the frightened man. He was no longer screaming or breathing so hard, likely relieved to see the two policemen and…Bastian, at any rate.

"Hold up, T, something's not right," Bastian said, quietly enough that he hoped the lab tech wouldn't hear him.

"Yo, T!?" Z raised his voice, getting T to slow

down and glance over his shoulder at his partner. Z quickly joined T as the man arrived and came to a stop. Bastian was close behind him, forced to keep his shotgun low so as to avoid friendly fire.

"Thank God you're here, officers," the man panted. He threw a frantic look back from whence he came. No sign of movement, either at the corner or farther down the hall. "I was hiding in a room, it was locked and secure, then one of those *things* fell through the ceiling, and I was forced out."

"They're using the crawlspaces," Bastian said, his bad feeling confirmed, unfortunately.

"Who the hell are you?" the man scowled.

"I work here, buddy. Or…did."

"Oh, you must be one of those meathead testers. Or a security guard…where's your uniform?"

"Want a third guess, shit-for-brains?" Bastian dug his ID card out of a back pocket and shoved it into the man's hands.

"B-Bravo Clearance," the man muttered, stuttering as the realization came to him. Not only was Bastian technically this man's superior, but he had military experience and was a lead designer. These things were also on the laminated ID card, next to his photograph and signature.

The man cleared his throat and gave the card back to him.

"My apologies, Lieutenant, I just—"

"Thurgood is fine, man, and no need. I get it. Shit's bad. Let's cut to it. How'd it look down the way you came? We're trying to get to the armory in one piece."

"Security? Oh, uh…I really don't know. I've been inside that room for over an hour. But I've heard quite a bit of shooting, well before you three must've come this way. I fear the worst for the men on security tonight."

Bastian gulped and looked over his shoulder at T and Z, who lingered by him, anticipating his strategy.

"What's your name?" Bastian asked.

"Jeremy Lowell," he replied.

"Jerry L?" Bastian raised his eyes. "Yeah, I've heard good things about you from some of my peers. You do solid work. Can be kind of an ass sometimes, but hey, who isn't in this line of work?"

Bastian punctuated his long-winded, oddly casual if not a little sarcastic statement with a firm slap to the guy's arm. He was possibly the same age as Bastian if not a few years younger, but physically was about six inches shorter and at least fifty pounds lighter. He was clean-shaven with a disheveled bowl-cut, however, the sheer terror and distress that the man—Jerry Lowell— had recently experienced was its own wear-and-tear that nobody could overlook.

"Yeah, I, um," Jerry's brow furrowed and he rubbed his arm, "I've heard of you, too…Thurgood…"

"Excellent. That makes intros easier." Bastian smirked, almost crazily, and turned to indicate his comrades. "This is T and Z of the SDPD. Got a ring to it, huh? Easy to remember, at least."

Now it was not only Jerry who regarded Bastian with a dubious expression. It was clear that he was just shy of going off the deep end, despite his moment of clarity minutes ago, and T's advice.

In Bastian's mind, while he had not completely let his sanity get away from himself, there was a reason behind his behavior. He had to admit that it wasn't necessarily excusable, however, not when he was essentially the leader and superior of this group, which now included someone who might as well qualify as a civilian, unarmed and untrained. Nonetheless, his reason if he had to give one, had become unsettlingly obvious—the enemy could no longer be dismissed as mindlessly feral creatures. Whether all along, or just developed recently, they were dangerously sentient and capable of strategy.

"Hey, buddy," Z said, eyes wide. "Got something you wanna share?"

Having realized that he must've been zoning out rather conspicuously, or otherwise aloof to how Jerry had initially come to them, Bastian snapped out of it.

His voice became fortified again, and the fortress of a man that he had been to T and Z, for the most part, returned in the blink of an eye.

Internally, Bastian allocated his strengths and all of the qualities, trained, honed, or simply inherent, that made him such a commanding leader and effective soldier. Simultaneously, with the weaker traits and infirmities, those he could not jettison, he buried and discarded the shovel.

*Game face, Bastian.*

A little self-motivation could go a long way.

"Get behind me, Jerry," he motioned, shouldering the shotgun in a combat stance. "T and Z, behind him. Watch our asses, but also up top. Remember…they're using the crawlspaces. Some of 'em, anyway."

Scared half to death, but respectful, Jerry gulped and slinked behind Bastian.

All of a sudden an LED fixture at the end of the hallway flickered, catching their gazes. It then dislodged from the ceiling and sparks showered the floor. Two seconds later, the entire ballast dropped and the lights shattered.

"Speak of the devil," Z muttered loud enough for everyone to hear.

"It might be a ruse," Bastian said, his voice low and husky.

"Uh, how so?" T asked from about six feet behind him.

Bastian started to advance, slowly, his knees bent slightly and the shotgun firmly shouldered, barrel pointing down the hall but not up at all.

"Remember what I said about the doors earlier?" His head didn't pivot but his eyes darted left and right, acknowledging the intermittently placed doors. They were premium steel with alloy bearings and internal dead-bolts that activated upon lockdown.

"Yeah," Z said. "Not to bother with 'em 'cause of lockdown."

"Well, that kinda still stands—don't even try to open any. They won't, unless from the inside. But I wouldn't put it past one of those big fuckers to find a way through."

"W-What? Impossible." Jerry's face lost color.

"Not through the door itself, of course," Bastian said. "They've got tungsten dead-bolts. Strongest metal on the planet. Attached to a steel frame, surrounding the door. But…the *walls*, well, that's a different matter. Might not be drywall, but remember what that one did back there—and it was wounded, then."

Jerry frantically looked over his shoulder, peering between the two officers that covered the rear of their formation. He could see the chunks of wall debris from the demolished corner.

His eyes widened.

"W-Wait. One of those *things* did that?" he exclaimed under his breath, now staring at the back of Bastian's head.

"The big ones, yeah," he replied without turning his head. "One of 'em, anyway. Shot to shit, but still managed to shoulder-charge through the fucking—"

Another light fixture flickered ahead of them, this one no more than twelve feet from Bastian, who immediately stopped in his tracks. Jerry accidentally bumped into him at the same time. Bastian shook his head but kept his gaze fixated on the ceiling. However, his shotgun remained pointed down the hall at shoulder-level.

*I ain't fooled.*

The light fixture fell to the floor like the one before it, shattering. Now the last quarter of the hallway was saturated in darkness. Just beyond where the first one had come down, at the next T-intersection, there was still light. With the absence of two ahead of them, however, as illuminating as they had been, what was really only twenty feet now felt like forty.

"Keep close, but not too close," Bastian said hurriedly. "Try not to clip anyone's heels. We're moving, though. It ain't gonna get any lighter anytime soon."

Before anyone could protest, Jerry's mouth already open, Bastian began jogging forward.

"*Move*, Mr. Lowell," T commanded, essentially walking into him. Z helped guide the man into motion, until he got the gist of it himself, and the fact that this decision was not only nonnegotiable but also the right one. The only one, unless they decided to stand still and wait to be engulfed in darkness, then culled in a narrow abattoir.

Bastian risked a glance over his shoulder just before his right foot reached the last illuminated tile. He saw Jerry gain speed and grow some sense all at once, though not without the aid of T and Z. T kept behind them, frequently checking their six, while Z jogged to the right of Jerry, his pistol low but his eyes frequenting the doors along the walls on either side of them.

It was in this moment that Bastian felt the most confident in the two policemen, and couldn't be more grateful for who had happened upon him those hours ago. Hours, supposing it hadn't already been weeks. For it certainly felt like it. And years, since—

*No. They might as well have died two seconds ago*, Bastian grieved in thought.

It was immediately suppressed.

Through literal darkness he now trekked, and any

time he glanced above him, there was only more shadow. The abyss around him through which he moved, and that above. It was disheartening, especially to acknowledge the possibility that at any moment he could be plucked without ever seeing the enemy.

If he had more ammunition to spare, he would've lit up the whole ceiling before making this run. As it were, he simply counted his steps as he neared the end of the hallway, and thus the last few feet shrouded in darkness.

He slowed down before reaching it to look behind him. Jerry's face was awash in as much fear and panic as it was a warped shade of hope—seeing the light behind Bastian, and knowing they were less than a hundred feet closer to the security armory.

Behind Jerry, T and Z were just reaching the first part of the hallway doused in darkness. Their faces were not so dissimilar from Jerry's, except for less panic. More determination.

Z was a good ten paces ahead of T when the wall to their right exploded. Large chunks of debris struck T midstride and he was thrown against the left wall. The pistol in his hands clattered to the floor and his jog reduced to a stagger, while he choked on and coughed through the dusty debris. He bled from a cut on his brow and a stream of red exited his right ear, running down his neck.

Simultaneously, the cause of the breach charged into the hall directly behind T. Its glowing yellow eyes were unmistakable through the dust, and light from the large, jagged hole in the wall poured into the hallway.

Z hadn't realized what had happened until he was within ten feet from Bastian, just as Jerry shrieked in terror and ran past him. As Z skidded to a stop, Bastian reached out to try and grab Jerry's arm or lab coat but was unable to.

"Jerry, *freeze!*" Bastian shouted after him, but didn't wait to see if he complied. He immediately heard gunfire from Z's pistol as he shot down the hall, up at the creature that dwarfed T by three or four feet.

Bastian raised his shotgun, knowing that he would have to aim even higher to avoid the risk of hitting T in the process.

"Ruuuun!" T yelled, waving at the stationary men as he felt his legs lose power.

Bastian fired off a shell before contact was made, and what few pellets peppered the beast's skull had no penetrative effect.

T was maybe fifteen feet away when the beast caught up to him, seizing his right shoulder with its large, clawed hand.

"Jaaaake!" Z screamed just as his pistol's slide locked back and smoke poured from the empty chamber. Every shot he had landed was unflinchingly disregarded by the beast.

It pulled on T's shoulder with its right hand, while its left wrapped around his face. In an instant the creature ripped his arm off, and he howled in pain, his voice scratching but muffled behind the beast's hand. T's blood jetted out of the wound and sprayed the opposite wall.

Z and Bastian were dumbfounded, and Z, out of

ammunition, was forced to stare in horror. Bastian was almost as frozen with shock, but irately began walking toward them and firing into the beast's upper chest and face as it lifted T off the floor by his head.

The shotgun clicked empty and the beast bled profusely from buckshot-perforated flesh, in addition to the several bullets that Z's pistol had landed. But it didn't suffice. The monstrosity still breathed, haggardly, and its eyes glowed just as its veins did. T's legs kicked only a few more times before the creature's left hand closed into a fist, crushing T's skull between its clawed fingers. The gore spewed through and dripped to the floor, skull fragments and brain matter making nauseatingly wet sounds before T's limp body slumped to the tile.

Z backpedaled, his eyelids fluttering, and his stomach in all kinds of knots. The pistol fell from his hands and he stumbled into the wall. Bastian shifted and caught Z from hitting the floor. He tugged one of the man's arms over his shoulder and helped him up, and together they did the unthinkable—

Bastian turned their backs on the creature and urgently hobbled down the hall.

Unarmed and deprived of all hope.

# 9

Reaching the end of the hallway felt like an impossible task until they did, and the light-scarred darkness illuminated entirely. The three-way intersection offered them the choice to continue down the same path or hook a right and head for the armory. It was about sixty feet from where they now stood, bathed in stark-white LED light, not unlike the path before them.

Jerry was halfway down, dismayed and weeping, but alive. All in one piece, contrary to the three colleagues of his littering the floor around him. They were badly mauled, one of them beyond recognition.

Bastian knew that he and Z, and soon Jerry, would be the same if they didn't hurry.

Of course, time seemed irrelevant. The beast could have caught up to them by now, and ripped them apart as they had Jake Taylor.

Pulling Z along with him, down the well-lit and intermittently blood-dappled hallway, Bastian could feel the man shiver up a storm. He was sobbing quietly and had nearly abandoned the use of his legs. Had Bastian not caught him, he would have hit the floor and possibly passed out. Bastian couldn't fathom hauling Z's unconscious dead-weight down the hall, all the way to the armory, supposing they could make it there.

How they had gotten so far was beyond him. Unless…

*They're toying with us. Like fish in a barrel. Thinning the herd, one by one.*

Bastian hated being right sometimes, and this easily took the cake. Their enemy had proven to be far more strategic than any of them thought possible at first. Much like their bodies, he wondered if this cognizance was something they were gradually developing.

If it was, his—and humanity's—worries were tenfold.

*At least they're still learning. And every soldier knows not to toy with the enemy; never underestimate.*

Bastian could see the security room from here. The armory was inside, essentially half of the secure room itself, the other half being an array of surveillance cameras.

"It-It's locked, I-I couldn't get in, it-it wouldn't let me…" Jerry was a bumbling mess. He was visibly shaking and the tears painting his face had pooled together with the mucus bubbling from his nose.

He had been locked away in his room indefinitely, likely since this whole thing began, and hearing was different from seeing.

*Seeing is believing.*

All the screaming and chaos he had heard for hours, locked in his lab, didn't compare to the carnage he now stood at the center of. Of course, to Bastian, three bodies paled in comparison to the utter bloodshed he, Z, and T had previously navigated. Not to mention the horrors they had *witnessed* themselves.

Still, it was a first for Jerry, who Bastian assumed must have come down the other hallway when his room was infiltrated.

In his panic, he had beelined directly past this hallway. Perhaps he had seen Bastian and the others from afar, down the long hall, and it was the only beacon of hope he needed to stay on that path.

Regardless, they were together again—more or less. Z himself was hardly intact, but with Bastian's occasional mumbling, gently demanding that he keep it together, that they were "so close," helped Z stay conscious.

Jerry's lips started to move as Bastian got closer, Z still under his arm. Once within earshot of Jerry's tremulous and hushed voice, Bastian realized he was trying to get out the question "what happened?"

As simple as the two words were, Jerry knew full well what had happened, or could just as well deduce it. The guilt of cravenly fleeing earlier now caught up with him, although even in the back of Bastian's mind he knew he couldn't blame the man given the circumstances. Jerry was untrained and unarmed, defenseless, with no way of helping even had he truly wanted to.

It was for this reason—in addition to simply not having the time or patience—Bastian didn't berate Jerry for his decision.

Instead, he just kept walking past him, until he was about ten feet away and he paused. He looked over his shoulder and gestured at Jerry to follow.

Jerry started fidgeting his hands and didn't know how to respond, until the heavy yet slow footfalls of the large creature drew near, down the hallway from around the corner.

"Yeah," Bastian said matter-of-factly, trying not to sound spiteful, "it's still alive. And we're all outta ammo. Wanna give me a hand with him?"

Jerry now rushed to help, but as if triggered by Bastian's words, Z snapped out of his traumatized daze and abruptly stood up. He did so, so fast, that he nearly toppled. He stumbled off to the side, caught himself on the opposing wall, and then regained his balance.

"I can manage," he finally said, at a gratuitously high volume.

"Good," Bastian said rather coldly, not caring for it himself, but in that moment relieved nonetheless. He took advantage of Z's conscious independence and rushed down the hall to the armory, a room on the left.

This hall was a dead-end, just a few feet from the large bulletproof, shatter-resistant glass pane offering a view of the armory. It stretched from a steel beam under the ceiling down to about waist-level, and from there to the floor was a steel barrier. The entire room was encapsulated by a concrete shell that prohibited entrance or infiltration from any feasible intruder, any which way they might try.

The door itself was just as impenetrable, and the keypad affixed to it had a thumbprint scanner that would pop out after a certain code was entered. Urgently, Bastian entered the four digits, requiring two tries due to his shaking hands. Then the scanner ejected and he pressed his thumb to it. Unlike the code, this was specific to whoever was accessing the armory, of course, thus enforcing accountability.

As if the cameras weren't sufficient.

When Bastian heard the error tone and the light around the keypad illuminated red, he cursed quietly.

A glance to his left lent him the sight of Jerry struggling to get a few words through to Z, and about twenty feet behind them, the approaching shadow of T's killer.

Bastian imagined that as soon as it saw him trying to access this room, while it likely wouldn't be able to grasp the intricacy of it, he feared it would do the math so to speak—and stop fucking around. It would charge them, making damn sure they didn't get into whatever room they were desperately trying to enter.

So he wiped the sweat off his thumb and tried again, slower this time, which aggravated him to do so. Then the keypad illuminated green and it chimed accordingly. The door unsealed with a hiss, and then a loud clang as the internal locks disengaged.

The sound resonated through the hall.

Bastian heard a grunt and a growl, then a shriek from somewhere that seemed quite close, but the source was unseen.

He shot a glance to the ceiling.

"Let's *go!*" Bastian shouted, beckoning the men, who stood about ten feet away.

Z headed out in front of Jerry, nonetheless pulling on his arm. Even in his dilapidated state, Z tried to help the man to safety before himself. Just shy of essentially throwing Jerry out in front of him, a ceiling panel crashed above Z and a Crawler descended in its wake.

A graceless ambush of one, however effective. It parted Z's grip on Jerry's arm, and not smoothly. Jerry's elbow fractured in the opposite direction, bone jutting through flesh. He screamed as he fell back, and the pain paired with fear overwhelmed his senses.

Z was thrown off guard and balance, but kept his footing and somehow his wits, too.

Bastian watched, jaw dropped and eyes wide. He looked inside the armory, his gaze searching for a quick if even temporary resolution.

A pistol left on the desk under an array of surveillance monitors. He snatched it without checking the chamber and rushed back to the door, keeping one leg across the threshold to prohibit it from automatically shutting.

He witnessed Z get swiped at by the Crawler and forced to teeter backwards, unscathed. From where Bastian stood, Z's back was turned to him, unknowingly obstructing his aim of the creature as it pounced on Jerry. It wasted no time towering over its defenseless victim before it was upon him.

"Get inside, Z!" Bastian shouted.

Z hurriedly backpedaled, unable to take his eyes off the Crawler and Jerry, likely feeling guilt that he was unable to help him. Just as he had been futile in saving T. His partner and best friend since high school. A friendship and camaraderie that survived deployments and girlfriends, breakups and fights, and then the academy.

As far as Z was concerned, in that moment, he wasn't worth a damn to anyone if he couldn't have saved T.

If Bastian could read minds, he would tell Z that he knew how he felt, and that, if he really addressed it unbiasedly, he would assure him of its bullshit.

Now was neither the time nor the place.

As soon as Z backed up to stand in front of Bastian, he brought the pistol up to aim, but it was too late. The Crawler was already dragging Jerry down the hall, in the opposite direction. Jerry's skull had been severed by the jaw, the Crawler's clawed fingers stuck into his palate. It dragged him like a ragdoll, its back to Bastian and Z.

The sight of Jerry's unnaturally gaping mouth and split skull, the blood and his lifeless tongue flopping in his mouth, was enough to traumatize anyone.

Z tasted bile but found himself feeling more faint than sick.

Bastian noticed this and immediately began firing the pistol. The gunshots so close to Z startled him back into a full state of consciousness. Bastian managed to plop two rounds into the Crawler's back before it released Jerry to skulk on all fours and shrieked.

In that moment, much to Bastian and Z's surprise, the large beast made its appearance.

Not from around the corner, however.

Which would explain why it had taken its time to arrive. Because for the last minute or two it was navigating rooms down the other hall, likely bypassing doors by slowly and as quietly as possible pushing itself through walls.

Now it was less covert about it, and crashed

through the wall directly opposite the security room. Z stumbled back into Bastian, who was just as startled, and the two teetered into the room.

The beast shook off wall debris and dust, its glowing yellow eyes still unmistakable. It roared briefly, like a provoked grizzly, except that its vaguely humanoid features somehow made it even more frightening.

Seconds after the doorway was cleared, its sensors made the detection. The steel door started to whir shut, but not quickly enough. The large beast lunged forward, pressing part of its wide torso into the doorway. The steel frame wouldn't budge, but Bastian knew that it might very well dent if the beast persisted.

And then the door wouldn't necessarily seal.

He clambered up from where he had fallen next to Z, and firmly gripped the pistol in both hands. He elevated his arms, elbows locked, and began frenziedly firing into its face. Its humanoid jaws gnashed as it struggled to force its shoulders through the doorway, but it would be an impractical task.

Bastian emptied the pistol's magazine into the beast, first its upper chest and even throat, then its face and skull. The pistol only held ten rounds but still, the beast proved disturbingly relentless.

He could even see the bullet marks in its rocky flesh from where Z had struck it earlier in the hall.

Almost as soon as the pistol's slide locked back in Bastian's hands did Z step forward, perilously close to the beast. It frightened Bastian as much as it startled him, and he began to shout at Z, but then he saw what was in his hands. A Benelli pump-action shotgun raised, and just shy of shoving the barrel into the wounded beast's mouth, Z closed the distance—

And squeezed the trigger.

No quip or expletive before he blasted the creature's skull into wet fragments, all over the door frame and the glass to Z's left. Several of the monitors were splattered, too, and his police uniform was also stippled bright red.

He knew it wouldn't matter in a few seconds, anyway.

Almost like black magic, shortly after the beast's headless corpse slumped to the ground, all traces of it dissolved. It left behind only a clumpy pile of ash and little red-orange embers that fluttered in the air before evaporating themselves, just as the security door clanged shut and sealed with a hiss.

Down the hall, an inhuman skirl could be heard.

Yet no creature came to see what had happened, or to avenge the fallen beast. Either they knew better, or a strategy was being constructed by a greater force.

Bastian hoped for the prior, but naturally dreaded the latter.

With the door immovably sealed, he and Z were relieved with a breather.

"We were...so close..." Z mumbled, trudging away from the door. The shotgun dangled at his side before it clattered to the black-tiled floor and he slumped into a wheeled chair. Tears tarnished his face and his eyes were puffy.

"Goddammit, I'm sorry, Z," Bastian shook his

head and repressing the tears that welled up beneath his own eyes. It was like Z's emotional pain made the air thick with grief, and he could feel every bit of it. "I hardly knew you two, but T was a good fucking man. And we...*you*...did *everything* possible to—"

"Y-You don't...get to call him that..." Z mumbled, his nose wrinkled and his brow furrowed. He didn't look up at Bastian as he sat slumped in the chair, but his aimless glare was expressive enough.

Bastian's nostrils flared and he wanted to retort, but held it back. He firmly set the empty pistol down on the desk and, like a reanimated statue, plodded toward the back of the half-moon-shaped room.

With his back to Z, he spoke in a low, grating voice that was, still, not bereft of emotion. Raw and palpable, there was so much to his voice that any sensible human could detect, if not feel.

"I get the defense. I don't blame you. We say anything in moments like these. But don't you *dare* protest my empathy."

Bastian punctuated his statement by vigorously removing a weapon from its designated cubby. One of eighteen set into the aerated metallic wall, floor to ceiling. This action, paired with the last of what he said, drew Z's attention. He spun around in the chair and then sat up more rigidly.

"What are you doing, Bastian?" Z asked, his voice nasally but stanch.

"My mission."

Z scoffed. "You're not a Ranger anymore, man.

Nor a SEAL. You're retired. Cut the macho-man bull-shit and sit your ass down. We're safe in here, and your plan is batshit crazy. Accept it."

"The only thing I can accept, Zavala," Bastian said, his back still turned but his voice clearer than before, "is that these things are evil. Alien, demonic, fucking spirits from another dimension, doesn't matter if they're made of earth or fire, flesh or stardust. I'm gonna do everything in my power to kill as many as possible."

He turned, then, to face Z.

"And I *am* going to make it to that Monolith. Dead or alive. I have to see inside of it. I have to."

"So…you're a tourist?" Z said, gritting his teeth, forcing himself not to address or even acknowledge anything else that Bastian said.

"Sure, Z," Bastian simpered madly. He brandished a shotgun in one hand and a compact assault rifle in the other, at the same time. A bandolier of 12-gauge shells hung around his neck and shoulder like a strap to a purse, especially with the satchel at the end, dangling above his right hip. In it were spare magazines for the rifle. "A tourist armed to the teeth, with a short fuse and zero-tolerance for bullshit."

"You're crazy, B," Z said, shaking his head. "But I guess that's why I like you so much. T liked you, too."

"He shouldn't, and nor should you, but I can't reject your sentiments. You're good men."

"And you're not?"

Bastian's smirk wavered before disassembling, and he turned his back on Z again to finish stocking up.

Beneath each weapon cubby were a pair of stacked drawers, and various versions of ammunition inside, correlating to the weapons above them.

It was an extensive arsenal, capable of fending off even a large-scale terrorist attack on the facility above or below, but only given ample warning and man-power. Today, they had been offered neither; nor was their enemy even human.

And in a most unsettling way, they seemed innumerable.

If Bastian's theory, outlandish as it was, had any truth to it, then the enemy's forces might very well be endless.

*Using our own planet against us.*

He didn't want to entertain the theory too deeply, of course, or he would get sucked into a vortex of thoughts. Like a multiverse of questions, doubts, fears, and ultimately, fatal pessimism.

A gauntlet leading to a dead-end that he couldn't afford right now.

Even if that was exactly the route he was going to take, physically.

"Answer me, dammit," Z insisted, forcibly standing up. The wheeled chair rolled across the floor and clashed with the desk.

Bastian sighed and finished packing supplies. It wasn't burdensomely heavy, as he didn't want to cripple his mobility. Nor did he want to necessarily rely too much on this arsenal when his ultimate goal in the facility was the Bravo Vault.

A serious upgrade to even this.

"Good or bad, moral or immoral, isn't the question," Bastian said.

He finally turned around to face Z again.

The compact assault rifle, a SA58 Mini, was slung over his shoulder, and in both hands was an AA-12 automatic shotgun, with a twenty-round drum magazine. While rigs and holsters were kept elsewhere in the armory, he hadn't taken the time to find them and equip himself more properly. So the pistol he had chosen was now tucked into the front of his slacks, and spare magazines were tossed into the bandolier satchel.

"It's about decisions and capabilities, now," he added, which didn't seem to register for Z.

"The hell does that mean?" Z scowled.

Bastian walked toward the door, and the motion alone, especially without saying anything for a few seconds, drove Z to urgently begin stocking up at the armory wall.

"It means," Bastian said, half-turning to face a bewildered Z about twelve feet away, and using the base of his fist to strike the 'open' button by the door, "I'm not fit to burden the lives of anyone else with my reckless decisions."

The door whipped open and Bastian stepped through. Z choked on his words as he tore away from the wall of weapons, rushing toward the door. It closed again and sealed seconds before he reached it. On the other side, Bastian sealed it with a quick code and thumbprint confirmation.

Z stepped over to the side, between the door and security monitors. Bastian glanced down the hallway to see shadows shuffling around the corner of the intersection. His heart started to race for a different reason than it did when he looked at Z, now through the reinforced glass that Z pounded the bottoms of his fists on. His face was distorted with desperation.

Despite the window's thickness, their voices were still audible to each other, albeit muffled.

"You're crazy, Bastian, don't do this! You can't go out there alone! Let me the fuck out!"

"It's more than an armory, Z. Think of it as a panic room." While Bastian didn't yell the words, his collected demeanor alone settled Z down to listen. "There are rations in the corner, MRE's and water bottles, under the med-kit. There's an air-tight disposal compartment on the opposite wall, for recycling spent casings and defective ammo, for regular pick-up. Anyway…you can use that for waste disposal, in the meantime."

Z gulped and shook his head firmly.

"Don't…do this."

Z had stopped pounding on the glass, seeing how calmly Bastian stood there. It was almost infuriating in itself, but it started to come over Z how and why he was acting so detached. Knowing, deep down, that Bastian, of all people, was absolutely the opposite of emotionless. No matter how cold he looked or acted.

"I hope you reunite with your family, Z. You deserve their love as much as they do yours. And so does T's family." Tears visibly welled up in Bastian's eyes, blurring his vision of Z on the other side of the glass. Maybe this was best.

Z fumbled with his words, but ultimately Bastian cut him off, respectfully.

"Taylor was a good man, Z. He lives on through you. And goodness oughtta prevail."

# <u>10</u>

There was no listening to Z after he started walking down the hall. He knew the door wouldn't open for anyone except himself, or an employee with higher clearance. Which made him think of the Deputy Director. While he had to pray that Bowman was safe and unharmed, possibly not even in the building anymore, he also knew he couldn't afford any search-and-rescue endeavors.

His tasks were straightforward and, more or less, linear. Reach Bravo Vault on Sublevel 4, then zip back topside, and from there, somehow, make it to Calipatria. It was about an hour and a half drive with no traffic, which he knew wouldn't be the case, but equated it to his level of zero-tolerance urgency. An unmatched sense of haste and impatience.

By the time Bastian was within fifteen feet of the intersection, opted with going left or right, he could no longer hear Z at the other end of the hallway. Neither his screams nor his pounding fists, supposing he still exercised both.

As much as Bastian hated leaving him behind, mostly because it left himself alone, emotionally and tactically, he did not second-guess the decision.

Besides, perhaps being emotionally independent

was his best option given the circumstances and his objective.

It was bad enough as it were that he felt like the only sign of life in this facility. However, Jerry had been a survivor forced out of his room, so as far as Bastian knew, many more were scattered throughout the installation. It was, afterall, a massive compound with a complex floorplan, and five levels below the lobby. The fifth was primarily maintenance.

The fourth was his current goal.

He needed to make it back to the elevators, however, not venture further through this level. Which would be the case if he took a right turn at the intersection of corridors. Fortunately, that was the side where the shadows could be seen, splashed against the opposite wall, white and well-lit around the inhuman silhouettes.

A small party of the creatures, lying in wait, or scheming an imminent attack.

Surely they had heard or otherwise detected the security door opening and shutting, followed by Bastian's voice. But, he had kept stoic, despite the maelstrom inside of him.

Now sufficiently armed, contrary to earlier, and a waypoint concreted in his mind, he could let that storm out—in waves.

With both of his hands on the weapon he had chosen ideal for close-quarters situations, he knew there was no time like the present. And what a wretchedly chaotic present it had become.

Teeth gritted and blood boiling, Bastian lowered

his head as if charging through a barrier, and bolted into the intersection. He approached it from an angle, so that he could stride down the hall from whence he and the other had originally come, without sacrificing momentum. Yet he did so, too, while throwing a glance over his shoulder, still not risking any loss of speed.

A glimpse was all he needed, and he almost wished he had not even looked at all.

The throng of four Crawlers were immediately attentive to his presence, and made gurgling yelp sounds as soon as they saw him. They then shrieked louder, as if calling for backup, and began bounding down the hall after him. He minded his footing around blood spills, bodies, and debris, as he headed down the hallway, crossing intermittent sections of lightlessness, all of his newly attained gear rattling on his body.

Part of him certainly wished he didn't have it all, so that he would be lighter, but that notion vanished immediately.

Especially when he glanced behind him, turning a corner and stumbling over debris, witnessing the four Crawlers in pursuit.

When he redirected his attention to the path ahead of him, knowing that he was just one more hallway from the elevator foyer, he felt his heart race faster. He felt his muscles vacate of strain and exhaustion. The adrenaline became a drug that his body hungered for.

It was only when he came close to the end of this hallway that he realized the next was essentially a bottlenecked slaughterhouse.

He caught his breath as his shoes—*thank you so*

*fucking much, T*—scuffed and skidded across the clean tile, trying to slow down before careening around the corner. In the process he lost his balance and stumbled into the opposite wall, forcing himself to accept a breather.

A very fleeting moment of reprieve.

He looked down the hall to his left, from whence he just sprinted, and saw only two of the Crawlers galloping on all fours. One on a wall, and the other using the floor. He frantically wondered where the other two were, and then saw a light fixture twenty feet away flicker all of a sudden.

*The crawlspace.*

They were trying to get the drop on him, literally. It was evident to Bastian, then, that the creatures were treating him like a special kind of prey instead of a rogue survivor to be herded and slaughtered.

He needed to use this to his advantage, and prove that he was indeed a force to be reckoned with.

*Not to be fucked with.*

Bastian, resentful but in a way invigorated for the same reason, proceeded down the next hall, feeling more like a predator than prey. The stench of incipiently rotting corpses and coagulating blood down this corridor was almost as unbearable now as it had initially been—almost.

He reminded himself that he was unstoppable. He had to be. No matter how absurd, it was a necessary evil type of illusion that he took to heart.

The sixteen-pound automatic shotgun he hoisted

in both hands, grateful for the twenty-round drum magazine. Like a Tommy Gun that fired 12-gauge buckshot. He listened for the encroaching Crawlers from around the corner and then spun, hip-firing the AA-12 instead of shouldering it due to the recoil.

The first Crawler hissed shrilly as if it recognized the threat. Already loping on all fours, however, made it a prime target. The first two shells unloaded into its face and shoulders, shearing away flesh and muscle at an eight-foot distance. It tumbled back, crashing into its compatriot.

Bastian turned around the corner again and began striding through the bodies to make his way to the other end. The sneakers skidded through a slowly drying puddle of blood halfway through and he nearly lost his balance. The added weight to his person definitely didn't help his grace.

But it sure helped his cause.

A glance over his shoulder lent him the sight of one Crawler careening around the distant corner, so fast that it slammed into the opposing wall. This actually made Bastian smirk, but the arrogance was given an immediate rebuttal.

In addition to a Crawler descending through the ceiling about ten feet behind him, a second dropped down directly in front of him. His momentum carried himself into it, and both bodies staggered down the hall. Unfortunately, he was just a few feet from the end, thus when he fell, he didn't hit bare tile. Part of him guiltily felt thankful for the corpse that cushioned his impact, but the sensation was gruesome and repulsive.

The Crawler, on the other hand, was far more graceful. It landed on all fours like a cat, except that its lanky limbs protruded out from below its body, in an inhuman fashion. Its claws skittered across the tile and it hissed its hideous face at Bastian less than ten feet from where he slid to a stop. He was on his right side, planted into some poor man's disemboweled corpse.

Bastian stifled the urge to retch, as he picked himself out of the body, whose face was missing an ear and eyeball. The flesh had already begun to decompose, and the odor alone was enough to fluster most folk.

Bastian Thurgood was not most folk, but he had certainly seen, heard, felt, and smelled more than his share of tolerable horrors today.

He had no concept of time down here, especially now that he was alone. But he had to guess that it was at least nine o'clock.

He vaguely recalled it being around seven-thirty when he was with T and Z topside, watching the TV in the lobby.

At any rate, it was time—

*To get the fuck outta here.*

Unfortunately, at present 'here' simply meant this level. He still needed to go even deeper into the compound, before he could leave altogether.

The Bravo Vault was his beacon of hope.

Sufficient motivation.

"I don't have time for this, fuck-face," Bastian muttered, just short of growling it, as he stared at the skulking Crawler ten feet away. He had risen to all fours himself, still not entirely out of the bemiring corpse beneath him.

As soon as he pulled up the shotgun, albeit using it as a crutch to get himself into a three-point stance, the Crawler shrieked and launched itself at him. Bastian was a quick-draw marksman in his prime; while the circumstances were not ideal, and he was understandably off his game, there were some traits that never faltered. Like a duly notorious gunslinger, he drew the pistol from the front of his slacks and fired it before the creature closed the distance.

Two rapid shots cleaved the creature's half-skull from between its temples. Its head whipped back on its scrawny neck, spraying the clean white floor with a yellow and red mist. It fell, twitching, supine. Within arm's reach of the pistol's smoking muzzle.

He got to his feet, wielding the Kimber Tac-II pistol in his right hand, and dangling the shotgun in his left. The black semiautomatic was a custom, tactical variant of the classic Colt 1911. His thumb rubbed the textured grip, anticipating the need to fire it again.

That had felt too easy, in a manner of speaking.

Behind him he heard the approach of the other two Crawlers.

Without looking over his shoulder, Bastian forfeited caution to exchange it with adamant haste. He marched forward, almost nonchalantly, and blindly double-tapped the creature in the face as he walked past it, into the elevator foyer. The creature's half-skull bounced against the tile under the shots, and its entire body disintegrated seconds later, as Bastian hit the call button to the freight elevator.

He had three rounds left in the pistol before needing to reload it, but that would be a cinch with the spare magazines he had in his satchel.

He was grateful that the security armory had a decent supply of pre-loaded, expendable magazines for most of the weapons provided. He knew, too, that oftentimes the security personnel had little to nothing to do, especially the night crew, so they would occasionally be tasked with manually loading magazines, cleaning weapons, and arranging them best in case of an emergency.

In the six years that Bastian had worked here at CHERI, nor in the decade prior, not once was anything in that armory needed…

Until now.

Needless to say, he was indebted to the security personnel.

He had yet seen any of them, alive or dead, and assumed he would notice. Their tactical uniforms were all black, which made them stick out like sore thumbs in this mostly white facility.

He heard the two Crawlers in pursuit of him careen around the corner to his far left, their motion alone drawing his gaze.

He had holstered the pistol, so he turned to face them and raised the AA-12. His finger curled around the trigger just as the freight elevator lurched to a stop in front of him. The heavy metal doors peeled open, and he glanced inside to confirm that it was unoccupied. When he looked back at his targets, they had split up.

One was ceiling-bound, crawling to him like a four-legged spider, hissing. The other zig-zagged as it charged him across the floor.

Bastian fired the automatic shotgun at the one on the floor, sweeping his aim and liberally expending ammunition. He knew it was the only way to hit it with all of the movement. Eventually he did, just as it came within a lanky arm's reach of the shotgun's muzzle. Buckshot had peppered its body enough at that point to reduce it to ruins.

Instead of engaging the one on the ceiling out in the open, especially realizing how close it had gotten, Bastian backpedaled into the freight elevator. He dropped to his knee against the back panel, and shouldered the shotgun, aiming high.

The elevator doors finally pulled shut, but not before the creature swung inside. Bastian yelled incoherently, a war-cry preceding the raucous firing of the shotgun.

Two rounds caught it, center-mass, airborne.

Before it even landed inside the elevator, it was thrown back, albeit against the now shut doors. Its bright red blood had spray-painted the inside of the elevator, including Bastian. He kept his mouth shut and squinted his eyes.

For this reason alone, in addition to the obvious ones, he yearned for the Suit.

Even when, upon death, the creatures' blood vanished without a trace. Still, it would be wonderful to never risk getting it on his face again.

The Crawler's torso had been practically oblite-rated by the successive shotgun blasts, and it dissolved seconds later. Bastian impulsively spit its blood from his lips, scowling, only to look down at himself—and the shotgun—to witness every drop of blood disappear.

He was appreciative of that, at least.

Contrarily, it meant there would never be physi-cal evidence of their presence.

As long as they were caught on film, and with enough survivor testimonies, there would be no way of covering this up or suppressing the reality.

Having caught his breath, Bastian stood up and punched the S4 button on the panel. The elevator lurched and he glanced up at the level indicator above the door, illuminating as he descended further into the facility. He bypassed Sublevels 2 and 3.

A quick ammo check revealed that he had only six rounds left in the AA-12 drum, which was half trans-parent. He began reloading, shell by shell, via the bandolier around his torso. The drum magazine was re-loaded as one might a fixed-cylinder revolver.

He had managed to load eight more shells before the lift lurched, and he glanced at the level indicator. It was between S3 and S4, moving exceptionally slow. This wasn't unusual for the freight elevator, especially when operating during a lockdown, on low power. But the lurch was caused by something else.

He heard rattling above him, and impulsively stepped to the side just as a ceiling panel crashed and a creature descended into the elevator. It was a Vulture, wings flapping, beak-jaws hissing all around it as it spun to face him.

Had Bastian not been so startled and taken aback, he would have blasted it to hell without a second's hesitation.

One of its wings managed to whip toward him and draw blood from a gash on his right forearm. Bastian cursed under his breath and extended his right foot, kicking it in the chest. It being a little smaller than Crawlers was especially evident right now, and Bastian felt like a giant despite almost rivalling its size.

With another kick that sent it staggering into the closed doors, Bastian gave himself some room to breathe—and enough to elevate the shotgun. He hip-fired it, squeezing the trigger once and then letting off. The single round of buckshot tore through the screeching creature's wings, turning the membranes into Swiss cheese. Coincidentally, the foul creature was already about that color.

Except now it bled the same bright red hue that its comrades bled.

This satisfied Bastian something fierce.

Scowling and growling and more or less grinning through that warped expression, Bastian lunged out and struck the creature with the buttstock of the composite shotgun. It wasn't as heavy as he would've liked, but it managed to further unbalance the Vulture.

More importantly, to Bastian at least, it staggered away from the doors. He didn't want to risk damaging them, as durable as they were.

Now he aimed down and fired another round into the Vulture's slender, vaguely avian skull. Everything was decimated at this range, from the tip of its beak-like jaws to the base of its spindly neck. The headless body slumped and evaporated just as the elevator realigned and reached Sublevel 4.

Bastian shrugged in an aggressively arrogant fashion, feeling victorious, and even a little unstoppable. Or at the very least, unyielding.

He proceeded over the threshold and into the elevator foyer. Unlike Sublevel 1, 4 was much smaller— a lesser number of hallways, but each one was longer. This was because the rooms had to have more space between them, for safety purposes. Most of the rooms were ranges and testing chambers.

Bastian knew exactly where he had to go, which was an advantage.

Unfortunately, by the looks of it, he imagined \ the enemy was just as abundant down here as they were above. If not more so, which was greatly troubling.

The elevator foyer alone was more red than white, the latter being the common motif of every sublevel. The amount of mutilated bodies were too many to count, and at one glance-over, Bastian couldn't spot any two tiles not tarnished by gore.

His body began to shake where he stood.

Jaw clenched, his teeth grinded against themselves to the point that he was hurting himself. His temples throbbed, blood racing, but all in a stasis of futility.

*They probably figured they were safer the deeper they went.* Bastian shook his head and bared his teeth, spittle bubbling behind his lips. His mind became clouded with splenetic thoughts. *But that's where they're coming from…* inside *the fucking Earth.*

Not that the surface was any safer.

His stomach turned and he heard overlapping screams erupt from down a hall.

Like every Sublevel elevator foyer, it branched off into two hallways, and from there the maze began. Except that this one was less complex. The one to his right—the source of the screams, according to his hearing—eventually branched off into two more. Unlike Sublevels 1 and 2, 3 and 4's corridors did not have a route that circled around to the elevators.

The hallway to Bastian's left was no-outlet, and did not branch off at all. It was mostly maintenance closets but included one extensive testing range. Then, at the very end, not unlike the security armory where Z was still confined—*for his own good*, Bastian assuredly thought—was a dead-end, and the Bravo Vault.

The floorplan was a little different than the security armory, however; the dead-end itself was the Bravo Vault. A floor-to-ceiling, wall-to-wall security door. It opened vertically, at the center, with pressurized locks sealing it. Access required a PIN that only select personnel with Bravo Clearance or higher had, and of course a thumbprint scanner.

The screams down the hall to Bastian's right drew his focus. Despite his thought earlier about not being able to afford or risk any search-and-rescue tasks, this he couldn't ignore.

He hastily proceeded to the hall on his right, but didn't need to go far to find the source of the screams.

The hall was twice as wide as the ones on higher Sublevels, and by average nearly twice as long. Looking down it now, as strewn with corpses and body parts as it was, his eyes played tricks on him. Dizzied by a vertigo effect, the hall stretching itself before him, he staggered briefly at its opening.

Another scream thrusted him back into reality and he fixated on the upright subjects eighty feet away.

His vision corrected.

Two women and a man, all appearing worse for wear. One of the women was still in her lab tech attire, white coat down to her knees, but the others were in plainclothes, likely having changed already at the end of their shifts, ready to go home.

And then all hell broke loose.

*Literally*, Bastian couldn't help but quip.

There was, however, not a shred of humor in this situation.

He rushed down the hall, yelling wordlessly at the top of his lungs, to draw the creatures' attention. While he didn't see any from this distance, he assumed they were nearby, and had probably flushed the people out into the hall, as they did Jerry.

The closer he got, the sooner he realized that the three people were alone, huddled together and trying to get a grip on themselves. Their screams were instigated by the visual carnage in the hallway, and as far as Bastian could tell, nothing else.

"Who are you!?" one of the women shouted, with a thick Indian accent, and Bastian immediately recognized her. She was the one still in her lab coat.

"Adhira, it's Bastian!" he shouted, now about twenty feet away.

Her expression went from dumbstruck and terrified to hopeful and relieved.

Adhira Laghari was seven years younger than Bastian, but one of CHERI's lead tech engineers. She had been a friendly colleague for the past four years, after she transferred from a DARPA facility in Nevada.

"Oh, thank God," she exhaled, her dark eyes lighting up.

The glowing yellow eyes behind them were even more luminous. The tall, wide-shouldered beast turned the corner ten feet from where they stood and growled with a hot huff of breath.

Bastian's shoes slid through a pool of blood before he came to a stop about fifteen feet from the trio. He didn't recognize either of Adhira's company, but that didn't make them less important.

"Everybody, behind me, run!" Bastian yelled, shouldering the AA-12.

The beast roared more thunderously, and began lumbering toward them. It took the second woman longer than the others to finally start running, as shock had seized her. Once she did, though, Bastian's aim was unobstructed. He fired at the incoming beast, aiming high instead of low. The boisterous reports reverberated in the hallway, likely deafening the second woman as she had barely cleared him when he began firing.

Neither T nor Z had gotten a chance to pitch names for this abomination, but Bastian had a few bouncing around his head.

Legionnaire came to mind.

He remembered how it had practically commanded the small multitude of lesser creatures, about an hour ago. And how it braved the most challenging routes of attack. Also, more common and seemingly more combative than a Baron.

As absurd or unfitting as the name might be to others, should he ever get a chance to air it out, it stuck in his brain like a thorn.

Four shells he had spent into its chest and shoulders before Bastian decided to turn and run. Somehow the Legionnaire was still mobile, and not fazed by its blood loss.

Far more inexorable than the one he and T had faced down in the parking lot.

Of course, bottlenecked like this, Bastian felt like he and the unarmed personnel were at a disadvantage.

Bastian had to remind himself this wasn't the case, at least for himself. That he was armed to the teeth and smaller, more mobile than the beast. Lastly, none of the creatures had any projectile attacks. They were ultimately beasts, no matter how methodical, and had to be within close range to deal any damage.

From afar, all they had to offer was intimidation and fear.

*And I'm beyond that*, Bastian tried to reassure himself.

The others obviously weren't, and reasonably so. He watched them reach the end of the long hallway, much faster than he expected considering the slaughterhouse floor they had to traverse. But then the trio careened left, into the elevator foyer. He heard screams overlap.

"No! Keep going!" Bastian shouted. "Bravo Vault!"

He glanced over his shoulder to see the beast slow down a little. Its blood loss was significant, and Bastian was reminded that, despite its atrocious nature, it was still mortal.

In layman's terms, *killable.*

Bastian's brow furrowed and he gritted his teeth. He turned his feet and skidded to a stop, a body pushed aside against the heel of his right shoe. He solidified his stance and shouldered the AA-12.

"Get to Bravo Vault!"

Punctuating his exclamation, all while staring up at the slowly approaching Legionnaire, Bastian squeezed the trigger. He was aiming higher than usual.

The buckshot spread was wider than most tactical shotguns, but at this range—and increased fire rate—he couldn't complain. Double-ought pellets sprayed the Legionnaire's dome of a skull, some of them peppering the ceiling tile above it. A light fixture shattered and sparks sprayed the large beast. Its beady yellow eyes still glowed, and when it roared defiantly, Bastian stumbled back. He saw that distinct orange glow from its throat and its veins embossed, gleaming like streams of magma.

He threw a frantic look over his shoulder and witnessed Adhira rushing down the hallway leading to Bravo Vault. She was tugging on the arm of the other woman, whose short blonde hair had matted to parts of her sweaty face, obscuring her vision and adding to her disorientation.

He didn't see the man, however.

"Fuck," Bastian muttered, and turned back to face the Legionnaire. It had taken another couple of steps closer to Bastian, and now dropped into its own three-point stance, a clawed fist crushing several tiles. Bloodied saliva dripped in viscous red ropes from its jaws.

Languidly, it looked up at him, now about his same height.

Bastian lowered his shotgun to aim directly at the beast, but it surprised him with a last-ditch effort of agility. Its jaws lashed out, head and neck like a snapping turtle, and they clamped down around the shotgun, demolishing it. He let go, saving his hands, and stumbled back, almost losing his balance. As his shoes slid through blood and his knees locked to keep him afoot, he drew the pistol from his waistband.

The beast purged its mouth of the plastic and metal debris. If it had a tongue, he imagined now it would lick its lipless chops.

*Rest in pieces, AA-12*, he grieved.

It had served its purpose, but he would have liked to rely on it more.

The Legionnaire snarled and Bastian could have sworn he saw the rigid corners of its mouth curl into a diabolical grin. His stomach turned but he answered tersely, firing the pistol at its face.

From nine or ten feet away, the results were promising. The .45-caliber ACP bullets smacked the

Legionnaire in the brow and the space between its eyes and upper teeth. It began shaking its head as if a dog with tape on its nose.

Three rounds never felt so satisfying.

The pistol's metal slide locked back and smoke curled out. Bastian didn't curse or exclaim, but he did slowly regain his balance and start backpedaling through the bodies while reloading. The ejected, empty magazine fell to the floor, more rather, on top of an eviscerated corpse. Only minutely shaking, he deftly drew a sleek seven-round magazine from the satchel dangling over his right hip, and slammed it into the base of the pistol's hollow grip. It clicked and his thumb swiped the slide latch, snapping it forward and loading a round into the chamber.

Immediately, the Legionnaire propelled itself forward, using its downed fist as leverage.

Bastian fired rapidly, but meticulously. Despite the terrifyingly close threat, his knees didn't wobble nor did his aim waver. He focused on the big dome of a skull, until the .45-caliber bullets punctured bone enough to split it open. Brain matter discharged in a yellow arc of fluid, and the Legionnaire's glowing eyes suddenly dulled.

Its body crashed into the floor, pancaking bodies beneath it and crushing tiles.

Bastian felt the impact vibrate up his legs and he teetered briefly before concreting his stance. He fired one more round into the inert body of the beast, a split-second before it started dissolving, slowly. The pistol's slide locked back again and he quickly reloaded.

A loosely masculine scream pierced the ringing in Bastian's ears from all the gunfire.

He pirouetted at the end of the hallway he occupied and swung into the elevator foyer, reloaded pistol aiming in both hands, elbows locked.

He spotted the man in a far corner, swinging a red fire axe at a Vulture that fluttered around in front of him, backing him into a corner. The axe was heavy, eight pounds, which in the hands of a frightened man like this one might as well be sixteen. Still, he hollered irately and took wildly desperate swings. The Vulture easily evaded them, but still pestered the man.

Staccato screams sputtered in the opposite direction, leading to Bravo Vault, where Adhira and the other woman headed.

Bastian jerked his gaze back to the Vulture and whistled with his tongue to his teeth. The Vulture hissed and turned away from the man, wings flapping.

All of a sudden the man moved forward and swung the axe horizontally, striking the Vulture midair. The blade cleaved the Vulture's right wing membrane before lodging itself into the slender torso, and the momentum drove it into the wall, anchoring it there. Blood splattered outward and dripped down the axe, which the man understandably abandoned.

He rushed toward, Bastian, who lowered his aim and couldn't help but smirk, impressed.

"Hell of a swing, Bambino," he said, motioning the man to come to him.

Bastian didn't want to forget these people's faces. Their voices. Their names. Except that he hadn't learned this man's name, and wouldn't. The Crawler that crashed through the ceiling seconds before he reached Bastian crushed him under its weight, but not fatally. He screamed out and tried wrestling the creature off of him, but a second creature descended, knocking Bastian back and scratching him in the process. His right forearm stung but the cut was not deep. He dropped his pistol unintentionally, and it slid between the legs of a Crawler that now stood upright, between him and the man, who was wrestling with the other.

Bastian growled, knowing he didn't have any more time to waste, especially with the women down the other hall, where he heard more screams.

He took a swing at the creature, punching it in the jaw, which hurt him more than it, but did still bemuse it some. Then he unslung the compact assault rifle, shouldering it and hunching forward to grip it stably. He bent his knees and aimed high, firing a burst into the Crawler's left shoulder. It spun like a top and then he centered his aim and hosed its sternum with half a dozen rounds. The armor-piercing 7.62mm ammunition ripped holes in its frail torso and it fell into its compatriot. The man groaned out and managed to roll from under them as the uninjured one fought to push off the dead weight of its fallen brethren.

He sprung to his feet, livelier than Bastian expected. He proceeded to push the man toward the other hallway, but all of a sudden he wouldn't move.

His face went pale and blood rolled down his lower lip. He clutched at his stomach, which started to open up. He had been clawed across the gut and didn't realize it until now. The laceration gaped and his eyelids fluttered.

Bastian snarled an expletive under his breath, saliva bubbling down his chin. He aimed down at the two Crawlers, one of them finally getting to its feet. The other was still alive, but moved sluggishly.

Bastian fired indiscriminately, not aiming anywhere in particular on the creature's body.

Meanwhile, the man a few feet to his right fell to his knees, and then his side. His entrails steamed on the floor.

The upright Crawler's legs cut out from under it as Bastian swung his aim low, then high again, as if trying to spell something with the spent lead. He ultimately emptied the magazine into the two Crawlers until nothing but embers and ash remained. But he hardly waited for that process to begin, before he rushed toward the other hallway. Passing by the poor man's corpse so indifferently angered him further, not to mention the fact that he couldn't save him, either, despite being so well armed.

He stared down the hall, which featured a canted bend along the right wall at the halfway mark. This kept the Bravo Vault door out of sight from where he stood.

*Who the fuck designed this place? Dr. Seuss?*

Bastian shook his head and glowered as he hurried down the hall, which was virtually untarnished. A few smears of blood on the walls here and there, suggesting that some wounded people had made their way through it, probably en route to the elevators, possibly even herded in that direction.

No bodies, though.

Not even when he reached the bend and had a straight-shot view of the Bravo Vault at the end of the hallway. A distance of roughly sixty feet.

The only bodies occupying the hall, besides Bastian, were the two women. Adhira was currently typing her passcode into the keypad on the control panel to the right of the massive gunmetal door. She was occasionally pushed or bumped into by the blonde woman, who wasn't handling panic well at all.

"Hurry!" the blonde woman shrieked.

"I'm trying, shut up!" Adhira shouted back, frantically. She seemed logically sound earlier, but now she was crumbling, and the other woman wasn't helping at all. Or else they would have likely gained access by now, Bastian imagined.

He began jogging down the hall, grateful it was empty, at least.

And then the blonde woman shrieked again, looking in his direction. But he didn't need to second guess it to realize that it wasn't himself that alarmed her. He slowed down and looked up.

The LED fixture above his head flickered before popping, sparks showering him. He raised his arm and rifle to shield his face. His eyes traced the ceiling panels leading down the hall. They rattled in their frames and eventually other LED fixtures flickered before popping and going out, like clockwork.

Indicative of the creatures traversing the ceiling on the other side of the panels.

Unlike other parts of the facility, there were no

crawlspaces in Sublevel 4. Which meant that the creatures had to navigate a claustrophobic path of beams and wiring to take that route.

This abated them, and caused shortages in the lights they passed over.

Giving him time.

"I'm coming to you!" Bastian shouted, resuming his jog. Exhaustion and the weight of his gear started to wear him down. But he wasn't about to succumb to it now, of all times.

"Hurry!" the blonde woman screamed.

*No, I think I'll take my time.*

One of the ceiling panels about fifteen feet from her fell and so did the Crawler that was behind it. It landed in a tumble, far more acrobatic than Bastian would have liked.

Not that he liked any of this mess.

The creature caterwauled and launched itself at her. Bastian still ran, faster now, rifle up to aim.

"Down, get down!"

It was no use. Adhira screamed and threw her back against the wall near the keypad. Bastian noticed the thumbprint scanner protract and Adhira was too horrorstruck to see it.

Bastian witnessed, as she did, the Crawler tackle the woman into the door. Her scream was bloodcurdling.

"Scan your thumb!" Bastian shouted. "Adhira! Your *thumb*!"

Adhira's eyes widened and her gaze shot over to Bastian, who enclosed on the others. He saw her turn toward the keypad, but then shifted all of his focus onto the Crawler. He fired into its back right leg, clear of the woman, and it wailed out, wetly, turning around to swipe at him. One of its long claws missed his shin by inches as he leapt back, and then fired three-round bursts into its body once it cleared the woman.

He caught a glimpse of her.

She was awfully mauled, but not necessarily fatal. There were med-kits inside the Vault.

He heard the pneumatic hiss of the pressurized locks loosening, and then a loud beep followed by the mechanized opening of the door.

This cacophony caught the Crawler's attention, foolishly diverting its eyeless gaze from Bastian to instead stare behind it.

He lunged forward, driving the buttstock of the rifle into the back of its head, disarraying it. When it looked back up at him, still on all fours, he fired into its gaping brain cavity, pushing its abhorrent thoughts through its throat. The exit wounds caused by the bullets were grisly, and lethal.

The creature crumbled and he rushed through its dissolving mass to help Adhira lift the poor woman from the floor, even if it meant dragging her across the threshold.

A crash sounded behind Bastian and he paused on the other side of the door to witness two more Crawlers descend from above. They landed upright and hissed at each other before loping forward.

"Fucking hell," he muttered, and reloaded. The hefty rectangular magazine clattered on the floor. He unearthed a fresh one from his satchel, which was officially much lighter now. As he reloaded the SA58, he looked at Adhira. "She's inside enough. Go close the door. I'll hold 'em off."

Adhira gulped and nodded, sweat pouring down her dark brow, black hair matted to her perspiring face.

She carefully eased the woman's head down, who mumbled incoherently as she bled from her multiple wounds, mostly on her face and shoulders, her attire torn in several places.

As Adhira moved across the wide antechamber to secure the door, Bastian held his ground and began burst-firing into the hallway. He clipped the creatures a few times in the shoulders before aiming lower as they maintained upright positions, gangly running and gaining speed. He shook his head "nuh-uh" and knee-capped them with well-placed two-round bursts.

One of the Crawlers hit the deck hard, both of its legs obliterated at the knees.

The other bounded over its fallen sibling and began galloping toward the door. A loud beep sounded and the large gunmetal door panels began closing, one from the ceiling and the other from the floor. They would eventually meet at the center, and seal horizontally.

*They take their sweet fucking time, though.*

Bastian stopped with the bursts and began sweeping his aim, left to right, at about knee-level. With the Crawler on all fours, running as it did, this was perfect. Eventually the creature struck a stream of bullets that managed to at least slow it down.

Even with blood in its lungs, it still advanced.

Finally the doors came within a few feet of shutting, and Bastian couldn't see the Crawler anymore. He began backing up, and then it lunged into view, crawling up the lower door half and trying to pull itself inside the Vault.

"No, you don't," Bastian sneered, and fired. One round struck it in the shoulder and then the gun clicked empty, the ejector bolt locking open. He mumbled something to himself and marched forward, then clubbed the creature's head with the retractable buttstock of the rifle. It was so lightweight, and with Bastian's force behind it, that it broke upon impacting the creature's half-skull.

The desired effect was delivered, though.

The creature found itself hung up on the door as it raised, but given two more seconds and it would have been able to crawl off, the opposite way.

Would have.

Instead, the doors sealed, with the Crawler's neck between the unyielding edges. It was severed with ease, and the lopped off head bounced across the floor, past Bastian's feet. He looked down at it and Adhira gasped, while the Vault door hissed and locked.

The creature's head came to a stop, its slender tongue lolling out with a wet sound, before it and the blood trail behind evaporated completely.

Adhira looked up, wide-eyed and bemused.

"Yeah, they do that."

"Upon death?" Adhira asked.

Bastian nodded. He dropped the SA58 Mini at

his feet, and shrugged off the bandolier, along with the satchel.

"What's all that?"

"Ammo. Unwanted now."

"Bastian, what the *hell* is going on?" Adhira demanded, moving away from the keypad to tend to the woman. She crouched beside her.

"Hard to say. But it's bad. And not local." Bastian's gaze swept the innards of Bravo Vault. His heart rate climbed with anticipative excitement. But the reality of everything kept his enthusiasm at bay.

He looked down at Adhira, who now wept quietly. The woman below her was unflinching. His insides tightened.

"Who is she?"

"Was," Adhira murmured through a cry.

"I'm sorry, Adhira. I tried. It seems…" Bastian frowned angrily and made a beeline for the center of the Vault. There hung a cylindrical encasement from the ceiling, with a four-foot gap between its rounded base and the floor. He tapped a passcode into the dark green shell that wrapped around it.

"It seems what?" Adhira demanded, almost as irately, as she stood, her heels to the woman's corpse.

"That I cannot save anyone." Bastian pushed the words through his teeth as his nostrils flared and the protective shell retracted from the encasement.

"Why am I standing here, then? And Maggie? Eliza? Are they waiting outside?"

Bastian scoffed and laughed unevenly. He turned his back on the helmet to the INFERNO Suit, propped by a skeletal pedestal inside the reinforced glass case. The Suit itself was located elsewhere…

"They're *dead*, Adhira," he said, facing her. The insane, hopeless smirk devolved into something worse. More loathing than grieving. "*Butchered* by those *things*. And *I* couldn't save them. 'Outside?' Are you fucking crazy? There *isn't* an outside anymore, Adhira. It's worse up top than it is down here. It's…"

Tears streaked his cheeks and he turned his back on her again to face the encasement.

"It's all gone to shit," he mumbled.

He didn't hear anything else from her for several minutes. She was probably trying to process all of that, which must have been hard especially since she had family in the area, and she had been *friends* with Maggie for over two years.

He imagined that she hadn't caught what he and the others did on the TV, either.

She was essentially clueless.

Part of him wished he was so lucky.

Yet so burdened by the unknown…

Bastian started to turn away from the encasement and almost walked right into her. She had strode up to stand beside him.

Her face was a mess of lamentation. She started to struggle with her words, to get something out.

"I'm…I'm sorry, Sebastian. I'm really—"

She stopped trying to form words and just hugged him. She feared for her husband's life and although they didn't have any children, that was enough to turn her world upside down. She had grandparents in

Tierrasanta, too.

Bastian contemplated how much he should tell her. As he reciprocated her embrace, hoping to console her to some extent, even microscopically, his eyes meandered around the Vault's interior. Every weapon festooning the walls was encased in protective glass. At the point of entering the Vault, they were all accessible without any additional security. Obviously that wasn't the case with the INFERNO Suit, or even the helmet, which he had now unlocked.

And then his eyes fell across a digital clock in a corner, by the main door. Though it flickered and glitched occasionally, the red numbers were an accurate readout. By deduction, he was sure of it.

9:47.

Immediately, and taciturnly, Bastian slipped out of her embrace. Just short of pushing her off, he rigidly collected himself and focused on the reason that had brought him here.

"W-What are you doing?" Adhira sniffled.

"Take a guess," he said, his apathy swelling. It was a veneer that served a purpose under dire circumstances, he assured himself.

Especially given his recent experiences.

He couldn't afford surrendering himself, even momentarily, to those occasions of weakness. He would rather avenge the dead, than grieve for them.

Especially with the tools to do so.

A few taps on the keypad that had unlocked the helmet encasement beckoned a pedestal from the floor under it. The encasement hanging from the ceiling shifted back, thanks to a hidden rail system. Below, the pedestal rose to a height of seven feet, a rounded white column with black apertures. From these air hissed out, and the front of it came open, thin doors dividing down the center.

Ultimately exposing what was kept inside.

The INFERNO Suit, affixed to a metallic spine, for support. Similarly designed ribs extended from it to bolster the sleeves. The Suit's interior was composed of a black Kevlar webbing, whereupon the armor plating was sewn, with spaces between the shells for mobility.

"You're going back out there," Adhira said, scoffing in disbelief. She struggled to grasp the insanity of it. "But to what extent?"

"This...*thing*, Adhira...this whole catastrophe, it's bigger than Miramar. It's bigger than SoCal, even. The tremors are reaching other countries, farther inland than you'd think. Sinkholes, hundreds of them, *birthing* these creatures en masse."

Everything he said, she believed, and had no reason not to. She trusted him as much as anyone who had ever gotten to know Bastian well, and the pain in his voice, in his eyes, spoke volumes more.

And from this absorption of knowledge, Adhira began to feel sick to her stomach. Shaken to her core.

"But they know the source of it," Bastian added, turning his back on the Suit in the column, and undressing. First the tanktop went, and then his slacks, down to his briefs. In a way it felt relieving to do so, knowing that in minutes he would feel like a shelled crab crawling into a new carapace. Being reborn. This zeal, despite the negative emotions accompanied with it, livened his voice. "In Calipatria, a monolithic structure of unknown origin has landed. It's digging into the earth…or something, I don't know. But it's protected by some kind of EMP field. I have to find a way inside. I have to end this, if I can."

"I…I don't know what to say," Adhira murmured, tears running free.

"There's no need, Adhira. Not even *I* can say anything worthwhile anymore." He started to step back, holding his arms at his sides, a few inches from his body. "This doesn't call for speeches. Only actions. And I'm done feeling futile."

Bastian stepped back into the open Suit. He was beyond grateful for the Pumas that T had given him, a size too small as they were, but this was the perfect fit he had awaited.

The Suit detected his presence and the fabric molded to his body. The armor pieces adjusted accordingly, but with him it was like a meticulously tailored suit. He had worn it and tested it for three years. Not a steady schedule, but three years nonetheless, at any intermittency, was a long time. Enough to develop tolerances for its snugness, and its weight, to train himself to carry it like a second skin, more than an exoskeletal suit, which was what it boiled down to.

Once the posterior part of the Suit had conformed to his body, he stepped out and the rest unfurled from the back to curl around his limbs and, eventually, his torso. The separate chest plates met at his sternum, sealing as if with a mind of their own. The Suit's armor mechanisms were fueled by a single ionized plasma cell located at the base of the nape, in a detachable compartment the size of a mouse. As with the armor plates composing the Suit, this compartment was tungsten. However, it was more porous than the plating, so that it could power the Suit.

It was basically a hivemind of ionized particles, augmenting strength and mobility in the operator's arms and legs.

*Or, in layman's terms, I have the strength of five men,* Bastian mused confidently. *Five champion body-builders, that is.*

The cell had an indefinite lifespan. It was theorized to last up to two years of constant use, day in and day out. But not even half of that kind of use and exertion had been put into the Suit. The plasma cell was currently being developed into ammunition for energy-based weapons, but the instability of it outside of containment made that kind of technological advancement implausible.

At least for a few years to come.

And the one currently in play with the INFERNO Suit was still not officially qualified for active combat. Bastian knew this as much as he disagreed with it.

Adhira knew it, too.

"What if that thing proves to be more unstable than you think, Bastian?" she asked, while it sealed itself around his body. The jungle green plating was dull, not shiny, after a lot of testing and refinements. It was an effective, functioning prototype that had yet been buffed for the public eye.

"Then at least I'll go out with a bang," he said, unable to resist the quip. He even winked at her as the collar sealed below his throat, covering his neck.

"You're crazy, Bastian. Why can't you just stay here? It's a *Vault* for a reason. Nothing can—"

A commotion stirred outside the doors. Infernal voices, chittering and growling. No dialect. A savage medley. It wasn't unbeknownst to Bastian that they were capable of communicating, however, it wasn't with any traditional language, or even a foreign one.

Just noises.

And communicating, much less strategizing, that way, made them even more terrifying. And never to be underestimated—especially as time passed.

Particularly if Bastian's theory had any truth to it at all.

"You may be right, Adhira," he said, stepping out of the column, now wearing the suit.

It added ten inches to his height, and each footfall descended with a soft *clang*. Despite the ostensible weight of the Suit, to the operator it was hardly any different from wearing a few layers of wooly turtlenecks, sweatpants, and stilted boots, all over skintight long-johns. But somehow it felt 'natural' and even comfortable. Of course, that adjustment didn't come to Bastian until about eight or nine months of weekly testing.

As if the Suit had given birth to him.

He respected it as much, too.

"But I can't just 'ride this out,'" he added, reaching for the helmet. He retrieved it from the encasement, and slid it over his head. It clicked with the Suit's collar, both externally and internally, sealing it with a hiss.

The visor composed eighty percent of the helmet's anterior, promoting maximum visibility for the operator, including wide peripherals. The visor itself was reinforced, shatter-proof glass. It had been tested against armor-piercing bullets, flame, and IED blasts at close range. The Suit's absorption of impact damage made it virtually incapable of being crushed, whether by debris or a concussive force such as grenades or other explosives.

Speakerphone enhancements were currently in the works for the helmet, but presently the only way to talk and be heard was through a perforation below the visor. This sealed automatically when the Suit detected atmospheric changes, such as an explosion, gaseous or otherwise. A very small oxygen reserve was stored under the back carapace of the Suit for such instances, but higher volume canisters were currently being developed for it, in addition to respirators and the like.

"I have to *act*, Adhira. You must trust me on this." Bastian sighed and rolled his shoulders as he adjusted to the weight and snugness of the Suit. It was momentarily claustrophobic, every time he stepped into it, even after so long, but this was short-lived.

Especially when he really threw himself into the job. As he would have to now, except that it was more than just a job from here on.

It was life or death, but for more than himself. If he truly believed in his objective...it was *far* more than his life at stake.

"I've always trusted you, Bastian, but this...you

have to admit it's crazy. At least a little."

Bastian smirked, visible through the thick but transparent visor.

"A little? No, Adhira. It's *super* fucking crazy."

Both of them abruptly looked at the door when they heard something slam against it from the other side. All of the moving parts in, below, and above it, unseen, now rattled loudly.

They looked at each other.

"Speaking of 'super,'" Bastian said, "where's the Supe?"

He immediately backpedaled away from Adhira, already feeling at home in the Suit. He spun on his metallic heels and looked around the Vault.

"Um…traditional ballistic weapons are, uh…Bay 3. F-Far right corner."

He heard her voice behind him, as well as he would without the helmet, thanks to the enhanced earholes. These would also seal automatically, in the event of atmospheric change, as the mouthpiece would.

Bastian made a beeline for Bay 3, which was a section of wall in the Vault that displayed ballistic firearms currently in development in Bravo Labs. This included both nascent models and prototypes edging on public exposure. Then, those between—combat ready, but not sufficiently tested.

Such as the Sevin and Arbalest.

The latter was in Bay 2, he believed.

His retention was a little scrambled at the moment. But he was beyond relieved that he innately remembered the passcodes to the security armory, the

Bravo Vault door, and the INFERNO Suit.

Three different codes, all one thumb.

They were numbers he had memorized, as well as he knew his SSN or birthdate, even.

As he armed himself, the Vault door continued to clang and rattle.

"Bastian…what if they get in?"

"They won't. That door is impervious."

A loud, shrill metallic sound caught his attention and he slowly, apprehensively, turned to face the broad antechamber and the door there. He could see the gunmetal halves of the door vibrate, and the sealed seam between them started to move.

Whatever was on the other side was trying to manually pry it open. How something could be that strong baffled him, but when he pictured two Legionnaires, or one Baron, it wasn't so unfeasible.

He couldn't fathom a Baron somehow getting down in here, as it was too big. But two Legionnaires? Quite possible, especially with how wide this hallway was, to accompany the Vault door.

The thought of them infiltrating this chamber unsettled Bastian to the core, especially with Adhira here. He looked around, and gulped.

The Vault itself was as spacious as half a 747's interior, window to window, seats omitted. There was no cover or shelter to take, except for two large ammunition repositories on either side of where the helmet was encased. These were about six by six feet, square containers that rose to about waist-level. However, they reached eight feet below the floor, which was partially hollow, primarily composed of automated conveyer belts that transferred ammunition based on the selections made topside.

"Adhira," he snapped, gesturing at one of the ammunition repositories. "Climb into the ammo-dump. I'll—"

A discordant grinding sound, worse than nails on a chalkboard, interrupted him. He shot a look at the Vault door in time to see a gap form between the two halves. Bony claws pushed through, acting like crowbars, as above so below. The door began to pry open. The pneumatic locks on the outside hissed before combusting, which would likely kill or knock out any man standing within a ten-foot radius. It hardly fazed the beast, however, which appeared to be a Legionnaire, only a little bigger.

*And stronger.*

Bastian obviously wasn't a scientific expert on these creatures' capabilities, but something about this one, aside from its slight size increase, was different than the Legionnaires he had faced thus far.

Therefore, all the more troubling.

"Quick!" He shouted at Adhira, and she moved toward one of the repositories.

Bastian wielded the Supe, grateful for the conservative gloves, despite the bulky gauntlets. Otherwise, operating weapons would be impossible.

Then again, several features of the INFERNO Suit were, from a third party perspective, virtually impossible.

Or, as Bastian liked to say, technological triumphs. He of course had the engineers to thank for the realities constructed and perfected from his designs.

The Exoblade attachment integral to the left gauntlet provided a retractable, serrated melee option for close quarters combat. The blade itself was sharpened tungsten, operating via a sectional function that allowed it to stow inside the gauntlet without protruding much. By forming a fist and using his thumb to depress a button on his left forefinger, it would protract rapidly and forcefully, like a switchblade. Only much larger—three inches wide and fourteen inches long. Pressing the button again would retract it in the blink of an eye.

It was basically a retractable bayonet, except on his arm instead of at the end of a rifle.

While the Exoblade was strictly a combative piece of equipment, the chainsaw attachment was, though more experimental in functionality, an environmental tool. He had proposed the design rather excitedly, to a board of directors who laughed in his face, but after nineteen months of development and perfection, he showcased it with exceptional results.

Attachable to his right gauntlet, the chainsaw was obviously not as easily hidden as the Exoblade, instead folding to conform to the length of his forearm. When in use, it would swing out and protrude from his gauntlet, six inches longer than the Exoblade, and twice as wide. The teeth ran with great speed and power, fueled not by gas or electricity, but the ionized plasma cell. This allowed it to cut through obstacles with ease, and without sacrificing mobility to the operator, who could saw an obstruction with his right arm while engaging enemies with a gun in his left.

The concept of using it as a weapon had never entered Bastian's mind until now. He may have become a passive weapons designer, seeing everything strictly from a functional and almost artistic perspective, but his history was combat. And his present had become it again, however terribly.

"It's full!" Adhira shouted from one of the repositories.

"Try the other one!" Bastian barked back. His eyes scanned the Vault, looking for the chainsaw attachments. There were teeth variants for different uses, from wood to steel.

"They're both fucking full!" she exclaimed, shrilly, panic addling her.

"Dump them! Uh, hit the 'empty' button twice to confirm!"

She was shaking, constantly looking up from the repository to gawk at the widening Vault door.

Bastian saw it now, too. And the beast roaring in through the gap. It had the body of a Legionnaire, but the head was different, and somehow far more terrifying. Certainly less humanoid.

Choosing instead to focus on gear—the whole purpose he was here, aside from the Suit—Bastian began stockpiling.

At least to get the basics down.

With a downward flick of his wrist—controlling the effort in his exertions so as to keep himself from breaking anything—Bastian opened the double-barrel shotgun. He scooped up two of eight shells from a foam tray under the weapon's place on the wall, and dumped them into the twin barrels. With an upward flick of his wrist, he closed the barrels and armed them simultaneously. The trigger action offered the ability to fire the barrels individually or simultaneously. And of course there was the barrel extension that he had enthusiastically told T and Z about earlier in the car.

Right now he just used the protruding foregrip below it for improved handling. As if that was really needed while he was in the Suit.

"It's not working!" Adhira screamed frantically, repeatedly jabbing the 'empty' button on the repository.

"Dammit," Bastian muttered. "The receptacles must be full. I forgot, they normally recycle and clean them overnight."

"What do I—"

Adhira was interrupted and so was Bastian's subconscious as the door halves were pried open. They vibrated and malfunctioned, sticking open but not all the way. Sufficient space for the large, bipedal beast to duck through.

Two Crawlers as well, one on either side.

"Fuck me," Bastian mumbled, bug-eyed.

The beast was a Legionnaire from neck to toe, except for its slight size and bulk difference. Its skull, however, was remarkably and disturbingly distinct. Its mouth was a grinning cage of bony teeth, composed of the same material that its skull was. From each prominent brow, which seemed permanently furrowed above angular, black cavities of eyes, curled broad horns that tapered back. They weren't long, not even half the imposing length and size of a Baron's, but they added to the beast's imposing look all the same.

Its body was a shade between soil and clay, yet the skull, from pointed chin to stubby brow-horns, was a lighter hue, like raw bone, yet splotched with brown and black, as if wear and tear.

The muscular, horned, demonically mouthed beast marched into the Vault, its broad chest heaving, deep rugged breaths spewing through its jaws. The bony teeth interlocked perfectly when its mouth was kept shut, making it all the more terrifying a sight.

Bastian gulped again and clipped the Supe shotgun to the Suit's waist. There were several parts of the Suit's armor that offered magnetic links, presently only designed for certain CHERI weapons. This freed the operator's hands when needed, and optimized the ability to carry more weapons than any man might.

He hurriedly snatched the ROT-20 from its place on the wall, and began loading it, trying not to shake. Fortunately, any physical shortcomings such as the shakes or other imbalances were absorbed, distributed, and compensated by the Suit.

*Yeah, there's a good fucking reason I've been pushing the INFERNO Project to finality.*

He knew that the major obstacle for DARPA was revealing their experimental plasma cell to the public without further testing it.

He understood this, from a tentative standpoint. He just didn't care, at least not as much as they did, and certainly not right now.

Presently, he focused on arming himself as adequately as he could manage, before the threat became too personal to ignore.

"Sebastian!" Adhira screamed, backing up against a wall. Particularly, Bay 1. His eyes shot in that direction, after glimpsing a Crawler make its way toward her, and the second at him, much faster. Meanwhile, behind it, the Tyrant, for lack of a better moniker in the heat of the moment, very slowly advanced.

He studied the wall behind and above her, belonging to Bay 1. They were all prototypal 'small arms'—from pistols to submachine-guns. Including two experimental revolvers.

"Fight back, Adhira!" It was all he could think of. The only other option, aside from hiding. Which had proved futile.

Bastian turned his back on the encroaching Crawler, which was an insane act of bravery, and continued loading the ROT-20. Additional ammunition would have to be retrieved from the repositories, supposing he survived this encounter.

He could hear Maggie's voice echo up through the caverns in his mind.

*"Patience is a virtue,"* she cried out, half in panic and, it at least seemed to him, half in mockery. Her playful way of jeering him. The echo bounced off the wet walls of his brain. *"Patience is a virtue."*

Bastian shook his head.

"Not right now it isn't."

# 11

Three barrels, six 20-gauge shells each. Bastian couldn't help but think of T, and Z, as he finished loading the rotary shotgun in record time. He had practiced and trained with it so much that it had become second nature, and he felt like part Olympian doing it. The gauntlets were only bulky because of the attachable options, whether chainsaw or Exoblade. But the gloves themselves were designed with weapon usage in mind. Still, he wished T was here to handle the ROT-20 himself, or the Supe for that matter.

Ultimately, the sentiment came down to Bastian wishing T was here, period. Alive.

Z the same, but by his side.

At any rate, he knew Z was alive and, as much as he hated to admit it for Adhira, in better condition than her.

Already he felt the pang of guilt that he might not be able to save her, either.

Leaving her to her own devices, or the enemy's for that matter, at the end of that hallway, however, would not have been any better than now.

*It ain't over yet*, he convinced himself.

When Bastian spun on his metallic heels to face the Crawler that had leapt for him from some ten feet away, he acted with violent haste.

*I don't have time for you, either, wretch!*

Bastian took a swing at it with his left hand, fist formed, and struck it in the jaw midair. The creature was thrown to the floor into a barrel-roll, likely dumbfounded at what just happened.

Bested by a human.

Except that in the INFERNO Suit, Bastian was at least five men. And none of them had the raging emotions that currently surged through his veins.

It was an inferno of determination.

The horned Legionnaire—*Tyrant, yes, foul beast*—now stood still and unleashed a thunderous roar. Of vexation, no doubt.

It was beyond the state of intimidation.

Especially seeing what Bastian had become, a proper adversary, additionally. Supposing such a concept was even feasible in the monster's mind.

Bastian heard Adhira scream before gunfire erupted. He looked over at her in the corner, in front of Bay 1. She had a lean frame, not that that meant she had no business using a firearm, of course. But Bastian knew her history and, despite being a chief engineer at CHERI, she had a strange aversion to firing guns. She wasn't opposed to their existence and use, of course, but was simply displeased with operating them herself.

The paradox was now in play.

She wielded a submachine-gun that was in its latter stages of testing. The bullpup style SMG rattled in her hands, dispensing recoil through its central frame as opposed to the buttstock, making it easier to handle at full-auto. Instead of properly shouldering it, given the frantic circumstances, she squeezed the buttstock under her right arm. Nonetheless, she controlled it well, and her trigger finger wasn't shy.

The charging Crawler received its fair share of lead, and then some. A steady stream of 12mm ammunition tore it to shreds by the time it hit the floor, reduced to ash and embers in the coming seconds.

Bastian nodded to Adhira, whose face was awash with a contradictory panic and triumph.

It didn't last long. Her eyes darted to her right before realigning with Bastian, twenty feet across the Vault, and then widened. A moment before she screamed, Bastian was on his toes, already knowing what to expect.

The Tyrant was done waiting.

It couldn't rely on its smaller comrades anymore. In a way, neither could Bastian—not in reference to T or Z, of course, but himself. And he would not have to rely on the rudimentary version of himself again, so long as he occupied the Suit.

His masterpiece, finally being treated as more than just an exceptional prototype.

While Adhira was right—he didn't know just how stable the plasma cell might be under the extreme duress of live combat—he couldn't stand idly by any longer.

*Actions, not words.*

Bastian turned to face the Tyrant, whose dense shadow came over him a split-second earlier. His trigger finger was heavy, and the ROT-20 opened up at point-blank range. Its cylinders spun with a cyclical *click* sound, like a revolver's under steady fire. Except that he didn't need to strike a hammer each time—just squeeze the trigger. The shotgun's single muzzle flashed steadily as shell after shell of 20-gauge buckshot struck the Tyrant in its broad chest. Bastian held the shotgun at the hip, angling its barrel up.

In the Suit, he now had a few inches' advantage of an upright Crawler, and came close to standing nose-to-nose with a Legionnaire. As it were, this new abomination had a good foot over him, not including its horns.

Still, Bastian no longer felt so inadequate standing his ground, trying to gun one down.

As this thought passed through him with a vote of confidence, the Tyrant roared in his face, hot breath fogging his visor from the outside, and its clawed hands seized him—the Suit, more rather—by his right shoulder and left hip, then spun him around like a discus-thrower. With another roar and pivot on its heels, the beast flung him across the Vault. He landed on top of a repository, dealing a blow to his ribs, and rolled over it, barreling across the floor another eight feet before coming to a stop.

The breath was knocked from him, due more to surprise than impact. Aside from that he was uninjured, thanks to the Suit's impact resistance.

Still adjusting to the combative mobility of his body in the Suit, he struggled momentarily back to his feet. Once upright again, he felt ready to square off with the homely creature that now charged him. It roared en route, but about halfway to him received a barrage of 12mm bullets to its right abdomen. It staggered briefly, pausing midstride to look at its attacker.

Bastian did, too.

Adhira had gifted him a few seconds to reorient from being tossed across the room like a ragdoll.

A virtually indestructible ragdoll.

Bastian was grateful, but as the SMG in Adhira's hands ran dry, and the Tyrant held her in its abyssal gaze, he knew she was regretting the action. He sympathized, for her sake, but wasn't going to let her be his martyr.

He rushed the beast from the side, it now more than distracted from him to instead focus on her. He had dropped the ROT-20 upon being hurled across the Vault. But as he rushed it—his metallic, heavy yet agile footfalls catching its attention—Bastian didn't feel defenseless. His left hand formed a fist, thumb pressing the designated button, and the Suit's Exoblade protracted with a metallic *shing*.

The Tyrant had just enough time to pause midstride, its heavy clawed feet thudding on the metallic floor, before Bastian struck it with a hard swing of his left hand, as if going in for a jab. The Exoblade made contact before his fist ever did; the clip-point, sharpened tungsten tip punctured flesh with ease, and even the dense muscle of the Tyrant wasn't impenetrable. The Suit's plasmatic power source augmented the momentum behind Bastian's swing, and he took advantage of this, as he wasn't a weak man. Nor, even after such a harrowing and exhausting day, was he running on fumes.

Somehow, now more than before, he felt genuinely invigorated.

*Not 'somehow.' The reason was obvious.*

The INFERNO Suit was his blessing, and the enemy's kryptonite.

He only wished he could have gotten to it sooner. Considering all of the obstacles and horrors he had to face, and wade through, between his home and this Vault, he knew that was out of the question.

That sort of hindsight would only serve to haunt and hurt him right now.

He focused on the present, and the impending future.

With an additional iota of pressure behind his initial punch, Bastian drove the Exoblade all the way in. Fourteen inches of serrated, three-inch-wide tungsten buried itself into the Tyrant's right side, between ribs. It faltered briefly and snarled at nobody in particular, before reaching down and taking a swing at Bastian's head. He ducked, leaning to the right, and twisted the Exoblade in its flesh. He imagined a vital organ being shorn in the process, and the beast's reaction was proof.

It lurched and abruptly dropped to a knee. Blood spewed from between its odious grin, which was not an expression but merely the arrangement of its jaws.

Bastian briskly jerked the Exoblade out of the beast's side and its body twitched in that direction. It vomited more blood, its grotesque head bowed less than five feet from the stagnant Adhira. He gave her a quick glance through his visor, which would be fogged up from his own breathing if it weren't for advanced technology.

"Find me a flat-cart, if you can," he said rather simply to her, retracting the Exoblade.

She gulped and nodded before darting away.

The exchange was brief, but as soon as she moved, the Tyrant growled like a revving Harley and jerked its head up, gaze tracking her.

"Wrong target, buddy," Bastian mumbled, and, standing directly next to its right side, likely in a blind spot, reached out to grab both of its brow-horns as if getting ready to—

Hop onto its back.

Bastian did this immediately, but before the Tyrant could react properly, he jerked his hands back, and broke the stubby horns off above its eyebrows. It made a sickening *crunch* sound, of bone fracturing, and yellow fluid started to ooze from where they broke. The beast bucked him off and started wildly shaking its head side to side, slinging the yellow fluid across the floor, while irately snapping its jaws.

Bastian rolled once before springing to his feet, and then darted for the ROT-20, which he spotted near the repository he had struck earlier. He scooped it up and circled around to the other side, about ten feet from where Adhira stood, with an orange flat-bed cart she had retrieved.

The Tyrant rose to its feet and stumbled in his direction, jaws frantically snapping. Blood poured between its bony teeth, and the yellow ooze now dripped down its eyebrows from the broken horns.

It was in a world of pain, and it was about to get fatally worse.

*Consider this a mercy killing, then, barbarian*, Bastian thought, hoping that the creature was somehow telepathic in that instant.

He shouldered the ROT-20 and immediately discerned a vague look of fear in the beast's wretched face. As appetizing as it was to witness, Bastian didn't want to dilly-dally. And he definitely didn't want to give the beast the chance to rake in another breath, however agonizing it was to do so.

He squeezed the trigger and the three smooth-bore barrels rotated rapidly, without requiring acceleration. In the span of two seconds, before he released the trigger, four shells were expended. The 20-gauge buckshot volleyed the Tyrant in the face and upper chest. Chunks of flesh were blown off its broad breastplate, and its bony skull was dismantled into something that Bastian would call "art."

Its body slumped to the metallic floor with a wet sound, until its heavy skull, though reduced to ruins, struck with a harsher *clang*. Bastian only turned his back on the defeated monstrosity once he glimpsed the first sign of its dissolution.

While embers danced into the air behind him, he faced Adhira standing in the corner by Bay 1. She wore an expression of sheer awe.

"I think we can phone in Bowman," Bastian said, rather proudly, "and motion the INFERNO Project for approval."

A duality of shrieks caught their attention, pulling their gazes to the large Vault door. It was still open halfway, more than enough space to continue welcoming intruders. Waves upon waves of them, if they so wished, and could produce.

An unsettling feeling in Bastian assured him that they very well could, and would, so long as he remained inside.

The exact opposite of his intentions.

"I gotta get outta here, Adhira," Bastian said resolutely, glancing back at her. "It's nonnegotiable."

"You've always been awfully stubborn," she said with a wavering smile, tears on her cheeks.

"Figure out a way to hide in the repository. I'll…seal the door behind me. They will probably follow me out. I've given them something to fear."

That wasn't pride speaking. It was fact.

Adhira gulped and nodded speechlessly.

"Thanks for the cart," he said. "I'll do the rest. Now go."

"Be careful," her voice shook softly. "However you can."

"If I can risk it, I will," he said without lying.

She scrambled to the other repository she hadn't tried, and immediately began working the buttons on the side.

"It's working! It's emptying!" she exclaimed excitedly, relief flooding her.

"Good," Bastian said, filling up the flat-cart, which had high railings. It was about six feet long and four wide. It would have to do.

The sources of the shrieks they heard earlier now entered the room through the gap in the Vault door. One Crawler, earning its name as it sleekly crept over the lower half of the door, and one Vulture, gliding in. From its fanged, beak-like jaws discharged a screech that probably scrambled Adhira's brain to some extent. For Bastian it was a bit more muffled than if he didn't have the helmet on, not to say that his hearing was impaired any.

He snatched a rifle from the wall in Bay 1, a prototype he had not mentioned to T or Z, mostly because he knew it wouldn't serve much of a purpose in this ordeal. It was too long, nearly five feet, and too heavy, for most men anyway. It was a conceptual modification of the CheyTac Intervention, coined the Divination, a long-range, anti-material, armor-piercing sniper rifle.

He snatched one round from the foam tray under the weapon's place on the wall and slid it into the open chamber. He cycled the bolt with meticulous dexterity, grateful for the touch-sensitivity of the glove's Kevlar fibers, and shouldered the rifle.

All in the time that it took the Vulture, which had a lead on the Crawler by a few meters, to reach the repositories. Apparently it had made a beeline for Adhira instead of him—an easier target. This boiled Bastian's blood and exacerbated his abhorrence for these creatures. He heard her scream as it came within six feet of her, just on the opposite side of the cubic repository, a split-second before he squeezed the trigger.

The rifle wasn't fitted with a scope, which was mounted separately, as it was currently under separate development. He used the integrally illuminated iron sights for lining up his shot, which came to him swiftly—

And accurately.

The report from the fluted muzzle brake thundered in the confines of the Vault, rattling Bastian's eardrums even with the helmet on. Thanks to the Suit, he was able to sustain the monumental recoil without a hitch in his step.

The .50-caliber BMG round struck the airborne Vulture in the right shoulder, but almost its entire body exploded. The nebula of gore splattered the white repository and the gunmetal floor, as well as misting Adhira's horrorstruck face; she had her hands up, too, cupping her ears.

"Sorry," he called out to her, genuine in intention but realizing it seemed sarcastic in the moment.

He swung the rifle to face the Crawler, which, unlike the Vulture, had its eyeless gaze set on *him*.

He was unable to snatch another round from the tray before it reached him, erecting in hopes of facing him at equal height.

It was possible that, in the INFERNO Suit, to these creatures he was no longer a pesky human to be culled. But a different kind of enemy. Something not to be underestimated; something to be feared.

Even for the eyeless Crawlers, its sense of smell, supposing it had such, or when its slender tongue licked the air, to taste the change in atmosphere, he wondered, was it possible that it detected an irregularity? The Suit used an ionized plasma cell for power, afterall, and the armor sections themselves likely had a particular scent. As for its hearing, Bastian knew that the metallic footfalls of the Suit, even while potentially nimble, were louder than any boot.

Regardless, this Crawler experienced a moment of surprise right away. It rose to its feet, and found itself still a foot shorter than Bastian. He was already an imposing man, but in the Suit he was a different breed of warrior.

Despite having no eyes, the Crawler instantly realized its miscalculation, and Bastian could discern this in its wretched face. It caused a two-second hesitation that he gladly took advantage of.

He struck the Crawler in the chest with the muzzle of the thirty-pound rifle, in a battering ram motion, knocking it back several paces. Buying him another two seconds. In that time, he dropped the rifle to the floor and stepped over it, driving his left hand in an uppercut manner. He formed a fist before making contact with the Crawler's lower chest, and protracted the Exoblade. It was clean again, after the Tyrant's blood disintegrated with the rest of it, but only for a split-second before it impaled the Crawler. He grabbed its left shoulder with his right hand, pulling it closer to him, making sure that the tungsten blade went all the way through. He looked down its back to see that it had; at least eight inches of the fourteen-inch blade protruded between its gaunt shoulder blades, glistening bright red.

Stuck on the clip-point tip of the blade was what appeared to be the creature's heart. Or a similar organ, pulsing, mauve and pink, oozing blood and other fluids.

The Crawler shuddered around the blade, against his left fist and in his right hand. Blood poured from its mouth and he felt its stance weaken.

Bastian put his helmeted face next to the creature's temple. He spoke on impulse, anger, and a lick of arrogance in his voice, not second-guessing whether it could actually hear—or understand—him, much less as it took its final breaths.

"Looks like the tables have turned, fuck-face."

When Bastian extracted the Exoblade from its body, 'holstering' it altogether, both the organ and the creature itself slid off. They collapsed on the floor, disintegrating in the same instant.

Bastian straightened his posture and surveyed the Vault. There were no other enemies, but he knew that soon even more would funnel through the door.

He glimpsed Adhira preparing to enter one of the repositories.

He shifted his focus, and energy, on loading the flat-cart.

First went the ROT-20, and he skipped the tray under it, instead going for the drawer. He ripped it right off the wheeled rails and tossed it into the tray. It landed with a resonant, metallic *clang*. Inside were fifty-four shells, which equated to three full reloads. The drawers under each weapon on the wall, excluding the small trays, contained two to three full reloads for it. These were maintained at all times by Vault personnel, twice throughout the day. Some were frequented more than others, but these ammunition drawers were typically used for small-scale testing sessions. Any larger exercises, especially ones that involved blanks or dummy rounds, and the repositories were accessed.

*I don't have time for that shit.*

Especially with Adhira in here.

As much as Bastian hated to act like he was the only hope against this Monolith thing, he felt like that mindset was the best form of motivation he had.

As it were, he devoted himself to the concept that, as long as he wasn't in Calipatria trying to infiltrate the Monolith, then more people would die by the hundreds. Especially with the military's futility, so far.

Hence his mentality that time was critically essential, and patience hardly existed anymore.

He didn't regret helping Adhira—and trying to help the others—but looking ahead, he might have to force himself to avoid taking those diversions in his itinerary.

As coldhearted an act as it might be...

Hell, he wasn't even sure if he would be able to avoid the attempt to help someone in need. Especially now that he had the means, all the more.

It was a constant juggle of priorities and morals in his mind...in his soul...on this harrowing, disquieting journey.

Focusing on the present helped.

Like right now, as he stockpiled the flat-cart, to its limits. It would eventually become much heavier than any man could haul, or push, but so long as it rolled, he didn't have an issue.

After the ROT-20 and its drawer of fifty-four

shells—numbers of this kind also soothed his tormented mind—went the drawer under the Supe. Since the sawed-off, double-barrel prototype could only handle two at a time, the drawer contained an ample eight full reloads. So, twenty 12-gauge bolo shells. He decided to carry the Supe itself with him while he pushed the flat-cart, as he could one-hand it more easily than any other weapon, something that no man would be able to do due to the imposing recoil.

Leaving the Supe clipped to his waist, he shifted to the Sevin. Despite the term 'minigun,' it was basically a portable version of the Gatling-style rotary chaingun mounted on attack helicopters. The portability, of course, was arguable, and presently the main caveat holding it back from combat readiness.

However, in the hands of a Suit operator, as Bastian could testify, the Sevin was usable. Its problematic heat output, recoil, and weight became a non-issue with the INFERNO Suit. The same applied to the Arbalest and, although he wouldn't be taking it, the Divination.

Taking the Arbalest railgun was a debate he breezed through himself. Its primary use was medium-to long-range engagements, which he didn't anticipate on his journey to Calipatria.

*Better safe than sorry.*

Afterall, this enemy was completely unpredictable, and part of him feared that, once it realized the threat he had developed into, it would throw its worst at him. Tenfold.

He tried not to let this worry him, even if he was just one man, in the Suit no less.

The weapons at his disposal helped mitigate his worries.

Unlike the previous two weapons, the Sevin didn't have a drawer. It had a backpack. Which itself was composed of an alloy frame, covered in jungle-green canvas; when fully loaded, it weighed about sixty pounds. Its contents included three cooling fans and a thousand-round, disintegrating-link, looped belt of 7.62mm ammunition that would feed into the Sevin's loading port. Due to the Sevin's size and weight—four and a half feet long and fifty-five pounds—it offered a curved bar above the seven-barrel housing for grip.

Without the Suit, it was required to even wield the Sevin in a stationary state. In the Suit, however, it could serve as a carrying handle.

Putting the Sevin and its correlating backpack into the cart just about filled it.

He had two more stops—the Arbalest in Bay 2, and a particular handgun in Bay 1.

The Arbalest, while about half the weight of the Sevin and twice the effective range of the Divination, was shorter than both. It was crossbow-shaped, but the magnetic rail system which propelled the 20mm-diameter tungsten slug at 7100-feet-per-second generated enough heat to melt the skin off any operator.

Fortunately, this was no issue in the Suit.

The drawer of ammunition for the Arbalest contained sixteen rounds, in four separate clips. Each clip was composed of four slugs, linked together, and fed into the exposed magnetic rail chamber from above, in the same manner as a World War II-era M1 Garand.

The effects and potential, of course, were immensely different.

Each shot from the Arbalest could penetrate a tank's armor, or an entire battalion of Humvees lined door-to-door. What it would do to flesh, wearing body armor or otherwise, was nothing shy of overkill. There was a designated testing range on this level for the Sevin and Arbalest, the largest in the entire facility. Its back wall was built of reinforced tungsten to slow the slugs' momentum, and behind that concrete to finally absorb its trajectory.

Bastian was comforted by having these weapons at his disposal, but knew that he had to put a lot of faith in the endurance and soundness of the INFERNO Suit. Without it, he knew that he would truly fail.

However, he also had to put a lot of faith in himself. He wanted to convince his own mind that nobody else could do this, simply because they had the Suit. *He* was experienced with it, *he* had tested it and all of these weapons, thoroughly, and when it all came down to it, *he* had nothing to lose.

Except for the internal, automatic promises he had made to those he saved along the way. From Z to Adhira to…

The list was painfully small.

Bastian moved to Bay 1 and glanced at the repositories in the center of the room. Adhira was essentially wading in one, hanging onto the edge, waiting to descend. She would require him to seal it from above. It was not airtight, so she would be able to breathe down there, but the only way out for her was either a lifting of the lockdown, or manually from above.

"I'm almost done," Bastian announced, returning his attention to Bay 1.

The cart was full, save for a few gaps between the weapons and their drawers. What he would be taking with him could be magnetically clipped to his waist, opposite the Supe, and a little smaller. He would just about not even fool with any handguns for this type of endeavor, but combat-tested prototypes were worth the hassle.

Now he was merely torn between two choices—the 12-gauge revolver or the .460-caliber pistol. Given his two shotgun selections, and the increased hassle of handling another cylindrical weapon, he bypassed the debate by snatching the semiautomatic pistol. It was essentially a sleeker, nickel-plated Desert Eagle with major advancements. And yet again, due to recoil alone, only ideal for a Suit operator, at least to be wielded in one hand.

It was coined the Duke, and some CHERI personnel fabricated an acronym for it: Depleted Uranium Killer Elite. Bastian couldn't reasonably object. The pistol utilized solid .460 Magnum depleted uranium rounds, capable of piercing light to medium armor plating. Due to the ammunition's density and the sheer weight of the nine-pound pistol, the loaded unit proved too heavy to wield as a backup sidearm for most infantry, and especially for sharpshooters.

For this reason, it was still shelved as an incomplete prototype.

Bastian had some experience with it in the Suit,

however, and wasn't remotely hesitant bringing it with him. He magnetically clipped it to the left side of his Suit's waist; while ambidextrous, he favored his right hand. With the Supe on his right, however, it took priority. In the Suit, at least, weight of an object was hardly an issue.

The impact compensation integrated into the Suit's armor not only allayed damage from falls and strikes but also made extreme recoil almost nonexistent. Additionally, it helped that while in the Suit, Bastian's legs might as well be pillars of stone.

A spine composed of tungsten alloy made all of this possible.

Bastian ripped the drawer out from beneath the Duke's place on the wall. Three six-shot magazines clattered loudly inside, as he redirected the drawer into the cart. The Duke, as with every weapon in every Bay, was displayed empty, for safety purposes.

A glance over his shoulder reminded him that Adhira was still lingering in the repository. He was at least gifted with the sight of inactivity by the door, however, a second before he turned his head back to the cart beside him, he heard more sounds. An infernal cacophony of skirls and growls from down the long hallway.

Impending.

"That's enough chitchat," he mused to himself, surveying the weapons in the cart, and then those left on the wall.

He took a deep breath and drew the Duke from his waist. He ejected the magazine and nearly fumbled it in his gloved hands. He was beginning to shake, but it was quickly subdued. He pulled the tray and used his Kevlar-snug fingertips to pluck each depleted uranium slug from the foam. He meticulously, manually loaded the magazine until all six gleaming silver rounds were secure.

With a grunt, as if prefacing a building war-cry to get himself ready, he slammed the magazine into the base of the pistol's hollow grip, and it locked with a click. He racked the heavy steel slide and 'holstered' it against his left waist.

He began to turn away from Bay 1 when something caught his eye. A glint of metal, at a vertical angle that reflected the light just right. He raised an eyebrow and paused, narrowing his gaze.

There, mounted on the wall between Bay 1 and 2, was the chainsaw gauntlet attachment. It was nestled between the Bays in a narrow nook, likely to keep things from snagging on its sharp teeth. It had only recently been approved as a standard attachment for the Suit, so a proper case had yet been made.

He approached it and lifted it off the mount, and then affixed it to his right gauntlet. There was a secure *click*, and a low humming sound, just audible enough for Bastian, as the Suit's power adapted. Since most of a regular chainsaw's bulk was the motor housing and fuel storage, this was considerably conservative on size and weight. The blade itself, though nearly twice as long and wide as the Exoblade, folded back along the length of Bastian's arm when not in use.

He had to be mindful of it when bending his right arm, as it protruded several inches past his elbow, but if anything it felt more of a comfort than a burden.

He cleared his throat and turned away from the wall, putting both hands on the waist-high handle of the flat-cart.

"Adhira," he raised his voice, pushing it in the direction of the Vault door. "It's time."

"I know you're not a religious man," she said, hanging onto the ledge of the repository from the inside, standing on the raised platform below. "But I will be praying for you."

"I cannot object to that, especially at this point," he said, his voice as soft as it could be. "Thank you for everything, Adhira. Not just in these last few moments, but your friendship and support over the years."

Tears welled up in her eyes.

His head bowed and he glanced over at the woman on the floor. He still didn't know her name.

*Perhaps it's best that way*, he thought, rather selfishly. For his own peace of mind. For his own mental composure, which nonetheless already seemed irreparable.

An audible gulp later and Bastian turned his head back toward Adhira. He tapped a small button on the side of his helmet and the visor raised, unobstructing his face in the frame provided.

"I'm…I'm sorry I couldn't save her. Or the man. I…I didn't know them, but—"

"Sebastian," she said, bypassing the awkwardness of calling him such a formal name, as it simply felt natural in the dire moment. "Stop. You can't…you can't save everyone. You just…do what you *can*, right now, and I have faith that whatever happens…you'll find peace in the end."

She was getting choked up, struggling to finish her little speech. One that struck Bastian in the biggest of ways, and worked under his skin. He took it to heart.

A firm nod later and he resealed his visor before taking a step back and observing the repository controls. He tapped the necessary buttons and then gave her one more nod.

"You'll be safe," he said, stifling tears.

She was speechless, but offered a weakened smile, as the platform she stood on lowered into the floor, and the repository sealed over her.

He headed for the Vault door, which he knew would require some finessing—literally speaking, some brute strength—to grant him *and* the cart passage. The lower half was stuck in its place, coming to about his stomach on the Suit. The gap was sufficient enough for one of those beasts—the Tyrant—to get through, so there was no doubt that he could fit.

A glance down at the cart, however, reminded him that it wasn't that easy.

He stepped around the cart and solidified his stance, knees slightly bent. He curled his gloved hands around the top edge of the door's lower half, and ex- erted, pushing down. The heavy steel door made a loud, low groaning sound as it grinded against its locking mechanisms beneath the floor. It had already been pried open to this extent, now it was being forced the rest of the way. Finally Bastian got the right amount of lever- age and with the unabashed help of his Suit, shoved the door partition into its floor compartment. There was a hissing sound below, like a blown pneumatic spring. It was quite possible that, at any moment, the door would be forced up again, and likely inoperable after that.

Just short of the lockdown being lifted.

Bastian didn't hesitate. He pushed the cart over the thin gap in the floor, and the hard plastic wheels rattled loudly as they crossed it. Then it was smooth sailing—the flat-tread wheels glided over the hallway tile, though he knew that in instances where corpses littered the floor, it wouldn't be as effortless.

He paused a few feet from the Vault door and turned to go pull it shut. All of a sudden he heard a loud metallic hiss and pop, followed by the lower half of the door shooting out of the floor. As soon as it reached its height limit, whether by internal trigger or sheer vibration, the top came down. The two halves met at the center with a thunderous *clang* and emergency latches previously not in use now clamped together. They weren't as unyielding as the pneumatic locks, though even those had been 'bypassed' by the Tyrant, but they were as good as it was going to get.

Bastian had to leave it at that.

Hope had become his strong suit over the years with Maggie and Eliza. However, in the last several hours, it had devolved into cynical ruination.

Nevertheless, Bastian forced himself to collect some hope and optimism that Adhira Laghari would be safe in there.

He bequeathed himself with a boost of confidence in a manner that most would consider suicidal.

That Adhira's chances were even better now that he was headed out into the storm.

If his departure from the Vault, and eventually from the facility—assuming he could survive that exodus—also lured the threats away from CHERI, then so be it. He had to count that as a little victory in itself.

He turned his back on the door and proceeded to push the orange, high-railing flat-cart down the hall. In it was his next-gen arsenal, his livelihood as it were.

The Suit was his insurance.

And together, with Bastian Thurgood at the center of it all, he started to cheer up. It was a dismal twist on how things had come to be, but he knew that if he had any shot of making it to Calipatria, he couldn't risk pessimism and self-doubt.

With each heavy, yet somehow graceful step, Bastian injected himself with the fact—no longer merely a notion—that he was an unstoppable force.

# <u>12</u>

Reaching the elevator foyer was too easy. Bastian had a feeling that either the enemy was strategizing from afar, or somehow otherwise lying in wait. His journey down the long hallway between the Vault and elevators was urgent, sans running. He never paused his stride, or even slowed it. He didn't vigilantly observe the ceiling to anticipate the descent of more Crawlers. He certainly expected it, but he didn't let it…slow his roll.

"Whoa, honey, slow your roll," Maggie would say if he arrived home upset. It was a rare occasion, as he usually defused before stepping through the door. Especially for Eliza's sake, and her precious peace of mind, which always prioritized over his own.

But on occasion she was still at school or on a playdate so when he got home, he became a chatterbox. Ranting about this or that, vexation getting the best of him. The issues were always trivial in the end; something about Bowman, or the denial of a project to move forward, or the rejection of an idea.

Of course, Maggie never knew the details.

Even in his irate rants he censored himself from being too explicit about his work at CHERI. Still, it was his rapid-fire monologues that would show Maggie how worked up and passionate he could be about his job. It never equated to physical violence, and his words seldom took a profane turn.

"Whoa, honey, slow your roll," she would say nonetheless, usually more amused than anything. It almost never took Bastian more than a few words from her, or even a couple of glances into her eyes, to simmer him down.

He would admit his foolishness, and they would embrace like none of it mattered. Like the whole world didn't exist beyond them.

Occasionally it would spiral into something steamier, but as Bastian thought about it, he was simply placated. Any part of his body that had felt tense or on edge now melted into a state of tranquility.

*Slow your roll. But not literally.*

He reached the elevator foyer and was reminded, immediately, of the carnage painting its floor. Not to mention the rotting bloodshed down the opposite hall. Unfortunately his sight glazed over the man's face, whom he couldn't save earlier, and how his eyes had rolled back, and the color sapped from his skin, was unsettling to say the least.

Whatever serenity his memory of Maggie had brought was now cast to the abyss. He paused only now, and only for a moment, turning his head. His gaze hit a clean spot on the floor, between his foot and one of the cart's six wheels.

He was grateful for his visor, and the obstruction to his olfactory senses.

His sight, however, was as pristine and hawk-like through the visor glass as it was without it.

Of course, Bastian had to take that as a good thing. Because the quality of observation during combat, or even between engagements, shouldn't be overlooked.

He reminded himself of his mission, and the criticality of it.

He didn't know what the enemy was up to, and why his trek to the elevators was so quiet—*too quiet*, he couldn't help thinking—but he had to be grateful.

Quickly, he pushed the cart toward the freight elevator. He tried to circumvent the bodies but unfortunately had to roll over—or through—some of them. The resultant sounds were repulsive and saddening in their own right.

Upon hitting the call button, which chimed, two ceiling panels behind him cracked and a pair of Crawlers descended in their wake. They squalled and landed in the bloody mess rather gracefully, but that was where their composure ended.

Bastian spun on his armored heels, squeaking in blood, and wielded the Supe. He squeezed the dual trigger, firing both barrels simultaneously. The Crawlers were about six feet away when the twin muzzles flashed, and the sawed-off shotgun kicked. The Crawlers' bodies all but exploded from their gaunt waists up, spraying the floor with their bright-red gore and chunks of infernal meat.

They barely even had a chance to growl, much less scream.

Bastian smirked triumphantly, satisfactorily, and with a flick of his wrist popped the barrels open. In that same action, the ejector sprung the spent shells out, and they clinked to the floor, trailing tails of smoke. As much as he wished he had grabbed a bandolier or something from the Vault, he hadn't, and was simply left with the drawer. He opened it, resting on top of the ROT-20, and scooped two fresh shells out. He left it open, but at an angle that would make it easy to grab from, without risking it spilling.

The elevator *dinged* and the doors opened.

It was empty, thankfully.

He reloaded the Supe, flicked the barrels shut, and singlehandedly pushed the heavy cart into the freight elevator. It was just barely wide enough to fit them both inside. He then jabbed the L button, eager to leave Sublevel 4 and return to the lobby.

Ground level.

Coincidentally, that would feel more like hell than what he had experienced below. Only because up there, he was reminded of the civilization and humanity which was rapidly being crushed under the wretched heel of this horrific enemy.

While in the elevator, he again thought of Bowman, and wished he was safe, but a pang of doubt resonated in his bones. He shook it off quickly, even if merely a façade of reassurance, and as if on cue to remind him of being vigilant, gunshots rang out above him. Not in the shaft, but somewhere in the building. He shot a solemn glance at the levels indicator and impatiently awaited the illumination of the 'L' badge.

Bastian's brow furrowed and he two-handed the Supe, shouldering it. He anticipated the doors opening, sweat beading on his brow but quickly evaporating. Despite the snugness of the Suit, the helmet and spine were fitted with small air-conditioning units.

Regardless, Bastian blazed with vehemence.

Still, he was miraculously collected. And poised, ready for action.

Subconsciously, he admitted the uncertainty of what type of action it would be—and how to handle it. The echoes of gunfire suggested security guards, or other survivors that had managed to arm themselves and made it onto the premises.

The lift lurched once it reached the lobby level, and the heavy doors peeled open.

"Oh, thank God!" some man in a ruffled suit panted, rushing into the elevator.

"Wait, sir, this isn't safety. The rest of the—"

"Holy shit!" the man gawked up at Bastian and his look of terror shifted into one of awestruck relief. "Y-You're wearing the INFERNO Suit! Holy fucking shit!"

"Uh, yeah," Bastian said, not recognizing the man, who was at least fifty and worse for wear. At least he didn't appear to be injured.

"Maybe all hope isn't lost," the man said, suddenly sounding disgruntled. He reached for the control panel inside the elevator but Bastian stepped forward to obstruct him. He scoffed and looked up at Bastian, scowling. "Look, man, we're better off down there! Wouldn't you say?"

Gunshots not too far off.

Bastian perked up, staring through the elevator

doors, and when he spoke, his voice monotonous, he didn't look down at the man.

"Quite the opposite, sir. Everyone's fucking dead."

The man fumbled with his words, practically choking on them. He backpedaled a few paces until his back hit the wall and then he slumped down.

"Who's shooting?" Bastian said, abruptly looking down at the man. "And where'd you come from?"

"Parking lot," he mumbled. "I was…on my way out. Had…had a meeting with Bowman…"

Bastian's brow furrowed, though it had hardly lifted since the doors opened, and he briefly lifted his eyes in rumination.

"Wait, are you from DARPA?"

The man nodded and started to sob. "We…we gotta get outta here."

"*Who* is *shooting*?" Bastian demanded to know, speaking slower and more emphatically, as if the man was hard-of-hearing.

He gulped and gawked up at the green-and-black giant standing beside him.

"The…the security guards. I…I don't know their names, b-but—"

"Listen, I'm sorry to have burst your bubble about the staff below. But it's true. As far as I could discern. With the exception of two people I managed to save. Now forget what I said about the elevator, and stay put. Once it *starts* to go down, pull the emergency brake and wait this shit out. In the—"

More gunshots, closer, and shouting.

Bastian took a step outside of the elevator, peering to the right. The elevator foyer continued on a right-hand turn, past the stairwell access door, and down the north wing. Towards system maintenance and the connected warehouses.

All of a sudden the man *crawled*, on his hands and knees, faster than Bastian might have expected, out of the elevator right under his nose. Panic had quickly returned to his bones, and consumed him like a disease. He crawled, rather madly, muttering all the while, out into the elevator foyer of the lobby.

Bastian called after him under his breath.

"Mister! Get back here, you nut!" Bastian reacted whimsically, frustrated.

Here he was again, once more delaying his own progress to help another.

*But I* do *have the means*, he tried to reassure himself, as he pulled the cart out of the elevator, and then left it on the tile to pursue the man. He managed to crawl into a doubled-over stance, catching his breath and righting his posture.

Bastian reached out to grab his arm but at the spur of the moment he pulled away, scrambling down the hall.

In the direction of the intermittent gunshots, which still gradually neared, and what was even worse, a discordance of inhuman sounds.

Bastian had to imagine that the man had originally come from that way, according to his previous statement, yet there he was, scampering off from whence he came.

A crashing sound caught Bastian's attention, in that direction, around the corner. He was maybe ten paces from it when the man disappeared around the bend.

"Ahead!" someone shouted, sounding livelier than the man's voice had been.

And then another cry, this one more likely coming from the middle-aged man.

*What the hell is going on?*

Bastian tentatively raised the Supe in both hands, just as the man returned, careening around the corner. His face was bereft of all color, aghast.

A creature turned the corner, looking far meaner and more atrocious than any Crawler, but about the same size. Its humanoid outline was not to distract from its impious design—jaws that began as open mandibles on its lower face, and then proceeded down its torso, both sides lined with thick, sharp teeth. As if its entire upper body was a voracious mouth.

It latched onto the man from behind, its jaws snagging his left side, from under his arm all the way down to his waist. The teeth sunk in, through his suit and flesh, and blood jetted out of each wound. Its bite pressure was shockingly immense, despite its lean figure.

Bastian had no shot at this range, with the creature behind the man, so he clipped the Supe and drew the Duke.

A Crawler descended through the ceiling to Bastian's left, a few feet behind him. His reaction was both knee-jerk and trained; he swung his left arm out, fist enclosed and Exoblade protracting. The Crawler hissed wetly and lunged. In the same motion, Bastian's arm swung toward it, and the Exoblade made contact. It cut through the Crawler's lean neck as if a hot knife through butter. The creature's head flew through the air behind him, and its body collapsed.

Bastian was quick, but not enough to save the man. He turned back to face him in time to witness the creature, for all intents and purposes, eating the man. Its skin was a homely shade between pale purple and gray, and its eyeless face was quick to nuzzle the space between the man's neck and left shoulder.

He was essentially paralyzed, twitching in place as the creature slowly but firmly chewed him from behind.

In the same breath it clamped its vile, bifold mandibles onto the man's neck. Instead of biting or chewing, it whipped its head back, and a geyser of blood shot out. The creature appeared delighted to bathe in the red fountain, jaws agape.

Bastian hardly had a shot, but at this point knew it was better to risk it than not at all.

Everything had happened so fast, he couldn't quite blame himself, but the guilt crept into his veins nonetheless, like liquid lead.

There was a minuscule drop of relief when he fired the big pistol. A hand cannon for sure, it thundered and the slide kicked back, then forward, like a tank's barrel recoiling. The result was almost mesmerizing, especially with Bastian's elite marksmanship, even under such dire conditions. The Suit definitely helped enhance his aim.

The shot was spot-on.

The creature's ghastly skull would have whipped back from the impact had it have been from a regular pistol. Instead, the depleted uranium slug annihilated everything from scalp to collarbone. Its body fell back with a wet splash before disintegrating almost in the same instant. Along with its corpse, all of the yellow brain matter and bright red blood disappeared.

Its victim, unfortunately, would be left behind to decompose, chances were.

Bastian cursed, not under his breath but out loud, infuriated at the man for panicking, and at himself.

The report from the Duke would have left his ears ringing for minutes if it weren't for his helmet, regardless of the openings. So with his hearing intact, he immediately detected the approaching footsteps, and deduced two men running in this direction.

Shadows fell over the tile ahead of him, quickly followed by their sources. Two security guards in all-black uniforms, with obscure CHERI patches on their biceps, stitched in white to stand out. The black uniforms made this certain already, in a facility with a primarily white motif.

The men's feet skidded to a stop inches from the nearest pool of blood from the slain man's neck wound.

Their hard yet flummoxed faces immediately shot up to lock on Bastian. In the blink of an eye their perplexity intensified.

One of them even raised his weapon to train it on

Bastian, who had since lowered his pistol.

"That would be a bad idea, buddy," Bastian said.

"So, you're human?" The man tentatively lowered his pistol, which was half the size of the Duke at most, and he only dropped his aim to Bastian's legs.

Not only did Bastian roll his eyes, visibly behind the visor, but so did the other security guard.

The man that had spoken was African, with a heavy accent.

"Of *course* he's human," the other security guard said, with a strong British inflection and uniquely hoarse voice. He scoffed and shook his head, which featured a red-orange Mohawk a few inches high, and a cryptic tattoo on the left side of his scalp.

His posture ultimately relaxed and he looked down at the man's body. He cursed under his breath.

*Security guards. Alive. This is good.*

"Was he with you two?" Bastian asked, raising a hand to hit the visor button on his helmet. He took a couple of steps closer, making the African man flinch, but then relax. Bastian wanted to comfort them as much as he could, even the redheaded Brit, with the fact that he meant no harm.

"More or less," he said, sighing. He holstered his pistol and squatted by the body. He fidgeted with his scrappy, red-orange goatee. Tattoos on his fingers and knuckles. His face was quietly distraught.

"He was panicky," the African man said, finally lowering his pistol all the way, but not holstering it. His gaze was ever watchful of their surroundings, if not in a paranoid fashion, but justifiably so. "He was in his car, a nice one I might add, when one of those *things* jumped on the hood."

"But we blew it straight back to hell," the other man said, sneering and standing up.

"You think they're demons, too?"

"What?" The man raised an eyebrow. "Uh…no, I mean, I was just being figurative."

"Oh, demons, this is for certain," the other man said, eyes wide, nodding.

"Christ, not this shit again," the Brit rolled his eyes and kneaded his forehead. He had striking blue irises, but otherwise his pale face was bleak with experience. Whether it was war-related from a past in combat or simply what had transpired today, he was clearly not someone who simply shrugged off hard times.

"Doesn't matter," Bastian said, glancing over his shoulder at the cart. When he looked back at the two security guards, he noticed that they had also glanced at it.

"So what *does* matter, stranger? The survival of you, and just you, is that it?" The Brit slowly reached for his pistol. "Just who the hell *are* you, anyway?"

"Bastian Thurgood. I work here. Thought it was obvious. Don't draw that."

Bastian spoke rapid-fire, but composedly.

The Brit's eyes narrowed on him and he eventually stayed his hand.

"Look, mister," the other security guard said, pistol holstered and palms facing forward, but taking a closer step, "we mean no harm. We work night shifts only, with lobby-level clearance, and nothing else. We don't know what goes on here, but our guesses seem confirmed. Just got hired two months ago. That's when I met this *bozo* here. But we are not enemies. We can be a team."

"Quite communicable, now that you know I'm *human*, huh?" Bastian said, raising his eyebrows. He then clipped the Duke and nodded at the man. "What're your names?"

"Abby, you can call me Abby," the African man said.

Bastian wasn't going to argue.

"Fields works for me," the Brit said. "Now can we cut the shit and get to it?"

"Can't object there," Bastian said. He returned to his cart and resumed pushing it. "As you can see, I have someplace to be. And I've already wasted enough time—"

"Had you saved that man's life, would you still be saying that, you coldblooded asshole?"

"Fields, right?" Bastian said sternly. He didn't pause long enough for Fields to even nod; only long enough to gather breath for an aggressive rant. "I don't need to justify *shit* to you. While you two have been prancing around up here, I've been down *there*, knee-deep in the dead, wading through blood and bodies, trying to save people, failing to save people. I managed to help two, but couldn't even save my own wife and daughter, so stifle your therapist mentality and get with the program right-quick, or get the *fuck* out of my way."

Bastian was about to blow up even more had he

not finished talking when he did. He pushed the heavy cart forward, and the two men parted to avoid being run down.

He reached the edge of the corner, making the turn down a wider hall, when Fields called after him.

"Thurgood, is it?" Fields asked, compassion warming his previously embittered face.

"Bastian works better."

"Right. Bastian. Apologies on me, and maybe beers sometime in the future. For now…"

"Don't worry about it," Bastian sighed. "But seriously, time is critical for me."

"We'll talk about it en route," Fields said, shrugging.

Bastian started to retort but Abby came up to his left, drawing his gaze and interrupting his breath.

"Yeah, but on one condition," Abby said.

"Listen, I'm not really putting anything down for negotiation. I'm headed for Calipatria. That's where the—"

"Yeah, we've seen the broadcast," Fields said, looking glum again. "The Monolith, right? A.k.a., the Mothership."

*Abby says demons, you think* he's *crazy, but you say aliens, and he thinks* you're *crazy.*

*We're* all *fucking nuts.*

Bastian's mind was clouded with more thought than he could articulate.

"Right. The source of the scourge," Bastian said. "Well, at least I hope. Maybe with this Suit—a functional prototype, like these guns—I can bring it down.

Gotta try at least. Nothing left to lose."

"Sounds like a plan," Abby said matter-of-factly, and without a hint of incredulity.

Bastian stopped midstride. He smirked, more skeptically, and shook his head, waving his hands.

"Crazy, sure," Fields butted in, before Bastian could get out a word. "But ballsy. I'm down."

Bastian looked down at Fields. He already wasn't a tall man—maybe 5'9"—but from the Suit's perspective, he seemed awfully short. His carriage was tall, however. His personality had a commanding quality that couldn't be ignored.

"You were right the first time," Bastian said. "It's insanity, not bravery."

"Same bag, far as I'm concerned," the Brit said with a nonchalant shrug. "Especially with the way things are going 'round here."

"True as that may be, to an extent—"

"Look, mister Bastian," Abby said through a tired sigh, "we've been all over these premises. Ground level at least. Everyone we've come across is either dead or dies right after we make contact; panic has weakened everyone. Rightfully so, so we can't bear any blame. We just have to do our best, and keep moving. You seem like a man with a plan, and the means, by the looks of it. Like you said…time is crucial. So let's stop bullshitting, and get on with it."

"Abby is right. Besides, where are we gonna go?" Fields said, clearly battling his own emotions as he struggled through his next few sentences. "I've got family in Oakland. Or did. Heard the quakes were spreading inland, and farther north. Managed to phone them before the lines went dead. But not before I heard screams, theirs and…something else."

Fields cleared his throat and furrowed his brow, gathering his bearings.

"So yeah. Nothing to debate. I'm tagging along."

"I have a sister and her husband in Seattle," Abby said. "Grandparents, safe in Nairobi. Hopefully safe…"

"But Seattle is—"

"Why do you think I'm adamant on coming with you? I cannot do anything to help them from here. And Calipatria is a much closer drive."

"Okay. So your points are made. I shouldn't have protested in the first place."

"Time wasted, see?" Abby said.

Bastian smirked briefly. "Right. Well, I can't ask for much, nor expect—"

"Nothing to answer, or live up to," Fields said. "Our itineraries are the same. Let's leave it at that."

"Well, in that case," Bastian sighed, looking down at the cart before him. He buried the regret inside of him, for leaving Z locked in the armory, but ultimately resided with the idea that it was a decision best for them both. "I come bearing gifts."

"Thought you'd never say it," Fields grinned, looking at the cart and rubbing his palms together.

"As I started to mention earlier," Abby said, "I would tag along, on *one* condition."

"Naturally," Bastian said, unable to hide a smirk, unless of course they couldn't see from below.

Abby was about six feet tall, even, with short

black hair but otherwise clean-shaven. He had kind brown eyes but a burdened weight on his brow, which Bastian at this point knew he wasn't misinterpreting.

Nonetheless, the two security guards' acceptance of his Suit, sans any elaboration, was both surprising and actually relieving.

"I imagine you guys are low on ammo?"

"Last mags, each," Fields said. "We've been conserving, and sharing our spares, since we both have the same SIG's."

"Good guns, but inferior to mine. Wish I could say I wasn't bragging. I designed most of these. But that's another story altogether."

"No shit?" Fields raised his eyebrows.

"The suit too?" Abby asked.

Bastian nodded. "Yeah. The Suit, too. An even longer story. But let's focus on getting you two better armed against the horrors standing between us and Calipatria."

"I feel like a kid at an ice cream truck," Fields muttered.

"Just be easy on the triggers, yeah? Limited ammo for the journey." Bastian surveyed the weapons and realized that the options were pretty slim, since the men didn't have the handling capabilities of the Suit. He reached for the ROT-20, lifting it with his left hand. Simultaneously he unclipped the Supe from his right waist, but then crossed his arms, handing the weapons off. "Take 'em. No objections. We should hurry."

"Uh, I'm not asking for a user manual or anything, but…" Fields mumbled, looking over the ROT-

20 as his hands scrutinized it.

"ROT-20," Bastian talked fast. "Three barrels, rotary-action, automatic. Twenty-gauge buckshot. Six shells each barrel."

"Damn, boy…" Fields whistled low.

Bastian glanced over at Abby, who looked dumbfounded at the heavy shotgun in his hands.

"It's called the Supe," Bastian said, again rapid-fire. "Double-barrel, sawed-off, obvious shit. Twelve-gauge bolo rounds." He indicated the fore-grip below the folded barrel extension. "Grip and twist to increase range. Break-open action. Kicks like a wild mule so try to anticipate that. Watch the triggers; squeeze the rear, then the front."

"Works like an elephant rifle, then? I've used one before. Been ages, though."

"Same action, yeah. Just about the same recoil, too." Bastian scooped out eight of the twenty shells from the drawer in the cart. "Stuff these wherever you got 'em."

"Those are twelve-gauge, yeah?" Fields said, removing the empty bandolier from around his torso. "Use this, Abby. I'll pocket mine."

"That's great," Bastian nodded.

Abby donned the bandolier and loaded the loops with the eight shells that Bastian handed him.

"Is it already loaded?" Fields asked, looking for the magazine.

"Yeah, both are loaded," Bastian said. "And Fields, yours loads through the port on the right side. Once the barrel is full, manually rotate to the other, and so on. Ejection port is on the left."

An unnatural shriek and some clattering noise down the hall, out of sight.

The corridor they currently occupied was about twelve feet across, and eleven high. There were no doors for the next forty feet. Then some maintenance closets, before the hall forked into a T-intersection. The lighting was intermittently intact, a few bulbs shorted here and there. Not much debris in the hall itself, except for a few scattered blood smears and footprints.

"Eighteen is a high count for a shotgun," Bastian spoke fast, addressing Fields as he dug a few shells from its drawer in the cart. "I've got fifty-odd extras, make every one count. I'm only giving you twelve, for now."

"Alright, bossman," Fields said, accepting the shells and stuffing them into his pockets.

"I take it you had a shotgun at some point before?" Bastian asked, in reference to the bandolier he gave Abby.

"Yeah, a nice Mossberg pump."

"Ran out?"

"In the parking lot, yup. Tried to salvage it but one of those toothy things swiped it. Bastard."

"Toothy things? Oh…like that one?" Bastian's voice tapered off, as he thumbed over his shoulder.

"Yeah, one of those," Fields said.

"An Eater," Bastian said, off the top of his head.

"Huh?"

"I'm calling it an Eater," Bastian said. "My first time encountering one, to be honest, but seems fitting. For call-outs."

"Right. And what else?" Fields asked, finished pocketing the 20-gauge shells and trying to get comfortable wielding the prototype shotgun.

"Crawlers," Bastian said. "The humanoids with half a head. Vultures, the winged ones. Uh…"

"What about the biggies?" Fields asked.

Bastian started to push the cart, gesturing with his head that they keep moving.

Abby and Fields quickly caught up, passively accepting this decision, and increasing their vigilance.

"Hooves and black horns, red skin, I…" Bastian paused to think of T and Z. "Well, just been calling 'em Barons. Not a common sight, though."

"Yeah, that's news to us," Fields said.

"Doesn't sound pleasant," Abby added.

"None the least," Bastian shook his head.

"And the bald ones?" Fields asked.

"Legionnaires. Bossy leaders."

Fields acquiesced without saying anything. Abby appeared more inquisitive, but didn't voice it.

"And before you say it, the toothy, horned version of the Legionnaire, I call a Tyrant. Can't say why. Seemed fitting."

"That's new to us, too," Abby said. "Can't wait to meet it, though."

The sarcasm was right up Bastian's alley. It consoled him to know that such brave, yet witty, people were still holding it together in this mess. And that he had the pleasure—the honor—to cross paths with some of them.

"So, where are we headed, Bastian?" Fields

asked, his husky voice rather quiet.

"Loading dock, north wing. We need a vehicle. Something with a small trailer, or a bed."

"We haven't been that way yet," Abby said. "Restricted access, those warehouses."

"I must've forgotten my ID card below," Bastian said. He then brandished his fists, including the obvious chainsaw attachment, though folded against his arm. "But these should suffice."

"I tried to resist asking at first," Fields said. "But I can't anymore. Is that—"

"Yes, a chainsaw."

"Where's the gas stored? Or is it electric?"

"No gas, nor quite electricity. It's actually—"

They were about twenty feet from the intersection when the ceiling opened up directly above them. The nearest LED fixture popped loudly, sparks flying, and two Crawlers descended, entangled in each other. Not the most graceful creatures, but unrelenting nonetheless.

Abby and Fields were genuinely startled, staggering back, each catching themselves on opposing walls. Bastian, however, hardly flinched. He was only irked by the separation between himself and his cart, thanks to the two creatures, now getting to their feet amid a cloud of white dust.

In the Suit, his strides were twice as far as they were out of it. He took one forward, and closed the gap between himself and the nearest Crawler, which swung at him. Its claws slashed the chest-plate of the Suit, like nails on chalkboard. There was no effect to Bastian himself, and the look of surprise in the eyeless creature's face was immediate.

Bastian, in the INFERNO Suit, became a shadow falling upon the Crawler.

He seized the hand that had swiped him, with his right, and used his elbow to break its arm in half. Its own elbow compound fractured, bone jutting through flesh, and the creature wailed. He swung his left fist around to connect with its temple, protracting the Exoblade simultaneously. Its half-skull was impaled, bursting like a maggot-infested watermelon in the same instant, dwarfed by the blade.

As Bastian relinquished himself of the slain Crawler, the other darted out of his path, avoiding him altogether and going for Abby.

"Coward," Bastian growled, and reached out for the Crawler.

Abby hip-fired the Supe once he had remotely regained his footing, and the Crawler's gaunt stomach blew out its lower back. The torso collapsed into its legs, and the two halves fell back with a wet splash. The entrails and blood disintegrated, along with the bisected corpse, seconds later.

Abby stood up, eyes wide, and looked down at the Supe, then up at Bastian.

"I'll be damned," Abby muttered.

"No, my friend," Bastian said. "With that, you *do* the damning."

Abby mustered a devious smile, while Fields' face lit up.

"Let's hoof it," Bastian said, reinvigorated. He reconnected his hands with the cart and began urgently pushing it down the hall. "They're likely hot on our trail. Above, in front, behind, doesn't matter. They can be trickier than you might think."

"Are they…getting *smarter*?" Abby asked, catching his breath as he and Fields started jogging on either side of Bastian, to keep up with him.

Despite his size, and the lumbering weight of the Suit, they were surprised at how nimble he was.

"I'd say it seems so," Bastian said, and they reached the T-intersection. He peered down both ways, holding a fist up to signal Abby and Fields to hold back. He saw no hint of the enemy down the left hall, but down the right he glimpsed shadows at the end of the forty-foot stretch. A few light fixtures flickered down that way, but the ones to his left were all lit.

"Clear?" Fields asked from behind him.

"As far as I can tell," Bastian sighed. "Enemies to the right, out of sight. Doing something. Hopefully just lost."

Bastian looked back at Fields, and then Abby.

"Crawlers seldom act very smart, or strategic. Same with Vultures. I think, individually, they aren't real sharp. But under the command of, say, a Legionnaire…or Baron…they pose a greater threat."

"Leadership goes a long way," Fields said.

"Yeah. So…let's just not underestimate them, shall we?"

"Sounds reasonable."

"Which way, then? Left, yeah?" Abby asked.

Bastian gulped and nodded. "Yeah. To the loading docks. Let's go. Keep it tight. Abby, hold the rear. If they drop in close, hip the Supe like you did a minute ago. If they're a ways off, *grip and flip*, extend the barrels and don't be shy. Might wanna reload now."

Abby grunted and complied, while Bastian went ahead and filed down the left hallway, leading with the cart. He kept both hands on it, knowing at any point he could quick-draw the Duke for anything at a distance. Closer than that, he had the Exoblade and his sheer strength to defend himself.

While Abby reloaded the left barrel of the Supe, his hands shaking, Fields stood beside him, keeping an eye on the right hallway.

"Don't go too far," Fields called out to Bastian, who was advancing down the left hallway by himself. He kept a steady pace, haste in each step.

"Keep up," was all Bastian had to say.

Fields cursed under his breath and shook his head. He made a quiet "can you believe this guy?" comment to Abby, who merely sweated profusely and shook his head, albeit simpering sarcastically.

Finally he secured the Supe again, snapping the barrels up and locking it.

"Ladies first," he said, beckoning Fields ahead of him.

Fields smirked wryly and filed down the hall, shouldering the ROT-20 but keeping his aim low, with Bastian in mind. He was a steady fifteen feet or so ahead of Fields, so he accelerated to play catch-up.

Behind, Abby pulled in their rear, frequently

spinning on his heels to face the opposite direction. He backpedaled like this for as long as he could, before he feared tripping, and then faced forward again. He maintained this maneuver as the three men advanced down the sixty-foot hallway.

At the end, which Bastian now approached, gratefully without confrontation, were a pair of aluminum swinging doors. Both had a small oval window, through which Bastian looked forward to observe the warehouse foyer before actually entering it.

There was light on the other side, he glimpsed its reflection on the glass, making it hard to see past.

And then a large figure obstructed both windows, and the double-doors flapped open, in the wake of a Legionnaire. It ducked to pass under the lintel, and walked slowly, as if marching into an arena, burly arms at its sides.

Beneath the bright LED lighting, its features were illuminated.

Bastian spotted bullet holes in its pale, yet bloodied, dome of a skull, and in other places around its broad shoulders and upper chest.

*I found him, T.*

The same Legionnaire from the parking lot, over an hour ago at this point. Possibly two.

Time had evaded Bastian.

But not the beast—it wasn't just mortal, but it had no healing properties. This was comforting.

"Oh, shit," Fields's voice muttered behind him.

"Hold," Bastian said, and lifted his hand to hit the visor button on his helmet. It closed, but his view of the beast remained clear.

Fortunately, it didn't take the raising of his arm as provocation. Instead, it had stopped several strides from the double-doors, breathing haggardly, its big chest heaving noticeably.

"We got incoming!" Abby called from the rear, backpedaling to stop about eight feet behind Fields.

"How many?" Bastian asked, without moving a muscle or taking an eye off the Legionnaire fifteen feet from the end of his cart.

"Two, uh…two Crawlers, and one Vulture thing. They're, uh, they're coming in hot."

"Range?"

"Forty feet, closing."

"Grip and flip, Abby. Once they're at twenty feet, let it rip. Fields? Back-up your boy. I got this motherfucker."

Fields stuttered, trying to say something while Abby successfully rotated the Supe's barrel extension, locked it in place, and shouldered the shotgun…

Before Fields could even finish his thought, Abby fired the Supe, a thunderous roar that bounced off the walls. It immediately kicked the Legionnaire into high gear, and it threw its arms back, roaring, head pushed forward.

Bastian took the opportunity and quick-drew his Duke. He fired it and the depleted uranium round struck the arrogant beast between its glowing ember eyes. Its skull parted like the Grand Canyon, and yellow brain matter sprayed the ceiling. It teetered on its legs, like a giant tree somehow refusing to fall despite being—

*Chainsawed.*

As if a light bulb suddenly illuminated Bastian's mind, he clipped the Duke and darted forward, to the right of his cart. He swung his right arm at the teetering beast, but the chainsaw attachment didn't unfold.

He had never used it in combat, and although hypothesized by some of his colleagues, it had yet been approved for CQC testing.

Somehow the Legionnaire was still alive, although its eyes no longer glowed, and were a dim yellow at best. It still managed to function in defense, seizing Bastian's right arm before it came close. A croaking growl spilled from its jaws, which leaked a fluid comparable to bile.

Bastian clenched his jaw and tried to pull free from the Legionnaire's grip on his right arm, but couldn't.

*No worry.*

He drew the Exoblade and plunged it into the beast's gut, down to his fist. In the Suit, he could nearly stand nose-to-nose with the dome-headed monstrosity, though now its skull was not so spherical. Also, due to its vertical lobotomy, its composure was sacrificed.

Its legs constantly wobbled, knees weak and footing shaky at best.

Bastian took full advantage of these changes. Now, with the entirety of the Exoblade buried in its stomach, the pain at least caused it to loosen its grip on his arm. It staggered back, freeing itself from the tungsten blade, but Bastian wasn't going to let it off on a slow death.

*Places to be. Things to kill.*

He heard gunshots behind him, from the Supe to the ROT-20, both with distinct reports. The click-clacking of the ROT-20's rotary barrels cycling was as unmistakable as the Supe's break-open barrels, and empty shells clattering to the tile.

Bastian was almost shocked at how meticulous his hearing was in the helmet.

He shifted his full focus to the Legionnaire, just as it—almost lazily—bowed its ugly face to take a chomp out of him. Try as it might, Bastian doubted it would even slightly puncture the helmet's carapace.

At any rate, he didn't give it a chance to try. He yanked the Exoblade out, an easy motion as its serrations cut through the beast's fragile organs, and then lifted his right foot and kicked it in the chest. Had it not been doubled over, he wouldn't have the ability, but it was just the right height. The Legionnaire tumbled back, releasing a pitiful sound as it did.

Bastian leapt over its legs and came down on either side of its head. He lifted his right foot and brought the heel down into what would be the Legionnaire's nose. Its upper jaw and brow caved in, crushed beneath the armored boot. Bastian scraped brain slop and skull fragments off his sole, across the tile, before walking forward and turning around to face the rest of the hall. His perspective was briefly scarred—no, gifted—by a handful of dancing embers, before they, too, evaporated.

Then he took in the sight of his new comrades mopping up the others.

Since Bastian initially engaged the Legionnaire, more than Abby's first call-outs had emerged. In the wake of a Crawler's corpse disintegrating, not far from the ember remnants of a slain Vulture, two more creatures were on the move—in addition to the second Crawler Abby had originally spotted. Witnessing the extended-barrel Supe in action was a dream come true, but given the circumstances, he couldn't feel as thrilled about it as he would've preferred.

Nothing about the situation was dreamlike, unless likened more to a nightmare.

Nevertheless, Bastian was grateful for the weapons, and his competent acquaintances.

Abby seemed to have gotten down the reloading action of the Supe, which was simple enough, but for a beginner it could be a hitch. Bastian recalled Abby mentioning his experience with a break-action elephant rifle in the past, so he imagined that was where the easiness came from.

*Nothing about this is easy*, he thought to himself, naturally. It was a given, but, compared to others, they did find themselves in a relevantly comfortable niche. In the throes of combat, Bastian felt composed. When he was fleeing, or unarmed, or even just waiting around, his disposition was worse off. He felt reduced to a state of fragility.

It was only then that he was morbidly reminded of his mortality, and he hated it.

As Abby reloaded, after devastating the torso of a Crawler with a 12-gauge shot of bolo rounds, his fellow security guard wiped out the last two threats. The cyclical ROT-20 found a home in Fields' hands, as he already got the hang of it, favoring three-round bursts.

He didn't have remotely the amount of training as Bastian, in or out of the Suit. Nor the recoil control gifted by wearing it. So, naturally, he wasn't able to use the ROT-20 as a semiautomatic weapon, which required those things and firm trigger handling, but given the circumstances Bastian was impressed with Fields' use of the prototype.

It gave him further hope for CHERI's projects in the near future, supposing they—or the company—survived this catastrophe.

Once the gunsmoke cleared, and only frail embers flitted through the hallway, the two security guards turned to face Bastian.

"All clear," he declared, and thrusted a thumbs-up gesture toward the men.

Adrenaline-fueled, triumphant smiles manifested on their worn, seen-better-days faces.

"Ammo check?" Bastian asked, while the two men regrouped.

At that point, not a single corpse or drop of blood spilt from their slain enemies remained. It was almost disappointing, to not have that grisly reminder of their victories.

"I fired…nine rounds, I think," Fields said.

"Three for me."

"Only three, Abby?"

He nodded, eyes widening.

"This is…a very efficient weapon."

Bastian grinned behind his visor, too small for

them to see, and nodded.

"Oh, I know."

"I'm kinda jealous," Fields admitted, "but to be honest, I think this gun has stolen my heart."

"It does that," Bastian said. "Speaking of stolen things, let's go hijack ourselves a truck."

Nobody had any objections to Bastian's urgency. They just as eagerly followed him through the double-door flaps, which he pushed open with the end of the flat-cart. Each man was about as avid as the next to finally leave this building.

Upon entering the warehouse foyer, however, they realized that was going to be easier said than done.

Before entering the warehouse itself, one required basic security clearance to access the foyer door. It was thick steel, with a push-bar handle, but integrally locked unless the keypad beside it received the right code. An ID card could be swiped through the mag-reader; alternatively, it also took a four-digit PIN.

Bastian would have used the code, but paused in the white-walled foyer, which was basically a ten-foot cubic hallway, between the two entrances. However, the aforementioned steel door was no longer in place—it had literally been ripped off its hinges, exposing the irreparably bent internal steel bolts.

Bastian imagined that only a Tyrant or Baron could have done this.

Regardless of how, it had been done at some point, and free access through the warehouse was granted.

Slowly, Bastian passed through the gaping doorway. He didn't have to duck, or even turn sideways. The door wasn't simply torn away, but it had taken much of the frame with it, too.

His gaze lifted to the high, arched ceiling of the warehouse, where metal beams crisscrossed beneath barred, inaccessible skylights. Below them hung LED fixtures. All but two strips nearest the loading docks were off, as the backup generator for the facility was scarcely routed here.

The warehouse covered about half an acre on the floorplan, and fifty percent of that was racking for the storage of freight.

There was another warehouse beyond this one, which required higher security clearance, and was used for the transference of more delicate materials.

Once all three men had entered, they fanned out and stood still, taking in the sight.

Eleven bodies were strewn across the floor, some on top of large crates, one in a forklift, and two up on a racking ten feet off the ground. A wheeled ladder was toppled nearby. The actual blood spilt was profuse, not to mention the grisly maiming.

The warehouse personnel had not been given a chance to hide or defend themselves. The enemy had gained access from outside, by the looks of it, and after that they were just fish in a big barrel.

One of the three large, ribbed, steel roll-up doors for the three loading docks was breached. It was the farthest from them, with a jagged hole somehow torn through it, five feet off the ground. The gap was maybe eight feet wide on all sides, just enough space for several Crawlers and Vultures at once; even a Legionnaire might have been able to squeeze through that.

A flat-nosed freight truck with a large white trailer about ten by twenty feet had wrecked headlong into the second rollup door. It bent outward and essentially molded itself around the cab, but otherwise did not budge. The panel doors to the back of the trailer hung open, and more bodies were inside, brutally slain.

There were no other vehicles in the warehouse, however, Bastian was willing to bet there was at least one outside the docks. At any given point there were usually a couple, either waiting to be unpacked, or left overnight to be loaded.

Bastian could *hear* Abby gulp.

"Focus, gentlemen," he said, beckoning the two security guards to follow him toward the first, and nearest dock. "Let's get this door up and see if there's a truck on the other side."

"W-Wait," Abby said, pausing and holding back, while Fields mutely followed Bastian.

"What is it?" Bastian said, sighing impatiently. "We gotta go."

"Shouldn't we…at least…" Abby tried to keep the tears at bay, as he struggled more to grasp his words. He looked around at the butchered men and women in warehouse garb, some of them so mutilated—or eaten—that their attire was indiscernible.

"What, Abby? Shouldn't we *what*?" Bastian hated, in retrospect, how irreverent he sounded. But he had already gone over this in his own mind—and out loud, with them, albeit more bluntly.

*Time is essential.*

"Like…check the bodies…make sure…" Abby spoke in gasps.

Bastian shook his head, and imagined that he now acted as much as he looked it—like a robot.

"No," he said firmly, and then took one emphatic step forward. "They're all *dead*, Abby. Every single one of them. These creatures…these *monsters*…they do not leave behind stragglers. Not like this, at least."

He could tell that Abby believed him, he just didn't want to accept it.

Fields had begun to walk past Bastian and go to the door, but now he returned, hoping to reason with his colleague. His friend.

"He's right, Abby. Let's just…try to focus on the path, not the scenery."

"Scenery!?" Abby exclaimed.

Fields sighed and kneaded his brow with a free hand, although absentmindedly he found it a bit difficult to tote the ROT-20 in just one.

"You know what I meant, man," Fields looked up. "C'mon. Let's go. Let's…focus on *avenging* these people, not wallowing over them."

Bastian's brow wrinkled and his head pivoted to the left. He looked down at Fields, who was unbeknownst to his gaze.

*I like the way this guy thinks.*

Abby clearly took it to heart, too, and in a good way. He frowned powerfully, but also appeared angry. And not at Fields or Bastian. Instead, at the enemy.

Presently out of sight, but certainly not out of mind.

Bastian wondered if they could ever be completely forgotten, especially to survivors like him and his current company.

Hoping, of course, that they in fact endured this to see its end. It was then that Bastian remembered Z, and Adhira. He gave them his best thoughts and wishes, for what it was worth.

"Fine," Abby said resolutely, on approach, and Fields looked appeased. "Let's go kill—"

Abby's well-placed, malevolent statement was interrupted by the sound of tires screeching, and two seconds later, something heavy struck the rollup door they stood thirty feet from. It rattled loudly, including the chain used to operate it.

Fields, Abby, and even Bastian were genuinely startled.

Then the sound of a big engine revving, more squealing tires, and again a discordant impact to the outside of the door. This time it didn't just rattle, but it popped out of its frame. The chain screeched as the lock sprung off and it was yanked up, followed by the door itself. Then one side caught on the frame railing and jammed in there. The rollup door scrunched to the right side, stuck about halfway up the twenty-foot height of its frame.

Beneath the ten-foot gap drove a burgundy pickup truck, a heavy-duty model with dual wheels in the back, supporting the eight-foot bed. It had a yellow light-bar on the roof, which shone into the warehouse. Fog lamps were mounted on the brush-guard, which were shattered now after ramming the rollup door. The headlights behind the brush-guard remained intact, however, and with the bar on the roof, temporarily blinded the three men inside the warehouse.

They stood still, waiting, unsure how to act.

Bastian's visor redirected most of the light and he was able to see through it, until seconds later the idling truck parked and killed the headlamps. Due to the lack of sufficient illumination in the warehouse, the driver kept the light-bar on.

Two of the four doors on the cab opened, and a man and a woman stepped out. They paused beside the open doors, while three men hopped out of the bed. Their boots slapped the bare concrete of the dock floor.

The other two docks had raised ramps, so driving in and out wasn't feasible. This dock was usually used for UPS and FedEx shipments, though.

In the three men's hands were weapons.

Bastian noted two pump-action shotguns, and one Colt M1911.

"Look around," the driver said to the men, who lingered around the bed, on either side. The driver didn't turn when he addressed them. The hovering glow from the light-bar on the roof kept Bastian from discerning the man's features, besides a large beard, red flannel shirt and jeans.

The woman had shoulder-cropped dark brown hair, straight but disheveled, a white tanktop, and jeans.

"There's nothing to find here," Bastian spoke out, his voice almost like a thunder. Especially funneling through the helmet's small mouthpiece.

The driver drew a large, stainless steel revolver from the tail of his jeans and audibly cocked the hammer, holding it at his left side.

"I'll be the judge of that, RoboCop," he said, his voice just as authoritative as Bastian's, sans the reason.

"Honey—" the woman started to say, her voice not as shaky as someone might have guessed.

"Listen to your wife, buddy," Fields said.

Bastian clicked his tongue against his teeth and bowed his head a little, as if to say *"should've kept your mouth shut, Fields."*

"Better put a leash on pumpkin, there," the man retorted, taking a step forward.

The men that had fanned out from the truck were now at a standstill, their weapons not raised, but their hands attentively gripping them.

Now that there was some distance between them and the truck, with a couple of little glances, Bastian could discern their features.

They were all in their upper twenties or thirties, at best. With the exception of possibly the youngest, they looked rugged.

*What is this, a lumberjack convention? Or just the SoCal douchebag assembly?*

Bastian bit his tongue to keep that remark solely in his head.

"We don't want any trouble," he said. "But I'm telling you—this building has no resources, only danger. There are likely still hostiles on the premises."

"Looks to me like *you* got some mighty fine resources, buster," the driver said.

"I do," Bastian nodded. "But you can consider me...*stingy*." He paused. "Unless...you want to tag along."

"Where are you headed?" the woman asked, and immediately her husband snapped at her.

"Carla!"

"What? Look at them. We could use their help, Sam. And they could use ours, I bet."

"Goddammit, Carla," *Sam* growled.

"Calipatria," Bastian said.

"I don't give a fuck where you're—" Sam said, but cut his own sentence short when Bastian suddenly raised both of his hands, the motion alone startling everyone present. Sam immediately trained his revolver on Bastian, and the two shotgun-wielding men fifteen feet behind him and off to the side shouldered their weapons. Carla gasped and even against the glow of the truck's light-bar, Bastian could see the look of concern on her face.

And then Bastian simply removed his helmet, and cradled it under his right arm, against his waist.

Now bathed in the unforgiving illumination provided by the truck's light-bar, every one of Bastian's features became the scrutiny of the strangers. From the hint of his age to the evidence of his tiredness and even grief. The area around his eyes was pink and slightly swollen, with a light sheen, suggesting the excessive purgation of tears.

Despite these, what some might call flaws or signs of weakness—humanity, simply—the fortitude in his gaze was still unmistakable.

"Look, mister," Bastian said, as genuinely as he could, "I'm just a man, okay? Trained, yeah. Experienced, sure. But not for, and not in, this fiasco. I used to work here. All this hardware is next-gen shit. Half of it is unusable unless you're in this Suit. Which is literally tailored to me."

"Mighty convenient," one of the shotgunners said, sneering in his voice alone.

But Sam shushed him with a curt whistle.

"Go on," he then said, albeit still with his revolver pointed at Bastian.

Unfazed by the three weapons trained on him, and likely his now exposed head, Bastian nonchalantly continued. However, the details of what he spoke of were not channeled through him so effortlessly.

"I get why you wouldn't wanna go to Calipatria, probably the source of all this mess. Or why you wouldn't trust a man like me, in a thing like this. But these are unprecedented times, mister, and, speaking of time, I'm running *real fucking thin* on patience."

Bastian's expression warped, unambiguously.

"My wife and *daughter* were…*slaughtered*…by those *monsters*…as was a friend, in front of my eyes. I've been virtually powerless until now. So don't for a single goddamn *second* think that just by pointing a gun—or three—at me, that I'm gonna stand down."

Bastian lifted his helmet and returned it, sealing it with a hiss, but pressed the button to lift his visor. By that point, Sam's gun had lowered.

He then whistled and said: "Lower 'em, boys."

Bastian saw one of them comply, but the other,

the man who said something earlier, was unyielding.

"Not a fucking chance," the man muttered under his breath, barely audible.

Sam spun around and yelled at him.

"Goddammit, Ed, put it *down!*"

This Ed fellow snorted and then lowered his shotgun, scowling all the while.

"You gonna trust this asshole, Sam? Just 'cause he fed you some sap story about his wife and bitch-kid—"

Bastian drew his Duke faster than a racing heartbeat and everyone snapped back into action, from Abby to Fields to the other shotgunner and even the younger man with the pistol.

Sam and his unarmed wife were the only ones not engaging in this standoff.

And Ed—though the shotgun was still in his clutches, as fast as Bastian had drawn on him, he wasn't able to match it. Not under the fear of having his head blown off upon trying.

Sam waved his hands in the air and cursed at Ed, who was a few feet higher than Sam, not in height but location. He and the other guys occupied the raised concrete floor on either side of the dock, by the rollup door.

Which meant that, while Sam was technically between Bastian and Ed, with about fifteen feet from each, Bastian had a clear shot at his target.

His added height in the Suit made it even easier. Though, he knew nothing was easy about this situation, which was spurred by emotion, not logic.

"Take it easy, man," Fields said, the volume of

his voice evidently addressing Bastian.

"Maybe I was mistaken," Bastian said, loud enough for the others to hear, yet barely moving his lips—or any other part of his suddenly rigid body. "And I should find another transport. Just let us pass, without action or saying *another fucking word*, and we'll pretend like I don't want to obliterate your friend's skull with this Desert Eagle-on-steroids."

"First, the asshole's my cousin," Sam said, rather civilly, "and second, I think my wife was right, we should team up. You'll have to forgive *me* and…just *forget* Ed."

"Sam," Ed said weakly, fearfully.

"Just stop talking, dumbass," Sam grumbled.

Bastian took deep breaths until he slowly lowered the Duke.

"Obviously I can't fit in the truck," Bastian said simply, clipping the Duke to his waist. "And I'm about four-fifty with the Suit on. So let me and my men, and the hardware, occupy the back. Your guys can fill that XL cab. And we'll keep any of those freakshows off your tail for as far as you'll drive us. Even if it's just 'til we find another transport of our own."

It was a rapid-fire, yet articulate spiel that seemed to strike the right chord in Sam, and assuage the other men, Ed excluded, who still appeared begrudged but at least mute.

"I…I think we can make that work," Sam said. He slowly walked away from the truck, and beckoned Carla over. Once his face was clear of the lights, Bastian discerned that, despite his voice and beard, and his initially rude disposition, he had rather soft features.

"My name's Bastian. I'd offer you my hand, but…"

"Fine by me," Sam replied, still a little bitter, but not even half as resentful as his cousin. "I'm Sam Ferguson. This is my wife, Carla. Ed, yeah, you've already met him. The kid with the pistol is his boy, Cory."

Bastian clearly misinterpreted their ages.

"The other guy is James. A neighbor."

"Y'all just looking for supplies?" Bastian asked. He looked around, and then back at Sam, who nodded. Bastian shook his head. "I wasn't pulling your chain earlier. Trust me, you won't find anything worth salvaging here. Have you hit a grocery store yet?"

"Not yet. We live just outside the Miramar property. Pops used to work here, before the cancer. Anyway…grocery store was gonna be our next bet. Figured, ya know, this being a military base—"

Bastian shook his head. "You drove to the wrong end. This facility is mostly tech research and shit. Not much beside what you see on this cart, and I meant what I said earlier about the Suit. Just the way things are being designed. I'm sorry. But I wouldn't mind—"

The ground shook beneath their feet, though it was passing. Mostly because of the foundation below the facility, deflecting the tremor. However, the sound of splitting asphalt caught their ears. Unlike the parking lot out front, beyond these docks was just a one-way road that led off the property—less than sixty feet from the rollup doors.

Beneath that, susceptible earth.

There were still roads there, albeit tarnished by the wear-and-tear of eighteen-wheeler traffic.

The sinkhole formed fast, stunning everyone in the warehouse, staring under the rollup door stuck half-way up its frame.

From where Bastian stood, directly in front of the truck, he could not see what they did. Sam and his wife had parted ways just to look past the truck on either side, and gawk in awe.

"Sam, Carla," Bastian said. They didn't hear him. He could, however, hear the sounds of various creatures crawling—likely *pouring*—out of the sink-hole, about eighty feet from where he stood. He realized everyone, including his own comrades, were gorgon-ized by what they were witnessing. So he raised his voice. "Listen to me!"

It sufficed to snatch their attention, and snap the others out of their dazes.

"We need to do one of two things," he said.

"How about one, Terminator, and it doesn't in-volve you," Ed sneered, already climbing behind the wheel of the truck.

"Ed, don't even think about it!" Sam snapped.

"We need to speed the fuck out of here before those things—" Ed was shouting from just outside the cab, standing on one of the running board steps, and holding onto the open door.

He was interrupted by a thunderous roar, fol-lowed by audibly heavy footfalls.

Bastian could have sworn he felt the ground

shake, even through his Suit. Then again, it *was* quite receptive…

"We wouldn't make it," Bastian said, his voice low but Sam heard him clear enough, for he turned to look at the man with wide eyes, at least now respecting what he had to say.

*I was going to opt we either hop in and try to engage them on the run, but…*

Bastian shook his head. "We only have one option now. Bottleneck."

Sam's brow furrowed and he nodded.

"Everyone, fall back," he called, gesturing for a regroup.

James was quick to assemble, staying close to Carla, and constantly glancing at her. Bastian didn't need to know them for longer than five minutes to tell that there was something there, whether reciprocal or not. Unimportant at the moment, of course; Sam was, meanwhile, busy trying to reel in Ed, who was now demanding that his son get in the truck.

Cory was torn.

"Fine, get in the fucking truck, but stay put!" Sam finally gave up.

"They won't be safe there," Bastian growled. "My wife was—"

He heard the bone-chilling cry of his name, by Maggie, moments before she was abruptly crushed to death. It echoed up through the abysses of his memory, as he inadvertently unearthed it in warning Sam.

That was why Bastian's voice hung up, however,

the arrival of threats from outside quickly took precedence, and silenced everyone, shy of incoherent shouts.

Carla was among the very few who didn't exclaim. She instead reached behind James and suddenly withdrew a pistol that Bastian presumed he had kept in the tail of his jeans. It was a weathered Colt .45, the same as Cory's.

Two Crawlers had entered the warehouse on either side of the truck, hissing and darting back and forth on all fours.

Gunfire started to pop off, erratically at least; Bastian had to be grateful that they weren't panicking and firing at will.

Unfortunately, the ones engaging were James and Cory. The latter of whom was still up on the raised part of the floor, at its edge, about eight feet from where Ed stood on the side of the truck. James, meanwhile, had stepped out in front of Carla, in a protective gesture, but slowly fanning out, farther from the group fifteen feet in front of the truck.

Bastian and Sam were among them, including Fields and Abby to his right. They were trying to get a clear shot of the Crawler presently dodging Cory's pistol rounds, taking its time. Toying with the young man. Cory's marksmanship was incompetent at best, and his composure was stripped before their very eyes, making Bastian sick to his stomach, fearing the worst.

James' pump-action shotgun was going off every five seconds, missing each time. The Crawler nearest him was doing the same thing, biding its time, simultaneously observing the rest of the group.

Bastian was sick of waiting.

*Haven't I already said? Time is critical.*

He drew the Duke with his left hand, elbow locking and aiming it down. In nearly the same motion, he fired it at the Crawler ten feet in front of James, at Bastian's eleven o'clock. The first round struck it in the left shoulder, shearing its arm in a spray of blood, and the depleted uranium slug passed through its torso, nearly cutting it in half. It somehow remained intact, save for the arm, but it was severely wounded, bleeding abundantly and regurgitating red sputum.

James was wide-eyed, glancing at Bastian before redirecting his aim and executing the immobilized Crawler with a well-placed round of buckshot.

Bastian, meanwhile, shifted gears and side-stepped to his right, directly behind Fields and Abby, respectively. He stopped a few feet to Abby's right, and a little behind him. He had a clear shot at the Crawler about to pounce at Cory, and he didn't hesitate.

"Cover your ears," Bastian mumbled, and Abby dropped the Supe just in time to pinch his ears shut before the Duke boomed.

The Crawler was caught in the throat just as it rose to lunge at Cory, whose pistol had gone empty. The Crawler's head popped off like a Lego, trailed by a bright red arc, rolling across the concrete as its body stumbled a few steps before falling.

Almost all eyes were on Bastian.

And then a Vulture screeched, gliding into the warehouse after flying under the stuck rollup door. It rose above the truck, wings out.

Bastian adjusted his aim but it was Carla that took it down, wildly firing up at it with both hands on the pistol. Four rounds later and the Vulture dropped, crashing into the truck's roof and shattering the light-bar. Three bullet holes riddled its body, two in its right wing and one in its bulbous chest.

It twitched and gurgled blood as it lied on the truck cab's roof.

"I got it, babe," Sam said, waving his left hand at Carla. He rose the revolver in his right, then put his left on it, and squeezed the trigger.

Bastian let him have this one.

He popped the Vulture, and it rolled off the back of the roof, into the bed, where it would disintegrate seconds later.

The other Crawlers were doing the same now.

That raucous roar and heavy footfalls from earlier returned with a vengeance, punctuated by the appearance of its source.

"Everybody, get *back*!" Bastian demanded, waving.

Sam grabbed Carla, and they shifted behind Bastian. James joined, too. Cory started in that direction, but paused when he looked to his father, Ed, who had stumbled out of the truck only to stand like a statue, gawking at the beast as it entered the warehouse. He was unresponsive to his son's yelling.

The Baron had ducked under the rollup door, its red back nudging it open further in its passage, and now stood, albeit still a little hunched, and marched around the passenger's side of the truck.

Hot breath visibly spewed from its flaring nostrils, saliva dripping in thick ropes from its exposed teeth.

Clawed, red-skinned fists flexed by its sides.

Bastian turned to face it on its calculated approach. The Duke was in both hands, but only partially raised. He knew that as soon as he brought it all the way up, the Baron would charge.

"What do we do?" Fields asked quietly from behind him.

"If my shots don't take it down, when it charges," Bastian whispered, unmoving, "I'll step outta the way—then hose it with what you've got."

"Will do," Fields muttered.

Bastian felt poised, and ready, as the Baron slowed about fifteen feet away, just staring him down, when all of a sudden something robbed his attention.

Not just two, but three more Crawlers, entering the warehouse at once, to his right, from under the rollup door. One of them pounced onto the roof of the truck, startling Ed into falling back. Another leapt into the bed of the truck, its chassis rocking, and from there onto the raised floor within arm's reach of Cory, who screamed.

It was too much, too fast.

The Baron roared and charged.

*Fuck.*

Bastian spun to fire at the Crawler near Cory, risking exposing himself to the Baron. He clipped it in the shoulder, and the Crawler spun away from the young man, scratching him in the process. As he staggered, Bastian fired a round into the Crawler's chest and a jagged, gaping hole bore through it.

Out of his left peripheral vision, the Baron's red mass loomed.

He dove out of the way, forward.

Behind him, he heard the ROT-20 cycle, spitting out shells, and the thunderous Supe fired off both barrels simultaneously.

*Atta-boy, Abby.*

He rolled onto his back to face the action, and saw the Baron's charging path delayed by the onslaught. The combined torrent of 12-gauge bolo rounds and 20-gauge buckshot chewed through its muscular chest, and battered its already ghastly face. It roared, even made a yelping sound, and lost its balance.

Bastian heard screams and gunfire separate from the security guards, who were suddenly reloading.

Behind them, Sam and James concentrated fire on the two other Crawlers. One was bouncing between the roof of the cab and the bed, resulting in a lot of gunfire striking the truck itself. The other was darting from the raised platform and the dock floor, nearer Ed, who was struggling to his feet, and sobbing in trepidation.

He had left his shotgun in the truck, Bastian presumed, as he was now defenseless.

The Crawlers were far too agile, and diabolically animated, to be caught by the slow gunfire from the panicked civilians.

Bastian briefly wondered if this was their first actual confrontation with the enemy. Regardless, it was pending to be their last, if he didn't do something.

He reminded himself how unstoppable he was, or at least drove his body to do the convincing.

Essentially popping to his feet like a spring, Bastian drew the Duke only to realize it was empty, upon squeezing the trigger. He remembered that the slide didn't lock back like every other modern semiautomatic pistol, due to its weight and recoil.

He cursed under his breath and clipped it back to his waist, then uttered an animalistic war-cry as he charged the nearest Crawler. It took a swipe at Cory, barely missing him, and then Bastian was upon it, tackling it to the ground. When he came up, pinning its shoulders to the floor with his knees, he reached down and grabbed its head with his gloved hands. His thumbs dug into its mouth, and then he parted his hands, as if cracking open a coconut. The flesh inside wasn't white, though, it was bright red and pale yellow.

The Crawler's long, pink tongue flopped out, and its body below him went limp.

Carla screamed, a piercing sound.

Sam shouted something and rushed past Bastian, madly firing up at the Crawler on top of the truck.

Bastian looked around, and saw the bleeding Baron retreating behind some stacked wooden pallets and crates. Abby and Fields had reloaded, but now the latter was slowly approaching the horned beast, firing the ROT-20 in controlled two-round bursts every five seconds.

He wanted to tell Fields to stop, but his gaze circled around to Cory, who was on his side on the floor, less than ten feet from where he knelt. The young man—the kid—must have been eighteen or nineteen, twenty at the most.

His stomach was split open, organs pushed to the thin gash, fluids and blood having made their way out.

His eyes had rolled up, and he was unmoving.

*The Crawler didn't miss. It had just barely sliced him in the gut...*

Bastian was furious. He rose to his feet and turned in time to see the Crawler on the roof dart to the hood of the truck, then have its left knee blown out from under it by Sam's revolver, which proceeded to make clicking sounds. The creature crawled off the hood and rolled toward the weeping Ed, who was supine, still on the floor.

With a big stride forward, Bastian protracted the Exoblade and swiftly decapitated the Crawler. It slumped to the floor, and its head rolled a few feet.

"Bass!" Fields shouted.

*Not the fish. Me.*

Bastian hadn't heard that nickname before, but couldn't complain. Especially now.

He rushed toward Fields, who was now retreating from where he had been approaching, and then his armored heels skidded to a halt on the concrete. He spotted the wounded Baron reemerge from around the stack of pallets, with a Tyrant at its heels.

Bastian assumed it must have come from inside the facility, through the doors they used earlier. Regardless, it was here now, and Bastian was about ten strides from his cart of weapons.

"Sam!" Bastian shouted, without turning around or breaking eye contact with the slowly impending beasts. "Get everyone in the truck!"

"What about us, boss?" Fields asked, gulping. He stood a few paces to Bastian's left, still slowly backpedaling. Bastian, however, remained like a statue.

"Ammo low?" Bastian asked.

"Real low," Abby said, maybe ten feet behind him. And then Fields chimed in the same.

"How 'bout this—give 'em something to look at. Run under the racking to your left. Draw their gazes. Worst case, they'll fail to follow you. I need a gun."

"So, we're bait?" Fields asked.

"Either that or hop in the truck. Your call."

"No, this is more fun," Fields said with an uneasy chuckle.

"You're nuts, Flynn," Abby said, which Bastian assumed was Fields' first name. And then Abby sighed. "But I guess so am I."

"Kiss on your own time, boys, get ready to run," Bastian joked, and then spread his arms wide, bending his knees. The two beasts put all four of their eyes on him, though he knew that wasn't going to last.

"Gonna say when?" Fields asked.

"As soon as one of them makes a—"

The Tyrant rolled its head on its stout neck, roaring, its patience evaporating. It rushed Bastian, and immediately his comrades bolted for the racking to his far left.

"Move," Bastian exhaled.

The Baron roared even more thunderously, and

lumbered toward Bastian, while the Tyrant took the bait and redirected after the others.

Behind him, and a bit to his left, Bastian heard the pickup truck's turbo-diesel V8 rev.

If Sam was behind the wheel as he suspected, then there might be a chance he would wait for him. Ed, not so sure, but after losing his son, Bastian doubted he was in any shape to drive. He had to thank Sam, at least, for being able to herd everyone into the truck at this point.

Including Cory's body, which Bastian didn't see when he scanned the area en route to the weapons cart.

He reached it and swiveled his head to the right, spotting the Baron. It filled his field of vision, startlingly closer than he had expected.

The truck's headlights flashed on, right to the high-beams. The Baron snarled and teetered to the right, raising its left arm to shield its beady, soulless neon-green eyes.

This granted Bastian a couple of seconds, and he took advantage of every one.

Reloading the Duke was painless; he ejected the heavy magazine, even empty, and slammed a new one home, leaving two more in the drawer. As soon as it was loaded, while kneeling beside the cart, he lifted it in his right hand and fired at the disoriented Baron. The first slug caught it in the abdomen, lodging into its muscle or flesh, but not passing through.

"Oh, so you're a tough fucker, huh?" Bastian growled. He aimed low and fired twice, in rapid succession, at the Baron's left knee. The hocked joint made it resemble a goat even more—until the two depleted uranium rounds blew through it. Thick hide, sinew, and even bone, now like putty. The Baron released a howling roar as it toppled to its left, catching itself on its hands, one fist actually cracking the concrete.

Abby had somehow climbed on top of a rectangular crate on a shelf of racking fifteen feet off the ground. He suddenly whistled, and the Baron impulsively turned its ugly head to look up at him, on his far right. Bastian's left—and he glanced, too, spotting Abby standing up there, like the king of the world, shouldering the Supe. Its barrels were extended and a second after the Baron locked its gaze on him, he squeezed one of the triggers.

There was less light up where he stood, but the muzzle flash from the Supe was bright.

Bastian saw the bolo round catch the Baron in the face, and tear a chunk of its skull out from under its left horn. It immediately dropped onto its back, gurgling blood and twitching, arms splayed.

Fields hooted in victory, and immediately cursed just as loudly, as the Tyrant trying to catch him came terribly close. It proved to be more agile than he had expected, or Bastian for that matter, pursuing Fields under the grating, around beams and crates.

"Come back, Fields! Draw him to me!" Bastian shouted, while he glimpsed Abby try to find a way down from where he was.

Movement caught Bastian's eye to his right, and he witnessed the wounded Baron defy reality as it crawled toward him. Half a face and one-legged, the abominable beast still breathed a combative breath.

Defiance in his blood, Bastian neither chose a weapon from the cart nor drew his freshly reloaded Duke. Instead, he stood up, rigid, and resolutely approached the crawling Baron. Its large black claws scraped the concrete, trying to pull itself toward him. Its partially destroyed skull gazed up at Bastian, blood and brains leaking out of the jagged cavity.

Bastian dropped to his knee directly in front of the beast and, without pause, punched down at its face, the Exoblade protracting in the same instant, impaling its skull through its intact eye. The serrated tungsten blade blew out the back of its skull, bright red blood splashing the concrete. Yellow chunks of brain dripped from the wet blade.

The Baron ceased its crawling and slid off the tungsten, what remained of its cranium clicking against the serrations on the Exoblade.

"ETA right fucking now!" Fields hollered.

Bastian stood and spun. He saw Fields essentially leading the lumbering Tyrant out from under some racking. It was hot on his heels, a consistent ten feet at best. Just barely out of its arms' reach.

"Run right past me!" Bastian barked, retracting the Exoblade and drawing his Duke.

"No objections!" Fields shouted, and bolted right past Bastian, on his left.

All of a sudden the Tyrant lowered its shoulder and launched itself at Bastian. A maneuver he had not expected the slightest. Not to mention the sheer speed that it exercised in that instant, despite having chased

Fields around the warehouse.

Bastian fired the Duke in the same breath, but it missed. The Tyrant struck Bastian in the chest with its lowered, rocky shoulder, and then swung its arm out, flinging him through the air.

His vision blurred as his view of the warehouse twirled around him, until he struck a stack of wooden pallets, back-first. It knocked the wind out of him, and the stack toppled. He crashed through several, wood splintering and cracking around him, until he hit the floor. And the rest of them fell upon him.

The Suit was impact-resistant, but he had sufficiently been disordered by spinning through the air. Crashing into the stack of pallets, while not necessarily painful, was upsetting enough. Landing, then, in addition to all of that, and the rest of the stack falling on him…

Bastian was out of breath.

Additionally, the air he drew in was thickened by a smog of dirt and dust.

He fought blacking out, as his head spun, and he felt nauseous.

Screams from the security guards and civilians, including a horn honking and sporadic gunfire, kept him in the game.

That and hope. Some version of it.

*And impatience.*

# <u>13</u>

Through the rubble of wooden pallets, a visible haze of dust, and his own fleeting despair, Bastian rose. He returned to his feet—his armored feet—and was immediately reminded just how unstoppable he was. Or at least how deserving of that mindset he had come to be, after everything he had faced and the odds he overcame.

Now he was essentially in the company of more people—*humans*—than he had seen, much less interacted with, since the start of all this.

And while they were armed, too, to an extent, he was the flaming sword of defense and vengeance that stood between them and their common enemy.

All of this coursed through him like an ocean funneled into a creek. The overflow translated to adrenaline and he gathered his bearings.

It was faster than it seemed.

So were the two Eaters that had since infiltrated the warehouse from whence Bastian and the security guards had originally come. More from inside the building, as he predicted, they had not all been exterminated.

*Fucking pests.*

He of course referred to the various creatures as a collective. A scourge of evil.

This particular kind was new to Bastian, but ultimately they were one in the same, far as he was concerned. They were a heinous pestilence that needed to be extinguished.

Bastian's eyes widened as one charged Abby. It moved much more radically and frantically than any Crawler, absence of even a semblance of poise. This, combined with its grotesque appearance, made it an all the more appalling enemy.

Even from afar, an iota of this fear had infected Bastian. Still, he didn't let it paralyze him for more than a millisecond. He unclipped the Duke a heartbeat before Abby's Supe roared and half of the Eater was blown away—particularly, its right arm, all the way to its innately gaping, toothed sternum.

Bastian nonetheless elevated the Duke and fired at the second Eater, charging Abby *through* the remains of its fallen brethren. The creature dissolved into embers, which then floated around the other Eater as it mindlessly lunged at Abby. Bastian's shot missed by inches, miscalculating the creature's maneuver.

Abby was trying to reload when the Eater swiped the Supe out of his hands. A few fingers went with it, severed at the knuckle, spurting small fountains of blood. Abby clutched his right wrist, screaming.

The Eater howled a piercing, nerve-wracking sound less than a foot from his face, enough to traumatize most men. And then bright red blood misted Abby's features when a depleted uranium slug eradicated the creature's entire skull. Several of its ivory-like, curved teeth had mottled Abby's uniform, blood and brain goop acting as an inadvertent adhesive.

Meanwhile, smoke curled up from Bastian's Duke, and Abby stumbled back, beyond disoriented, in addition to of his throbbing pain.

Bastian took a step toward him but his focus was drawn left, to where the pickup truck was still parked. He could hear the engine sputtering under the dented hood, refusing to start despite Sam's frantic attempts.

Standing directly outside the cab's backseat door, on the passenger side, was the Tyrant. It punched through the glass and seized James, pulling him out of the backseat. James dropped his weapon inside and flailed wildly, hollering. He inadvertently kicked Ed in the face during his panic, while feebly struggling to punch or claw the muscular, earthly arm that hauled him through the window.

The closeness of the Tyrant's horrid face flooded James with fear.

Bastian aimed the Duke, but then heard the distinct sound of the ROT-20 firing. It was Fields, to the Tyrant's far left, about fifteen feet away, his back to the partially open rollup door. He was firing low, so as to avoid hitting the truck or, farther to the Tyrant's right, Abby, who had now crumbled to a sitting position. Bastian glanced at Abby, seeing him bandage his fingers with a torn piece of his uniform.

When Bastian looked back at the Tyrant, all in the span of seconds, he saw that it had sustained a few 20-gauge shells' worth of buckshot to its burly legs, but somehow still stood.

And Fields had stopped firing.

*Out of ammo. Should've given him more.*
*...Trusted him with more.*

Carla screamed from inside the truck and suddenly leaned out of her window, firing the pistol into the Tyrant's right side. In her panic, she accidentally struck James in the arm, a split-second before the beast dropped him entirely. He crumpled to the concrete, groaning and whimpering, bleeding from the bullet wound but moreover from the clawed divots in his chest and shoulder. The Tyrant had sustained quite a grip on him to pull him through the window, but now it was growing cantankerous from Fields' gunshots.

He had transitioned to his standard-issue pistol. It was like throwing rocks at Plexiglas. The Tyrant snarled in his direction, turning away from the truck.

Bastian elevated his aim and fired the Duke high, to avoid hitting the truck, or James for that matter. His aim was just shy of excellent, though his timing wasn't as good as it could have been.

So much was happening so fast.

He blew off the Tyrant's right horn, merely inches from walloping it in the back of the skull. Nonetheless the wound was enough to splash the roof of the truck with yellow fluid, and cause the beast to release a strident roar. The pitch of the vocalization actually startled Bastian.

The truck's engine rumbled to life and Sam threw it into reverse.

"Wait!" James screamed from the concrete.

The front right tire ran over James' leg, crushing it, and he howled out. Sam cursed and impulsively hit the brakes. Carla threw open her door to help him, making Bastian pause to demand she get back inside, fearful of her safety.

The Tyrant took advantage of this pause and, yellow ooze coursing down its face, blood leaking from wounds to its legs yet somehow still upright, it drove its flat, clawed foot down onto James' head. His skull pancaked against the concrete, his features bursting to the side and brain mush spilling out.

Carla had shut her door a split-second earlier, and now screamed in horror.

Bastian yelled incoherently and fired at the beast's head, but in his panic missed.

Sam abruptly reversed, and the Tyrant reached out with its left hand. Its clawed digits grappled the corner of the brush-guard, and the truck's rear dual tires squealed against the concrete.

The Tyrant roared, all but in the face of a petrified Carla, who sunk in her seat, sobbing.

Sam screamed incoherently and kept gassing it while spinning the wheel, but the Tyrant, even wounded, was too strong.

Fields had stopped firing to deal with a Vulture and Crawler that had entered the warehouse from outside. Bastian's attention was likewise scattered, unsure who to help and how.

Panic and adrenaline stormed through him simultaneously.

Despite the air-conditioning inside the Suit, he sweated abundantly.

Abandoning reason, Bastian charged the Tyrant

from behind, clipping the Duke and unfurling the chainsaw on his right gauntlet. He armed it, revving the toothed chain, and sidestepped to his left, when the Tyrant glanced to its right.

He brought the chainsaw extension down on the Tyrant's right arm, just below the elbow. The revving teeth chewed through its flesh and muscle with surprising ease, then caught bone, hanging briefly before cutting through it, too. The action lasted less than three seconds before the Tyrant's burly arm was severed near the elbow, spewing blood and thus relieving the truck of an anchor.

It fishtailed backwards, however, Sam's frantic acceleration in reverse abruptly caught up to him. The hitch and rear bumper collided with the lower edge of the rollup door frame. The truck came to a stop and its inhabitants were at a loss.

The Tyrant, despite its wounds, was not as fazed. It started to turn toward Bastian, on its left, but he wouldn't have it. He flipped the chainsaw attachment back to fold against his right arm, and then sidestepped to yet again elude the Tyrant. Before it could figure out what was going on, Bastian vehemently punched the Exoblade through its lower back. At fourteen inches, it wasn't quite long enough to make an exit wound in the Tyrant's stomach, as its body was too wide.

This, of course, didn't keep Bastian from maddeningly twisting and turning the serrated tungsten within the beast's midsection, churning its insides. Blood started to spurt through its bony teeth, a cage of a mouth now unable to contain its own death.

Fields suddenly ran up to Bastian's left, startling him. Blatantly, Fields elevated his pistol, the muzzle half a foot from the beast's left temple, and fired twice in rapid succession. The .45-caliber double-tap sufficed to knock the Tyrant off its feet. It collapsed to the concrete in a heap, reduced to ash and embers seconds later. The process took a little longer for its massive body, compared to a Crawler, but as soon as it began, it was safe to turn away from it.

"Dammit, Fields, you startled me half to—"

"You're welcome," Fields said in a haggard breath, before running past Bastian to meet with Abby, who had started to stumble in their direction.

"You crazy asshole," Fields said, embracing him before observing the makeshift bandage on his hand. "How many?"

"T-Two," Abby mumbled. "Index a-and middle. At the knuckle."

"Fucking hell."

"Wishing I was a lefty right about now," Abby smiled weakly.

The pickup truck drove forward a few meters and Sam leaned out of his window.

"Get in the fucking truck!"

Bastian glanced at Fields and Abby, who stood motionless about ten feet in front of the bent brush-guard.

"Fucking hurry!"

This time the person shouting was Ed, which warranted more of a surprised reaction from Bastian and the others, but instead it just kicked them into gear.

Or at least Fields and Abby, while Bastian momentarily zoned out. He glanced down at his chainsaw attachment, pleased that it was no longer dripping with bright red blood and chunks of vibrant flesh. He then watched Fields escort Abby to the passenger side of the truck, and insisted he climb into the backseat with Ed.

The two security guards and Bastian did their best to avoid looking at the poor corpse of the late James. Carla, meanwhile, wept into her hands in the passenger seat, slumped down.

As the truck's engine idled and the brake lights emanated a red glow into the night outside the rollup door, Sam leaned over the center console to try consoling his wife.

Bastian snapped out of his stupor and stepped forward to help Abby into the truck. Fields started to shut the door but Bastian's large, gloved hand kept it open.

"In you go," he said firmly.

"Oh, hell no, I'm—"

"There's no room for you, Fields," Bastian said. He glanced back into the bed of the truck. Cory's body occupied the front left corner. Essentially directly behind where his father sat in the backseat. Bastian gulped and returned his gaze to Fields. He raised his visor. "Get into the truck. Slide the back window open so we can communicate. Time's wasting."

Bastian didn't wait on Fields to comply.

He knew he would, after that.

He made a beeline for the ROT-20 that Fields had dropped earlier, out of ammunition. Then he rushed past the truck again, toward the flat-cart of weapons, and the Supe on the ground.

"C'mon!" Sam yelled out of the window.

"Turn it around!" Bastian snapped back, returning to the flat-cart at long last. He deftly reloaded the ROT-20, then the Supe.

Meanwhile, Sam turned the Super Duty pickup around. It had a wide radius, but the front left tire was able to mount the raised part of the floor briefly to achieve the angle. Once the truck was facing the stuck-open rollup door, its headlights illuminating the night outside, Bastian was cast in a red glow. He lifted his head from the cart, kneeling beside it, and lowered his visor to deflect the bright taillights.

He pulled the flat-cart over to the truck, thankful for Sam turning it around and then backing up as far as he could.

He opened the tailgate and squatted beside the flat-cart. He raised each corner individually, breaking off the wheels one by one.

Lifting the loaded flat-cart with his hands and arms alone would have required the assistance of at least three other men, if it wasn't for the Suit. The enhanced strength had the power cell to thank, and Bastian was a certain shade of grateful.

Once the cart was in the bed, and not rolling around thanks to the absence of wheels now, Bastian climbed into it and shut the tailgate. The pickup truck sank a little above the back axle, but was aptly supported.

He looked forward and, squatting, moved to the

back of the XL cab. Fields had slid open the rectangular window there. Abby sat between him and Ed, whose face was a reddened mess of dried tears.

Bastian peered past the backseat and to the front. He raised his visor.

"What's the towing capacity of this beast, Sam?"

"Twelve tons on the hitch," Sam replied, his voice low and morbid. "Can we get this shit-show on the road, please?"

"Sorry," Bastian mumbled, and then cleared his throat. "I'm in and the cart's secure."

Sam snorted and spat out of his window.

"Good," he said, shifting into gear. "Just…watch your step."

Bastian regarded Cory's corpse, which was unfortunately face-up.

Sam must have glimpsed Bastian in the rearview mirror, and seen him looking down.

"There's a tarp tucked under the mat, right side." After saying this, Sam drove out of the warehouse. "Watch your head."

Bastian ducked, just to be sure, but after the Tyrant had made its way through, there was a little more space. Once outside, the truck lurched to a halt.

"Which way?" Sam asked, calling it out.

Relieved that Sam was not only agreeing to give them a drive but also deferring their route to him, Bastian didn't know how to thank him.

*Just keep him alive, for starters*, he thought, but unfortunately, that was easier said than done.

It was still just the first day since the first sink-hole. Since the Monolith made contact.

Hard to believe all of this in just one day.

"Head northeast, toward the military grounds. The air strip is unmistakable once you start to cross the clearing between this building and—"

"Yeah, yeah, I'm familiar, remember?"

"Right."

"Hang onto your metal ass," Sam said, that snideness returning with a vengeance. He then mumbled: "Or whatever the hell that thing is made of."

Sam whipped the truck around to the right of the rollup doors, and gassed it in that direction. Gladly leaving behind this part of the Miramar base.

Bastian glanced over his shoulder, watching the CHERI facility slowly get smaller in the night, most of its exterior lights shut off.

"Hang tight, Z," he whispered to himself. "And Adhira…and anyone else…"

Bastian looked down at Cory's body, and frowned. He then scanned the interior of the bed, and knelt on the textured rubber mat before moving to the right. He investigated the edge of it, flush with the right wheel well. It was a little raised there. He dug a few fingers under it and pulled out a beige canvas tarp. It spanned seven by four feet, almost the surface area of the bed. He tucked the excess parts of it under Cory's body, the rest covering him snugly.

A deep breath later led Bastian to look at the cart in the bed, but movement drew his eye behind the truck. He pivoted on his knees to face the tailgate, and observe the night through which they drove.

Sam had started to drive the truck toward the quarter-mile clearing between the CHERI facility and the military grounds, including the airstrip. However, the fenced perimeter was impassable.

He diverted their route toward the suburban backroads just beyond the Miramar's outer perimeter.

"I was gonna tell you," Bastian said, leaning toward the open rear window. "The old fences were torn down and those barriers were erected in their place, two months ago."

"Whatever. We'll wrap around."

Bastian nodded. "Good. Heavy foot, Sam. We might get some company."

"You just put yourself to good use, Tin Man," Sam bit back, "and keep those freaks off our ass."

"I'll do my best," Bastian said, and looked down at Fields. "How's your ammo?"

"You're gonna laugh."

"What?"

"I've got one fucking round left," Fields said, glum.

Bastian couldn't resist grinning. It didn't last long, though. He felt bad, especially since…

"Sorry, man, but I can't give you anything. It's all too big for back there."

"I understand. Just…be careful."

"How romantic," Abby said, facing forward and not turning around.

Bastian smiled through a scoff and rolled his eyes, momentarily infected by the hazy sarcasm in the

347

air. Ultimately, he turned away from the window.

Whatever caught his eye earlier returned, this time more boldly. A pair of Crawlers bounding after the truck, on all fours, low to the ground and almost blending into the concrete drives they were on, having not yet reached the roads.

*Can I not have one fucking minute of Zen? No? Thirty fucking seconds?*

Bastian's sardonic musings shifted gears when he drew his Duke and aimed.

*Oh yeah, I forgot*—this *is my Zen.*

He fired at one of the Crawlers, successfully anticipating its juking maneuver, and the slug sundered its right collarbone. It tumbled back, bleeding all over the place. The gunshot alone startled Sam and the others, Carla shrieking briefly, but at least he kept the truck steady.

Or as steady as it could be as he slowed necessarily to hop a median and then skid onto the tattered asphalt of a backroad. The end of the truck fishtailed for an instant but Bastian was like a statue on his knees. And his aim, just as rigid.

He fired again, but missed the Crawler as it evaded, frighteningly agile on all fours. Knowing he only had three more shots before requiring a reload—*not even out of Miramar and already scarce with ammo*—Bastian readjusted.

He knew he had to start being more punctilious with his combat and tactics. In spite of his acceptance of urgency, he had to be more…

Patient.

Focused.

Raking in a deep breath, grateful for the refined air inside the Suit despite his perspiration, Bastian gripped the heavy pistol with both hands, elbows locked, and closed one eye…

The other peered through the visor, down the sights, and he exhaled slowly.

The Crawler leapt toward the bed, its calculation of speed and direction correlating to the truck perfect. It would have landed in the bed and crashed through Bastian's cart had he not fired when he did. The armor-piercing slug struck the gaunt creature at the base of the neck, on its right side; it didn't stop there. The round exited somewhere between its legs, halving its body right down the middle. The two lean slabs of meat and limbs flopped over the sides of the truck's bed, ultimately falling to the blacktop.

Bastian adjusted his aim to track the first Crawler he had shot moments ago, which was now playing catch-up. Bastian let it do so only to an extent before his patience paid off, and he landed a headshot that reduced it from a half-skull to a no-skull.

Amidst the night that trailed them, he could discern dots of red-orange in the darkness, like fireflies.

Embers of the dead.

Bastian looked down to prepare a new magazine for the Duke. He tapped a button on the right side of his helmet and the visor illuminated, like an LED screen, offering improved vision in dark environments.

As soon as his gloved fingers graced one of the two remaining Duke magazines in its drawer, the truck suddenly accelerated, its chassis lurching back. Bastian did not fall but his balance was temporarily forfeit, and he dropped the magazine into the cart, between weapons. He glared over his shoulder, about to ridicule Sam, when he saw it through the rear window and thus the front windshield.

Creatures coming at them from *ahead*.

He couldn't detect the amount, but the first was a Crawler either assuming the vehicle would slow down or swerve around it. The Crawler hugely underestimated the human driver.

Sam essentially floored it and before the Crawler could evade, the brush-guard struck it in the chest and its body was sucked under the truck. The hefty tires crushed arms and legs within the two or three seconds it was beneath the three-ton vehicle. Its corpse would have resembled processed meat after, had it not disassembled into ash and embers by the time the truck passed over.

The next two Crawlers were not terribly smarter. One of them tried evading but it had all happened too fast between its previous compatriot and itself. The front right fender caught its leg as it tried to dart out of the way.

Sam made sure to swerve in that direction and run over the rest of the creature with the truck's back right dual wheels.

This, however, gave the third Crawler a chance to predict the vehicle's approach and thus leap onto the hood. But one of its feet got caught in the brush-guard and Sam had no issue braking just hard enough to sling it off. Its ankle broke but the foot remained caught, rubber-banding its body back into the grill, and then under the truck. Its heavy chassis barely even bumped or rolled when crushing their bodies.

"Now that's how you drive," Bastian exclaimed.

"Glad you're still with us back there," Sam said with a quick glance to the rearview mirror.

"Watch it!" Bastian snapped, as a Vulture flew into the middle of the road, at windshield-level. Sam swerved just in time to miss it; hitting it at that height could have dealt serious damage.

Bastian's gaze tracked the Vulture's trajectory as it glided above the truck anyway, dragging its foot talons across the roof. Just enough to dig troughs in the metal, but not penetrate it.

He fired at it, aiming up with little space to move between him and the back of the cab in that short period. The Duke went off a millisecond before the Vulture collided with him, knocking it out of his hands. It clattered across the mat in the bed. The creature caterwauled as it struck Bastian in the face with its feet, talons raking the visor but not hard enough to cause any damage.

He reacted rapidly, unarmed but not defenseless. He seized the creature's legs and tugged, dragging it down to his level. Now it really screeched.

The bed of the truck was not big enough for both of them. Its wings constantly kept it airborne, that being, its feet off the mat. But not out of Bastian's control. Immediately vexed by its frantic motions, he abruptly skewered its right wing membrane with his Exoblade, causing it to droop to that side. Bastian rose to his feet for an instant—knowing it was unstable to do so in the back of the speeding truck, no matter the soundness of the Suit's posture—and reached, with his right hand, for the Vulture's head.

Instead, due to the slender, evasive neck, Bastian seized its throat. He pulled it down into the bed, inverting its position. Clawed feet grappled the back of the cab, curling through the rear window and startling the men in the backseat.

Bastian's encounter with the creature, though complicated, endured less than six seconds by the time he ended it.

He more than just squeezed the lean neck of the creature, he twisted simultaneously, and wrenched its head off. Blood fountained from the wrought jugular wound, and sprayed his illuminated visor. The bright red blood was, in that moment, made so brilliant a hue it was almost pink.

And yet no less disgusting.

Bastian, scowling, hurled the slain creature's headless body over the side of the truck. It of course disappeared from this physical plain nanoseconds later, including the decapitated head at his feet and the gore on his visor.

He retracted the Exoblade and felt infinitesimally victorious.

Thinking he was out of the frying pan so to speak and given a moment to catch his breath, Bastian was mistaken.

*Here comes the fire…*

He glimpsed something large emerge from behind a tree in someone's front yard to his left.

They still weren't out of the backroads bordering the suburbs that surrounded Miramar.

He knew they had to be quite close to hopping back onto the paved one-way drives that wove through the military base…but not yet.

"Nine o'clock!" Bastian impulsively yelled.

Abby and Fields in the backseat immediately reacted, yelling at Sam and pointing to the left of the truck.

Unfortunately, neither of them were in a physical position to fire their pistols at the incoming enemy.

By the time Sam caught on and noticed the charging Legionnaire—now crossing the street parallel to them, at a vicious speed—it was too late.

Bastian had pulled the Supe from the cart in the same instant that the Legionnaire made contact, lowering its shoulder into the left side of the truck. The impact was too severe to deploy any airbags, denting the left door behind the driver's seat, glass shattering inward and flaying Ed's face. He screamed and his body would have been thrown into Abby from the momentum of the impact alone, had it not been for part of the door warping inward and pinching his left forearm, anchoring it.

Ed screamed all the louder from this additional pain, while his face bled from several tiny wounds.

The impact forced the truck out of Sam's control for only a moment, but he regained it quickly. The Legionnaire lowered its head and hunched forward slightly as it ran to keep up with the truck, going maybe fifteen miles an hour at that point, after being slowed by the collision.

It snapped its disturbingly humanoid, sharp-toothed jaws directly outside of Sam's open window, and he could feel its slinging saliva dapple his face.

"Punch it!" Bastian yelled.

"Gladly," Sam replied, and violently accelerated. Tires squealed and the truck lurched forward, its chassis jerking back. Everyone sank into their seats as the truck accelerated and the turbo-diesel V8 roared. Bastian himself hunkered down into a squatting position to keep himself from losing balance.

With the acceleration of the truck, the bulky beast was unable to keep up.

The instant that the truck's cab passed it, it glanced right and essentially stared down the double barrels of Bastian's Supe. He fired both simultaneously, not wanting to take any chances, and the Legionnaire's dome of a skull was blasted into a vibrant plume of gore in the night.

Bastian didn't need to see it disintegrate to know that it was inevitable after that, but he sure would have liked it.

A tremor passed under the road, powerful enough that even Bastian felt the vibrations up his legs. He started to alert Sam of what he dreaded was happening, but the man was already struggling to control the truck. The quake caused the interior of the vehicle to rattle, and was reverberant enough to offset his steering.

Somehow, Sam managed to keep the truck from

spinning. Instead it slalomed, the steering wheel vibrating under his hands.

Bastian stood and with his left hand gripped the roof of the cab for stability. He saw the road ahead of them, illuminated by the truck's headlights, start to cleave down the center. A crack zigzagged, the sound itself painfully loud.

He knew that they couldn't just brake and let it pass, for fear that a hole would open up and devour them.

"Get off the road!" Bastian shouted. "Toward the base, toward the—!"

"I can't, I can't!" Sam hollered back, combating the vibration of the steering, just before the sinkhole opened up in front of them. The term sinkhole was hardly applicable anymore; Bastian knew this from the beginning, as the earth didn't just cave in, but violently erupt outward. Still, the word stuck with him.

*More like hellhole*, he would have propositioned.

Sam was unable to steer clear of the hole in the road, which spanned a ten-foot diameter. It had gaped the tarmac immediately in front of their path, leaving the truck nowhere to go. The front tires bounced up the raised, cracked asphalt, and then the three-ton vehicle nosedived into the opposite ledge, hewing the brush-guard and grille. Smoke poured from under the hood, which now dented outward, and the engine died.

The impact was quick and hard.

Sam, without his seatbelt on, was catapulted forward, through the windshield. He landed on the opposite side of the sinkhole, a few feet from what remained of the grille, and rolled across the pavement. Simultaneously, back inside the truck, Abby was thrown forward, between the front two seats and colliding with the dashboard. The front airbags had deployed, and Carla's seatbelt saved her life. The impact of the airbag gravely disoriented her, as did the shattered side window.

Fields and Ed were jerked forward, also without their seatbelts. Fields' head struck the back of Carla's seat and he was nearly knocked unconscious. Ed's left arm, still pinned by the damaged door, was torn at the elbow, tendons and bone severing. He felt a sudden warmth, an extreme burn, and pain jolted up his arm, snaking through his torso.

Bastian, meanwhile, was caught on the back of the cab, the impact jarring his stomach but the Suit compensating for it.

He was mostly dazed from the suddenness and shock of it.

The truck had wedged itself in the diameter of the sinkhole, at an angle. The back bumper and warped tailgate rested on the raised, cracked asphalt at one end; in the front, the grille basically sandwiched the edge of the torn road.

Smoke continued to pour out of the hood, obscuring Bastian's view of Sam. The metal creaked and the chassis groaned, its weight occupying the sinkhole, everything between the grille and back bumper suspended above whatever oblivion awaited below them.

*Hell itself, far as I'm concerned.*

Bastian grunted and gathered his bearings, while the inhabitants of the truck groaned and struggled to do the same. Ed's painful whimpers were the most prominent. Bastian knelt beside Cory's covered corpse in the bed, which had rolled face-down during the wreck.

He peered into the cab and reached through with his right hand to shake Fields, hoping to keep him from passing out.

He couldn't help but notice the red streaks around the hole in the windshield, in front of the driver's seat. This made Bastian wince, and fear Sam's condition.

"What the…fuck?" Fields grumbled, clutching his head and finally sitting back, grimacing.

Abby was surprisingly conscious, but bleeding badly from a forehead wound, which could be correlated with a smear of blood above the dashboard A/C vents. The makeshift bandage on his injured hand was now all red, though a dark shade, due to the black fabric. Abby himself, however, braved through the pain and groaned under his breath as he crawled toward the backseat.

He paused, basically straddling the center console, to check on Carla at his left.

Meanwhile, Bastian shifted his focus to Ed, hoping to help him somehow.

Twelve long seconds had passed since the truck came to a violent stop above the sinkhole.

A perimeter lamppost at the edge of the Miramar base to the truck's far right had been affected by the quake. It now leaned in that direction, at an acute angle.

One of the two LED bulbs flickered before going off, but the other stayed on, dimly illuminating the truck.

The partial darkness that covered Bastian's position, where the light's reach ended, was like an omen of what was to come.

Beneath the truck emanated another kind of glow—fiery orange, and pulsing.

Now the inevitable happened.

Bastian first heard the truck creak and groan on its chassis, and then he felt it actually rock side to side. Some low thumps and bumps against the metallic undercarriage.

His eyes widened and he withdrew from the rear window to reload the Supe. He ejected two spent shells with a quickness, one of them plinking his visor. He doubled over the cart of weapons and frantically searched for the drawer of 12-gauge shells. Once he found them, he inadvertently dumped the contents into the bed but didn't complain. He scooped two up and loaded the smoking barrels, just in time to witness a gang of Crawlers creep up around the sides of the truck, from below.

*Below.*

He couldn't fathom what might follow them.

There were two on either side of the bed, rising up around the large wheel wells. Two more on both sides of the XL cab, and a ninth—a *ninth*—crawling around a fender, and onto the hood.

Fortunately for Sam, wherever he was on the other side of the column of smoke, the Crawler faced the windshield instead of the road.

It felt like two or even three drawn-out seconds of just staring at the creatures now surrounding him, before Carla suddenly came to and screamed.

This punctuated their surge of motion.

They snarled and hissed as they vehemently crawled into the cab and bed, concurrently as if driven by one mind.

Bastian heard Abby repeatedly scream "no, no" as one of the creatures clawed through the airbag to overcome Carla. He tried to fight it off with his weaponless hands and arms.

At the same time, Bastian was faced with his own predicament.

The two Crawlers that poured into the bed over the left side, in front of him, were easily taken care of. He aimed down, not even giving them a chance to rise to their feet. At point-blank range, closer than the Legionnaire earlier, just one of the barrels sufficed against both of them. The Supe thundered and the discharged bolo rounds sheared through their heads and torsos, simultaneously penetrating the mat and lodging into the metallic floor of the bed.

The other two that crawled in behind him now latched onto the Suit, their lanky arms embracing him, claws scratching and teeth gnashing armor, to no avail.

It was nonetheless disturbing to be so close to enemies that would have otherwise torn him to shreds had he not been wearing the Suit.

Through the sounds of wet growling and the grating claws on armor, he discerned the struggle of the people in the cab. From Carla to Abby, to the severely wounded Ed, and Fields. They were all far worse off than Bastian, and utterly defenseless, save for a couple of weapons somewhere in the truck, likely since scattered after their wreck.

This thought came to Bastian like its own collision. He braced for it and then retaliated, motivated to defeat this small horde and save these people.

*Nobody else is gonna die on my watch*, he convinced himself, and suddenly doubled forward, reaching back at the same time, throwing one of the Crawlers over his shoulder. Its back struck the left side of the bed, bending unnaturally and breaking. Like a ragdoll it rolled off the truck. Bastian elbowed the other in its side with his right arm, inadvertently lacerating its flesh with the folded chainsaw. Then he put his back to the rear window, facing the Crawler less than three feet away. Tucking the Supe under his left arm, he fired it and the bolo rounds ravaged its chest.

He didn't pause to confirm the deaths of his enemies. He didn't even reload. Both threats and friendlies were at too intimate a range to risk firing weapons in the cab.

Bastian himself, in the Suit, was too large to crawl through the rear window and try to help that way.

He lunged around the right side of the cab, grateful for his extended reach in the Suit, and grabbed the Crawler currently wrestling with Fields, who was supine in the backseat. The creature hissed and looked back, then Bastian exerted his enhanced might through his right arm, and flung it out of the cab altogether. It rolled across the pavement to the right of the road.

Bastian stretched to grab the Crawler halfway through the passenger window.

Carla stopped flailing and screaming, and somehow managed to grab the pistol she had earlier, and put it to good use. Abby himself was startled by her maneuver, as she retrieved it from the floor by her feet, after the Crawler had practically shredded the airbag trying to get to her, and suddenly fired it at the creature. Bullets perforated its face, throat, and upper chest in the foray.

Bastian witnessed its body fall out of the cab and disintegrate half a second later.

He would have liked to feel triumphant for Carla, and Abby, but wasn't given the chance for even a fragment of such an emotion.

Two more Crawlers emerged from the hole below, crawling over the sides of the bed, favoring a low stance, attacking him like massive insects. They tried to yank his legs out from under him but his stance was too resolute, his footing surer than even theirs.

He turned around and immediately stomped one of their half-skulls into the mat with a firm heel. Though he almost slipped in the wet mess it left behind, he managed to knee the other in the face when it rose to try to take advantage of him. It staggered back, but not far enough that he wasn't able to take a swing at it, chainsaw protracted. The blades revved and caught the creature in the left bicep, chewing through skin and flesh and bone, then sticking into its side, above its ribs, and messily grinding through that.

Vivid red blood sprayed Bastian's visor.

The Crawler squalled a terrible sound as the chainsaw tore through its chest from the side, ultimately reaching its right armpit, where Bastian, his teeth vibrating in his skull, was able to wrench the chainsaw free, and witness his halved enemy topple.

He retracted the chainsaw and faced the cab again, not necessarily tired, but in a crazed state of bloodshed, wreaking it instead of wading through it for once.

He glimpsed the Crawler on the hood of the truck start to squeeze through the hole in the windshield. It used its hands to widen the gap, Plexiglas ripping its fingers and palms, but the creature seemed unfazed.

Unable to get to it from here, and worried about Ed and Abby, Bastian ducked to not only peer into the cab but reach in, too. One of the Crawlers had its jaws clamped onto Ed's right shoulder, claws digging into his legs. His back was against the seat, sitting upright, and the entirety of the creature's body was inside the cab. Bastian snatched it by the half-skull, digging his fingers into its cranium, pinching brain mass against bone, crushing much of it in the process. The creature let out a foul sound of panic and pain.

Bastian, gritting his teeth but really not needing to exert much, thanks to the Suit, pulled the Crawler toward him. Into the center of the backseat.

Fields, who had recovered not only his mindset but also the pistol he had dropped, now sat up and fired two rounds into the Crawler's right temple, aiming up at an angle. Bastian withdrew his hand a moment before, and the bullets missed Ed by a few inches.

"Noooo!" Abby screamed.

The creature in the front seat had overwhelmed Carla, severing the hand that held the pistol using its claws, and clamping onto her chin with its vile mouth. When it pulled away, it took her mandible with it.

Abby would have vomited had he not been overtaken with rage and adrenaline. He lunged at the creature, and somehow tackled it, wrestling it *through* the passenger window.

"Abby!" Fields shouted.

Bastian saw the other creature now crawling through the hole in the windshield. It had extended an arm in hopes of seizing Abby's leg or foot before he went through the window. But it was unable.

Bastian made sure that it would be unable to do anything ever again. With his head and one shoulder squeezed through the rear window, he reached down and drew the Duke.

"Ears!"

Fields complied, covering his ears. Ed was dying from blood loss and had surrendered any attempt of regaining control of his intact arm.

Bastian withdrew only so that he could aim the Duke properly, extending his wielding hand into the cab. He fired without being able to see his target, but just…knowing.

The gun went off like a thunderclap.

When he ducked to view the damage, he saw as he anticipated—the Crawler's brains on the windshield, which itself was barely intact after the gunshot.

"C'mon, Buddy." Bastian said, reaching for

Fields.

"Help Abby!" Fields snapped, frothing at the mouth.

Two more Crawlers rose up from either side of the truck. Both immediately entered the cab, one per backseat window. Bastian cursed under his breath and yanked on Fields' uniform, pulling him through the rear window. He kicked and exclaimed, frantically firing the pistol at the Crawler that reached for him through the window to his right.

The pistol went dry after two shots.

One of the bullets had caught the creature in the brow, not fatal, but delaying it.

Bastian let go of him as soon as his back hit the mat in the bed, and then blindly reached for Ed. Something sharp clamped onto his gloved hand, and owed thanks to the armored gauntlet.

Instead of immediately retracting his hand, he wiggled his fingers to confirm what was happening, and then reached…deeper.

Blindly fumbling through the rear window, his helmet pressed to the back of the cab, he seized what he presumed was the Crawler's tongue, at its base, and yanked it out of its throat. The creature regurgitated blood and other fluids onto the backseat. Bastian let go and ducked to witness the reality of what he had done.

To his regret, however, Ed was…

Not a hint of life existed in his eye. One of them had been torn, or eaten, from its socket.

Somewhere not too far off, Abby hollered. It was

a wordless utterance of ire—neither agony nor fear. Although, in Abby's current state, Bastian imagined that it did have its roots in pain.

Fields sat up fast.

Bastian stood and looked to the right.

Just then the truck rocked side to side. Something big emerged from below. A Tyrant rose out of the hole, its bulky shoulders nudging the truck's undercarriage but not dislodging it. Metal scraped and as the vehicle rocked to the left, Bastian almost lost his footing. The Tyrant climbed out and lumbered toward Abby, on the pavement twenty feet away.

Fields rolled around in the bed, less composed than Bastian, who dug through the cart for a weapon. He shouldered the ROT-20 and was about to fire when more Crawlers emerged from the hole. They didn't just crawl over the sides of the truck, however, some sprang into the air and others flooded it.

A certified horde of them.

Obstructing his aim and nearly overpowering him. The ROT-20 was knocked out of his clutches and, at least fortunate for Fields, they focused on Bastian. Trying to claw their way into his Suit. Or rip open his visor. Trying their damnedest.

The damned themselves.

Bastian cursed under his breath as he wrestled on his feet against the horde. He could barely see anything past the upright Crawlers trying to overpower him. Lurid faces deluging his vision. He managed to fling one or two to the side, and speared another on his Exoblade, wanting to use the chainsaw but unable in the foray to see where Fields was.

And yet, in between the storm of creatures, he caught a glimpse of Abby, although he wished he hadn't.

The Tyrant reached Abby, who had somehow slain the Crawler he had been wrestling with, using a knife sheathed to his thigh. It would not fare against the horned beast, however, although this didn't keep Abby from trying.

Bastian only caught glimpses, which was more than enough, and too much.

Abby jabbed the knife at the Tyrant, but it swung at his arm, breaking it at the elbow. The next thing Bastian saw was Abby—*I don't even know his full fucking name*—being impaled on the beast's right arm, its clawed fingers wiggling in the air, slick red.

Bastian lost his line of sight after that, and rage filled him something fierce.

*Everyone…keeps…dying…around me.*

He kicked a Crawler off of his Exoblade, elbowed another that had literally climbed onto his shoulder, and then drove the serrated tungsten down into a third's half-skull. It didn't just split like a cut melon; the Exoblade cleaved bone and flesh all the way down to the creature's sternum, where the tungsten caught. A bright red arc sprayed up into Bastian's face, coating his visor and armored chest with evil blood.

*Pure evil.*

Bastian simultaneously kicked the Crawler he had just elbowed, in the knee. The joint blew out and the creature let out a pained sound, but didn't fall. Its claws raked across Bastian's green chest-plate, the INFERNO armor unyielding.

Meanwhile, Fields took advantage of Bastian's popularity and snagged the ROT-20 from the mat, then *rolled* over the side of the bed. He alighted gracelessly, but managed to keep his balance.

Despite the man's small stature, he yelled something unintelligible at the top of his lungs, and one would have guessed he was a much taller, larger man.

Fields fired the shotgun twice into the air, gathering the attention of the Tyrant. Bastian glimpsed it again, this time witnessing it pull its forearm out of Abby—in a downward motion. The grisly cavity in his stomach merged with his pelvis, and there Abby's body parted before flopping to the pavement.

Bastian grimaced.

Fields wobbled. He wanted to charge the beast with all of his energy, but his body reacted differently. He vomited onto the asphalt, a few feet from the curb. And then he started to run, wielding the shotgun and stumbling at first.

"Fields! Wait!" Bastian shouted after him, but it was no use.

The Crawler with the broken knee now latched itself onto his left side, claws frenzying over his visor and armor. Another popped up from below, vaulting the right wheel well in the bed, and immediately latching itself onto Bastian. He was caught with his right arm down.

Two more of the gaunt, half-skull abominations sprung onto the hood of the truck, climbing up to the roof. They casted malformed shadows onto Bastian and the other creatures in the bed.

The vehicle groaned as the repeatedly added weight on it threatened to dislodge it in the worst manner. Bastian armed the chainsaw attached to his right gauntlet. The teeth spun madly, and he rose his arm between the Crawler's legs. The blade effortlessly chewed through its groin, and kept climbing, eviscerating it from below. The creature's body frenetically vibrated, and it howled a bloodcurdling sound.

Bastian tried to use his Exoblade on another creature, while the two on the roof prepared to pounce him, but another pair restrained him from behind.

They wouldn't be able to hold him for long, but he reckoned that the truck was going to fall at any given moment.

And Fields—

He tried to glance in that direction, but his view was blocked.

Then he heard gunfire, and hoped that Fields was able to somehow catch the Tyrant off-guard or at least buy himself some time.

But it wasn't the ROT-20 that lit up.

A volley of high-caliber bullets, every fifth round a tracer that streaked the darkness white-hot, tore through the Crawlers on top of the truck. Bastian witnessed their bodies birth holes the size of his gloved fist. They were ripped apart in the blink of an eye. Their vivid blood misted Bastian's helmet and visor.

This startled and confounded the creatures currently restraining him, which he took advantage of.

Except, he didn't just shake them off and go for the kill. He actually shoved them out of the bed, having to kick a third over the side.

Their bodies rolled or crawled away from the truck, whether by impulse or to assess the situation. This was something Bastian had already done, merely by looking forward and spotting the Humvee M1151 on the other side of the sinkhole, facing the truck.

Regardless of the Crawler's strategy—or lack thereof—they had made a grave mistake. Once they were clear of the truck, a barrage of fully-automatic gunfire perforated them until nothing remained.

Bastian's immediate surroundings were no longer obstructed.

He saw Fields kneeling on the sidewalk, hands over his head, as bullets flew around him. From Bastian's perspective, they were in no danger of hitting him. Whoever was firing the machinegun—Bastian recognized it based on the sound alone, confirmed by a glimpse of the armored turret mount—knew what they were doing.

However, the same couldn't be said for the Tyrant standing over Abby's body. Of course, it wasn't standing for long. A steady stream of .50-caliber rounds ripped into its body, reducing it to the size of a Crawler before its bloodied corpse smacked the pavement.

And then the firing ceased.

Bastian would bet that everyone's ears were ringing terribly, so he was especially thankful for the helmet.

With his bearings intact, he made sure that both

gauntlet attachments were safely retracted, and vaulted over the side of the bed. He landed on the asphalt, clear of the sinkhole, and hurried to check on Fields, simply waving at the Humvee and company—it wasn't alone— in front of the wedged truck.

"You good? You hurt?" Bastian asked Fields, stopping to stand beside him.

Fields slowly lifted his torso, kneeling on the pavement, and his gaze solidified on Abby's corpse ten feet away. The embers of the slain Tyrant were now being carried off by a gentle night wind. The dark, almost black ash on the concrete wafted until it was no more. But Abby's body remained in all its gruesome details.

Bastian saw Fields' head turn to the left, and his expression of grief warped into something meaner. He rose to his feet and brushed past Bastian; physically unable to literally push him aside, Fields nonetheless acted as if he wasn't there. And for a moment Bastian understood Fields' misplaced rage, so he let him by.

After a rugged sigh and shake of his head, Bastian took a deep breath and raised his visor. He turned to see Fields marching toward the two Humvees and tank opposite the sinkhole, where the truck remained lodged. The red-orange glow beneath it had completely diminished.

Fields was about ten feet from the nearest soldier, who was among three who had exited the Humvees, when he began yelling.

"Where the *fuck* have *you* been? Huh!?"

Bastian didn't need to see Fields' face to know that tears were bolting down his cheeks, eyes red and teeth bared.

"Where…the *fuck*…have—" His voice had shifted from screaming to growling as he neared one of the Marines, who were in their basic training fatigues, all of them idly carrying assault rifles. Fields collided with the dumbstruck man and he took a hold of his fatigues with both fists, shaking violently and abruptly screaming in his face. "Where *were* you!? Huh!? What…"

Another soldier rushed over to pry Fields off of his comrade, which didn't take much effort. Fields quickly crumbled, staggering back and almost falling, but then Bastian was there to catch him. Instead he rebounded off of Bastian's unyielding Suit, and braced himself on the front grille of the nearest Humvee.

He sobbed out the words "what took you so long?" with his head bowed.

Bastian took another deep breath and his gaze swept the two soldiers now standing in front of him, their eyes scrutinizing his Suit.

"I gotta thank you all for showing up when you did," Bastian said, his voice loud enough for the gunner on the nearest Humvee to hear. The perforated barrel of the .50-caliber machinegun was still smoking.

In addition to the headlights on the two Humvees, there were foglights mounted on all four corners of the tank, providing a stark white glow with a ten-foot radius. Additionally, a directional spotlight was mounted beside the gunner's hatch, but nobody manned it.

Despite Bastian's audible statement, which almost rudely contrasted what Fields had been exclaiming, there was no retort from him. Fields was simmering down and sorting through his own grief. Assessing the situation and prioritizing internally.

Bastian took this under consideration.

"Unfortunately," he added, his tone grim but loud and clear, "it wasn't soon enough…we've suffered terrible losses. As you…as you can see."

One of the three Marines now on foot, and farthest from Bastian and the other two, whistled. He grabbed all of their attention, save Fields', and then beckoned his comrades with a gesture.

"Check 'em," the soldier, about fifteen feet to Bastian's left, called out.

The two young men standing before Bastian nodded at what he presumed was their superior, and then dispersed. One of them broke off to his right, making a beeline for Abby's body. He was easily the most apparent casualty, but Bastian understood from a tactical—and respectful—standpoint, to confirm the fallen.

The other soldier joined his superior to check the pickup truck. The superior took the driver side, and he went to the other.

Bastian sighed and tended to Fields.

There were still uniformed men behind the wheel of each Humvee. They studiously observed Bastian, Fields, and occasionally their own comrades, from where they sat, behind the windshields. In addition to them, though each Humvee had a roof-mounted machinegun, only one was manned. The vehicles were a light beige-brown, and showed no wear or tear, although Bastian imagined—hoped—that, if their enemies weren't prone to evaporate upon death, then the armor would be covered with blood.

Yet for all he knew those that they just mowed down were the first threats these men had seen tonight. It seemed unlikely, however, given how much time had passed since the first quake.

*Feels like ages ago*, Bastian thought, remembering Maggie's death and cringing from it. *Feels like a minute ago...*

He was conflicted. Emotionally, the enormity was fresher than his last breath. But his retention was detached; mentally, recalling certain events along the way, and the moments leading up to his family's slaughter, it might as well have been a decade past.

"I'm the last to conform to clichés," Bastian said, hovering over Fields' shoulder, looking down at him. His voice was low, audible enough just for Fields, and maybe the gunner a few feet away. "But...there was *nothing* you could've done. Not even me. We were *overrun*. These guys saved our asses for sure. You have to—"

Fields sniffled and stood up straight all of a sudden. He backed away from the Humvee, and Bastian, by just a few steps.

He nodded briskly.

"Of course," he said. "Of course they did. I'm not blind."

Bastian nodded once. He looked around.

"They're confirming the casualties."

His gaze swept over the two Humvees, and then the tank, which he was pleased to see, but not terribly surprised. There were at least half a dozen stationed at the Miramar military base, in addition to a full battalion of Humvees. The surprise factor aside, he *was* however extremely relieved that these men managed to survive the debacle and make it out alive. Of course, their presence outside of the fortified Miramar perimeter gave him a bad feeling.

On top of all the other bad feelings, but he couldn't afford the nausea right now.

His eyes pivoted back to Fields, who seemed to stand there as if awaiting orders.

Bastian was unfathomably grateful for such loyalty. It also terrified him, too. He feared Fields' death more than his own at this point, but ultimately knew that it was he who needed to reach the Monolith, before anyone else.

The INFERNO Suit was the key, or so he had put all his faith into over the last couple of hours.

"You know we don't have time to grieve, though," Bastian said, his eyes connecting with Fields on a level that felt almost telepathic. "Or at least I don't."

"Don't think I'm backing out, now," Fields said firmly.

"I can't have you dying on my watch."

"You're not a babysitter. If and when I die, it'll be on my own goddamn watch."

Bastian stifled a smirk. He nodded.

"Better go get that shotgun. I'll snag the rest of

the hardware."

Fields got to it, adding nothing else. He was fueled now by his own vengeance, which Bastian might have normally tried to dissuade, but given his own trauma, he empathized.

Now it was Bastian who whistled, to snatch the attention of the three Marines on foot. The one who had checked on Abby, and was now conversing with Fields about the ROT-20 on the ground, only glanced. He then returned to talk to Fields, who, from Bastian's perspective, appeared to be apologetic.

Bastian returned his focus to the truck, particularly the back end, and the other two soldiers who now assembled by the tailgate.

"New tech, huh?" the man on his left said. He was probably in his upper thirties, a little grizzled but not even half what Bastian was, let alone before this mess.

Bastian imagined that all of their superior officers had died in the wake of this.

"Very new, but very tested," Bastian replied. "I appreciate you guys not being startled by me and trying to shoot."

The superior, whose insignia represented Lance Corporal, smirked briefly.

"Nah, we're not *that* green. We know about CHERI. I mean, from a speculative standpoint."

"Allow me to clarify," Bastian said. He wrenched the tailgate open, which would have taken several men, considering the damage it had sustained from the wreck. He then reached into the bed and seized the cart's handle. He hauled it out, the metallic wheel mounts grating across the mat, and then the tailgate. He hoisted it over before setting it down on the asphalt a few feet from the raised edge of the hellhole.

"Jesus, man," the Lance Corporal said. "What is that suit *made* of?"

"Tungsten alloy, mostly," Bastian replied nonchalantly. "Kevlar padding and interstitial knitting."

"Heavy?"

"Not to me," Bastian said. "I'd love to answer more questions, but me and my wingman over there are on a tight schedule."

"Oh?" the Lance Corporal scoffed, amused. "You've somewhere to be?"

"Calipatria, yes."

"Cali—" the man stopped himself mid-word. He raised his eyebrows and shook his head. "You have *family* there, or you just wanna commit suicide?"

"Have you even seen the broadcast, mister?" the other soldier asked.

At this time, Fields and the third soldier were approaching, side by side. The ROT-20 was in Fields' hands again. The other soldier's face appeared a little deprived of color, sickly even; Bastian guessed he didn't witness Abby's remains with an iron stomach.

"We've seen it, yeah," Bastian said, and gestured at Fields as he arrived. "And I've been over this with him, too. We're going to Calipatria, no matter what. If you can't afford to give us a ride there, I beg that you at least drive us 'til we find a suitable vehicle to haul us and our gear there."

It was the first time Bastian had enlisted the help of others, but given the armored vehicles and additional firepower, he couldn't ignore the opportunity.

The Lance Corporal took a deep breath and exchanged solemn glances with his two comrades, who were Privates. Despite their grim looks, they were not devoid of curiosity.

"What exactly…do you have in mind?"

# 14

Two up-armored military Humvees, each with fortified turret mounts, and an M1A3 Abrams tank. Fields supported Bastian's decision to request an escort, especially after he had simmered down and apologized to the soldier. Now that Bastian's suicidal plan was vented, there was little to debate. His urgency was as palpable to the soldiers as the chaos in the air, following the Monolith's touchdown. Its origins remained unknown, and unspoken. Not even the Marines that had agreed to escort Bastian and Fields to Calipatria were open to that discussion.

Fear had many faces, and no human was able to mask it so easily.

Bastian, with all of his military experience, and now even in the seemingly insurmountable Suit, was not immune to the face of fear.

He wore it bravely, though.

It was all anyone could do at the moment.

In spite of all this, the eight Marines present had no qualms with supporting Bastian's objective.

While his goal was undeniably suicidal—calling it "dangerous" was too much of an understatement—they couldn't argue his good intentions. They knew courage when they saw it, and there was an infinitesimally fine line between bravery and madness when it came to situations like this.

And this particular catastrophe was genuinely unmatched, which left the men with shaken rationale.

Bastian didn't have time to go through introductions with each of them, but their superior—Lance Corporal Henry Elam—was briskly communicative with his men. There were no objections to helping Bastian, as they had already given themselves 'to the cause.'

"We were in the showers when the first reports came in," Private Terrence Irving said, while Bastian and Private Brett Preston rigged together something for the tank to haul his cart of weapons. He had insisted that the tank take this responsibility, so as to liberate the Humvees from the burden of hauling something that might limit their maneuverability.

Nobody could object.

Standing in the area at the time was also Fields, Elam, and one of the other soldiers from the Humvees. The gunner remained, keeping an eye and ear out, but also heeding the conversation behind the tank.

The other two of the eight Marines in their group stayed inside the tank, not wishing to leave their stations. They were, however, privy to the conversation taking place, and the decision that had been made to escort Bastian.

All the details of his Suit had not been disclosed, but assumptions could be made without much room to misinterpret.

Bastian figured there was nothing wrong with that; it was pretty straightforward, his intentions, and his stubborn faith in the Suit—plus what Fields could testify—cajoled the Marines.

"It was crazy, to say the least," young Irving continued. "Thirty-some, buck-naked Marines rushing outta the showers, some throwing on towels, others not giving a fuck, to listen to this emergency broadcast. Some guys just made a beeline for the barracks to grab what they could and get out; lot of our ranks on base got families in the area, ya know? As soon as reports came in of…an *unidentified* enemy…well, that's when the shit hit the fan big-time, and those with families in the area, or even So-Cal in general, *split*. We 'lost' a lot of our senior officers that way."

"And we lost the rest, the worst way," Elam muttered.

"Y'all are all that's left of Miramar?" Bastian asked through his open visor, after securing the hitch behind the Abrams tank.

Irving shrugged and sighed. He wiped beads of sweat that glistened on his dark brow, with the back of his hand. The lights mounted on the tank washed them all in a white radiance that made them sitting ducks in the night.

Bastian previously suggested they hurry, adding to his preexisting state of urgency, lest another sinkhole open up nearby. Or directly under their feet, worst case.

This helped Bastian's cause for haste.

While none of the soldiers directly answered his

question, he was sharp enough to take the hint. The Marines certainly didn't want to admit that the two Companies in which they belonged were wiped out.

Bastian had heard enough, and didn't want to pry into the details of their losses.

These men came from C Company, 2$^{nd}$ Platoon. The grim looks on their faces spoke volumes of grief and bewilderment, which Bastian understood all too well, and could decipher as if another language. Although, he couldn't empathize on the same level. He had never suffered such losses like these while on tour.

"And the aircraft?" he couldn't help but ask.

Afterall, Miramar was not solely a military training facility. The base was primarily an airfield and grounds for various squadrons of helicopter and fighter jets, part of the Marine Expeditionary Force, a joint task force headquartered at Camp Pendleton, outside of Oceanside, California.

Bastian couldn't wrap his head around what was going on down there, or at all the other military bases around the country. How were they handling this? Clearly their attacks on the Monolith were futile, and they hadn't dispatched any ground units into the greater San Diego area yet, or maybe they just underestimated the enemy.

"Can't fly without pilots," Elam said, sullen.

Bastian grimaced and shook his head.

"So much for a fortified perimeter," he mumbled disgruntledly.

"Against ground troops, maybe," Elam said. He then scoffed and shook his head. He looked out into the night, beyond their nimbus of light. "Who knew an enemy without projectile weapons could be so fucking deadly?"

"I'm one of the last people to badmouth the U.S. military, but…" Preston started, but was immediately interrupted.

All of the other Marines present—even the Humvee gunner—scoffed and laughed mockingly. Some of them made remarks of disbelief under their breaths. Bastian didn't need to be a rocket scientist to deduce that Private Preston here was, in addition to easily being the handsomest of the men present, clean-cut and chisel-jawed, the big-mouth one of the group. Every platoon had at least one; a man who questioned everything and usually masked serious issues with crude humor.

Preston scoffed and shook his head at the onslaught of jeering from his comrades, while Bastian kept to himself and tested the hitched trailer's stability.

"I'm serious, now," Preston said, gesturing with palms out. "I *love* the U.S. military—total faith in 'em. But *this*…tsk, tsk. Whoever's pushing papers in D.C. and calling the shots needs to wise up. They're underestimating the threat big-time."

"I agree," Bastian finally said, sighing and standing up.

He took a couple of steps back from the two-wheeled trailer, which had previously been hitched to a civilian SUV across the road, loaded with lawn gear. It had a foot-high, steel mesh railing on all sides, and had certainly seen better days. But the axles were sturdy, and the tires weren't flat, miraculously.

When he realized that the other Marines, save a pleased-looking Preston, were staring at him in disbelief, he shrugged.

"The last part, I mean," Bastian added.

Everyone relaxed and mumbled incoherently amongst themselves.

Bastian glanced at Fields and together they simpered fleetingly before shaking their heads, as if reading each other's minds. Bastian then 'dusted off' his palms and stooped to retrieve the cart of CHERI weapons.

"Go on, go on," he heard one of the men mutter behind him, amongst themselves.

He slid the cart onto the trailer, which was louder than he would've liked, but when he went to shut the tailgate, the grating broke clean off. He rolled his eyes and tossed it onto the grassy median, so as to avoid making anymore unnecessary noise.

When he turned to look at the three Marines, and Fields, two of the soldiers were gently pushing the third toward Bastian, as if high school boys egging on their friend to ask a girl out.

It was strange, but then again, they were young Marines. Bastian didn't have that thought derogatorily; he fully understood.

Irving stepped up and cleared his throat.

"You said you were an ex-SEAL, right?"

Bastian nodded. "Army, too. Ranger."

Irving's eyes widened and he nodded. Then he clapped his hands together and rubbed his palms.

"Cut to it, Irving, for fuck's sake," Bastian said

bluntly, glancing at his gauntleted wrist, as if he was wearing a watch.

"Right, sorry. So…you know what a MOAB is, right?"

"Massive Ordnance Air Blast," Fields blurted. Everyone looked at him, taken aback. He just shrugged. "A tour in Afghanistan. Well, three years…"

Nobody said anything.

"I made some mistakes. Substance abuse. It was…a long time ago. Mentally, at least." Fields cleared his throat. "*Anyway*…yeah, a MOAB. What about it?"

Irving coughed and appeared mortified to elaborate. Bastian was intuitive enough to get the hint.

"You think they're gonna drop a MOAB on the greater San Diego area?"

Now all eyes were on Bastian, including Irving, who appeared the least surprised.

"Just to wipe out the ground threats," Irving said, his voice dry.

"You're talking…a few hundred civilian casualties, easy," Bastian said grimly. "Maybe as many as a couple thou, depending on how many survivors there still are."

Irving shrugged coldly, hating to admit his next statement.

"Would beat the hell out of losing more troops trying to sweep the streets."

Bastian scoffed and shook his head, heavily gloved hands on his armored waist.

"No…no, they wouldn't. Couldn't." He looked

up at Irving, but due to the Suit was still looking down at the tall, lean, young man. "They'd send Apache scouts first, clean up from the air. *Then* amass tactical ground teams."

"I wish I believed you. But…it's a whole hell of a lot o' ground to cover, so urgently."

Bastian felt his stomach curl. He turned his back on Irving and the others, including Fields. His aged yet acute eyes scanned the surrounding night. Nothing moved. Nothing gleamed, outside of the disc of light they occupied. His gaze pitched up to the Humvee gunner with the Private First Class patch. He was easily within earshot of their whole conversation, and despite his watchful surveillance of their surroundings, he appeared to have an active ear.

"PFC," Bastian said, drawing his attention. He was probably in his mid-thirties, with stubble and a pronounced brow. "What do you gotta say about all this shit?"

The gunner shrugged nonchalantly.

"Please, humor me," Bastian said, "just be blunt, though. I wanna scram."

"I do, too, hoss," the guy said, with a thick Bostonian accent. "Never been a fan of playing the sitting duck. Fifty-cal or not. But a Mother of All Bombs, right on Diego's head? I dunno. Washington *can* be cruel. I wouldn't put it past 'em. Greater good and all that shit."

*I like this guy. Who* is *this guy?*

Bastian just nodded, then looked at the other Marines and blindly pointed at the PFC gunner, as if to say "this fucking guy."

"Ah, yes," Elam nodded. "That there is Donnie. PFC Sean Donahue. He's got a mouth on him for sure. Whether it's used to spit wisdom or bullshit, though, varies greatly."

Bastian smirked. "I'd say the prior, for now."

"Humbled, buddy," Donnie said casually. "My word's not golden, though, I'll admit." He cleared his throat as he practically slumped over the machinegun, its belt of ammunition clinking softly, and nodded down at Elam. "But really, LC, can we go now?"

"That eager to help RoboCop here?" Elam asked through a thin sneer.

*If one more person...*

"Well, I can't argue with his motives, crazy as they may be, but no," Donnie said, "I mostly just don't wanna keep sitting still. It's a miracle they haven't tried to crash our party yet."

"I second that vote, LC," Irving said, raising a forefinger.

"The longer we wait," Bastian added, "the worse the situation gets."

"How sure are you," Elam asked, his voice down-tuning into something grimmer than before, "that destroying the Monolith will stop all of this?"

Bastian sighed and shrugged. "Look, for all I know, there's one of those things on every continent. Maybe even every country. Or...just Calipatria. I won't lie; the odds and doubts are lining out the door to take a swing at me. No matter what I...believe."

"A leap of faith," Preston said, devoid of humor. There was something genuinely sentimental about his words in that moment. "You're taking a leap of faith."

Bastian nodded.

"We all are, if we choose to help him," Fields said. "And for the better, for hope, in this hopeless shit-show."

"There's one problem, buddy," Preston said, firmly approaching Fields.

"What's that?" Fields asked, taken off guard but internally preparing himself to become defensive.

Preston stopped a foot or two from Fields and put his hand on the shorter man's shoulder.

"We're shy one gunner."

Fields broke into a chuckle.

It was the 'lightest' Bastian had seen him act since the truculent death of his friend and colleague of sorts, Abby.

Fields glanced at the other Humvee, sans a gunner, and then at Elam, Irving, and eventually Preston.

"Why not you? Or Irving?"

"I'm no good with it," Irving admitted, without a touch of shame.

"And I prefer shotgun," Preston shrugged. "The seat, that is, not the weapon."

"Right. Well…it's been a few years, but yeah, I'm down."

"No, you're *up*. Gotta stand, though."

"Am I tall enough in that thing?" Fields chuckled nervously. "Fucking bigger than any Humvee I've ever been in."

The two M1151A2's were about sixteen feet long, seven and a half wide, with an eighteen-inch ground clearance, and nearly five tons fully equipped. They were up-armored, expanded-capacity variants, a couple of feet longer and wider, not to mention remarkably heavier, than a standard M1151 Humvee.

"There's an adjustable platform between the seats, no concern," Preston grinned, playfully slapping Fields' arm. He then gestured up at Donnie. "He may *look* tall, but Donnie there's only 5'8"."

"Good," Bastian butted in, "'cause there's only enough room on that lil' trailer for me and the gear."

He glanced back at the pickup truck still wedged into the hellhole.

*Because that's what it fucking is*, he subconsciously convinced himself.

However, his focus was not the hole through which their enemy primarily surfaced, but the men and woman he had just about called a team. Short-lived friends, in every sense of the phrase.

The son's corpse in the bed of the truck, and his father's in the backseat. The cousin. The husband. The wife. The friend. The people.

Souls, condemned or freed, by their brutal deaths, he couldn't be sure.

An ugliness ran through his veins.

He looked back at the Marines, who seemed to await him eagerly.

"All doubts and admission of insanity aside," Bastian said, "you lot *do* believe the strategy of my plan, yes?"

"It's quite sound, really," Irving was the first to say, and then Elam stepped forward.

"If our Lieutenant was here, he would've jumped on it the second you mentioned it, and not have waited a moment longer."

"Hell, LC," Preston simpered wryly, "he probably would've cursed himself for not thinking of it himself, sooner."

"The EMP factor, you mean?" Irving asked.

"Yeah, well, whoever your Lieutenant was, wouldn't have known what we've been developing at CHERI over the last decade. The ionized plasma source of power has been of the utmost confidentiality."

"He was a paranoid man, though, that's for damn sure," Elam said. And then he muttered: "God rest his soul…"

"At any rate," Bastian cleared his throat, "it's the best and only plan we've got against that godforsaken structure in Calipatria. The invisible EMP field nullifies anything electronic, but my INFERNO Suit doesn't run on traditional electricity; the ionized plasma shouldn't be affected."

"Shouldn't," Preston said, sounding hollow as he repeated the word with solemn emphasis.

"Better than '*won't*,'" Donnie said. "And that's enough motivation for me. Now…can we *please* get the fuck outta here?"

His Bostonian accent was so strong that it was almost like another language, but when he said that last thing, Bastian understood it deep down.

"Might I advise, Lance Corporal?" Bastian said to Elam. "Lead with Donnie's Humvee, center the tank, and let Fields pull in the rear."

"Sounds mint to me," Elam said. He looked at the tank and whistled, then gestured above his head to indicate moving out.

"Which one will you be riding in?"

"The back Humvee," Elam replied. "I'll sit behind the driver. Help Fields reload."

Fields hadn't heard this. He was already boarding the Humvee and getting situated through the gunner's hatch. He appeared delighted, at least, that there were armored plates surrounding the hatch, likely different from the last one he was in many years ago.

*Not that these enemies even use guns...*

Still, the additional protection was a relief.

"And the others?" Bastian looked at the other Marines, who were already fanning out.

"Shotgun," Preston chirped, approaching the lead Humvee, where above Donnie was straightening up, eager to be on the move again.

Bastian watched Irving climb into the passenger seat of the other Humvee.

"I know I wanted to skip introductions," Bastian said to Elam, while the rest of his men got into position, "but I'd be remiss if I didn't know the names of the Marines putting their lives on the line for my wild cause."

"*Our* wild cause, Bastian," Elam said, patting the Suit's bulky left arm.

He had already moved the Marines through the insistence of calling him by his nickname rather than Sebastian or Thurgood. He merely hoped the other silly monikers wouldn't surface again.

"That said," Elam added, once the Humvees' engines started to rev and the M1 Abrams' own motor sounded off. "Tank crew is Arthur Wilson—that is, Private Artie—and Private Ralph Lemay."

Elam guided Bastian over to the lead Humvee, and he stooped to peer at the Marine behind the wheel. It was a shame that none of these men wore proper uniforms and equipment, not even helmets, just their training fatigues. The panic had been genuine, even at a place like the Miramar base, especially for these men, having been startled from the showers.

The driver was a heavily built, dark-skinned young man with solemn eyes, but a gentleness to him that Bastian couldn't overlook. He had a taut ponytail of dreadlocks, which Bastian imagined would normally be longer if he wasn't in the Corps.

"This here is Private Tray Arlington," Elam introduced. "Better at driving than he is at shooting, I'm afraid."

Arlington rolled his eyes.

Moving to the next Humvee, on the other side of the tank, Elam swiftly introduced Bastian to the eighth Marine, behind the wheel.

"And this is Private Brandon Mercer. Donnie's cousin."

"Twice removed," Mercer said with a shrug, and a light Bostonian accent. He clicked his tongue against his teeth and nodded in the direction of the other Humvee. "Donnie's a Southie at heart, before moving down here. I got outta there soon as I was eighteen."

"Lovely troop you've got yourself here, Lance

Corp—"

"Please, please, just Elam, will ya?"

Bastian smirked. "Will do."

"Now, let's adhere to your initial urgency, and hit the road, eh?"

"Can't argue there. I'll hop in that trailer and hope everything holds."

"Good luck with that. If we happen across a better option on the way—"

Bastian shook his head. "No. Remember…if we're not gonna stop for civvies, we're not stopping for fucking *anything*. If, by happenstance, the trailer fails us…or me, more rather…*then* I'll figure something out."

"*We* will figure something out, Bastian Thurgood. You may not be a Marine, but you're military, retired or not, and you've got the heart for it, so goddammit, we won't leave you behind."

Bastian sighed and nodded. "I'm grateful for your dedication and support."

"That said," Elam started to backpedal toward his Humvee. "If any one of my men gets injured, our entire force will not hesitate to do whatever it takes to help him. No matter what. Now if that means you and even Fields go on without us, so be it. Can't say I'll curse you for it, but can't say I won't either."

Bastian nodded. "Seems reasonable. Can't say I would, or wouldn't, help, either, for that matter. As we said about the civilians. Who knows? Maybe my conscience will win in the heat of the moment."

Their voices extended over the breadth of the

street until Elam climbed into the Humvee which was destined to drive at the back of their formation. Bastian, meanwhile, made a beeline for the trailer hitched behind the Abrams tank, but paused there, and glanced over his shoulder, up at Fields situated in the gunner's hatch of the Humvee Elam now occupied.

He jogged over to the Humvee, while Donnie sighed and clapped his hands together.

"Can we *please* get this show on the road, fellas?" He called out, surely knowing himself that the vocalization only announced themselves furthermore.

Bastian casually flashed his left middle finger over his shoulder, visible to Donnie even from the other side of the tank. It was eight feet at its highest point, which was as tall as Bastian in the Suit, until he reached above his head.

The Humvee itself was seven and a half feet at the roof, but another foot taller with the addition of the gunner hatch fortifications. And the gunner, in this case the short Fields, was only exposed from the chin up.

Bastian barely had to lift his chin to direct his eyes at Fields, who must have felt odd in the moment being the one to look down at the robust man in his Suit.

"What was his name, Fields?" Bastian asked quietly.

Fields' brow furrowed in confusion but it was transitory.

And then his expression sunk, dour.

His eyes had been on Bastian's when the question was posed, but now they wandered just past his helmet as the words came out.

"Abasi Barasa Abdi."

*A.B.A.*, Bastian thought. He then pronounced the first and last name individually, and part of him momentarily smiled.

"Abby," he said softly, his own eyes wandering now. Then he reconnected with Fields. "And you?"

Bastian recalled Abby calling him Flynn way back in the CHERI building, he believed. But he wanted to hear it himself.

Fields cleared his throat and gathered his bearings before telling Bastian.

"Flynn," he said. "But I haven't answered to Flynn since I was a kid. And occasionally to Abby, because he knew how much it annoyed me."

Bastian smiled.

Elam whistled.

"Yeah, yeah," Bastian called out, "heeding my own advice."

"Hang tight, man," Fields said as Bastian walked away.

"You, too, Fields. Watch our butts."

# 15

The column was one-part military, one-part research, and two-parts war machine. The Marines and their gear, from vehicle to weapons to ammunition, were an ideal convoy as far as Bastian was concerned. While he could easily have wished for better, given the circumstances he was unfathomably grateful. And while they were collectively too headstrong—and bewildered—to admit it, the Marines were just pleased to have the help of an ex-Ranger, ex-SEAL, next-gen weapons tech designer and his hardware itself.

Everything was almost too good to be true.

The fact of the matter was that their surroundings ruthlessly reminded them of how unideal their situation was.

No matter the plethora of things they had to be thankful for, the warzone of the greater San Diego area through which they traveled was dreadfully depressing. What had once, less than a day ago, been a beautiful place with minimal crime, home to various communities ideal for retired servicemen, and a cornucopia of bustling privately-owned shops, was now an extensive slaughterhouse. Civilian bodies and the occasional pair of law enforcement corpses littered the streets in nauseating numbers. Every block a hellhole could be spotted, long since used to its limit, though nonetheless given a wide berth by the column of vehicles.

Traffic light poles, signs, and lampposts were either slanted against their foundation, fallen altogether, and otherwise warped. An occasional flower of sparks flew through the night air as the vehicles drove past.

And they did just that—keep driving.

Bastian had more than made it clear earlier, that they would do their best to avoid stopping—for anyone. While this was agreed upon, almost indifferently and yet full of guilt, Bastian declared that he understood if the men disobeyed this pledge should the time come.

They weren't just military, they weren't just U.S. Marines, they were *men*—humans—with the means to defend themselves, and those around them, or at least given the opportunity. How they could simply ignore this for a vague 'greater good' cause was dubious at best; Bastian admitted to them, as he had to Elam minutes before the group's mobilization, that even he might break this cruel promise.

As the column of vehicles proceeded along their route, favoring backroads as per Bastian's insistence, the amount of debris—structural, vehicular, and human alike—became more than upsetting. However, what seemed to disquiet the men the most was the utter lack of enemy activity.

The silence, as if Death had grown mute, but still Its thick presence clung to the air with a sullen gravity. An infectious bleakness.

Bastian wondered if any of the men conversed

about this unexpected, dreary quietness among themselves as the vehicles droned on.

With no communications equipment, the Marines could only converse with whoever they sat beside, at best.

Despite the gentle rumbling of the three large engines, and the crunching of debris under thick tires and the tank's treads, it felt as though nobody wanted to utter a peep. They certainly weren't going to call out, from one Humvee to another, or honk their horns.

After fifteen solid minutes of no activity, or glimpsing any sign of life, human or otherwise, Bastian began to feel quite alone in his trailer. Although, he was certainly relieved of its durability, proven with each crossed intersection or mounted curb, or debris that it rolled over. The tank operators did their best to avoid such obstacles, of course, for Bastian's sake.

*Remind me to thank Artie and Lemay.*

Bastian even started to doze off, as he sat on his armored, padded butt in the treaded-steel trailer cart, all of a sudden wishing he wasn't in the Suit, but in his bed, or any bed for that matter.

He imagined he would never be able to go back home again, supposing he survived this turmoil. Even though his family hadn't died *in* the house, it still felt to him now more of a tombstone than a home.

Every time his eyes began to even flutter shut, the restful darkness behind them was scarred with a lightning-flash image of Eliza's pained face, her arm being torn off, and her screams, overlapping Maggie's, echoing through the void of his mind.

He jolted and forced himself to stay awake.

To stay vigilant.

With his back to the tank, sitting in the trailer and the cart of weapons between his legs, he faced the Humvee that drove at the rear of their formation.

Fields up on the machinegun, routinely spinning in a circle, the fluted muzzle sweeping their surroundings. His vigilance wasn't to be second-guessed, and didn't ever seem to falter.

Behind the wheel, through the shatterproof windshield, Bastian saw Mercer. He would occasionally connect eyes with Bastian and give a casual wave or nod, which was always cordially returned. Across from Mercer sat Irving, whose gaze appeared permanently glued to whatever they passed, through his side window.

It was comforting to see the Marines sustain their watchfulness, even while Bastian himself felt so weathered.

He knew the worst had yet to come, of course.

Reaching Calipatria, a wishful destination as bad as they came given the situation, would test him like a trial by fire. Quite possibly literally; he didn't know exactly what to expect, except for what he had glimpsed on the distant, shaky televised footage.

How the Monolith itself would welcome him, however, he couldn't fathom.

While Bastian wished he could simply divert his attention from such thoughts, he really couldn't. There was nowhere else to go.

He tried to focus on their ever-moving environment, which he hardly even recognized anymore. Before he realized it, they had entirely passed through Tierrasanta, and were already several miles southeast of it.

*Tierrasanta*, Bastian thought rather dreadfully. *'Holy Land.'*

The irony was caustic.

Bastian distracted himself with some calculations for their route. Surely mulling over the actual itinerary versus the dilemmas of the journey would keep himself from being consumed by melancholy.

He looked around, nonetheless, to gather exactly where they were. Unfortunately, just about every damn thing looked the same now, thanks to the maelstrom that had transpired. And still was, likely, just somewhere else, now.

*Or they're in hiding…dormant…planning an ambush…who the fuck knows?*

It took a few more minutes—time of inactivity that he wasn't expecting to be offered—until he was able to recognize a landmark. As soon as he saw the particular In-N-Out Burger joint, at the corner of the intersection they cut through—now an asphalt-lain mass grave—he knew exactly where they were.

It was farther than he had anticipated, too.

*An hour and a half*, he thought. *Maybe less if we keep up this progress.*

He wanted to relay to somebody this good news, but didn't want to stop the convoy. And then, as if Private Arlington had read his mind, he brought the lead

Humvee to a stop and the tank halted behind it. Bastian looked around, noticing Fields' puzzled look, and even Mercer at the wheel of the Humvee behind the trailer, making an "I don't know" gesture.

The column of vehicles stopped in the middle of the intersection, diagonally crossing it.

Bastian heard a door shut and some light commotion on the other side of the tank. He stood up and saw the heads of two Marines debating incoherently by the lead Humvee.

He hopped out of the trailer and gestured at the back Humvee to wait. He circled the tank to find Preston standing a few feet away, arguing with Donnie.

"The hell is going on?" Bastian asked after raising his visor. "Why are we stopped?"

"This genius wants to grab some drinks and take a shit," Donnie remarked.

"Not in that order, of course," Preston said matter-of-factly. He paused in thought. "Then again…"

Bastian rolled his eyes.

He heard a door opening but not shutting, behind him. He turned to see Elam, who had exited the back Humvee, and jogged up to see what was going on. He parted his arms as if to say "what the hell" without actually using words.

Bastian simply pointed at the In-N-Out and shrugged.

"Nature calls," he added.

Elam rolled his eyes. "Seriously, Preston?"

"I can tolerate this," Bastian said. He turned to Preston. "Be fucking quick, please. And don't flush."

"I'll grab some sodas on my way out." Preston jogged toward the building. "They got bottles here."

"Keep your voice down," Elam snapped at him in a whisper. He looked back at the Humvee he came from and gestured at Irving.

Bastian held up a hand and shook his head.

"I'll go."

Elam scoffed. "So you don't wanna stop for a civvy in trouble, but you'll stop to let one of our guys pinch one off?"

"I know," Bastian shrugged. "Not very sound conviction."

Elam smirked but then kneaded his brow.

Bastian jogged after Preston, who was just now reaching the front entrance. He entered cautiously, slowly enough to not trip the bell above the door. He propped it open, quietly, using a trash receptacle.

When Bastian arrived, watching his step—*so many bodies*; it was surreal—he could see Preston inside, crossing the interior. Nothing else moved, not a single sign of life.

Just the opposite.

He tried not to grimace and get lost again in the palpable despair of the situation.

He paused halfway across the dining area, about ten feet from the front counter, and scrupulously observed every booth. Every table. Every gray tile. While there was no power and the lights were out through most of the area, luminance from the tank outside provided a soft white glow within the small building. It hung above Bastian's head, almost as if bestowing a nimbus upon the In-N-Out.

*A halo for its dead.*

It was an odd sight, alright, one that Bastian could not ignore. The white and red motif was now mostly red and dark red. The white areas a brighter crimson than the already red columns and booths. Bastian had waded through warzones overseas and bodies of both soldiers and civilians alike, but…

There were always littered casings from spent ammunition, soot in the air and black spots on the walls from explosions. The amount of actual blood and gore from multiple bullet wounds, especially in the desert, wasn't extreme.

During his Navy years, every SEAL prided themselves with meticulous, tactical combat. Infiltration and defusing a bad situation; incapacitation or succinct neutralization of threats.

*Saving* civilians. *Rescuing* hostages.

Not this.

Corpses here were not bullet-riddled, they were cut up as if with machetes and meat-hooks. A messy, haphazard killing spree. Some bodies were bereft of limbs, heads, and even faces. Some were eaten, disemboweled, and the viscera…not everything was present.

Whatever this enemy was, Bastian thought with a twist in his gut, it had *zero* concept of morality.

Bastian did not know how long he had been standing idly in the middle of the fast food restaurant by the time Preston emerged from the hallway leading to the bathrooms. His reappearance startled Bastian, which made him realize that he had not been a very good lookout, severely detached from reality.

And yet, quite the same, *too* attached to what wretchedness reality had become.

The stillness, the disturbing quietude, was tangible. Overwhelming, even. The absence of noise was subcutaneously unsettling to Bastian; not to say that he preferred fighting for his life, or the cacophony of screams, but…

There was a strange comfort, that aforementioned soldier's high, to not being blanketed with eerie silence.

"Glad to see you," Bastian said, his voice low. "Now get back to the fucking Hum—"

A shrill, guttural squall split the quietness.

*That's not what I meant*, Bastian thought, his heart sinking.

"On the roof!" one of the Marines outside yelled.

"Fuck," Preston cursed under his breath, bringing his weapon up to his shoulder.

Bastian had not gone unarmed, either. He wielded the ROT-20 and looked up on impulse.

Then guns started firing in the intersection.

First Donnie's .50-cal.

Followed by other soldiers' assault rifles.

"There must be more than one," Bastian said, shooting Preston an angry look. Preston was unresponsive. Bastian snapped: "Come *on!*"

Preston blinked rapidly, nodded, and sprang into action. He followed Bastian to the door, but about ten feet from it, they staggered back when a bulky figure dropped from above, landing just outside the large front window. It shattered from the impact, blowing glass shards inward. Preston exclaimed under his breath and shielded his face, while Bastian just stared.

The Tyrant rose from a hunched stance after it had leapt from the roof, and now blocked his view of half the convoy in the intersection.

Bastian grabbed Preston's fatigues, careful to pinch fabric instead of shoulder, and yanked him to the floor, simultaneously yelling "Get down!"

He knew what was coming, and assumed that they knew that he knew.

There was no other choice.

The two Humvee-mounted .50-caliber machineguns lit up the Tyrant. Large bullets, every fifth round a white-hot tracer, volleyed the bipedal beast and ripped through the air above Bastian and Preston's heads, as they hit the floor.

In less than four seconds the Tyrant was in pieces on the ground outside the shattered window, disintegrating by the time Bastian lifted Preston to his feet.

"Thanks," he mumbled, dusting himself off.

No blood on his uniform, just beneath his boots, which he noticed as soon as he tried to follow Bastian to the door. A loud squeak as his foot slid, and he caught himself on the edge of a table.

"Good?" Bastian asked, half-turning.

Preston gulped and nodded, then wiped his boots off on the mat by the entrance. Blood, not dirt or mud, or rainwater; he wiped off human blood from his boots on the welcome mat.

His stomach turned.

Bastian tried to not think about it.

Which was the only saving grace, as he led Preston out of the fast food restaurant. The Marine had entirely forgotten to get a soda or two from the refrigeration unit in the far corner, which he initially passed en route to the bathroom. It had since shattered and vanished from his mind.

He just wanted to get back into the Humvee, its armored doors and frame his only source of comfort right now.

Even the loaded assault rife in his hands wasn't sufficient consolation.

The machinegun mounted to the roof of the Humvee, however…

It wasn't his to fire, unless he demanded to, but his faith in Donnie was satisfactory.

When they emerged from the In-N-Out, Bastian half-expected to be thrust into a fresh crossfire. As it were, the stillness following the slaying of the Tyrant was resolute; Bastian looked around and couldn't spot a single trace of the enemy. He imagined that if they actually left behind bodies—like anything else in this natural world—then they would be scattered over the edge of the roof, some draping, but all oozing blood from their fatal wounds.

Bastian twirled around to see not even a hint of the enemy in the vicinity. He presumed that the Tyrant had been the last creature to show its ugly face since the Crawler—based on the sound he heard—announced itself on the roof.

"How many were there?" Bastian asked Donnie,

calling up to him to be heard over the ringing in his ears.

"Six or seven. Mostly grunts up top, then that big horned fuck that dropped down."

Bastian guessed Donnie was referring to the Crawlers when he said grunts, or quite possibly a combination of them and Vultures, maybe Eaters, too.

"Sorry about the crossfire," Donnie added. "Didn't wanna take the chance of it charging us or—"

Bastian waved. "No worries. It was a tall bastard, anyway, and your aim would've missed us had we stayed on our feet. Well, Preston anyway."

Elam walked up, reloading en route. He nodded at Preston, eyebrows high.

"If you were constipated, I bet you would've shit yourself then, huh?"

Preston smirked and shook his head. The smile lasted for half a second before devolving.

"Get your ass in that Humvee, unless you wanna go inside and make yourself a milkshake, too," Elam motioned over his shoulder.

"Yeah, yeah," Preston sighed, and bowed his head as he jogged up to the Humvee. As he boarded it, Donnie slapped the roof and cheered him on.

"Hell of a place, ain't it?" Elam said.

"Huh?" Bastian didn't catch on.

"The city. What it's become. Less than a fucking day, too."

Bastian sighed and shook his head.

"Tell me about it." His voice was as glum as his expression, more visible to Elam in the moment since he had raised his visor. "So much has already happened, and yet…so little, when you really think about it."

Elam raised his eyebrows. "What do you mean?"

"This is San Diego, man. That's it. So-Cal might be fucked, groovy. I hate to sound so nonchalant about it, but let's accept reality, yeah? Meanwhile, the tremors and sinkholes—fucking *hellholes*, more like it—have reached up close to, and possibly over into, Canada, not to mention even more inland. This much we know. But the world's a big place, Elam. And like you said—*it's only been one day*. Hardly that. Now consider…*seven*. I guarantee you, if shit keeps happening at this pace, without relent or some kind of proper counterattack, the entire U.S. is compromised within a week. Easy. Half the population, wiped out—I'll give that a month."

"Christ Almighty," Elam muttered.

He looked around. His Marines were out of earshot, even Donnie being the nearest appeared unaware—more focused on staying a vigilant lookout.

When his gaze returned to Bastian, he frowned and his voice became a little gritty.

"Would you mind stowing that shit from my boys, mister? Morale is FUBAR as it is."

Bastian shook his head. "No, *not* FUBAR. That's where I come in."

Elam's dark expression transmuted into something brighter.

"That's one mighty high horse there, Bastian."

Bastian's cheeks lit up briefly and he rolled his eyes. Then he hit the button for his visor and it sealed. His voice still lucid, he said one more thing to Elam before returning to the trailer behind the tank.

"Better than dragging my feet among the dead."

Elam was left befuddled for a few seconds before Bastian climbed onto the trailer hitched to the tank, by which point the words sank into him the way they were intended. Motivated to some extent, Elam subconsciously agreed with Bastian, that even a crazy sense of pride or hope was better than the opposite, especially in his case.

He had to carry the burdened gift of that Suit, and whatever it might mean for him in the long run.

Elam also clearly realized that so much time had already been sacrificed for the sake of Preston's bathroom stop. He couldn't ignore the brutal necessity of it, but ultimately they had lost precious time and ammunition quite possibly because of it.

Bastian himself had not appeared terribly disgruntled by it, although Elam imagined that inside he was a mess of urgency.

With this in mind, and fully understanding where he was coming from if that was the case, Elam shouted "move out" and jogged back to the Humvee behind the tank. He got in just as the Abrams resumed its acceleration to follow the lead Humvee.

With thanks to the soundness of the Suit's stability, which fitted him like a snug sleeve, Bastian didn't have to brace himself when the trailer lurched forward. He was, however, also grateful for the tires and sustaining axle beneath the trailer.

Of course, the biggest thanks went to whoever drove the tank. He knew not just any Marine could hop in an M1 Abrams and drive it around the block, much less know how to operate and reload the cannon. So to the two men that Elam mentioned were in it, Artie and Lemay, he was indebted. Whoever was actually maneuvering it, the most; Arlington drove the lead Humvee and clearly avoided major obstacles very well, while maintaining a decent speed.

Naturally, Bastian wished *he* was driving, but knew that wouldn't be feasible considering his size in the Suit. Not even the confines of the tank would support him in a sitting position.

He glanced down at the stagnant cart between his legs in the trailer.

*Besides*, he mused, *I've got you, baby.*

The little bite of sarcasm was soothing, and only slightly resurrected the thought of Maggie. With the mere thought alone came his last memory of her, paired with the sound of shattering glass and crunching metal.

With a grimace behind his visor, Bastian exiled that fragment of his mind into the abysses below.

His gaze returned to his immediate surroundings, which were beginning to pass him even slower than before.

He realized that they had finally shifted gears so to speak and changed course. Not direction, but a change of scenery. There were backroads and then there was this—suburbia. Why Arlington had led their column down even narrower streets, flanked by rows upon rows of residential houses, he didn't know.

His guess was that Arlington had glimpsed too many obstructions—or just one big, impassable one— on the original path ahead. And, with the greenlight to use backroads as opposed to the highway, he chose the next best route.

At first Bastian would have been critical, but before he knew it they were picking up speed again. While they were maxing out at maybe twenty-five down these roads, as opposed to thirty previously, there were far less obstacles to avoid. Hardly any abrupt decelerations or slaloming. The sound of the trailer's tires bumping over wide cracks in the asphalt, or unavoidable corpses, or vehicular debris, became a historic memory.

*Smooth riding. Who would've thought?*

It was unexpected, especially on these smaller roads, but Bastian quickly developed a newfound gratitude for Arlington, and the tank driver, too.

It had certainly occurred to Bastian that, without radio equipment, there were no comms between these Marines. And with Lance Corporal Elam in the back Humvee instead of the lead, odd as that decision was, they had no direct line of communication.

*Hell, not even* in*direct.*

Afterall, it wasn't like the gunners could shout back and forth at each other, over the crunching sound of the tank's tracks, let alone its motor, and the two Humvees' engines.

So, Elam had to trust Arlington's judgment to a great extent.

Though, for all Bastian knew, these Marines knew each other as far back as boot camp. Or maybe they were complete strangers prior to deployment, whenever that was for them.

In some other life, or some other detached point

in time, *maybe* Bastian would have met these brazen men under different circumstances. And gotten to know them better, more genuinely, as more than just soldiers adhering to a creed of duty and honor.

As it were, he could only thank them enough.

He found himself zoning out as abandoned houses with scarred front yards passed him on both sides. Every few residences and there would be one with an unscathed lawn. Those were, ironically, the strangest sights of all.

He couldn't help but think of Z down there in the CHERI facility, or Adhira for that matter. He prayed that they were safe.

*Better than out here*, he thought, but quickly second-guessed that notion.

As if to confirm it, a screech that was neither metallic nor tire-related caught his ear. Quickly after it, two more pierced the stillness of the night, overlapping to produce a disturbing medley. His suited body immediately straightened and he pulled his legs in, rising to a squatting position almost effortlessly.

Through his visor and upon a pivoting head, he scanned the houses they passed. From the lawns to the front doors, to some of their shattered windows, to…

The rooftops.

He knew better, too.

Being in the military, especially serving overseas, every soldier knew to be deservedly paranoid of shooters on rooftops. Not just snipers, but hostiles in general. While the slanted rooftops of suburban houses were not as ideal for gunmen as those with flat roofs and parapets for cover, they shouldn't be ignored.

Bastian had been doing just that, too—ignoring them. Despite even the incident earlier at the In-N-Out. Since these enemies neither possessed firearms nor the capability for ranged attacks, it had completely slipped his mind.

*Grunts, indeed.*

He spotted a Crawler on every other house, now that he paid attention. Or maybe there were less than he noticed, and they were simply bounding from one roof to the other, on both sides of the road.

As soon as he spotted them, some of the other Marines did, too.

He immediately noticed Fields in the back Humvee behind his trailer, keeping a car's length apart from its end, swing his machinegun around to aim at the rooftops to their left. Bastian waved his hands above his head, catching Fields' attention; flicking his wrist, he made a rapid cut-throat gesture under his helmet.

Universal for *NO*.

Fields nodded but didn't relinquish his fixated aim on the rooftops.

The tank started to speed up, and Bastian presumed that the lead Humvee crew noticed the enemies, too. Hearing them was one thing, but seeing them was another. Now that they were alert and heeding the roofs, where Crawlers constantly bounded from one house to the next, Bastian wondered what their strategy was.

The enemy's and his team's own.

*We* are *a team, afterall*, Bastian reminded himself. With that to chew on, he shifted his focus to the advanced weapons at his disposal.

Although considerably hefty to wield, especially on this little trailer, the Sevin caught his eye and heart.

He reached for it, but a millisecond before his gloved hands could seize the metal, a tremor shook the asphalt whereupon they drove. It was powerful enough to unbalance Arlington's driving; Bastian couldn't see it, but he heard the lead Humvee's tires skid and then what he presumed was it crashing through a mailbox.

The tank was only mildly affected by the tremor, fortunately not enough to destabilize the hitch or Bastian's trailer itself.

He noticed that Fields' Humvee, driven by Mercer, swerved briefly before regaining traction.

Although the tremor seemed to have passed, its consequence was not so transient. He could hear asphalt splitting like massive sheets of paper in the stillness of the night, which was no longer very quiet.

He tried to spot where the cracks were widening, but couldn't, until a few seconds passed and then, their column of vehicles decelerating, some spider-webbed out from under the tank. The sight would have been impossible had it not been for the tank's four-corner foglights.

The cracks, however, did not stop at the curb.

Wooden fences split and an entire house cracked in half, previously intact glass shattering in the process.

This produced a second tremor twice as bad as the first, and Bastian heard—on top of a rising chorus of Crawler shrieks—what he assumed was a sinkhole opening.

*Hellhole*, he reminded himself, and the connotations were unsettling.

For Bastian, it was also somewhat invigorating. He shifted gears and acknowledged the INFERNO Suit he wore, along with its capabilities, unafraid to embrace the egotism of wearing it.

He figured that it was a lesser evil in the face of what they were up against.

When he heard the unmistakable sound of a man screaming, Bastian bolted to his feet. In that moment he was able to see over the top of the tank, and glimpsed Donnie howling as the lead Humvee was *hurled* into the air.

The tank halted, skidding to the side in the process, and the trailer jackknifed. They hadn't been going fast enough to make it break the hitch, but along with the second tremor it sufficed to knock Bastian off. He landed soundly and recovered fast, the ROT-20 in his right hand, quickly joined by his left, just in time to witness what had flipped the lead Humvee.

It was a massive beast, a little bigger than a Baron but nothing little about it.

Bastian immediately shuffled behind the tank as he heard the lead Humvee land, its chassis groaning loudly. He spotted it on the front lawn a few feet from the porch of a house, to the right of the road. It had miraculously landed on its wheels. Donnie was, just as surprisingly, still standing through the gunner's hatch, but he was stupefied and then some.

The men inside were all extremely disoriented.

The Humvee must have completed a full barrel

roll midair before landing on its wheels.

For this much, Bastian was grateful, as it could have been much worse.

Bastian strode behind the tank's left side as it had stopped long-ways across the road. He peered around the front corner of its armored tracks, while the cannon rotated to adjust aim.

*There's no way they're gonna be able to track that thing.*

The illumination from the tank's lights not only doused his helmet and shoulders with a white glow, but offered them a clear view of this new abomination.

Its body reminded Bastian of lava flow. The dull, ashen black surface of its 'skin' was head to toe, and its gnarled horns were even darker. The eyes, unlike the Baron that it resembled, glowed red-orange, as if embers from the pit of Hell itself. The beast's gray-black body was interrupted by cracks which glowed a similar color, suggesting that its veins were composed of flame or magma.

Bastian wouldn't doubt it, at least not until he saw it get cut down by large-caliber bullets.

Unfortunately, the beast's most prominent characteristics were its arms. Instead of hands, it possessed long, barely curved 'spears' of...bone, or the same solidified lava, or igneous rock, that composed the rest of its body. These were engulfed in flame that did not dance too far from the sharp-tipped limbs, adding not only to its menacing appearance but also its danger in combat.

The tank found its aim but the bipedal beast

waited until the last second to move. When it did, the tank's chassis recoiled from the cannon shot, and a 102mm high-explosive round obliterated a house less than a quarter mile away, at the end of this street.

"Hold the big gun!" Bastian shouted, slapping the outside of the tank. "Hop on the LMG!"

As he said this, he heard one of the Humvee's machineguns start spitting fire.

*Speaking of fire…*

The beast with the blazing swords of rock for arms—each one about eight feet long, from elbow to tip—had evaded the tank only to bound into the front yard of some house to Bastian's left.

Out in the open.

Fields hadn't wasted the opportunity to light it up with his .50-cal.

Bastian watched the Pyro—*fitting name as far as I'm concerned*, he thought—as it tried dodging the volley. Quick on its hooved feet as it was, the beast couldn't elude the full-auto onslaught of .50-caliber rounds. Several caught it in the chest and abdomen, staggering it, and most—but not all—of the bullets cut right through it.

Onto the asphalt spilled thick streaks of magma instead of bright red blood.

*Close enough.*

He strode out into the open, clearing the tank, and shouldered the ROT-20. The Pyro snarled at him, its truculent gaze whipping in his direction, before the rotary shotgun opened up. A close-knit barrage of 20-

gauge buckshot pelted the Pyro in the chest and shoulders, threatening to drop it, while Fields shouted for a reload.

Bastian thought he was going to drop it until he heard Donnie's accented voice yell "hey, one fucking more!"

His heart sank and he shifted to stride behind the inert tank, just as one of the crewmen rose to man the mounted machinegun topside. This comforted him a bit, to know that the Pyro wouldn't be left untouched during its wounded stupor.

Bastian skidded around the end of the tank to witness a second Pyro climbing out of another hellhole that had emerged ten feet from the lead Humvee. The gaping crater reached from the edge of a front lawn to the roadside curb. The beast, despite having no traditional hands, still managed to clamber out of the hole with surprising dexterity. The torched arms lacerated the grassy earth of the house's front yard, as it hauled itself out.

Donnie was still dazed from what had happened, but that didn't keep him out of the fight.

He began firing at the Pyro with the mounted machinegun, and at that range, the .50-caliber rounds perforated it with ease. The beast roared, an orange glow emanating from the pit of its throat, and it lunged at the Humvee.

Bastian fired the ROT-20, squeezing the trigger, hard. The rotary barrels cycled fast, click-clacking as they did, a sound muffled by the actual blasts from the muzzle. The shots walloped the beast before it could connect with the idle Humvee, diverting its attention. It snarled and turned to face Bastian.

"Get us fucking moving!" Donnie shouted, kicking the back of the driver's seat. He slapped the roof of the Humvee. "And I need a goddamn reload!"

Inside the vehicle, Arlington threw a fit of panic as he relentlessly tried the engine but it kept stalling.

Simultaneously, Preston frantically climbed between the seats to assist Donnie with a fresh belt of ammunition.

Meanwhile, on the opposite end of the tank, the mounted machinegun fired rapidly at the other Pyro.

Bastian suddenly found himself in a bind. The rotary barrels still cycled even after clicking empty, their ammunition depleted.

"Fuck," he muttered, lowering his aim.

The Pyro still focused on him, and began lumbering in his direction. It was severely injured, missing chunks of its hardened, magmatic flesh, leaking globules of incendiary blood and yet it seemed unfazed.

Bastian retreated to the trailer, vaulting over the side and kneeling beside his cart of weapons. The trailer whined as it struggled to support the impact of his weight. Instead of focusing on reloading, he swapped the ROT-20 for the Supe. He deftly confirmed that it was loaded, just as the Pyro circumvented the tail end of the tank, the torched tip of its right arm scraping the top of the Abrams. The armor held against the inadvertent contact, but the grating sound was strident.

Somebody, somewhere, whistled loudly.

Bastian's gaze shot up and saw the Pyro now

looming over him turn, too.

Donnie, about thirty feet behind it, racked the firing levers on the machinegun.

"Come and get it, fuck-face!"

Bastian smirked behind his visor and dismounted the trailer, bending his knees upon landing.

Donnie opened fire. A torrent of armor-piercing rounds battered the Pyro in the face. Donnie's aim was precise. It was a tight spread, the strayer bullets either striking the beast's large horns or its bulky shoulders.

Bastian, about six feet shorter than the monstrosity, now rose to his heels and aimed high.

Another tremor swept beneath them.

He teetered back, but still squeezed the trigger. The Supe went off, and the fired bolo rounds tore into the Pyro's abdomen. Viscous, fiery blood stippled the asphalt, where it sizzled.

The tremor ceased only when another hellhole opened nearby. Bastian's gaze swept the area but he couldn't spot it, and with the overlapping sounds of gunfire, there was no tracking it with his ears.

He looked back at the severely wounded Pyro in time to witness half a dozen tracers from Donnie's stream of bullets chew through its skull. The horned beast's head exploded and its body slumped onto the tank before smacking asphalt.

Whoever manned the machinegun on the front end of the tank was momentarily distracted by this, and the injured Pyro he was firing at was given a breath.

Bastian shifted his focus, absentmindedly grateful for Donnie, and circled the tank's right side to put eyes on the other Pyro. It was in a three-point stance at the edge of the hellhole through which it had originally emerged.

The Marine on the tank-mounted machinegun re-oriented and began firing immediately.

The discombobulated Pyro snarled in Bastian's direction before receiving several more rounds to the side of its face and right shoulder.

Seven bullets to be precise.

And then the machinegun jammed.

"This can't be fucking happening!" the Marine exclaimed.

The tank's cannon began redirecting.

Bastian saw the bleeding Pyro's gaze divert from him to the Abrams. The sixteen-foot-long barrel slowly adjusting aim drew its eye. The muzzle would ultimately stop less than ten feet from where the Pyro knelt.

Easily within reach.

Discarding tact, Bastian shouted and rushed the Pyro. It ignored him and snarled at the tank, rising to its feet, defying its own injuries.

An explosive sound staggered him and impulsively lassoed his attention in the opposite direction. He spun on his heels and witnessed a house two spots down the road erupt as if a wrecking ball passed through it. The two-story building rained down shards of wood and glass and chunks of brick, around the Pyro that had charged through it.

*The other hellhole.*

At the same time, four Crawlers crept out of each crater within sight.

Eight more enemies on top of the one wounded Pyro and now another, irate and unscathed.

"Son of a…" Bastian mumbled, hoarse in the throat. His pulse raced.

He heard a roar behind him and spun in time to see the Pyro lunge at the tank, seconds before its aim aligned. The cannon fired anyway, and he had to applaud the panicked decision by the operator. The concussive report from the blast flustered the Pyro, proving that even these foul beasts still had mortal senses. It stumbled directly in front of the cannon, and Bastian noticed only then that its left horn had been blown off from the muzzle flash alone.

Bastian fist-pumped at the tiny victory, and then gritted his teeth as he charged the wounded Pyro.

Behind him, he heard Donnie shouting something incoherent, and then the roar of a turbo-diesel V8.

The approaching, stomping steps of the other Pyro closing in were unmistakable.

He used them as fuel to his own fire.

Motivation of sorts.

He reached the wounded Pyro and fired the Supe's other barrel into its left leg. From less than ten feet away, the blast tore through its limb, all but severing it at the knee. The beast released a harsh growl of surprise and pain and anger, before it doubled over. One of its torched arm-tips stopped at the asphalt, like a crutch. The other met with a crack and wedged into it, sinking a few feet.

Bastian took advantage of its briefly anchored, gravely injured state, and clipped the Supe to his waist.

He protracted the Exoblade from his left gauntlet, and before the beast could gather what was happening, he drove it into its destroyed-horn wound. The serrated tungsten sank in all the way, piercing the beast's skull and straightening its spine. Its head jerked back in the same instant, those ember-like eyes flickering like light-bulbs.

Unsatisfied, Bastian reached up and grabbed the Pyro's bottom jaw with his 'bare' hand. The Suit's armored digits and Kevlar gloving held as he gripped the beast's mandible, his fingers curled around its bottom incisors. With enhanced strength, Bastian knelt below the Pyro and roared as he pulled down. He ripped its bottom jaw off, splattering the asphalt with magmatic blood and chunks of black flesh.

He didn't need to release its body or withdraw from it. The slain Pyro quickly began its slow disintegration three seconds after he had stabbed into its skull through the horn wound.

"Holy shit, dude," the tank gunner said in disbelief, looking down at Bastian.

Bastian took a deep breath, although to his own pleasant surprise, wholly thanks to the INFERNO Suit—and its many engineers at CHERI—he wasn't actually exhausted.

At least, not physically.

Just emotionally and psychologically.

All of a sudden the Marine's face warped with ghastly surprise. Bastian reacted lightning-fast, side-stepping and swinging toward the Crawler that had charged him from behind. In the back of his mind he swore he had heard its panting breaths close in, but was himself having a moment of mental rehabilitation.

Now he impaled the Crawler's gaunt chest on his Exoblade, which was almost done shedding the dissolving blood of the Pyro. The Crawler's tongue flopped out of its mouth as the wretched life exited its body.

"More!"

Bastian heard the gunner a split-second before he saw it.

Seven Crawlers now ran amok, two hopping onto the back end of the tank, while the other five pursued the lead Humvee, which was driving in a wide arc about fifty feet up the road. On the other side of the nearest hellhole.

Behind it, the other Pyro was being walloped by bullets from a freshly reloaded Fields.

The beast, however, was proving awfully nimble. And Fields, not the best gunner, was having trouble tracking even such a large target.

Bastian couldn't blame him. His own stomach knotted at the sight of the bulky abomination juke and dodge Fields' volleys.

He started to run for the trailer on the other side of the tank, when he heard the Marine gunner curse and struggle with the mounted weapon.

It was still jammed.

*For fuck's sake.*

Bastian stopped and reached up to grab the armored ledge of the tank. He hoisted himself onto the vehicle, causing it to tilt to that side. This alone startled the two Crawlers that had mounted the tank, and their eyeless gazes diverted from the Marine to him.

One of them shrieked and didn't hesitate.

It lunged at him, bounding over the tank's cannon mount. Bastian sidestepped and swung at the creature's head, missing it by inches.

*Damn half-skull.*

The creature skittered behind him, almost falling off the side of the tank. Instead it latched onto his shoulders, and rode him as if they were playing piggyback.

The other one took the opportunity to redirect its attention to the Marine still struggling with the machinegun. It hissed wetly and charged him.

Bastian reached back and gripped the Crawler clinging to him, by its own shoulders, digging his thumbs into its flesh, forming hooks. He then ducked and flipped the creature over his head. It landed on its back and he immediately brought his heel down onto its half-skull, squashing it like a bright-red pumpkin against the tank's armor.

Just as he looked up—to see Arlington frantically drive way up the road, in the background so to speak, trying to lose his pursuers—the Marine had drawn his sidearm and began firing at the Crawler. The pistol barked rapidly, and the dark-skinned, wide-eyed Marine's jaw hung open in panic as he emptied the magazine into the creature. It was only able to evade a few rounds before the majority connected, and it dropped off the side of the tank.

The Marine froze briefly before frantically reloading.

"What's your name, man?" Bastian asked, stepping over the disintegrating Crawler on the tank's armor.

"Ar-Artie," he stammered, gawking up.

"Thanks for the help, Artie. Do me a favor and stay below deck for now. We'll fix that gun later. Help Lemay reload, if he hasn't already, and try to hit this fiery fuck."

Bastian spoke fast, but coherently. He glanced over his shoulder to see that he was running out of time. The beast was getting mighty close to Fields' Humvee, which just began driving forward.

As if Mercer read his mind.

"I'm gonna do my best to lure it out in front of ya," Bastian said.

Private Artie gulped and nodded. He glanced around Bastian at the Pyro, as it pursued the Humvee toward the front end of the tank.

"*Now*, Artie," Bastian insisted.

"You got it," the Marine replied, donning his game face. He descended through the gunner's hatch, pulling it shut over his head.

Bastian leapt off the tank, trailer-side. He alighted without even a tickle of impact pain and then reached into the trailer. He scooped up two shells for the Supe, their red casings immediately recognizable amid the gunmetal weapons, and the green ones for the ROT-20.

He reloaded on his way around the back end of the tank. He had snapped the barrels shut just as he bumped into a stray Crawler, possibly from one of the rooftops.

It snarled and slashed at his chest, claws grating against the armor but dealing no damage.

Bastian brought his knee up, driving it into the creature's stomach. It stumbled back a few steps, and as much as Bastian wanted to annihilate its torso with the Supe, he idealized saving ammunition for the Pyro. So he swung at the creature's neck, Exoblade connecting. The head was lopped off, bouncing across the asphalt, trailing an arc of bright red blood. It was almost luminescent under the light from the tank.

He rushed past its body before it even began to disappear.

The road ahead was quite a chaotic mess.

Less than a quarter mile down, Arlington was giving his Crawler pursuers a run for their money. Testing the limits of their nickname, though really it was just Bastian's moniker. Meanwhile, from the roof, Donnie fired bursts from his reloaded machinegun.

The creatures, despite not being able to quite catch up to the Humvee, were nimbly dodging most of the bullets.

Much closer, on the opposite side of the nearest hellhole, the other Pyro pursued Mercer's Humvee. He started to drive it in a circle, around the edge of the hole, either trying to get the beast to fall in or—

Lure it out in front of the tank's cannon.

Bastian gestured at Fields to relinquish the machinegun altogether, for now, and drop into the Humvee. Bastian feared potential crossfire, even though Artie was now below deck and he knew the Suit was bullet-resistant, a .50-cal had yet been tested.

Besides, with Fields inside the Humvee, he wouldn't have to worry about any sonic damage from the tank's main gun.

Bastian now rushed the Pyro just as Mercer drew it between the idle tank and the nearest hellhole. The space was maybe fifteen feet wide. However, the Pyro shifted gears, both mentally and physically, as it neared the tank.

It wised up, spur of the moment.

Or perhaps it had known all along.

In a punching motion, the Pyro jabbed at the tank. The tip of its flaming arm dented, but did not puncture, the armor. The Abrams skidded back ten feet, its tracks grating against the asphalt; luckily, it didn't overturn. Bastian was knocked back, caught off-guard, the moment that the Pyro struck the tank.

But he did not fall.

The Pyro roared in surprise and defiance, arms stretched wide, either as an intimidation technique or an omen of another attack. Possibly both.

Bastian wasn't intimidated.

He fired into the Pyro's stomach, left side, at point-blank range. The bolo rounds tore through hardened flesh and ripped into its insides. There was shockingly no exit wound, however, the beast *did* falter. It was a quick second that Bastian didn't waste.

He performed the same motion that the Pyro had done to the tank ten seconds earlier, except with his Ex-oblade. Having feared that it might not puncture the beast's tough exterior, he went for its Supe-blasted wound. There, the serrated tungsten dug in, and the Pyro, more responsive than its previous ilk, released a guttural howl and swatted at Bastian. The incendiary arm-spear walloped him in the chest-plate from the side, as opposed to its tip, and the armor absorbed the impact. Still, he was thrown back. He landed on his armored shoulder blades, and slid across the asphalt several more feet.

As he got up, looking down at the Suit, he nodded to himself with a detached sense of delight.

*Flame-retardant, indeed.*

Fields had returned to the roof-mounted machinegun and began firing at the Pyro again, this time from its right side. Bullets climbed up its bulky, ashen black shoulder until they battered its horned skull. It shook its body like a wet dog, growling thunderously, and then briskly turned.

With such force.

One arm extended.

Bastian's heart leapt into his throat as he watched Fields nearly get decapitated. He dropped down in the last second, and the machinegun was instead demolished in the wake of the Pyro's flaming arm. It clattered to the asphalt thirty feet away, fire licking its destroyed parts.

Two seconds later, its ammunition belt started popping off like firecrackers.

The Humvee rocked side to side on its axles from the near-impact, momentarily disorienting the men inside.

The Pyro grunted, snorted, and smoke billowed

from its nasal cavities. Breath hotter than Bastian could fathom also spewed like steam from its jaws.

He began to charge it again, and it swung at him before he could get close, forcing him to backpedal several steps. The beast took this chance to attack the Humvee again, just as Bastian saw Mercer return his hands to the steering wheel.

"Get outta there!" Bastian hollered, not necessarily meaning abandon the vehicle, but to drive away. However, Fields reacted in a fit of panic and dove out of the Humvee from the other side, rolling across the asphalt just as its thrusting, flaming arm speared the vehicle through the passenger door windows.

With Elam, Irving, and Mercer still inside.

In the path of the blazing arm, Elam's entire torso was obliterated before his brain could comprehend what had happened. Irving and Mercer screamed but barely had time to react otherwise, before they both caught fire from proximity alone. Its vehemence immediately devoured them head to toe, Mercer receiving the worst of it. Still alive, he howled in pain and flailed. At one point his foot slammed into the gas pedal, and the Humvee lurched forward, but the Pyro didn't let it go anywhere.

Likely with little strain, the powerful beast lifted the Humvee into the air, hurling it over its head.

Finally, the tank accelerated.

Bastian slammed his shoulder into the armored end, giving it a much needed push. The tracks skidded across the asphalt, spitting up gray smoke, a split-second before the Pyro slammed the Humvee directly behind the hitched trailer. Bastian stumbled back, clear of the impact by a mere few feet. Shards of shrapnel scattered in every direction, something sharp colliding with his shoulder and not piercing the Suit's armor, but spinning him like a dreidel.

The Humvee was crushed in so many ways that no inhabitant could have survived.

Regaining his balance, Bastian was nonetheless struck with dizziness. In his blurred vision through the visor, he glimpsed a horrified Fields slowly crawling back on his elbows and heels, twenty feet from where the Pyro stood.

And then his gaze swept back around, past the Pyro and the tank circling to likely retrieve Fields, until he took in the sight of the demolished Humvee. Most of the wreckage was up in flames, and the bodies inside were indiscernibly destroyed carcasses.

An unparalleled rage surged through Bastian in that moment.

Even when Maggie and Eliza were killed, he had not been quite this consumed with anger. But at that time, he was more victimized by grief and sickness.

He felt sadness now, but it was dwarfed by a violent fury. Besides, he currently had neither the time nor the space in him to lament. So he surrendered to a paroxysm of rage, and unleashed a grating war-cry as he charged the horned monstrosity.

It looked down at him, tilting its large head, and although Bastian did not want to admit it, he could have sworn the beast smiled in that instant.

*Not for long*, he assured himself, and collided with its left knee. The leg buckled, and the Pyro dropped forward, supporting itself with its torched arms, like crutches, as the other had before it.

*And so shall you die.*

Bastian's armored feet skidded across the asphalt just a few paces shy of the nearest hellhole's edge, and he turned back to face the beast. Its backside was less notably streaked by fiery veins, and it almost blended into the night, now that the tank wasn't here. It was behind Bastian now, skirting the other side of the hellhole, Fields occupying the gunner's hatch.

He had glanced over his shoulder to catch this sight, in addition to something far past the tank.

A speeding Humvee.

Arlington and company; Bastian hoped Donnie and Preston were still alive.

He returned his embittered stare to the Pyro ten feet in front of him. It rose to its feet and started to pivot to face the formidable human.

Bastian drew the Supe and, in the same motion, flipped the barrel extension. He locked it into place just as he brought it up to aim, high this time instead of low. He squeezed the trigger before the Pyro could react properly, and the bolo slugs blasted away the top of its skull, between its horns. A thick bowlful of magmatic gore sloshed out of the wound, sizzling the asphalt that it splashed behind the beast's heels. Its feet scuffled back, while both ember-like eyes flickered, and for the longest breath it was as if a chopped tree uncertain which way it was going to fall.

Deciding to aid the decision, Bastian swiped up

and across, with his Exoblade. It tore through what remained of its gaping abdominal wound and like a Pez dispenser halfway down its body, the Pyro's torso jerked back.

It fell with this sudden shift of weight, and the life force inside of it finally gave up.

Bastian all but punched the visor button on his helmet, and then spit onto the corpse seconds before it began disintegrating. He wore a distorted, spiteful expression as he marched around the edge of the hellhole toward the tank.

Arlington's Humvee arrived before the Abrams even moved, and Preston popped out of the passenger seat, wielding a pistol.

His fatigues were torn from one shoulder, giving him a one-sided sleeveless look. There were some shallow lacerations down that exposed, pale-skinned bicep, but otherwise he was unscathed.

"Ignore the new fashion look," Preston said nonchalantly. "Fucking eyeless grunt ripped my sleeve off, trying to pull me out of the goddamn Humvee. Took my rifle, too, it's all fucked up. How about—"

Bastian just let Preston rapid-fire his way through the words until his eyes spotted the wreckage. He paused midsentence and sidestepped to peer around the drab green statue of a man that Bastian was, especially as he stood there inertly, waiting to gauge the Marine's reaction.

"What…what hap…" Preston trailed off.

His eyes began to gleam with wetness.

The tank's foglights fifteen feet behind him,

paired with the Humvee's headlamps even closer, back-lit Preston.

This somehow only made his features darker than they became as he realized the deaths of Elam, Irving, and Mercer.

And then Arlington's door sprang open and the big man climbed out. He, too, looked rough, but uninjured, save for a cut above his brow and a bleeding lip, probably from earlier when their Humvee barreled through the air.

Despite not being devoid of grief, Arlington handled it better than Preston, who appeared to have partially shut-down.

When Arlington collided with Preston, his bulky arms wrapping around the leaner Marine, some mumbling words were shared. Whatever Arlington said to Preston, Bastian wasn't sure, but he trusted they were weightily consoling.

Because a few seconds later, Preston sniffled and toughened up. He two-handed his pistol and, glowering, turned away from the blazing sight.

Bastian could neither see nor hear any other Crawler in the area. And he did look.

Once Arlington and Preston were back in their Humvee, and the tank had come around to idle beside it, Bastian joined.

He strode between the two vehicles and swapped solemn glances from the tank crew's surveyor portal to the passenger's side window of the Humvee. Then he raised his visor.

"I can't apologize enough for what's happened,"

Bastian said, the tonality in his voice alone carrying genuine, severe weight. "But neither can I change it. The future, however, from near to distant, is still in our hands. At least for this little corner of the world."

"Bastian, for the love of God," Fields sighed from the tank's gunner hatch. "Stop with the speeches. Just get in."

He couldn't help but crack the smallest, driest of smirks in response to Fields. His gaze swept over to Preston, who rode shotgun in the Humvee.

"For the record, I like it," Preston said, the simplicity in his voice and expression almost amusing.

Bastian's simper grew a few millimeters. He looked up at Donnie on the roof-mounted machinegun, who still appeared deeply troubled by the deaths of his comrades. His friends. In a way, likely, his family.

"Just…get in," Donnie eventually said.

Bastian's smirk vanished and he nodded, grimly but empathetically. He glanced over his shoulder at the hitched trailer that remained.

When he looked back at the two vehicles between which he stood, words struggled to part his lips.

Yet nobody rushed or tried to interrupt him. Ultimately he gave up on what he was going to say originally, and cleared his throat.

"Who's the next highest rank among you?"

It definitely wasn't a question he wanted to ask, but felt obliged to.

The Marines exchanged looks that were neither of uncertainty nor intrigue. They knew, they just didn't seem to care much. To them, probably nobody was present that really fit the bill of leadership. Especially of themselves, and in the midst of such catastrophe.

"Aw, hell," PFC Donnie sighed. "I guess that's me, then."

"You know the way?"

Donnie nodded. He then kicked the back of Arlington's seat.

"Worst case, Arlington's got the best sense of direction."

Bastian nodded. "Good. We'll follow, then. If you or Fields spot anything suspicious, anything that *might* be a threat, give a whistle. I'll hear."

"We probably won't, then," one of the men inside the tank said. It wasn't the voice of Artie, who Bastian had briefly familiarized himself with earlier, so he presumed it was Lemay, the tank's main operator. The man sounded young but not necessarily a greenhorn, especially with how he drove the Abrams. He had a strong southern accent, and if Bastian had to guess, given his and Maggie's time there, he would say Texas.

"Donnie will give a hand signal, so keep a lookout," Bastian said. "Worst case, I'll give a gentle tug on the hitch."

"'Gentle,'" Fields muttered, mildly amused.

"That armor sure is something, huh?" Preston said, shaking his head and ogling the Suit.

"More than you can imagine. I only wish I'd been…" Bastian glanced over the hood of the Humvee, in the direction of the other one, its wreckage casting an orange-hearted pillar of black smoke into the night sky.

Bastian's breath seeped, barely audible. "Faster."

"You and me both, buddy," Arlington said, his voice sullen and his eyes damp.

"That's behind us now. Speaking of which…let's haul ass." Bastian lowered his visor and looked around. "Should reach Calipatria in an hour, two max, supposing we aren't met with any more…resistance."

"How are you on ammo back there?" someone inside the tank asked, Artie presumably.

"Uh…" Bastian lifted the Supe and broke open the barrels. Two spent shells ejected, trailed by thick curls of smoke. Finally he replied: "Manageable."

"That's good news," Donnie said. "Try to sound more convincing next time, though. Where we're going, in this capacity, with these losses…we can't handle much more demoralization."

Big words from Donnie, and Bastian was thankful. He could easily identify the authenticity in Donnie's voice and expression. Then his body language stiffened as he attached himself to the mounted machinegun in a far more attentive manner.

"You're right. Will do."

Bastian also tacitly agreed that the time for speeches and long-winded statements of gratitude was over. While Donnie technically had superiority over these surviving Marines, with the death of their Lance Corporal, Bastian selflessly believed that *he* was seen as their leader. Considering the Suit and his next-level weaponry, it certainly wasn't illogical.

Implicitly, he accepted this responsibility, but

would lead from the background.

He hopped into the trailer hitched to the tank and began reloading while assessing his weaponry.

The lead Humvee growled as it accelerated, and then the tank did, too. Internally, Bastian vied for patience, the kind that honed his senses and sharpened his aggression, as opposed to dulling them.

He would need both to make the most of this.

# 16

Driving. Watching. Riding. Wading. Dreaming. It all melted into one act for Bastian Thurgood. The oblivion through which they ventured, the wasteland, was a nightmare that clung to the skin and infected the brain with its diseased insanity. Should he look away for too long, in hopes of not witnessing the next piece of evidence that the world was past dying, that it was dead, then he feared falling into a bottomless abyss…

From which escape was not feasible.

As it were, they had driven for more than thirty solid minutes without glimpsing any sign of life along their route.

Human or otherwise.

The concept of survivors no longer existed to them, and the presence of their infernal enemy had so quickly become something of the past. Their recent past, albeit, history all the same. Like a sour, desiccated memory.

It hadn't occurred to Bastian that the vehicles were actually stopped until he awoke.

The fact that he had in fact fallen asleep was almost beyond comprehension. He felt a grave shame come over him as he pulled himself from the pit of un-consciousness. His limbs and nervous system were slightly sluggish, not just to move but to again accom-modate the Suit encasing him.

For the first few seconds he feared that he had somehow slept through the deaths of his company, or, worse yet, the extermination of the world around him.

Finally he regained motor functions, and full consciousness. His vision corrected, and he acknowl-edged that the Suit's visor was down. This at least helped keep the internal air regulation sanitized and un-corrupted, which would explain why he so easily fell asleep in the first place.

The aid of dullness and nothing actually happen-ing definitely contributed, too. Especially since he wasn't one driving, he simply rode along, forced to be a passenger.

But also a lookout.

*Lousy fucking lookout* you *are, Bastian.*

The disgrace dissipated once he realized that he wasn't the only one who had fallen asleep.

After stumbling over the side of the trailer, which rocked and creaked a little in the stillness of late night air, he caught his balance in the middle of the...

It was then that he realized they weren't on a road anymore. The two-vehicle column, if it could even be called that anymore, had pulled off to the side in a small suburbia for some respite in a local park. There was a fenced playground less than ten feet from the Humvee's grille. Its headlights were off, as was its engine, and the tank's weren't on, either, dousing their position in natural darkness.

A few streetlights surrounding the park that had not shut off or been destroyed, offered a brushstroke of illumination from afar.

Bastian could have sworn he saw one of the swings swaying, as if someone had just been using it, but he reassured himself it was just the wind or his own dazed imagination.

*Maybe even a ghost.*

Almost immediately after that notion, he snapped himself from whatever stupor he residually submitted to.

He reminded himself of the honed senses and sharpened aggression that he last recalled being so important to his current being.

His itinerary, and theirs, but ultimately his burden to bear, awaiting him in Calipatria.

He looked around and wished that he could recognize the area, but didn't. He did, however, recognize the look of utter fatigue on Fields' face as he had recently drawn himself out of sleep's hold. He was sitting on top of the tank's armored tracks on its right side, a few feet from the open gunner's hatch. He kneaded his scalp with dirty fingers and breathed haggardly. His previously rigid Mohawk, though only a few inches high, was now disheveled and sweaty.

"So," Bastian said, foregoing a whisper but also not shouting, "whose bright idea was this?"

Fields smirked dryly, and looked as though he either wanted to fall asleep once more to recharge, or do so and never wake up again. He then looked to his left, ahead of the tank, where the Humvee was parked.

"Arlington couldn't keep his eyes open. Wanted to switch with Preston, who was in no better shape to drive." Fields shrugged and looked back down at Bastian. "You were out of it at that point. We saw no purpose in waking you. Took the hint and pulled over for some quick shuteye."

"Fucking hell," Bastian removed his helmet and took a deep breath, then sighed. Cradling the helmet under his left arm, he kneaded his temple with his right gloved hand. The gauntlets were fixed to the sleeves, part of the Suit's entirety and not capable of individual removal. This ensured the Suit's airtight fashion.

For this moment alone, Bastian wished that wasn't the case.

Sometimes it really was the small things…

"You look rough, boss," Fields said.

"Shit, you look like how I feel." The new voice belonged to a husky man with a Texas accent, peering out of the tank's gunner hatch. He nodded at Bastian, who mutely nodded back. Then he said: "Private Lemay, by the way. Although I don't think rank has any purpose anymore. Not in this shit."

"Agreed," Bastian admitted. "Anyway…did you and Artie get some shuteye, too?"

"*I* did. Artie said he's been awake, though." Lemay grunted. "Restless."

"I can imagine why. Shocked at myself…that I was able to sleep, too. Dreamless, but still, sleep."

"We've all been up since this whole thing began," Lemay shrugged. "At least, I assume you've been, too."

Bastian nodded. "Unfortunately. Uh…with the exception of the little bit of time that I passed out after…"

He cleared his throat and looked away. He actually pivoted his entire stance, turning his back on them, and gazing out past the trees bordering the park. He focused on nothing in particular, but did find himself peering past the wind-rustled canopies to the houses nearby and their cramped front yards. A car or two that he spotted appeared completely unscathed by this madness. He briefly wondered where the owners were, or if they had died, or stayed inside this whole time.

Maybe they were in a cellar or shelter beneath the house. And they were wise enough to wait this out a few days, at least.

Bastian could only hope that this was the case for a lot of California residents. And elsewhere, for that matter, wherever this heinous disaster affected.

He then heard some muttering behind his back, and while he didn't decipher every word, he caught the gist of it.

Fields was telling Lemay, and likely audible enough for Artie on the other side of the tank's surveyor portal, about Bastian's family. No grisly details, but enough to explain why he suddenly gave them the cold shoulders.

A moment of reflection and distraction, to keep himself from spiraling into a fit of lunacy and sadness.

"I suppose," Bastian abruptly announced, speaking so loudly that it startled Fields and Lemay, as he turned to face them again, "that we all underestimate the needs of our bodies under such duress. And our minds, under such distress. Even an hour of sleep can do wonders. That said..."

Bastian whistled low, and then briskly high, a strident note that immediately stirred the three men inside the Humvee. Donnie popped up through the gunner's port, only after bumping his head on the metallic ceiling first and cursing loudly under his breath. He emerged rubbing his head and scowling.

The Humvee's driver and passenger doors popped open. Preston groaned and coughed, brow furrowed, as he extended his legs outside and leaned forward, sitting on the side of the passenger seat. Arlington actually got out, and circled around the back end of the vehicle, stretching simultaneously.

"That said," Bastian repeated, now at a lower volume, "can anyone tell me *exactly...how* fucking *long* we've been out of it?"

For the first few seconds Arlington, Preston, and even Donnie were simply bemused by seeing Bastian without his helmet for the first time. And then his question sunk in, and they wore expressions of first pensiveness, then confusion, and finally disappointment.

Something metal grinded, the sound catching everyone's attention. And then the commander's hatch opened on top of the tank, and Artie emerged. He hoisted himself up onto the armor, sitting there with his legs dangling inside the hole. He stretched and rolled his shoulders, then his head, and took a deep, ragged breath.

"About two hours," he said at last, and immediately, without even second-guessing him, everyone cursed, upset with themselves.

"How are you sure?" Bastian asked, holding off his own reaction.

Artie's sleeves were rolled up, but not until he actually exhibited the wristwatch did Bastian notice it.

"As Lemay mentioned," Artie added, drearily yet coherently, "I've been awake the whole time."

Preston swore under his breath, standing akimbo, shaking his head.

Now it really sunk in.

That they had been *sleeping*, despite their previous sense of urgency, much less in such a potentially hostile environment, for two long hours.

Bastian did his best to contain the anger and disappointment with himself, although as he had just admitted, the rest was likely a necessary evil. Still, it was critical time that could not be gotten back.

Successfully practicing placidity, at least from the outside, Bastian simply nodded repetitively until asking his next question.

"What time is it, Private?"

The use of rank in his already commanding voice helped reinject some gravity to their situation. He hoped maybe it would motivate them, instead of upset them. Much to his relief, it certainly didn't do the latter.

They seemed to respect him enough—*despite my*

*failures to save their fellow Marines*—to not take offense. And, probably, to see his underlying intentions, and the good of it.

"About four," Artie replied, observing his watch. "Uh…say, five 'til."

Bastian shook his head and mumbled something. He then looked toward the Humvee, but past it. His eyes searched the darkness of the playground, and then beyond it.

"Where are we?"

"On the right path," Arlington reassured, rather idly. After a few seconds, he shrugged. "I didn't veer off. We just keep heading—"

He started to point, indicating the road that circled the park in the direction that the Humvee was facing, but Bastian interrupted him.

"You rested well enough, now?"

Arlington took a deep breath. "Yeah."

"Certain?"

"Absolutely."

"And about the direction?"

"A hundred percent."

"It's uncanny, really," Donnie said. "Just *how* good his sense of direction is. He's a fucking human GPS."

"It does help that I've lived in the area all my life," Arlington added.

"Yeah, but I'm as good with a gun as you are anything with wheels," Donnie said. "Yet I never touched one 'til I was nineteen."

"Nineteen? Shit, last time I heard it was sixteen."

"Whatever. My point is—"

"Made," Bastian said. "Your point is made. Now, let's get back on the road. I won't say that we've *wasted* time, but, we've definitely used it up. We need to cut the shit and get going again."

"Can't argue there," Donnie said, leaning over one of the armored plates surrounding the gunner's hatch, and slapping the roof. "All this latency got me bugged as fuck."

"Ditto," Bastian muttered. He put his helmet back on, and sealed it. He kept the visor up, though. He addressed Fields while Artie slipped back down into the tank, and Lemay descended through the gunner's hatch. "You satisfied where you are, Fields?"

The CHERI security guard who had transitioned into something much mightier by this point now nodded and proudly returned to the mounted machinegun.

He checked the loading port and racked the firing levers.

"Feels like a home away from home, frankly," Fields said.

"Good. That's the best anyone can hope for at this time."

"And you?"

"That rickety trailer isn't the most inspiring," Bastian admitted, "but as long as I'm with those weapons, I can't complain."

"Speaking of which," Preston added, still leaning on his knees through the passenger's door, while Arlington returned to sit behind the wheel. There was something toxic about his voice. "When are you gonna actually *utilize* that shit? Or is it just for show? LC, Irving, and Mercer never got the chance to see any of them in action. Except that revolver shotgun thing. I wonder, are *we* gonna get to? That is, before we die, too?"

"That's enough, Preston," Donnie snapped.

"No, no, he's right, I mean, I get it," Bastian said, nodding and shrugging. He slowly approached Preston, who only then straightened up where he sat. Bastian hadn't expected this kind of reaction from Preston so belatedly, but it sure as hell surfaced all the same. "But, to answer your question, *Brett*, it just depends…"

"On what?" Preston asked, standing out of the Humvee, chin up, as if threatened.

Inside the vehicle, Arlington mumbled and shook his head, face-palming.

"If we make it to Calipatria alive," Bastian said, gathering the energy inside of him to amount to something positive instead of negative. "Because that's what I'm saving them for. I'm already low on ammo for the ROT-20 and Supe. Nevermind that, though. The rest of the weapons, the really advanced ones, I need to reserve for the horde guarding the Monolith."

Bastian started to back up, and only then did Preston start to defuse.

"That's a battle I have to do alone, because of the EMP." Bastian, however, remained in high gear, idling but still fervent. "But you guys help me get there, in one piece, and I *swear* I'll give my *all* to make it count. I can't bring back your fellow Marines—your friends—

447

just as I can't bring back my *wife and daughter*, but god-dammit, I'll do everything in my given power to avenge their deaths and keep others from suffering the same fate."

"Hey, Bastian," Fields called from the tank's gunner hatch. Bastian turned to look in his direction. "Scratch what I said about the speeches. That was a good one."

Bastian smirked for a split-second before his rugged face returned to a state of disheveled yet genuine, raw emotion.

He faced Preston.

"Do I have your support, Private Preston?" Bastian asked. "From an ex-Ranger, an ex-SEAL, and lately, a widowed father."

Preston sniffled and lifted his chin. He saluted firmly, at the risk of appearing melodramatic, but for Bastian it was interpreted sentimentally.

"To my last breath," Preston added.

"At ease," Bastian murmured, and Preston relaxed to an extent. He cleared his throat and straightened out, while Bastian took a few steps back and looked over the two vehicles, along with the men—the Marines—who remained devoted to his cause. He raised his voice a little. "That shouldn't be necessary."

Arlington took the moment to be punctual. He keyed on the engine and everybody present was grateful to hear the turbo-diesel growl to life.

Like a chain reaction, the Abrams tank started up, too, and from its exhaust a brief chain of smoke spewed out.

Bastian circled the Humvee and stooped to peer into the cabin on the driver's side.

"What's our ETA, you think?"

"No stops, thirty to forty minutes to Calipatria's outer limits," Arlington said.

"Solid." He looked across from Arlington to where Preston now pulled himself back into the Humvee. "You guys good on water?"

"Got some bottles bouncing around here," Preston said, leaning forward and scooping up two from the floormat. One was dry as a whistle, the plastic crumpled, and the other was about halfway depleted.

"Canteens?" Bastian asked.

"Nah," Donnie chimed in, from above. Bastian stepped back to look at him, swiveling on the gun mount to face that side of the Humvee. "Our exfil from Miramar wasn't exactly well-planned. We're all just wearing fatigues, for fuck's sake. Nobody's got a canteen on 'em."

"Except maybe Lemay," Arlington added. "That dude's always prepped."

"Yeah, flask, too," Preston chuckled. "Water or rum, who knows."

"Thanks. I'll drop in on 'em."

"You want a sip? I swear, it's not piss," Preston said, handing Arlington the half-empty bottle.

"Nah, I don't want to take your last fluids."

"We've got some in the back, too," Arlington said, thumbing over his shoulder. He shrugged. "Warm as fuck, but water's water."

Bastian nodded. "True that. Well, then, sure. I

could use a sip or two."

Arlington uncapped it for him and then handed over the half-empty bottle.

Bastian appreciated the offer and could only turn it down once. He put it to his lips and upended the bottle, draining the plastic in two big gulps. Then he exhaled loudly, flinging the bottle over his shoulder.

"Littering and," Arlington said.

"Very funny. And I'm sorry, but look around. Pardon your ethics while I say *fuck it*, but we got bigger fish to fry."

"Speaking of bigger fish," Donnie said. "Y'all hear that? Sounds like engines. Not too far off. Lot of 'em, too."

Bastian perked up, and wasn't the only one.

He then saw Fields back on the tank gun, appearing particularly wary.

Everyone stopped talking, or making any other noise for that matter, with the excusable exception of the vehicles' loitering engines.

Bastian didn't need to remove his helmet again to detect the distant sounds, and their approach in the night. Donnie was right. A throng of vehicles, not terribly far away, and, slowly, getting closer. Thus, louder. Clearer, too; given a few more seconds and Bastian would bet his life savings—for what little it was worth now, anyway—that at least one of the vehicles was a tank.

"Friendlies," he announced, hoarsely at first. Then he caught his breath, now irrigated a little, and donned an expression that had a semblance of hope.

"There's a tank, at least one tank! Friendlies!"

"No shit, I think he's right," Donnie said, still trying to focus on listening.

"Everyone, gear up," Bastian said, and whistled. He jogged back to hop into the trailer. "Move out!"

Despite his excitement, Bastian was still essentially bound to the trailer. The only thing that kept this from being depressing was the arsenal beside him. Secretly, he sympathized with what Preston had said earlier; as much as he yearned to use the Sevin or Arbalest, he recognized their true purpose was in Calipatria.

Of course, he had to actually survive to even see themselves that far.

Once Arlington got the Humvee going, the tank lurched forward, and Bastian was at least relieved to be moving again. They advanced beyond the playground and left the park, in all its quiet eeriness, behind.

Proceeding down the residential road that Arlington had indicated earlier offered them a view of the highway about half a mile away. There were no bends, only a slope in the road, before the asphalt path rose and leveled out, the intersection just past that point, the streetlight miraculously still lit up. It was a flashing yellow light that served as a sort of milestone as far as Bastian was concerned, but it wasn't his focus at that moment.

As soon as they crested a small incline on the road, a few hundred feet before the downward slope, they felt a wave of relief.

The remarkable column of military vehicles was definitely a sight for sore eyes.

It ground to a halt, the lead tank about twenty feet from where Arlington stopped his Humvee.

Bastian was the first to have boots on the ground, and seeing him initially struck awe into several of the soldiers exiting the other vehicles. Within a couple of minutes, Bastian and a reluctantly dismounted Donnie met with six soldiers from the first two vehicles, between Arlington's Humvee and their tank, an M1A2 Abrams.

He removed his helmet and cradled it under an arm, first to emphatically express his gratitude and relief, secondly to assure them that he wasn't a threat.

Not to them, anyway.

"Bastian Thurgood, Miramar, DARPA engineer," he introduced himself, keeping it succinct. However, the soldiers' bewildered gazes made him realize that he may have to be a little more thorough than that. "Uh, retired SEAL. The Suit is my pride and joy, our star project at the facility."

They were still generally speechless.

One of the soldiers, a tall dark man with gray sideburns and freckled temples, stepped forward. The insignia on his uniform indicated that he was a Master Sergeant.

"These are Marines with you, Thurgood?" the man asked, his voice somehow smooth despite being so deep. He, too, held his cap under his arm.

"They sure are. Some of the best, no doubt."

"PFC Sean Donahue, sir," Donnie saluted.

The man smirked briefly. "At ease, Donahue." he looked over Donnie's shoulder, peering at their

Humvee and tank, and the men inhabiting them. "How many of you are there?"

"Seven, sir," Donnie said, before Bastian could. "Including us."

"All the way from Miramar?"

"No, sir, we, uh…we've lost a handful."

"A fistful, certainly. A gauntlet's worth." The Master Sergeant sighed and returned his cap. "Marines are irreplaceable, afterall."

"Absolutely, sir."

"What were their names?"

Donnie cleared his throat and repressed the grief from manifesting.

"Lance Corp—"

"Their *names*, Donahue," he reiterated. "Not as soldiers, but as men."

Donnie wasn't expecting such a statement and it struck a chord deep in him. He cleared his throat again.

"H-Henry Elam. Terrence Irving, and…B-Brandon M-Mercer."

"Try to relax, Donahue. Were, uh, any of these men close friends or relatives?"

"M-Mercer, sir. He was a cousin."

"A loss is a loss, but I'm genuinely sorry for yours. And you, Thurgood. There's pain in your eyes. I can't imagine—"

"You probably can't, Master Sergeant," Bastian said. "I'm sorry to be so blunt, *sir*, but we ought to keep moving. It's critical that we reach Calipatria before things get—"

"Calipatria?" the man scoffed. He then peered at

the other Marines surrounding him, in full gear and wearing PFC insignia. "What are the odds?"

"Sir?" Bastian raised an eyebrow.

"Apologies, my name is Benjamin Avery, Master Sergeant, United States Marine Corps, stationed in Yuma, Arizona. The men with me are part of A Company, 3rd Platoon. We've lost twenty-seven men since our deployment."

"I'm sorry to hear that," Bastian said.

"This enemy is a wretched one, isn't it?" Avery sighed. "At any rate, it is an enemy nonetheless. One that we were ordered to confront, on the ground, in Calipatria, immediately after the structure now known as the Monolith was sighted. Once we were dispatched, attack orders were issued to the Air Force."

"We know about the Monolith, and the futile attacks, the EMP," Bastian said.

"That saves us some breath, then," Avery nodded. "But I doubt you're familiar with Operation Sledgehammer."

"Can't say that I am," Bastian said, and glanced at Donnie, who shook his head.

"Of course not, because only myself and select pilots were privy to that debriefing at 0300 hours."

Bastian's eyes looked up briefly in thought.

"About an hour ago," he said.

"Correct," Avery nodded. He looked at one of the soldiers standing beside him. "Private Hewlett, at what time will Operation Sledgehammer be executed?"

"At 0600 hours, sir," the Marine responded.

Avery nodded and turned back to face Bastian

and Donnie.

"You might want to gather your men for this, Thurgood, Donahue. It's critical to your mission, I imagine."

Bastian whistled and hand signaled in the air, motioning the other Marines to regroup on his position. In less than twenty seconds, the others had assembled. Everyone but Fields saluted Avery.

"At ease, gentlemen. I'm Master Sergeant Benjamin Avery, this is A Company, 3rd Platoon. Stationed at Yuma, Arizona. And then deployed to Calipatria. Whereupon we engaged the enemy horde surrounding the Monolith, for several hours on end. The expenditure of ammunition, and lives, was tremendous. While the enemy fell, so did they rise, eventually, and in greater numbers. Despite our grandest efforts, we could never lure them away from the Monolith. Enemy activity in the town itself, which was quickly evacuated, was non-existent, and for miles surrounding it, too.

"It became our belief, as much as Washington's, that the Monolith serves as the enemy's headquarters and command center. *How* it communicates with them, we don't know, but as of 0300 hours, this was no longer a hindering concern."

"You're gonna bomb it," Bastian muttered. He looked at Donnie, and the others. Particularly Preston. "Irving was right." He then looked back at Avery. "MOAB."

"You're either a great guesser, or..." Avery paused and sized up Bastian, head to toe, scrutinizing the Suit. "Something else entirely."

"Consider it an *educated* guess," Bastian said, giving Preston a brief glance.

"At any rate, yes," Avery finally confirmed. "At 0600 hours, the Air Force will deliver a Massive Ordnance Air Blast bomb to the Monolith. The detonation will occur *above* the presumed EMP field, so that the blast should still affect the structure itself, as well as the ground forces surrounding it. The blast radius is only six-hundred feet, but the composition and volatility of the Monolith itself is beyond our knowledge. Hence, our orders to retreat to the outer limits. We felt obliged to venture a little farther than that, and see if any civilians might be in need of our assistance. Worst case, we could mop up any enemies we should come across."

It was a lot to take in, but Bastian had already prepared himself for this type of possibility, especially after Irving had seeded that concept.

Although, that had been significantly different— then, they were discussing the deliverance of a MOAB to the San Diego area, not the Monolith.

As far as Bastian was concerned, this was worth the shot.

"Worst-case," Lemay said, "that's a lot of dead monsters on the ground."

"No, worst-case," Bastian hated to admit, "the Monolith is extremely volatile, and causes a much larger explosion that wipes San Diego off the map. Or…even worse…destabilizes the San Andreas Fault."

A few of the Marines cursed and mumbled quietly amongst themselves, on Bastian's side as well as Avery's.

"A necessary risk, I'm sure, Washington has considered," Avery added, his voice grim. "Nonetheless, we are merely following orders in a most unprecedented time."

"So that's it, then," Bastian said. "I'm expected to just lie down and wait?"

"Or risk a front-row-seat to the first combat use of a MOAB on U.S. soil."

Bastian looked at Donnie and the other men fanned out around him, in front of their Humvee. Even Fields seemed to shrink back a little. Bastian scowled and shook his head. He started to walk forward, toward A Company's tank. He put his helmet back on, visor down, on the way.

"I won't. I can't," he declared, his voice booming through the mouthpiece. "At the very least, I gotta keep going. Just in case…the bomb fails, and the Monolith *doesn't* detonate. Then I gotta…"

"What exactly was…*is*…your plan, Thurgood?" Avery asked, grimacing.

"Penetrate the horde's ground forces, infiltrate the Monolith, and from there, I don't know, find *some* weakness. There must be something."

"A suicide mission."

"That seems to be the favorite term for my task, sure. But it's better than having no endgame. It's better than walking this bleak earth, forced to inhale the stench of death, and continue suffering the memory of my wife's death and my little girl's *slaughter*."

Bastian refrained from punching something out of sheer rage. The nearest thing was the tank, which

Bastian, in his Suit, was better off not touching that way.

"So yeah, call it a death wish," he added, returning to his previous company, but continuing to walk after that. "But at least it has a purpose!"

"Fields," Donnie said.

Fields nodded and turned to catch up with Bastian, hopefully to talk some sense into him. But Donnie didn't know Fields well enough.

"Bastian, man," Fields said, just as Bastian reached the trailer behind the tank. "You're crazy, you know that?"

"Be that as it may," he said simply, without turning away from the trailer or his weapons cart in it. He didn't add anything to the open-ended statement.

"Your reasons are justified, I'm not protesting them. But we can't do this on foot. What do you propose, we just jack one of their Humvees? C'mon. We need *some* support."

Bastian smirked to himself, but let it fade once he turned to face Fields.

"You still want to come along?"

Fields nodded. "I'm in this. Just don't ask me to T2 that fence when the MOAB drops."

Bastian shook his head once. "We won't be getting that close, I promise. How the Monolith reacts, though, I can't be sure."

Fields shrugged. "Life is full of surprises."

# <u>17</u>

Persuading Bastian Thurgood was never an easy task, for anyone, ever. Not even for his best friends in boot camp, nor his rigorous trainer in the Navy. Not even his wife could say that it was ever an easy thing. The only person who could persuade Bastian with such little effort was Eliza Thurgood. Now that he was bereft of that little miracle, and of her mother, he felt alone in so many ways.

The plethoric company of Marines counted for a lot. And the others he had encountered along his journey, even more.

Flynn Fields had proven himself tenfold, not just as a fellow fighter but a brother-in-arms, of sorts, too.

Bastian was grateful to say the least.

Ultimately, though, he said very little.

Fields seemed to appreciate this, as he, himself, was a man of few words. It had already been established that actions were superior to words in whatever version of the world this had become.

Convincing anyone except for Bastian was a whole other task altogether. He opted for this undertaking instead of Fields, assuring the ex-security guard that he was better *equipped* with the means of persuasion.

Naturally, Fields couldn't object.

Part of him was even excited to see what Bastian might do to cajole the Marines to 'lend' one of their vehicles. While Fields preferred a tank, for speed purposes, Bastian favored a Humvee.

There was no debate between them.

After their succinct exchange behind the tank, Bastian thrusted a fully loaded ROT-20 into Fields' hands, as a gesture of appreciation at the very least. Then he equipped himself with a freshly reloaded Duke, strictly for intimidation purposes.

He returned to the befuddled gathering of Marines between the two convoys. Even more soldiers from A Company had purged themselves from their vehicles to assemble at the front of the column. In Bastian and Fields' absence, Avery had likely informed them of what was happening.

*And just what* is *happening, Master Sergeant?* Bastian mused to himself, before returning to the Marines.

He stood to the right of Artie, who stood to the right of Lemay and Donnie, Arlington on the far left. They all seemed to eagerly await whatever he had to say. According to the look on Donnie's face, Bastian would guess that the PFC already knew full well his decision.

"I'm heading there, regardless of what is said, or attempted, to stop me." Bastian took a deep breath and looked over the faces of the Marines present, on Avery's side. Their lead tank had two gunner hatches and spotlights mounted by each. They presently illuminated where everyone stood. "I could, however, really use a vehicle if you have one to spare. The M1A3 be-hind me is, while improved in many ways, a lighter version of your Abrams. It would mean a lot if you'd offer one of yours, and a Humvee. I of course would need a small crew to operate it, but—"

"You don't need anyone except us," Lemay said, matter-of-factly. He looked at his fellow crewmate. Artie didn't flinch. He did, however, nod minutely.

Bastian started to say something but was once again interrupted, although not in a cruel way.

"Before you go recruiting total strangers," Don-nie said, "just know that we're the first strangers to follow you into the mouth of hell."

"Well, seems like you're a popular man, Mr. Thurgood," Avery said, sounding both impressed and amused.

"Can't say I deserve it," Bastian replied, looking at Avery. He then glanced at Donnie and the others. "But I'm quite grateful."

"Gentlemen?" Avery said, peering at his fellow Marines.

Nothing else needed to be said.

At least not for a few of them.

Four men in particular stepped forward. The fourth tried to convince a fifth, but this particular Ma-rine refused to break away from the larger mass.

"Enough," Avery snapped. "There will be no co-ercion among my ranks. If you...so feel the urge to assist Mr. Thurgood, at the very least helping escort him to Calipatria, I will not interject. But know that your re-sources will be limited, and while I do wish for your safe return, no reinforcements shall be sent after you if needed or even requested."

"We understand, sir," one of the four Marines acknowledged. "But we humbly respect Thurgood's mission and request to join." The man had a light complexion but jet-black features, especially stark against the illumination provided by the tanks and Humvees' crossing headlights. He turned to face Bastian. "The four of us have been friends for eleven years. We…had family in Tierrasanta. From what we've learned…"

Bastian nodded sullenly. "I, too, had family there. *Had.* I am reluctant to risk the lives of anyone else eager to help me, but I cannot decline an escort, at the very least."

The four Marines nodded, almost in unison, and moved toward the front of the group, replacing those standing directly around Avery. They were all about the same age, in their low thirties, with the exception of a densely bearded individual. They appeared Hispanic, and the one who spoke had an unavoidable accent.

"Two of us can operate an Abrams, and the other two a Humvee," the same Marine who spoke previously, continued to. He then looked at Avery. "If that is permitted, Master Sergeant."

Avery nodded. "I believe we can spare two vehicles for your cause, Mr. Thurgood, as outlandish as you must admit that it seems."

"Perhaps, to someone who hasn't witnessed firsthand the capabilities of this Suit."

"Perhaps," Avery mumbled. He then elucidated his voice. "Perhaps, at another point in time and place,

I might be more understanding."

"I hope to shake your hand when this is all through, and the Monolith is but rubble at my feet. Maybe then I can change your mind."

"I look forward to it," Avery said through a chuckle. "And I envy your temerity, Thurgood. As rash as it may be."

"I'll be seeing you, Master—"

Bastian was tired of being interrupted, but this time it wasn't by another man. Or, necessarily, a creature. The ground shook, but in a manner that dwarfed previous quakes. Even the most sizeable one that he had experienced to date was significantly inferior to this one. Several houses on either side of the two-lane road crumbled in its wake, and broad, jagged fissures cut through the asphalt, bridging the gap between curbs with an even wider gorge.

It formed fifty feet from where Bastian stood, and even he now stumbled back. The other men present faltered much more severely, several of them falling altogether.

Bastian caught Avery, who immediately braced against the statue of a man in his Suit. They were equally in awe of this newfound cataclysm.

Half a dozen Marines screamed and twofold more hollered after their comrades as they tumbled into the gaping pit. An entire Humvee disappeared in its jaws right away, followed by another that tried to reverse from the jagged edge but couldn't escape gravity. The driver and crew inside screamed until the fiercely glowing depths swallowed them.

The back end of a tank teetered over the edge. The tracks spun madly against the asphalt for traction, but found none.

Bastian transferred Avery over to a pair of Marines before rushing down the column of vehicles. Most of them now accelerated, in the direction of the two vehicles belonging to Bastian's "team."

He had to dodge one Humvee that drove off in an entirely askew direction, which he quickly realized was caused by a gaping crack in the asphalt behind the vehicle. He leapt over this and reached the tank just as it tilted over the ledge. With his supplemented height in the Suit, reaching up to grab the cannon barrel with both hands wasn't a challenge, only to do so as urgently as he had to.

Bastian then swung back, and helped pull the tank's front half onto the asphalt again. The tracks accelerated until they found traction, and Bastian sidestepped out of the way. It lurched forward, past him, managing to pass over the other crack before it widened too far.

A few Marines who witnessed the feat hooted and cheered for Bastian, as well as the crew inside the tank.

Their little victory, which Bastian vainly began to give in and share, was short-lived.

A colossal mass lifted out of the pit, which glowed red and orange below. And then it came down, a couple hundred feet behind Bastian. He staggered back, gawking skyward, watching the solid black shape pass over him. When it impacted the ground, another quake passed beneath them, but no more gaping tracks tore through the earth, or the asphalt. This thing touched down in the park, crushing the entire playground beneath it.

Bastian only realized that it was a leg once two more lifted out of the pit, soaring above before crashing down around them. These two took alternating stances, one behind the column of vehicles about four hundred feet in the opposite direction, and the second off to the side, demolishing two houses with it.

The limbs towered at least seventy feet up before dipping into a U-shape, and then rising again to connect with a triangular mass of black flesh, if it could be called that. Bastian found a closer resemblance to igneous rock, and misshapen forms of it at that. The body appeared as if a basket of sorts, encompassing a lambent, magmatic mass inside.

A red-orange glow emanated around the colossal abomination, lighting up the night sky that it now towered beneath, the height of a 'small' skyscraper. A slender, rocky neck protruded from between two of the limbs and rose above in an arcing manner, as if a scorpion's tail. Yet instead of a stinger, this seventy-foot-long protrusion ended in a pentagonal skull of black rock, with a pair of gaping jaws at the front, and flames that lit up its throat. Atop its head was what Bastian could only describe as a crown of rocky protrusions, seven of them, cylindrical and slightly curved, tapering to a sharp tip.

The abomination was eyeless, but that was easily its least disturbing feature.

As soon as it had found its tripodal stance, the jaws hung open and a thunderous roar reverberated forth. The sound was tremendous, like an earthquake in the air, passing its stalactite-like teeth. Concurrently the flames in its throat flickered, but to Bastian's relief did not spill out.

*Good. Not a fucking dragon.*

Still, the Emperor of Hell as far as Bastian was concerned, or at least one of them—the thought of more of these things made him want to faint—was an imposing threat. It made every Pyro and Tyrant Bastian had faced seem like a wingless Vulture.

*Wingless.*

Seeing that the subterranean monstrosity, now having surfaced, had neither wings nor any extremities beside its feet, gave Bastian hope.

A light bulb flickered on in his head.

"A flawed creation, a true mutation," Bastian mumbled, nonetheless still gawking up at the colossus. He stood directly below its triangular thorax, which was about the size of five tanks gathered together.

"Now the fuck what!?" Donnie yelled.

Bastian was some forty feet away. He began moving back to his comrades, bumping into a few other Marines scrambling to get out of the way, leaping over several meter-wide cracks in the asphalt along the way.

At one point Bastian tripped over one and actually fell. He tumbled into a roll, however, and before he knew it had sprung himself back to his feet. Just as he did, though, the massive enemy's three legs *pivoted*. One of them dragged like a wounded foot, plowing through rows of houses to Bastian's left. He threw his arms up on impulse, as the sheer sound of the destruction was overwhelming, much less the added tremors.

"Get in the tank!" Bastian shouted at the top of his lungs as he rushed toward the Marines still gathered like a frightened flock of sheep. "Concentrate fire on the legs! The upper legs!"

"The what!?" Lemay hollered as he climbed onto the tank.

In addition to the overlapping discordance of turbo-diesel engines, Marines shouting at each other or screaming in general, a few of them futilely firing in a panic up at the behemoth, and the destruction caused, its sheer presence was loud. It breathed like rolling thunder and its mass moving through the air was a wave of disturbance.

From whatever unholy pit it had emerged, an obscure dissonance also spewed.

"The upper legs!" Bastian feverishly pointed. "Where they dip, that's where they're thinnest!"

"Oh, great!" Artie yelled, following Lemay. "The smallest target!"

"You got a better fucking idea!?" Bastian bellowed. He lowered his visor and focused on closing the distance.

Meanwhile, the gigantic atrocity voiced itself again, this time a shorter roar followed by the simple lifting of a leg before slamming it back down. It crushed a fleeing Humvee and the house it had driven close to, along with the entire front lawn and part of the neighboring property. Flames spat out around the circular, flat base of the limb, and several more Marines frantically fired up at it.

A pointless effort, but in their fit of madness, it seemed like the only thing to do, shy of fleeing.

"We stand a better chance speeding off, and outrunning this godforsaken thing!"

"Maybe, sir," Bastian replied to an aghast Avery, now just a few feet away, "but the people of this planet will be worse off for it! If you can get the word to them, order your Humvees to drive in a circle directly below it, force it to try and use its leg like it just did! It will stay still for this maneuver, and we'll fire then!"

"That's suicide, Thurgood!"

"Fine! Then *I'll* fucking do it, on *foot*!" Bastian practically spat. Spittle misted the inside of his visor.

While Avery apprehensively juggled this idea, the four Marines who had previously stepped forward to join Bastian now volunteered again.

Those who hadn't spoken then, were vocal now. Not a single one of the men, although horrorstruck by what was happening, expressed reluctance.

"We'll handle it, Thurgood! Just tell your men to be as accurate as fucking possible!"

"Of course!" Bastian replied.

"Two Humvees, just to make sure," one of the other Marines shouted.

"Two per!" another added. "We'll man the guns, too, short bursts, just to make damn sure it's paying attention!"

"Great idea!" Bastian responded.

"*Crazy* idea, Thurgood, but we're in!"

The men dispersed before Avery could say a word, heading back toward their convoy. There was only one Humvee that remained unmoving, which was where they had initially come from. All the other vehicles belonging to their column had either been swallowed by the fiery canyon or relocated.

Meanwhile, above, the giant roared again before dragging not one, but two of its massive limbs across the planet. The third acted as a crutch, pivoting with 'small steps' while it dragged the others in a circle, repositioning but not necessarily walking. Its massive head at the end of the arcing neck loomed over its body, peering down past its limbs to observe the throng of humans still beneath it, including the three vehicles.

One tank separating two Humvees.

"Wait!" Bastian hollered after the four Marines, seconds before two of them piled into the Humvee. Simultaneously, the other two replaced Arlington and Donnie in theirs, behind Bastian. "What are your names?"

"Intros later," the driver of the Humvee forty feet ahead of him shouted back, standing outside an open door. "Just call us the Bandits!"

He climbed into the Humvee, shut the door, and keyed the engine.

Bastian's brow furrowed and he looked over at Avery, who rolled his eyes. Bastian wanted to smirk, but the chaos of the moment was too intense to be even remotely distracted from.

"Come on, sir! In the tank!" two of Avery's Marines remained by his side, now trying to urgently usher him to their nearest Abrams, which had driven off the road but not far.

"We should still have comms," Avery called out to Bastian as he let his Marines lead him to the tank. "I'll order my Humvees to stay put, and not draw attention! I'll also share your strategy with my tank crews!"

"Remind me to buy you a drink sometime, *sir*!"

Avery smirked and briefly saluted before being assisted into the Abrams via the commander's hatch.

Meanwhile, the gigantic beast stopped and, instead of driving its leg down, swung it at a Humvee driving through front lawns about eighty feet from Avery's tank. Likely trying to drive off, in the direction they had come. The vehicle was going maybe thirty miles an hour, slowly gaining speed as it plowed through fences and fountains. The flat, rocky bottom of the tapered foot glided over the surface of the earth with maybe ten feet of room to spare.

Barely.

It clipped the roof of the Humvee, sufficient to cleave it in half, with a spurt of flame that appeared trivial in size compared to the massive leg.

Several Marines spectating tensely threw their arms up and cursed. They purged fits of anger and grief from their own corners of the neighborhood, most of them still beneath the giant's tripodal radius.

The few outside of it remained still.

Bastian hoped that Avery was able to radio them and communicate his haphazard plan.

Meanwhile, he shifted his focus to the Marines

in his current company, but wasn't sure what to do himself. Just then, the "Bandits" in Arlington's Humvee drove past, howling like coyotes.

"Crazy bastards," Arlington said, anxiously standing beside Bastian, head shaking.

The Humvee joined the other directly beneath the behemoth, not terribly far from the nearest ledge of the massive gorge through which it had emerged. They honked their horns and their gunners fired short bursts of .50-caliber rounds up at the rocky belly of the beast. And then the Humvees proceeded to drive in a close-knit circle, rousing dust and smoke in their wake, honking and shooting up a small storm.

Bastian watched as the monster's attention shifted to the Humvees below it, and likely realized that it could not attack them by swinging its leg, due to their position.

So it took one step back with two of its limbs, poising for another raised-leg strike. The backpedal destroyed four more houses in the process, and Bastian could only hope that they were empty at the time.

"I think we're better off on our feet," Bastian suggested to the men surrounding him.

Everyone but Lemay and Artie.

"Should we stay put, or run?" Preston asked.

"Whatever you want," Bastian said. "But I wouldn't run into a house. They're dropping like flies."

"Good to be small, then," Donnie said.

"Hell yeah," Bastian added. While not short like Donnie, and in the Suit he felt like a little giant of sorts among men, compared to the titanic beast above them, he was an insect. "We may not have wings, but neither does it. We're smaller, agiler. Size always matters; this time, it's the opposite of what you'd expect."

"Do you think the tank's ammo will penetrate whatever—?"

As if Artie heard Arlington, their tank's main cannon recoiled, firing. Donnie and even Bastian flinched, startled. Barely two seconds later, a pair of tanks below the beast, from opposite sides of the road, fired their cannons, too. It was a wonderful surprise to Bastian that they happened to be targeting the same leg; however, one of them missed, instead striking the central body. There was a small fireball against the rocky surface, but no apparent damage.

The other two high-explosive projectiles hit their target, only a few meters apart. The twin blasts enveloped the U-shaped portion of the leg, and the giant reacted as desired—

Maddeningly.

It made a thunderous snorting sound and descended its head, so low that the neck curled its skull beneath its body, between its tripodal legs, its rocky chin only forty or fifty feet above where the Bandits circled their Humvees.

Even now, still driving, howling and shooting.

The colossus started to roar in the direction of Artie and Lemay's tank, its eyeless stare coursing over Bastian and company, but then it paused.

The commotion directly beneath its chin caught its attention. It tilted its spiked skull and began to retract, only to angle its jaws down at the circling Bandits.

Just then one of the three tanks fired again, striking it in the side of the head. The explosion broke off two of its crown spikes, and the huge beast snarled in that direction.

The instant that it began to shift its legs again, the other two tanks fired, one a split-second after the other, probably watching and waiting for its cue. The muzzle flashes from the cannons were small fireballs of light in the flame-scarred night.

Now their goal was unmistakable—to focus on the weakened leg. However damaged it was, from barely at all to severely, they would see in seconds.

The two projectiles collaborated, explosively, on their target. The range was about eighty feet above them, but fortunately within their cannons' reach, as the barrels sustained accuracy only up to a 45° angle.

The result was satisfying, from where Bastian stood, and immediately he began backpedaling toward the tank that Lemay and Artie operated. Simultaneously, he watched the behemoth's leg crumble where it was thinnest, in that dip between its body mass and what might be called its knee. In addition to large chunks of fragmented rock and crust from the demolished limb section—about ten feet's worth—large globs of what Bastian predicted to be magmatic blood fell. Some of both kinds of debris came dangerously close to impacting where the Bandits continued to drive in circles below it.

The massive beast tilted to that side, as its severed limb toppled like an enormous tree. It fell to the right, ultimately crushing several houses in the process and flattening even more yardage.

Bastian could only justify this as the better out-come because, had they not acted, the giant would have proceeded to wreak its havoc well outside this area.

Now, the jaws of the beast shifted with its eyeless skull, fixated on the tank to the left of the road.

Finally, Bastian reached Lemay and Artie's tank, slapping the side armor and verbally applauding their marksmanship. Then he skidded behind the hitched trailer and hoisted the Arbalest out of his flat-cart, wielding it and stepping away from the tank.

Already the enormous abomination began to tee-ter, its shift of weight causing it to lean forward. As it did this, it realized it and the face displayed something that Bastian had to describe as surprise. He hadn't im-agined that the creature was even capable of expressing itself through its rocky, jagged face, but alas, that was what he witnessed.

Disturbing as it was, Bastian felt delighted that it could even feel what he would call a seed of fear.

With the Arbalest loaded and armed, Bastian re-called his limited training with it, and brought it to aim. It required bracing against his waist, wielding it with his left hand on a horizontal grip and his right on a vertical beneath its crossbow-shaped frame. He armed it via a switch with his right thumb, and the magnetic rail charged up with a high whirring sound.

"Oh, shit!" Preston exclaimed from the tank. He stood behind the back right side, peering around it. "Headshot that motherfucker!"

*Let's hope so*, Bastian thought.

He lined up his aim, grateful for the big target. As the gigantic jaws stemming an orange glow opened even wider, Bastian knew he couldn't chance a miss.

He fired.

The prototypal railgun recoiled something fierce, but against his Suit it felt more like a double-barrel shotgun, and not even the Supe. A hiss of smoke discharged from the hollow top of the Arbalest as the charged, magnetic tungsten slug shot out. At 7100 feet-per-second, the 20mm-diameter projectile reached its target in the blink of an eye.

To Bastian's displeasure, there appeared to be no effect. No exit wound, after the projectile vanished into the behemoth's mouth.

He gulped and lowered the Arbalest.

Not too joyously, he turned to face the tank, and spotted disappointed faces on both Preston and Fields. Meanwhile, Donnie was on top of the tank, on all fours, peering into the surveyor's portal, frantically talking to the crew inside.

Fields looked particularly discontent at his uselessness on the tank-mounted .50-cal.

Bastian looked around, not liking one bit that he, too, suddenly felt inadequate—and with the Arbalest of all weapons made it even worse.

When he spotted something that gave him an idea, he acknowledged the insanity of it in his mind but could not ignore the possibilities.

Urgently, he returned the Arbalest to the trailer behind the tank and rushed forward. Just as he reached the front of the tank, to his left, the cannon fired. It startled him, but even the concussive muzzle flash and pressure did not faze him. He was relieved to be in the Suit, and have the visor down, in that moment.

His gaze quickly switched from the tank to the beast, its head still lowered, its body teetering, as it struggled to maintain some kind of balance. And then the tank's high-explosive projectile hit its mark, through its gaping jaws, and the effect was easily more remarkable than the Arbalest's. A plume of flame erupted behind its rocky skull, where the head-like formation met with the neck, and several of its crown protrusions broke off.

The debris crashed to the asphalt below, where the Bandits previously were, but had since begun to drive away, toward Bastian and the others.

He raised his visor and the acridity of gunsmoke filled his suit. Something about it, in that moment, was actually aromatic.

"Hit it again!" Bastian shouted at the top of his lungs, waving at the tank, not just theirs but the two under Avery's command, on opposite sides of the road.

And then he lowered his visor as he made a beeline for the radical idea he had produced earlier. He neared one of the two intact limbs of the beast, this particular one awfully close to the edge of the gorge from whence it had come. He did not slow down as he reached it, however; he must have ran at least fifty paces full-speed—his strides and momentum enhanced by the Suit—by the time he lowered his shoulder and slammed into it. The tapered base of the limb was the size of a large oak tree trunk, but as the giant tried to establish balance, it didn't exactly have sure footing.

Especially after taking a 102mm high-explosive projectile into the mouth.

And then the tank opposite the one that Avery occupied fired its cannon, too. From its angle, it was unable to strike the beast's open jaw, but it did hit it from the side, the blast sufficing to knock its head asunder. The beast's carriage slanted, and Bastian's efforts were facilitated. His armored feet grinded against the road, forming troughs in the asphalt as he pushed the limb over the ledge of the gorge. It released a howling, guttural roar that sounded both prehistoric and other-worldly, as its weight pulled it back into the abyss from whence it came.

Bastian felt a momentous weight lift off his shoulders as he anticipated the beast's certain doom.

And then, somehow, its previously destroyed limb, where the stub remained, managed to catch the other edge of the canyon, propping it like a makeshift bridge across the opening.

There, it struggled madly, jaws gnashing at the air, bleeding magma from the back of its skull, and in denser flows still, from its severed leg.

Avery's tank fired, and almost simultaneously so did Artie and Lemay. He still had no idea which of the two men were responsible for driving and firing, respectively, but at any rate they were one hell of a team.

Bastian started to backpedal, watching in victorious awe as the two projectiles struck the behemoth almost at the same time. Avery's tank had hit it in the lower jaw, obliterating several stalagmite-like teeth in the process, while the other managed to deliver yet another shot *into* the mouth. This one exacerbated its previous wound, and part of the rocky skull dislodged from the neck entirely, yet somehow not cutting off its odious vocalizations.

The enormous abomination released one final, thundering roar of defeat as its body crumbled.

One by one, its extremities, from limbs to neck, began to dismantle, like the ingredients of a landslide. Until it no longer resembled any kind of lifeform, biological or terrestrial, subterranean or otherwise. Its giant mass disintegrated during its descent from which it came, the magmatic innards spilling out like exposed lava from an active volcano, yet lazily, ultimately returning to the bowels of the earth.

A few light tremors scattered beneath the surface, rattling houses and streetlights, but causing no further damage.

And then it all came to a rest, and while the chasm remained open, the glow from below dulled until it was no more.

Bastian now stumbled, lightheaded in a way, backwards. Farther from the edge of the canyon until the fear of falling in was nullified. While the gaping wound in the earth did stretch well beyond the roadside curbs, extending to the backyards of the houses on either side of the street, it was not impassable. They would simply have to either take another route, or force their own passage through backyards.

Presently, he was primarily focused on the relief

that not only he but most of their force also survived that appalling encounter.

He looked around.

They had obviously suffered casualties, but considering the incomparable and gargantuan nature of that enemy, and their lack of preparation, he chalked it up in the W column.

As he returned to the tank farthest down the road, in the direction of the park, the crew emerged with circumstantially jubilant expressions. Lemay especially. Artie looked more exhausted than anything, as he was likely the one loading the cannon projectiles, which were about twenty-five pounds each.

If Bastian had to describe Artie's face, it would be "relieved."

He wished he could tell them that their fight was over, but naturally, they still had a ways to go. And who knew, truly, for how much longer? Or if any of them would even get to see the end of it?

Of course, none of them *had to* actually tag along with Bastian, but at this point he wanted them to, for various reasons. He relished their effectual help, and had come to value their company as men. Even in as little amount of time as he had shared with them.

He couldn't help but wonder, now, if they would even want to continue with him. After that colossal horror, he would understand if they opted to hang back.

Then again, who knew, really, if or when another of those—*or something even bigger, even worse*—would surface?

Bastian feared that, in other parts of the state, or

country, similar beasts were already walking amok. There was no way for them to know, except to theorize that the worst versions of these creatures were only native to regions nearest the Monolith.

*Makes sense*, Bastian tried to convince himself.

He reached the tank and commended the crew's efforts. Though genuine and fervent, the recognition was brief. It didn't take a blind man to perceive that the urgency in Bastian Thurgood had yet dithered.

If anything, it was stronger now more than ever before.

"I can't believe you practically *pushed* its foot off the cliff," Preston said, flabbergasted.

"That's because I didn't, not really. And definitely not without help." Bastian looked up at Artie and Lemay. "Who's the driver, who's the loader?"

"Normally Artie drives and aims, but if we're stationary, I'll take the reins." Lemay shrugged. "He's got a better knack at mobile engagements."

Artie neither confirmed nor denied.

Bastian nodded and then turned when he noticed Fields' expression—and eyes—shift. He spotted Avery crossing the road toward him, after disembarking the Abrams now idling ten feet away. The man looked shaken but not completely discombobulated.

"Hell of a job, Thurgood," Avery said, before reaching him, and extending his hand.

Bastian raised his visor before shaking the man's hand, keen on being gentle.

"We're indebted to our crewmen," he replied, gesturing at Artie and Lemay, then looking to the left side of the road, where the other tank remained. Through the commander's hatch, however, emerged two men, one after the other. Then Bastian diverted his gaze and looked over Avery's shoulder to the Abrams he had come out of.

"Very true," Avery nodded. He took a deep breath and withdrew his hand, straightened his uniform, and looked over Bastian's "team." He nodded at each man individually, gestures of respect. "I must say, now, after that...*unparalleled* abomination...shit, you've got my full support. You're a madman for going after the Monolith, I can't deny it, but there's also a peculiar courage in it that cannot be overlooked."

"I guess I'll take the compliment while I can," Bastian said with a moderate simper. It evaporated as he looked around again, and his brow furrowed. "You lost several vehicles, and men, though. Great men, I imagine. I hope that your Marines don't find me, or our crossing of paths, to blame."

"Nonsense. If they did, they're no Marines under *my* command. No Marines period, for that matter. Hell, if anything, Thurgood, we're grateful. As awful and irreplaceable as our losses were. After you've gone, I'll regrettably do a roll-call and the absence of their names will sink like teeth."

Bastian exhaled forcefully through his nostrils and shook his head before letting it bow. It didn't have much space to tilt, with the broadness of his helmet on. The chin of it locked against his chest-plate and he found himself staring at the Master Sergeant's medal-adorned uniform.

"I best be going, then." He lifted his head and tried to breathe steadily. "You and your men have my best regards."

"Likewise. And if any of my Marines still wish to assist you, they have my support. There'll certainly be no shortage of honor to it."

"Thank you, Master Sergeant."

"Regardless of what happens at Calipatria for you and your men, Thurgood, your name won't be forgotten in my book."

"Nor yours, nor my men," Bastian said, not even mentioning all the others he had befriended along his warpath. From Eduardo Zavala to Jake Taylor to Abasi Abdi.

Avery nodded grimly, but not indifferently, and parted ways.

"Say, Thurgood?" He said before getting far. He paused, half-turning.

"Yeah?"

"That *was* your first time encountering such an enemy, correct?"

"Definitely. And you?"

"Oh, yeah. I must express my fear, however, that there are others like it…or worse…in the works."

"My bet is that they know we're getting awfully close, and this much of us might pose a threat. Greater than when you were already in Calipatria."

"Maybe it's you, Thurgood, had you thought about that?" Avery chuckled wryly. "A bit of notoriety for you, soldier."

Before Bastian could properly compute that possibility, Master Sergeant Avery turned back to his path and boarded the tank with the help of a Marine. And then Bastian noticed the other vehicles in the area, those not on the opposite side of the rift, start to assemble on the tank's position. He was envious of their communications equipment, but considering everything that he and *his* group had achieved sans a radio or even walkie-talkies, he was definitely impressed and thankful.

*Speaking of which…*

The Bandits, as they remained nameless but not for long, drove over. They did not assemble with Avery's group, but about forty feet over, in the middle of the road, where it was intact. Meanwhile, opposite the gaping, jagged gorge were two Humvees essentially stranded. Bastian assumed that Avery or his men were currently communicating with them.

Once the two Humvees with the Bandits in them arrived, their vehicles lurched to a stop and out stepped all four Marines.

They were each sweating torrentially, making their black hair and eyebrows stand out even more. One of them had a full beard, and another sported a neatly trimmed goatee. The other two were clean-shaven.

"Hell of a job, gentlemen," Bastian said. "Hell of a fucking job."

"Happy to help, boss," the goatee man said. He looked maybe thirty, thirty-five.

"Yeah, you guys are bonkers," Lemay said from on top of the tank. "But we appreciate you."

"More than you know," Bastian added. "So, the

offer still stands, if you boys want to tag along with us to Calipatria, we're happy to have you. But I can't guarantee—"

"We don't like guarantees, anyway," one of the clean-shaven men said, shrugging. "They leave no room for winging it."

"I suppose you're right. Can't argue there." Bastian cleared his throat. "One thing, though. Urgency is my main and only rule. I'm already running awfully late. A lot of shit keeps happening, can't blame anyone for it, but—"

"Then let's get to it, yeah?" the goatee man said. He looked at his comrades and they all nodded.

"Lemme just get your names, okay? I like knowing who I'm fighting with. And forego the ranks. They don't matter here."

"I like your attitude, Thurgood," the goatee man said with a pointing of his finger.

"I hope, then, that you won't mind calling me Bastian from here on. Anything else is a bit irksome."

"No worries," the bearded man finally spoke. "But we're kind of old-school. Surnames since boot."

"No objections, that's how these fellas are, too," Bastian thumbed over his shoulder. "And you are?"

The goatee man stepped forward, interrupting his heavily bearded comrade, and extended a hand.

"Jacinto Muñoz."

"Let's sound off, eh?" Bastian gestured at all of the men and raised his eyebrows. "Get the ball rolling."

He hoped the goateed Muñoz didn't take offense to his declined handshake. He didn't seem to; the man just smirked and nodded, stepping back, hands aft.

"Nice to meet you, though, Muñoz," Bastian added, cultured enough over the years to pronounce the name accurately.

"Likewise…Bastian."

They exchanged small smiles and curt nods. Bastian subconsciously admitted to liking the group of Marines' lighthearted disposition. Especially in spite of everything that had happened and was still occurring around them, both directly and indirectly.

It was kind of refreshing.

Definitely the needed morale injection for what awaited them; Bastian at least.

"Roberto Santi," one of the clean-shaven men said, probably the youngest of them.

"Diego Tielve," the other one announced. He was maybe a few years older than Santi, and less timid.

These were, of course, merely Bastian's preliminary readings.

The bearded man remained, who was not a challenge to analyze, at least not ostensibly. Although quiet, there was something veteran about him. While he wasn't quite as old as Bastian, he was easily in his upper thirties, low forties, and weathered. In more ways than one, Bastian imagined.

"Tommy Guerrero," he introduced himself rigidly, despite initially being the first, before Muñoz interrupted.

"Now that show and tell is over," Preston said, over Bastian's left shoulder, actually startling him too, "can we hit the road and get this shit-show over with?"

"Kitty can scratch," Muñoz whispered to Santi, and the two men chuckled.

Bastian turned to face an indifferent looking Preston, who simply rolled his eyes and returned to the tank. He realized, then, that the entirety of his *team* had been present for the introductions. Just looming behind him. He ultimately figured it was for the best.

And they could get better acquainted along the way. But Preston was right.

*Urgency, afterall*, Bastian reminded himself.

"Sure thing," he finally said out loud, and then whistled. It was so loud and strident that it even caught the attention of a few Marines surrounding Avery's tank. Bastian turned his back on the Bandits, nonetheless beckoning them to follow, as he returned to the trailer behind the tank, announcing: "Let's fall in and get going! We have ourselves front-row tickets to a demolition show!"

Some of the men theatrically hooted with excitement. It started with Fields, then a revitalized Donnie, and was quickly, unsurprisingly picked up by two of the Bandits. With the exception of the youngest and the oldest, Santi and Guerrero, respectively.

Bastian's declaration, bracketed by his whistling and the howling of his men, actually riled up several of Avery's Marines, too. He hoped that this wasn't interpreted as disrespecting their fallen comrades, of course, but merely motivating themselves toward their daunting objective.

While Fields remained on the tank machinegun, with Artie and Lemay inside, Bastian returned to his tank-hitched trailer and cart of weapons. He requested, though in a commanding manner, that both Humvees *trail* the tank, instead of leading it. This would also put him closer to the front of their formation, which seemed fitting, considering that this was, afterall, a mission instigated by himself. He felt more confident being the vanguard of their convoy, than the middle or end of it.

By this point, the Bandits and the other Marines from Miramar had arranged themselves in the two Humvees. Donnie manned the gun on one, Guerrero on the other. Arlington drove the one that Donnie occupied, his passenger Preston. Behind Preston sat Santi, not minding being separated from the rest of his crew. In the other Humvee, farthest back in the formation, which Guerrero manned the gun for, Tielve drove and Muñoz sat behind the empty passenger seat.

Bastian couldn't help but wonder just how talkative the shy Santi would become over the next thirty to forty minutes, during their drive, with Marines he didn't know at all.

It piqued Bastian's curiosity, in an almost playful manner.

As their column slowly drove past Avery's tank and his surrounding Marines, the commander's hatch opened and the Master Sergeant himself protruded. He saluted Bastian's team, and several of his Marines did, too. But just as the tank passed them, Bastian stood and whistled. Lemay stopped the tank with a lurch, while Bastian had a raised-voice word with Avery, about fifteen feet between them.

"I must admit, Bastian Thurgood," Avery said.

"What's that, Master Sergeant?"

"I am deeply hoping that your mission proves to be a waste."

Bastian scowled. "How, exactly?"

"Best case scenario," Avery explained, "the Monolith is destroyed without any collateral damage. Rendering your journey and mission a waste—of time, not life."

Bastian's foul expression alleviated and he smiled contentedly through his open visor.

Seeing this, Bastian illuminated by the tank's lights, Avery added a closing statement.

"I trust you'll make the most of it, regardless."

He then disappeared back into the tank, leaving Bastian smirking to himself, and ultimately shaking his head. He slapped the back of the tank before sitting down again in the rickety trailer. It continued to surprise him, its soundness. As did the resilience and resolve of these soldiers.

He had so much to be grateful for.

Maggie and Eliza would always be at the top of that list, even posthumously. Their memories, like residual energy in his bones. Good, not bad.

Passionately, he held onto this.

# 18

Calipatria awaited them like an abandoned ghost town. They reached it just shy of thirty minutes to six, on the precipice of dawn. The sun would peak the horizon in the next twenty minutes, and wash Calipatria with a sweeping amber blanket. Ten minutes later, a large explosion would occur near the town's eastward water tower. Where the Monolith stood, half a mile clear of any other buildings.

Bastian was glad he and his men had survived the night…those that did, of course. The others, he wouldn't forget. Their lives, and what they strove to accomplish, couldn't be forgotten. This enlivened him, as much as it could, considering the grim circumstances.

With dawn on approach, the darkness of the sky had finally lifted. The clarity of their surroundings was no longer reliant on the tank's foglights and search beams.

This was both a relief and a source of heartache, as the barren reality of Calipatria became unavoidable.

Their column drove down a main street on cautious wheels. They were mindful of their timeclock, but also paranoid of an ambush.

It was disturbingly clear, without the need of meticulous scrutiny, that Calipatria was just as Avery's men had left it: a casualty. Most of its civilian population had long since evacuated, those that weren't slaughtered in the process of the Monolith's occupation. So much time had passed since then, if an entire day could be considered a lot.

Numerically, maybe not, but emotionally and on all other fronts, it was immeasurable. From the loss of life to the trauma suffered by witnesses and survivors, to the sheer distress inflicted upon the earth itself. Violated by the Monolith, corrupted by it—somehow—and then used, like a carrier, for its evil.

Bastian could only theorize to an extent.

He was beginning to feel like some kind of mad-scientist cliché, except in geology, with his ideas surrounding the Monolith and its horde of abominations.

Regardless of these thoughts, the barrenness of Calipatria was nerve-wracking to say the least. It had always been a scarcely populated, small town; but this was uncanny. It was now more of a wasteland than ever a place of residence or civilization.

Vacancy held the town by the throat.

Most of the vehicles present were severely damaged, and mutilated corpses occupied them. Their desiccated remains suggested that the majority of deaths had occurred during the initial stages of the Monolith's touch-down. While the ground—from the desert earth to roads and sidewalks and entire buildings—was severely wounded via cracks and fissures, the town remained a whole. Like the scab of a wound, with a lot of traumatized flesh surrounding it.

The closer they got to the other side of town—

eastbound—the more soldiers' corpses and destroyed military vehicles were spotted.

Within a mile of the Calipatria-painted water tower, its gray, bulbous top visible over some ragged treetops opposite a garage building, Bastian signaled for a halt. The vehicles groaned to a stop, their engines idling. He stood up in the trailer, stagnantly stretching, and peered through his open visor. Through the residual darkness, past the water tower and over the rooftop of a warehouse at the end of this road, he could see a harsh red glow scarring the navy clouds.

It pulsed.

In the stillness of the paused vehicles, he could hear the heavy breathing of *dozens*—perhaps as many as a hundred—of execrable beasts.

The horde surrounding the Monolith.

Their sheer number and jumbled formation, which caused them to tread or march about dormant, produced subtle tremors in the earth.

Even through the trailer's wheels, the metal itself and the insulated INFERNO Suit, Bastian could feel a tickling of this reverberation.

It was unnerving to say the least.

He knew full well, too, that if *he* could feel it then the rest of the men absolutely did. Quite possibly, had already, before him.

"Time?" Bastian called out.

Fields was on it. "Five forty-eight!"

Bastian nodded. He glowered ahead, over the tank and in the direction of the pulsing red light.

"Increase speed," he growled out loud, his voice

elevated. "Be ready to disembark in less than ten minutes."

Lemay didn't hesitate to comply. The tank started up again, dust rising up from the tracks as they grinded against the tattered asphalt. As he had all this way, he continued to avoid wide cracks in the road, which became more common the closer they got to this side of town.

Closer to the source of all this madness.

The epicenter.

*Ground fucking zero.*

Any lightness previously occupying Bastian's veins now ran cold with resentment. He did not want to annul or belittle this spite; its vehemence was suppressed for now, at the sake of his composure, but in due time—quite shortly, he foreboded—its opportune moment would come forth.

He of course acknowledged the best case scenario, as suggested by Master Sergeant Avery, wherein there lied no need for confrontation. The MOAB would deliver its payload effectively, and at the very most, Bastian and his men would simply need to mop up survivors of the horde.

He longed to see this come to fruition.

Until it actually happened, however, he couldn't resist fearing—and poising for—the worst.

"End of the road!" Fields announced, seconds before the Abrams came to a halt.

The engine idled while the commander's hatch cranked open topside and Lemay lifted himself through it. He sat on the armor, legs dangling through, and nodded down at Bastian.

"How do you wanna handle this?"

"Is there any way around these buildings?"

Lemay grunted. "Fields! You see any other routes?"

"I think so. Some debris behind the warehouse, 'round that corner." Fields pointed at the large building, and its right wing.

At this point, ten minutes shy of six in the morning, the sun had woken from its slumber. Dawn bestowed upon them a warped semblance of light, which slowly but surely built with increasing clarity.

As per Fields' indication, Lemay and Bastian looked. So did the few men in the Humvee behind the hitched trailer, within earshot of their exchange. There were some tire tracks on the cracked asphalt, across a sidewalk and through a gravel parking lot. Like omens of a stampede, there were bent signs that looked as though they had been crushed or run over, and some disheveled cinderblocks near the building's far corner to the right of the road.

"Great eye, Fields," Bastian noted. He whistled low and hand signaled in that direction. "Lead, Lemay. I want eyes on."

"Wilco," Lemay said, and dipped back down into the tank. The hatch clamped shut over his head and then the vehicle turned, tracks grinding on the ripped asphalt. The Abrams redirected and, without minding the curb or signs, advanced toward the right wing of the warehouse. Virtually everything in its path was crushed with disregard. At that point Bastian knew the survival of the cart was no longer as necessary as it was before; still, bump and lurch as it did, it endured.

Bastian watched the two Humvees follow in suit. He knew they could speed out ahead of the tank, but he favored them slugging behind.

The tank was a tank for good reason.

Let it be the fortification of their column.

Within two minutes, it had journeyed the same path that Bastian imagined Avery's men had used hours earlier. They moved through the ruins of a junkyard's walls to the right of the warehouse, until they emerged on the other side.

It was almost like stepping—or driving—through a portal, and into another world. A desert planet of ruination and despair. Of terrestrial horror.

Lemay stopped the tank about fifteen feet beyond the outer junkyard wall. To their far right was the town's primary water tower, surrounded by a high chain-link fence and a couple of dry yet green-leafed trees.

The two Humvees followed, fanning out and stopping on either side of the tank. They hung back just a few feet, to remain closer to the trailer, whereupon Bastian now stood. He wanted as clear a view of this sight as Donnie and Guerrero had.

And then the commander's hatch of the Abrams opened, and out emerged the tank crew. Both Lemay and Artie, until they sat on top of the tank, their legs dangling over. Bastian climbed onto the back end of the tank, its chassis tilting a little, but Lemay and Artie hardly noticed. They were transfixed.

The inhabitants of the Humvees, with the exception of the gunners, also stepped out to take in the sight without obstruction.

"No photograph would do this justice," Preston said, bug-eyed. He raised his arms, elbows out, fingers dug into his hair.

"A MOAB should, though," Bastian said, his voice grating and raw with emotion. The statement alone, though open to sarcastic interpretation, was devoid of any humor. It made a few of the Marines look at him on impulse, only to feel themselves electrified with a mote of the same sentiment.

It was really an amalgamation of feelings.

Hatred. Fear. Awe. Shock. Nausea.

And more hatred.

The horde of beasts surrounding the Monolith had to count upwards of a hundred. Bastian's guess was fifty shy of two-hundred, at the most. Their variety was displeasing to say the least. From forty Crawlers to twenty Vultures, a dozen Eaters and easily fifty Legionnaires. Thirty Tyrants. Maybe ten Barons and a handful of Pyros.

There was a speck of relief in Bastian's heart that nothing bigger than a Pyro could be seen.

He of course couldn't fathom what might lie in wait beneath the surface of this dry, desert earth, however. He wouldn't put it past the Monolith and its preternatural powers to actually have something titanic in store for them.

Even more so than their last encounter…

Bastian did his best not to dwell on that notion. This sight alone was dumbfounding and disquieting enough in its own right.

The Monolith itself was just as unsettling as the concentrated ring of creatures surrounding it. They did not encircle the Monolith, but instead formed a crescent-shaped guard of their forces, packed tight together, and facing the town's outer limits.

Particularly, Bastian and his gathered men.

The gap between them was about two-hundred yards. Not nearly distant enough, as far as Bastian was concerned. Yet part of him wished they were closer.

With a little more scrutiny, and thanks to the rising sun's quilt of natural illumination, he could discern the horde's radius. Their formation did not extend beyond four to five-hundred feet from the base of the Monolith. With a gap of maybe thirty feet between them and where the black structure met the ground.

A ring of untouched earth.

Though, nothing in the area was truly untouched, since the Monolith had made contact.

"Time?" Bastian asked out loud, without diverting his gaze.

The Monolith was as hypnotizing as it was terrifying. Seeing it in the shaky, distorted aerial footage on TV over eight hours ago paled in comparison to this eyewitness experience.

Even from two football fields' distance away, with no obstructions on a partially cloudy morning, at first light, it was unrivaled.

Four-hundred feet tall at its highest corner; the

other was clipped, as if a rectangle with one 'ear' cut off. At its center, facing them, a large—bus-sized—red orb, pulsing vividly, and a line of the same severe color descending from this, straight into the ground. The circle above the line reminded Bastian of a thermometer.

He began to garner ideas about the purpose of it, but it muddied his focus.

"Bastian!" Fields snapped.

His voice finally snatched Bastian out of a stupor, luring him back to reality.

"Eighty seconds now!"

Bastian's eyes widened. He looked from the Monolith to Fields, whose own expression was dumbstruck. He glanced at the surrounding Marines, their body language collectively antsy.

"The blast radius won't affect us," Bastian announced. "It'll just barely extend the horde's ranks."

"But we don't know the stability of the Monolith itself!" Tielve exclaimed.

Bastian recalled Avery's words on the matter.

"You're right! Everyone, get inside, and prepare to drive off." Bastian hopped out of the trailer and stood beside the hitch, ready to break it if needed, for the tank's sake of mobility. "In which case, fan out! Don't return to the town. Avoid structures."

The Marines urgently returned to their respective vehicles, the drivers keenly ready to speed off.

The gathered roar of the horde, even from this range, was vociferous.

"Ten seconds!" Fields announced.

Bastian knew that the bomb wouldn't impact at

six o'clock on the dot. But the C-130 aircraft designated to deploy the MOAB would not miss the 0600 deadline by more than thirty seconds. This was implicitly assumed by the rest of the Marines.

Taking into consideration the altitude needed to drop the bomb for the desired effect, in addition to the elevation of detonation—just above the invisible EMP field—Bastian made a calculated guess. He reckoned eight seconds of travel from aircraft to target.

"Time?" Bastian called out, already knowing it was well after 0600 hours on the dot.

"Sixteen seconds past," Fields announced. A pause. "Twenty. Twenty-one…"

"Maybe they changed their—"

Preston was interrupted.

Through the amber-lit dawn clouds appeared a cross-shaped black object. Like a mote of dust at this distance. But as it neared overhead, its shape elucidated, and its identity crossed the beard-encircled lips of Tommy Guerrero.

He muttered it at first. And then his voice heightened with a hint of rugged enthusiasm.

"Hercules!"

Everyone looked at Guerrero before they caught on, and their gazes returned to the skies above the Monolith. Its red glow no longer held dominance against the morning light.

"Hercules!" several of the Marines hooted, some of them clapping and jostling each other.

Bastian wanted to remove his helmet but instead

kept it on for impending safety purposes. He left the visor up for a clearer line of sight. He keenly watched the Lockheed C-130 Hercules soar overhead, squinting against the warm sunlight. From below, the aircraft's 120-foot wingspan gave it a cross-like appearance.

His eyes widened at the glimpse of something black descend from it.

"Incomiiiing!" Bastian hollered, and then lowered his visor.

The thirty-foot-long, ten-ton bomb produced a shrill whistle as it fell. It detonated a hundred feet above the Monolith, clear of the EMP field. The blast yield was equivalent to eleven tons of TNT. The fireball extended out and down, carrying with it heaving clouds of disturbed air, concussive pressure, dust, and shrapnel. The air-burst detonation was a success. The proximity of the blast engulfed the Monolith and not even a skyscraper would have survived; even a solid steel structure would at least show signs of damage. The blast splashed the ground with roiling clouds of flame and pressure.

The horde barely had a chance to even react on a whim. The explosion occurred seven seconds following its deployment from the C-130, which now headed back to base. The ground shook briefly, but Bastian and his men hardly felt it; they did, however, detect a splash of heat and wind on their faces. Pebbles of dirt pattered the armor on their vehicles, waves of dust misting windshields.

From the initial explosion, surface damage was tremendous, as the antipersonnel weapon had fruitfully executed its job, all without penetrating the earth.

While Bastian and his men did brace for the blast and anticipate some kind of extremely volatile reaction from the Monolith, there was none.

Within thirty seconds, the explosion's resultant dirt clouds began to thin. A smog of smoke remained, polluting the air around the Monolith, but even through its ashen thickness, a red glow could be seen.

The clouds started to swirl until they lost their shape altogether. And through them, survivors of the horde bustled in an uproar.

This sunk the hearts of the men watching.

At the very least, Bastian was pleased to see so many of the creatures butchered by the explosion. Most of them had been obliterated or set afire, but by the time the clouds cleared, their bodies were almost done disintegrating. It was like some kind of unparalleled magic trick, or grand illusion.

Bastian was impressed, but only to an extent. Ultimately, he felt a high-caliber disappointment lodge itself in him like a bullet.

The Monolith didn't just remain, it stood with a cold indifference, miraculously unscathed.

Not even blood or dirt clung to its rugged black exterior.

Bastian's face distorted, bleakly.

He growled some incoherent breed of profanity under his breath.

"H-How?" one of his Marines muttered. He couldn't tell which, mostly because that same quiet question of disbelief was repeated among them.

"A-A-At least the horde's been affected," Fields

said through a stutter.

"Thank fuck," Donnie said. He leaned forward, staring intently, his eyes squinting, over the Humvee-mounted machinegun. "At least fifty percent of their numbers, wiped out."

"That leaves, what?" Fields gulped. "At least sixty. Mostly the big guys, as far as I can tell."

"Yeah," Donnie said, still squinting and observing. He had now raised a hand to his brow as a makeshift visor, against the onslaught of sunlight. "No more grunts. A few stragglers, but—"

Bastian had heard enough.

He doubled over the cart of weapons in front of him and began adorning himself with what he could carry. He disregarded the Duke and clipped the Supe to his right waist, then the ROT-20 to his left. He knew the other weapons were far too big to cooperate with that magnetic hands-free feature, besides, it was about damn time he put the Sevin to good use.

The two shotguns were fully loaded, but he knew that the Supe would become useless after two shots. The Suit was not fitted with pockets, naturally, and he never rigged together a bandolier for extra shells. So this would have to do.

He debarked the trailer and dust kicked up around his armored legs. All eyes shifted to him. He didn't announce his plan; it was already known to them, more or less. Instead, he leaned into the rickety trailer, subconsciously thanking it for its service.

Which was no longer needed.

He donned the ammunition backpack for the Sevin, which would have anchored any man beyond a few hundred steps, in addition to carrying the actual weapon itself. Which he now did, miraculously in his right hand alone, while left-handing the Arbalest. He felt like a bipedal tank, impossibly upright with nearly a ton's worth of equipment on him and in his hands, ammunition included.

"The hell are you doing, hoss?" Donnie asked from the Humvee to Bastian's right.

"Finishing this fight," Bastian replied firmly, neither pausing nor taking his eyes off the Monolith.

"Or letting *it* finish *you*," Donnie scoffed.

"Be that as it may, some type of finality is due." Bastian huffed. His course was concreted in his mind and veins. His waypoint, unmistakable. There, afar, the surviving creatures riled themselves up, roaring and shrieking and jostling in front of the Monolith.

"You ain't walking there, that's for goddamn sure," Preston said, loudly, from the passenger seat. He hung halfway out of his window, on the right side of the Humvee.

Bastian stopped in his tracks and took a deep breath. He turned to face the vehicle, ten feet away.

"Afraid I am, Marine," he said, through his open visor. "I appreciate the help and travel accommodations, gentlemen, but you all know the drill. EMP field nullifies anything electric. No vehicles past a certain point. Might get another fifty feet or so, then it's irrelevant. Explosively, I might add. Better to just stop here than be told to, in a ball of fire."

Some of the Marines cursed under their breaths, louder than likely intended. They either had not realized or, more probably, just forgotten that detail, amid all the chaos.

They began fussing amongst themselves, knowing full well they couldn't follow him into such a battle so ill-armed.

"Rest assured, guys," Bastian raised his voice. "I'm not as burdened as you might expect. This Suit…it really *is* my masterpiece. *Our* masterpiece. If I don't survive this, please speak highly of the boys at CHERI. In your prayers, even, or whatever, to yourselves. Just…give credit where credit is due."

Bastian smirked to himself and shook his head. He mumbled something unintelligible even to himself, and proceeded forward.

He had advanced maybe forty feet from the vehicles when he heard a whizzing sound, like very faint static. He paused midstride and bowed his head, ignoring the distant commotion of the detestable survivors. He rolled his shoulders, and felt a fizziness in the armpit regions of his Kevlar.

*Well, hello, EMP field. Or whatever the alienfuck you are.*

He had since dismissed the demonic concept of this enemy, given the otherworldly nature of the Monolith. Still, a myriad of questions needed answering. And he had a feeling he wouldn't get any, at least not with the clarity he desired.

Punctuating a deep sigh, Bastian threw a half-turned glance over his shoulder and raised his voice.

"Come here! Stop ten feet behind me! But fan out a little!"

They complied without hesitation. The vehicles drove up to stop exactly where he designated, in a divided formation. The tank was still centered.

"Any farther and you'll hit the EMP, so kill your engines! I don't want to risk it."

They followed his ardent suggestion.

"Try to cover me with your guns," Bastian said. "Lemay, Artie—wipe the sweat off your faces and dry those hands! I know y'all are elite at what you do, after taking down that gigantic son of a bitch an hour ago!"

The tank's main barrel raised slightly, the mechanical sound and motion like a nod to Bastian.

"Prove my confidence right," he added, baring his teeth. "Focus on the big, horned fucks."

He referred to both the red-skinned Barons and the dark, blazing lance-armed Pyros.

"Fields, Donnie, Guerrero—focus on the other major freaks. Try to avoid crossfire, I know this Suit is resilient, but let's not test any limits here. I've got enough to worry about."

"We've got you," Guerrero said firmly, and Bastian believed him. He had faith in the man he had never truly met or gotten to know, as much as he wished he had previously, or in some other life.

"Thank you, gentlemen, and I'll see you again…in this life or the next." Bastian gulped and shut his eyes. "Maybe even somewhere between."

# 19

Flynn Fields wasn't having this. He had come so far, he wasn't going to let this extraordinary example of a man venture into the Jaws of Hell, so to speak, with no help at his heels. He knew he could offer no comparison, in the flesh, with or without the armored Suit and the advanced weapons, but he couldn't sit back. He didn't hold this against the other men at all, but he knew just the same that Abby would not stay put, either.

And that shook him to the core.

Without even taking a full, deep breath, Fields dismounted from the tank's machinegun and gestured at it, to nobody in particular. He then ran to the hitched trailer and wielded the Duke, pocketing all of the spare ammunition once he located it.

He started to rush beyond their scattered formation when he heard one of the Bandits call out to him. Two had exited their Humvee to intercept Fields. Guerrero remained on the machinegun, and Santi stayed in his Humvee, apprehension consuming him.

"You're not going alone," one of them said decisively. It was Jacinto Muñoz.

"I'm no Marine. You don't need to risk—"

"Bullshit. It doesn't matter. We're coming."

Bastian stopped midstride, turning to witness

what was happening twenty feet behind him.

"Besides," Tielve added, "we're better armed than you. But you…you have a deeper connection with this guy. So consider us equally equipped."

"Thank you," Fields nodded.

Tielve nodded and circumvented the tank to attend Santi's side of the Humvee. He conversed with him briefly, then rubbed his head, gave him a gentle slap to the face, and left the man teary-eyed, but smiling weakly. Tielve came away with Santi's weapon and two spare magazines.

"Santi's donation," Tielve offered it to Fields.

"Gracias!" Fields exclaimed, taking the M4 assault rifle and ammunition.

Tielve and Muñoz exchanged chuckling glances. Meanwhile, Fields slung the strap of the weapon over his shoulder and stuffed the spare magazine under his guard belt.

Guerrero whistled, catching the trio's attention. He excavate some things from below the gunner's hatch of the Humvee and tossed them to Muñoz. He caught them—a semiautomatic pistol and a spare magazine. He gave Guerrero an unanswered smooching gesture, and then handed Fields the gear.

"A gift from Tommy," Muñoz said. "Just don't say 'gracias.'"

Muñoz and Tielve smirked.

Fields flashed a brief smile and simply thanked Guerrero with a genuine nod.

"You guys are fucking crazy," Bastian called out. "Don't do this."

"Says you," Fields replied. He stuffed the pistol into his hip-holster, where it fit snugly. He nodded back at the two Bandits who then accompanied him to re-group on Bastian's position.

Although internally grateful, Bastian feared for the men's safety and knew that this gesture wasn't needed to bolster their bravery and honor. Just the same, he knew that there would be no discouraging them from this.

"Morning, boss," Fields huffed as he arrived be-side Bastian. He shrugged, wielding the Duke in his right hand while Guerrero's assault rifle hung from its strap. "Couldn't resist. I know Abby wouldn't."

He also knew that mentioning Abby like that was a sure-fire way to daunt Bastian from trying to reject the help.

Bastian sighed and shook his head.

"Fine," he ultimately said, rather bluntly. "But…I'll thank you guys later, how about that?"

"Or *we'll* thank *you*," Tielve said.

"Right. A beer's a beer, then."

"Sign me up," Muñoz nodded.

"Fields. Two hands on that thing, please? Kicks twice as hard as a D-Eagle."

Tielve whistled low, impressed. "Got anymore toys to spare?"

"Afraid not, fellas. Last chance to wise up and turn tail."

"No wisdom here," Muñoz said, his accent as strong as the insane courage running through his veins. "Just guts."

"Speaking of which, get ready to spill theirs," Bastian said, motioning toward the now scattering semicircular swarm of beasts.

More than halfway to the horde, Tielve stopped midstride while Bastian and Fields continued, without noticing. Then Muñoz backpedaled and began chatting up a quiet storm with his comrade.

At that point, Fields paused, and Bastian didn't realize it until a few paces more.

"We oughtta mention," Muñoz finally said, raising his voice to catch Bastian's attention.

He turned on his heel and expressed confusion as to why they had fallen back.

"What is it? Can't you talk on the way?" There was an unyielding urgency to Bastian's voice and body language. "It isn't like they're gonna break formation, anyway. I think these ones are *bound* to the Monolith, like a Royal Guard."

"Which probably makes them more stubborn," Tielve added, his voice raised.

"Reminds me of someone, eh?" Fields muttered, glancing at Bastian but not receiving a hint of sarcasm in response.

Muñoz tipped his chin at Bastian as he proceeded, acknowledging him. On his way, he shrugged his shoulders and rolled his neck, trying to readjust to the impending danger. And the sheer severity of this recent development. By the time he caught up with Bastian and Fields, who now stood beside each other, he wore his game-face, and it weighted his voice.

He at least was not oblivious to the gravity of the

situation.

"We forgot to mention something, man," Muñoz said. Far behind him, Tielve took a moment before advancing. Muñoz addressed Bastian and occasionally glanced at Fields. "Back when Avery had us here, firing at the horde, expending all kinds of ammunition, I mean, we had mowed 'em down to only straggling numbers. Ten, fifteen minutes later, four or five sinkholes would open up beneath where they had stood, and in a matter of moments their numbers were replenished."

Bastian scowled. He took his eyes off Muñoz to glare at the scattered gathering of creatures fanned out in front of the Monolith. He raised his visor and spat on the ground, then returned his exposed gaze to Muñoz.

"Nauseating as this may be, it isn't surprising."

"Does it affect your strategy at all?"

Bastian shrugged. "Not really. Just…be more mindful of where you're stepping."

Muñoz shook his head. "They close up, though."

Bastian's brow furrowed.

*Well, that's new.*

"The ground around here, closer to that structure, it's *different*."

"Like a slave to the Monolith." Bastian was angry and disgusted and stupefied all at once. His rictus changed into a vindictive leer. He gathered his internal and external strength, while continuing to stand inertly, bearing the weight of the heavy weapons. "You said ten to fifteen minutes after you mowed 'em down, right?"

Muñoz nodded. Behind him, Tielve finally caught up.

"Then I say that makes our sense of urgency even greater," Bastian said. "I appreciate the head's up, fellas, I do…but I'm about done with caution. It can go fuck itself."

Bastian started walking again. Vigorously, he picked up speed.

Fields cursed under his breath, but not necessarily in objection. He jogged to catch up to Bastian, who, even in full gear and carrying such an arsenal, moved surprisingly fast.

The INFERNO Suit was more than just another layer of protection…

Bastian lowered his visor and glared through it, head bowed slightly, as he neared what he considered the outer frontline of enemies. He stopped about twenty feet from them, a cloud of dirt orbiting his legs. They were mostly Crawlers and a few Eaters that had somehow survived; a Vulture or two flitting up and down. Most of them were visibly wounded, though. The MOAB had certainly had an effect, it just wasn't enough to wipe out even a cluster of these anomalies.

There was something to be grateful for here, though—what he mentioned earlier, about their loyalty to the Monolith. Staying back, like dedicated guards, bound to a certain perimeter.

He would take advantage of this.

Somebody suddenly yelled behind him. It was a long, drawn out word that he couldn't discern. It did, however, snag his attention. He glanced over his shoulder, brow furrowed. Fields had stopped about ten feet behind him, and now looked back, too, a hand raised to his forehead to shade his eyes. About fifteen or twenty feet behind Fields were Muñoz and Tielve; they had dropped into the prone position, on their stomachs. From the ground, they signaled for Bastian and Fields to do the same.

In the fresh daylight, Bastian could see Guerrero and Donnie on the Humvee machineguns, waving in the air. And then Guerrero bowled his hands around his mouth and shouted something.

Bastian raised his visor and heard the previously shouted word with renewed clarity.

"Drooooop!"

Not droop. *Drop.*

Bastian's eyes widened. He let his legs buckle, descending to one knee and setting his weapons down. At this point Fields had fallen to his stomach and thrown his arms over his head.

"Fiiiiiire!" Bastian bellowed, a split-second before flattening into the prone position, too. He glimpsed muzzle flashes open up in front of Guerrero and Donnie, barely visible against the daybreak light. He turned his head to face the horde to his right. It was a glorious scene, to witness tracer rounds rip through the morning air and volley the frontline of smaller creatures. His memory was thrust back to when he first encountered the wretched Crawlers in his own home, and defending his family against them. He now adored the sight of their gaunt figures being shredded by .50-caliber bullets, which reduced their enemy to perforated flesh one second, embers and ash the next.

When a Vulture tried to flutter back from the

frontline, bullets would catch its wings and turn it into bright red pulp that misted the desert air.

Their cries were a sweet cacophony.

The gunfire from the two Humvee-mounted weapons was a distant roll of thunder.

They echoed until the last few bullets stopped whizzing over Bastian's head. He then heard a long whistle and he didn't hesitate to spring to his feet again. As he did, an overlapping commotion of shouts caught his attention, just as a large shadow loomed over where he stood, its form catching the sunlight and deflecting it. In that moment Bastian realized he had either gotten up too soon, or there was some mixed communication back where the vehicles were.

First Bastian heard the whistle of a projectile searing the air, then he glimpsed the Pyro looming over him, at the edge of where the Crawlers had previously stood. Those two things happened in a second and a half; next, he pulled himself out of the way, and in the ensuing blink of an eye, the 102mm high-explosive projectile struck its target, leaving behind a tail of smoke through the air, from the billowing muzzle of the tank cannon.

The impact was devastating, and the blast eradicated the Pyro from the chest up. A tall plume of black hide and fiery orange blood replaced its torso. Its horned head and jaws were nowhere to be found, and the explosion staggered two nearby Legionnaires, killing a residual Crawler in the proximity.

Fields started howling in celebration.

"Shit, why don't we just let *them* wipe 'em out

first, then we—"

Fields was interrupted by a passing tremor, punctuated by the sound of dry earth cracking. But it did more than just split; it sunk in, and then the edges curled outward, pushed up by the big shoulders of its travelers.

Bastian got to his feet. "*That's* why!"

He sealed his visor and left the Arbalest on the ground, in exchange for the Sevin, which he was initially going to use before Guerrero and Donnie chipped in. He braced it against his armored abdomen, gripping the bar above the barrel housing with his right hand.

"Either fall in or fall back!" Bastian barked. "Your choice!"

From the hellhole in the middle of the abated horde's ranks—reduced to maybe fifty now—two Tyrants and a Legionnaire emerged.

Bastian gritted his teeth and depressed the trigger on the Sevin. The seven linked barrels spun with a metallic whirring sound, each muzzle spitting fire. The tempest of 7.62mm armor-piercing rounds shredded any remaining *grunts*, while perforating the larger bodies of Legionnaires and Tyrants. They roared and tried to shift, but had no cover out here in the desert. Their precious Monolith would have sufficed, but instead *they* were the guards.

*More like bullet sponges.*

Bastian found himself beaming behind his visor as he mowed down half a dozen of each beast, from Legionnaire to Tyrant, in a matter of ten seconds. Large chunks of flesh were sundered from hefty bones, as he strafed the Sevin's aim left to right. A few Barons and

Pyros retreated behind the ranks of their more susceptible compatriots, while a couple of them actually lumbered between the firing chaingun to cushion some of the bullets.

The thousand-round, disintegrating-link ammo belt in Bastian's backpack did not last long. The exceptionally high rate-of-fire—two-thousand rounds-per-minute—paired with his unrelenting trigger finger, was merciless. On both Bastian's targets and his ammunition reserve.

In about thirty seconds, the Sevin's belt was depleted. Ashen smoke poured from the seven muzzles, as well as the backpack. The coolant system proved satisfactory from an engineer's perspective, although in that moment Bastian was strictly a combatant.

Perhaps regrettably, he had condensed his mentality to that of an emotionally-driven soldier bent on revenge and bloodshed.

Choosing not to dwell on this, instead finding victory in the effective use of the Sevin, he quickly shrugged off the backpack and dropped the chaingun to the ground.

Fields arrived behind him, agape and speechless. Muñoz and Tielve caught up, gawking at the seemingly effortless disbursement of ammunition and the massacre it had wrought. What they were used to seeing fired by an attack helicopter was just utilized by a *man* on his own two feet.

The variables, of course, had to be noted.

But still…it was a tremendous sight.

The results were also remarkably satisfying. The

enemy's numbers were, in thirty seconds, halved.

Bastian rolled his shoulders, not necessarily feeling tired or sore but just a crumb of strain. He then stooped to retrieve the Arbalest, his ears not *ringing* from the Sevin's onslaught, but nonetheless temporarily buffeted.

So he didn't hear the whistling and shouting from the three vehicles a few hundred feet behind him. He did, however, hear Fields shouting within arm's reach. He glanced right and saw the man doubled over, hobbling away.

Bastian put one and one together, then dove past the Arbalest before ever picking it up.

The whistling of another tank round piercing the air caught his ears. He glanced over his shoulder after he literally hit the dirt and saw it just *clip* the shoulder of a Baron, which didn't hinder its trajectory. The Baron stumbled, sans its left arm, blown off at the shoulder by the outright momentum of the 102mm slug. Its detonation didn't occur until a direct impact, however, which ended up being the Monolith, seven feet from the ground.

An explosion occurred, but there was zero effect to the black surface of the structure. Not even its seemingly exposed, brilliantly glowing, red *vein* was disrupted or damaged by the direct hit.

Bastian assumed Avery's men had already attempted this, supposing they'd been able to acquire an unobstructed shot. Still, with no results even hinting at the infliction of damage, he abandoned any idea of such a strategy.

*Back to basics. Head-first into Hell itself.*

Raking in a deep breath of ventilated, purified air inside the INFERNO Suit, he had his work cut out for him—a long letter of gratitude to his coworkers at CHERI. To the funders of DARPA, including the Commander in Chief himself and, as far as Bastian was concerned, even if not especially Deputy Director Bowman, too.

With all of this in mind, and then some, Bastian got to his feet again. He scooped up the Arbalest, wielding it as he had two or three measly hours ago, against that gigantic beast risen from beneath the earth.

"I don't know if it's Hell you ugly sons of bitches go to when you die," Bastian growled out loud as he glared at his scattered enemies. He marched closer to their now diminished frontline. "Or some other ungodly oblivion, but back from whence you came I shall fucking send you."

As soon as his right foot crossed that unseen line where the enemy seemed bound to stay behind, their remaining numbers went berserk. A boisterous hysteria of roars and snarls, shrieks and bellows. Shaking horned-heads and slashing of claws through the air. Like a horde of feral cats at the scent of genetically enhanced catnip.

They were hell-bent on not letting anyone or anything reach their beloved Monolith. Their frenzy was almost as nerve-wracking as Bastian imagined he was to them.

That was the mindset he had to accept, regardless of its arrogance.

*I am an unstoppable force.*

He aimed the Arbalest and fired. A charging Baron, not the armless one, took the magnetized tungsten slug to the chest. Its large body cleaved from throat to stomach, leaving a clean, oval-shaped hole through its seared flesh. It stumbled before collapsing into the dirt, past Bastian's feet. He side-stepped and, supporting the Arbalest with his right hand alone, swung at a charging Legionnaire with his left hand. The Exoblade protracted in time to catch it in its right side, like an axe burying itself between ribs. Bright red blood splashed the desert floor, and the beast squalled into the sky.

Just then a cluster of 5.56mm bullets rocked its dome-headed skull to the side, followed by another three-round burst to its neck. Red mist in the air punctuated the collapse of its body. Bastian's Exoblade was freed, and dripped blood until the beast's corpse disintegrated.

He glanced to his left, and saw Tielve advance, the muzzle of his assault rifle smoking. He kept it shouldered, peering down the sights, a rigid stare on his face. He reciprocated Bastian's respectful nod of gratitude, before another charging beast drew his aim.

Tielve put an easy ten rounds into the Tyrant's upper chest before his aim adjusted, climbing up its toothy-grinned face. Most of the bullets either lodged into the bone or ricocheted off.

To Bastian's right, Fields arrived, firing into the overlapping waves of beasts as they frenzied toward the frontline.

"Push!" Bastian roared, and started to move forward. He unclipped the ROT-20 from his waist with his left hand, drawing a bead on Tielve's targeted Tyrant. He put two 20-gauge shells into its gut, causing it to double over. He then clipped the shotgun and returned both hands to the Arbalest as the armless Baron teamed up with another Tyrant to charge him.

Simultaneously, Muñoz arrived beside Tielve and fired into the wounded Tyrant's black eye socket until something got through. Literally. The back of the horned beast's skull opened up in a spray of yellow and bright red, connected by fragments of beige bone.

Meanwhile, Bastian dropped to a knee and fired the Arbalest at an acute angle. The magnetized tungsten slug penetrated the armless Baron's stomach, going through and nailing a Legionnaire sauntering behind it.

*Two birds, one sharp fucking stone.*

The two beasts, fifteen feet apart, staggered until they dropped, mortally wounded, their torsos nearly severed from their legs. Viscera steamed on the desert floor before being reduced to embers and ash.

However, the charging Tyrant was not daunted. It collided with Bastian at the last-second, taking a few rounds from Fields after he managed to wound and hinder his own target. The Tyrant's momentum hurled Bastian back fifteen feet. He landed in a roll, dropping the Arbalest back where he was struck. He came up on his hands and knees, armor grinding against dry earth.

A fresh grimace scarred his face.

He glared at the growling Tyrant through his visor. Fifteen feet away and starting to march closer.

Fields stood off to the right, firing into its side, but it ignored them. Until it couldn't anymore, and *barked* at Fields, facing him, bleeding from its many bullet wounds.

Bastian breathed heavily, gutturally.

He charged the beast as it now ignored him in place of Fields. It reached out, while Fields reloaded in a panic, his body shaking.

To Bastian's left, as he enclosed on the Tyrant, Muñoz and Tielve were reluctantly advancing. Their assault rifles hardly stood a chance against these larger beasts, the Barons and Pyros especially.

He tunnel-visioned the Tyrant as it swung at Fields, who fell onto his butt and drew the Duke last-second. He fired it in both hands, the recoil actually kicking it out of his clutches. But the first round still hit its target—the depleted uranium .460 Magnum boring through the Tyrant's stomach. A divot of flesh and blood shot out of the exit wound in its lower back, and it paused midstride to grunt in pain, closing a palm over the entry.

Bastian collided, but not in a tackling motion. He slowed down just before reaching the beast, and leapt into the air. His feet cleared the ground a good ten inches. His left hand reached up and grabbed the Tyrant's right horn, tugging its head down. His left foot planted in the back of beast's right knee, pushing that leg to the ground. With his right knee, Bastian struck a cluster of smaller bullet wounds on its left side.

The Tyrant released a throaty roar of pain.

Bastian flicked the chainsaw attachment and it

extended with a metallic click. He armed it in the same instant, and connected the revving teeth with the Tyrant's throat. The blades rotated frenziedly, chewing through dense flesh until it sawed into its esophagus, and then its spine. Vibrant red blood jetted across the earth, and Bastian grounded his feet to the side, withdrawing the chainsaw attachment, which dripped wetly.

"Good shooting, Tex," Bastian said, nodding at Fields. "Now reload and up at 'em."

He didn't wait to see Fields smirk or comply and reload, as he already knew he had been in the process of doing so. Bastian hurriedly retrieved his Arbalest, stepping through the slowly dissolving remains of the Tyrant, while Tielve and Muñoz faced trouble.

Just then tracers walloped the bodies of a few larger beasts trying to flank the two Bandits. Bastian looked back, seeing Guerrero's machinegun open up.

He knew they had to be running low on ammunition.

With Bastian and the two Bandits now halfway to the Monolith, he acknowledged, too, that the tank crew couldn't risk another shot from the cannon. If it was just Bastian, maybe, but not the Marines, too.

Bastian fired the Arbalest into the Baron and Tyrant currently giving them trouble. Their assault rifles had sufficed in delaying the beasts' progress, which Bastian could chalk up as unintentional teamwork now that he pitched in.

At 7100 feet-per-second, presently less than fifteen feet away, the Arbalest's 20mm-wide slug did its job and then some. In *quicker* than the blink of an eye, both enemies were sundered at the waist, their legs toppling freely and their torsos rolling across the dirt, trailing spirals of blood and scorched entrails.

"Much obliged!" Tielve shouted, fumbling with his reload.

"Don't mention it! We're almost there!"

Bastian turned to face the direction of the Monolith, and an Eater wailed in his face, ropes of saliva dappling his visor. Behind him, a Crawler that had also miraculously survived the onslaught earlier suddenly leapt onto his back.

He kicked the Eater in its stomach, below the inverted triangle of teeth which doubled its torso as a vertical pair of jaws. It wobbled back, arms flailing. The Arbalest, in this moment, acted more as an obstruction than a weapon, getting in his way. He forced himself to drop it as the Crawler climbed up his back like a man-sized insect. He reached up, grabbing it by its bony shoulders. In one jerking motion, he pulled it over his head and much to his surprise its feet alighted on the ground in front of him.

It snarled aberrantly, an expression that Bastian returned amid a paroxysm of wrath, and pulled its shoulders in opposite directions. The Crawler split down the middle, blood and viscera not just spilling out but erupting violently. He knew that the gore on his visor would be temporary.

His fate, however, could be permanent if he let these fiends get the better of him.

Everything occurring so fast, he hadn't forgotten about Fields and the others firing their weapons and shouting in the vicinity, facing certain death if he didn't react swiftly enough.

The Eater had regained its bearings, albeit in a frenzied state, and lunged at Bastian. He sidestepped, swinging his Exoblade, nearly severing an arm in the process. Instead of leaving it to dangle there by a thread of sinew, the Eater unfazed, Bastian yanked it off and bludgeoned the creature in the face with it.

Whether or not the abomination could discern the lunacy of what just happened, he wasn't sure, but it wailed nonetheless, an animalistic dissonance before charging him again. Its torso-mouth gaped, the teeth lining it seeming to writhe sentiently.

Bastian didn't try to evade it this time.

Growling, he collided with the Eater nose-to-nose, so to speak. A head-butt dizzied the creature before he vigorously gripped the toothed edges of its torso jaws, and with a roar all his own, pried it open. Shrilly, bones cracked, and its chest gaped with a wet sound. Its innards gushed forth, steaming, and in their wake exposed the creature's glistening spine, as it howled a terrible requiem.

With a jabbing hand, Bastian enclosed his fist around the creature's spine, through its agape chest cavity, and manually removed it. The Eater's body crumpled gruesomely around his arm, briefly irrigating the dry earth. This, and the gore painting his armor, began to rapidly dissolve.

Feeling crazily invigorated and even a little relieved, Bastian wasn't given much of a chance to breathe.

A shadow came over him and Fields' strained voice called his name.

The Pyro took a swing at him, and he was able to duck it, barely. Flames whipped over his head, briefly blurring his vision. Any sense of triumph for dodging the attack was quickly recanted when the second arm followed faster than he anticipated. The broad side of the blazing, tapered, sharp-tipped arm struck him in the left bicep, throwing him into Fields. One of his unprotected arms dislocated from the impact, Bastian's Suit a dangerously heavy object itself. Fields cried out in pain and their bodies rolled across the dirt.

A Legionnaire roared as it climbed from the hellhole, which started to seal behind its heels, and immediately charged them. It kept its head low, clawed hands forming fists by its hips.

A high-explosive round from the tank struck the beast headlong, decimating its body from the waist up. The blast sent chunks of flesh, some swallowed in flame and others charred to the bone, flying in every direction.

The concussive shockwave from the explosion briefly disoriented the Pyro.

Bastian got to his feet and glanced down at Fields, who struggled, but was not out of the fight. Despite his broken left arm, he wielded the Duke in his right hand.

"Careful with that," was all Bastian said, feeling a pang of indifference as he turned his back on the wounded Fields to face the Pyro. Behind it, Muñoz tended to an injured Tielve, whose right arm had been torn from the shoulder. Bastian glimpsed the Baron responsible, slinging the severed arm through the air before bellowing at the Bandits, steam pushing through its orifices.

Bastian unclipped the Supe and marched toward the Pyro. It shook itself out of its mild stupor in time to take a swing at Bastian, but it wasn't recovered enough to land the blow. He juked around it easy enough, and fired one barrel up at its head. Yet to his surprise, the Pyro evaded most of the shell's bolo shot. One slug did connect, however, taking with it one of the beast's eyes. The socket discharged a viscous liquid that Bastian couldn't classify as magma, blood, *or* brain matter.

The beast shuddered and growled in pain, in frustration, and then maddeningly took another swing at Bastian. While he was able to dodge it, the flaming arm grazed the Supe's twin barrels and flung it out of his clutches.

Behind the Pyro, the Baron was joined by a Tyrant and together they ganged up on the two Bandits. Muñoz cradled his assault rifle, firing it and screaming simultaneously, tears scarring his cheeks.

The vehicles far behind them didn't have a clear shot at any of the creatures.

Bastian drew the ROT-20 and immediately began pumping shells into the Pyro's chest. Two, four, six. Fast. The cyclical barrels click-clacked as they rotated, spitting fire. The Pyro staggered back several steps, every two loads of buckshot clustering to connect the wounds, until they really started to deepen in its tough hide. The impacts were relentless, the ROT-20 delivering on its behalf.

This was exacerbated for the Pyro due to Bastian's incessant advancement. He continued taking adamant steps forward, his aim and recoil management unflinching.

The Pyro's back bumped into the Tyrant, which then toppled against the Baron as it loomed over Muñoz and Tielve. The domino effect drove the two latter creatures into the ground, the Tyrant flailing on top of the Baron, which vexingly lashed out against its compatriot. Meanwhile, the Pyro had landed on its back and now, like a turtle, struggled to get up.

Bastian saved the last handful of rounds he had for the ROT-20 and clipped it back to his waist. As well as the lone shell for the Supe. He charged the supine beast before it could rise again, and thrusted his Exoblade into the center of its groin, between its legs. Despite its lack of genitalia, the beast reacted with a jolt of pain, or perhaps sheer anger.

*Not entirely emotionless.*

Somewhere between a growl and a roar, Bastian released a throaty war-cry as he let the Suit's drive assist his momentum—

He mounted the beast's stomach, and dragged the Exoblade up its pelvis, keeping the serrated tungsten deep. Ultimately he stepped off its mountainous chest, dragging the Exoblade up its theoretical sternum, and ultimately twisting it beneath its throat. The vivisected Pyro opened up from groin to clavicle, a gruesome fissure that sprayed globules of magma up onto its own black flesh.

Bastian took a couple of big steps back while the beast writhed for a few seconds before death claimed it.

He didn't wait around to watch it dissipate. He could *hear* this process, just the same, as he wielded the Supe and approached the other two beasts. The Baron had risen to a three-point stance by the time he arrived, and thrusted the twin muzzles into its jaws.

Maggie screamed his name, an echo through the catacombs of his memory.

He squeezed the trigger and the horned beast's red skull gaped. The large, gnarled, black horns fell to the side, harmless. Everything in between was rendered crimson detritus, bits of its yellowish brain and cranium littering the desert floor.

Its hefty body fell like a sack of bricks.

The Tyrant roared in its stead, and he switched to his ROT-20, but not before it lunged at him. A dozen or so bullets emptied themselves from Muñoz's assault rifle, battering the Tyrant's legs. It teetered as it neared Bastian. He skewered its right shoulder on his Exoblade, stopping it in his tracks. It uttered a surprisingly shrill sound, and then Bastian stuck the ROT-20 against its throat before squeezing the trigger. The barrels rotated sluggishly against the beast's leathery flesh, spewing two 20-gauge loads of buckshot at point-blank range. The Tyrant's jugular opened onto the shotgun, filling the hot barrels with its gore, while the rest misted the air behind it. The decapitated head bounced across the earth until it rolled to a stop ten feet away.

Tielve cursed in Spanish, but festively.

Muñoz huddled over him.

Bastian looked their way. "Get him back to the others! Fields, too!"

Muñoz didn't object. Nor did the profusely bleeding Tielve. Before hauling him away, Muñoz hurriedly bandaged the wound with a strip of fabric torn from his pantleg.

Bastian turned away and faced the Monolith.

A single creature remained, like the last bullet in a revolver's cylinder. It stood about fifteen feet away, and several paces behind it was that clear space before the Monolith.

"Fiiieeelds!" Bastian hollered, without taking his eyes off the snarling, stagnant Pyro.

Fields adjusted the strap for the assault rifle, turning it into a makeshift sling for his broken left arm. He then wielded the assault rifle, with his right hand, hugging it against his side.

"Get back to the vehicles!" Bastian demanded. Even with his visor up, his voice exited the helmet with grating clarity.

"Bullshit! All or nothing!"

"Dammit, Flynn!" Bastian snapped.

The Pyro shifted its gaze to Fields, who approached its left side. Bastian started marching forward. He glanced over his shoulder. The Arbalest was on the ground, partially crushed, surrounded by a myriad of arcane footprints.

"Motherfuckers," Bastian mumbled.

He stared at the Pyro again, which huffed and puffed. It threw its gaze back and forth, between Fields and Bastian. Surely it could calculate that Fields was no genuine threat. Bastian, however…

The ground began to shake.

Bastian's brow furrowed. He looked down. The tremors were not fleeting. They centered below his feet, and when he looked up, he could actually discern an expression of bewilderment on the Pyro's dark, grotesque face.

Confusion promptly replaced by disappointment.

This gave Bastian an unnerving thought.

*The Monolith must protect itself. It underestimated me. No more horsing around.*

Beneath him, the ground loosened. He glanced over his shoulder to see that Muñoz and Tielve had made it halfway to the three vehicles.

When he looked back at the Pyro, he charged it in the same motion, shouting incoherently. Fields, in a panic, rushed *behind* the beast. Bastian was grateful for this, at least opposed to him trying to engage the Pyro; ideally, he wished Fields would have fled.

He now dodged the befuddled Pyro's first swing, before catching its second arm with his own hands. The heat of the flames, he could barely feel as warmth through his gauntlets. He tightened his double-handed grip on the arm-spear, and then put his shoulders into a twisting motion.

The Pyro roared and tried to pull away, which was a mistake.

Flesh and bone, or cartilage, or whatever composed the volcanic beast's anatomy, tore away at the elbow. Incendiary blood spewed out, scorching the desert earth as it trembled and began to crack beneath their feet. Bastian jerked the severed, flaming arm-spear, taking it for himself—and then returning it to the Pyro, via an upward thrust. The tapered point impaled the beast below the chin, rupturing the top of its skull, between its horns. The flame from its own severed arm now filled its head and burst out its eyes, licking from between its jaws.

As the slain Pyro toppled, the ground opened up below him. The quake, along with the gaping of the earth, staggered even sure-footed Bastian in his Suit. He stumbled back, just as the spike-horned head of another colossus rose from it. He would recognize that hellish skull anywhere, anytime, since their previous encounter.

With the rising of the rocky skull, attached to its lengthy neck, so did Bastian find himself elevated.

He was standing on top of the giant's spiked head! His legs felt wobbly, and he knew it was his own fear causing that, not the Suit's lack of integrity.

He glanced back to see the two Bandits reach the throng of vehicles safely. This offered a lick of relief, positive energy he used to battle that negative.

Down at the Monolith's base, he now stared. He teetered forward, both hands gripping two of the crown-spikes of earthen bone. Rocky crust. Solidified magma. Whatever the composition, it was rigid and fortified. Currently, Bastian used them as handles to stabilize himself, as he studied the front base of the Monolith.

Before the behemoth lifted too high, he established that there was no opening. Neither door nor gate, not even a fissure in its black surface, and the glowing red line down the center appeared impenetrable.

*Appeared.*

"Clear!" Bastian shouted and waved from the top of the beast's head. Fields had been frantically studying the Monolith for an entrance. He now gawked up at Bastian, and obeyed.

Using all his might, and the Suit's, Bastian *pushed* forward, his feet grinding against the rocky scalp of the giant, while his hands formed tight fists around two of the spikes. As close to the bottom as he could, each one about six feet from base to tip, ever so slightly curved.

From clenched jaws to grinding teeth, until his mouth opened and he expelled a thorough scream of exertion, his Suit making a *whirring* sound he hadn't caught before, Bastian pushed.

And then the spikes cracked at their base, discharging magma and chunks of crumbling rock. From there, Bastian's momentum drove him forward.

Over the edge of the giant's skull. It released a thunderous roar and shifted its head to face the direction in which Bastian fell. He bounced off its jaws, and fell an additional sixty feet.

When he landed on the earth, he had to be thankful not just for the Suit's impact compensation but the softening of the desert floor from the behemoth's emergence.

Otherwise he would have to admit an absence of

faith in the Suit's capabilities.

As it were, he stifled such doubts and got to his feet. Hurriedly, he raked in a few deep, ragged breaths, and gawked up at the beast as it continued to rise out of the gaping hellhole.

Suddenly a tank round struck it in the neck, drawing its attention and faltering it the slightest. The blast far above Bastian's head littered the fissure with chunks of rock. He teetered at the edge no longer; he strode forward, picking up speed fast.

On his way, he bundled the two six-foot-long crown-spikes into both arms like a battering ram, the sharp tips facing out.

The distance between him and the base of the Monolith rapidly closed.

Twenty feet.

Fifteen.

Ten.

He screamed and put all his might into a final jousting motion, not slowing down the least.

Paired with his enhanced momentum and the fortified composition of the bundled crown-spikes, part of the Monolith gave way. It was but a small section of where the black surface met with the ground, breaking away and leaving behind a jagged threshold that resembled cleaved onyx. Through it Bastian stumbled, impulsively letting go of the spikes, but he caught his footing before he went too far.

Below the visor, the helmet's mouthpiece sealed without his realization, and the small oxygen reserve filtered into the Suit.

Hands on his knees, he caught his breath. Having punctured the Monolith's surprisingly thin shell, proved to be no easy task. It took a lot out of him, physically, which meant that the Suit's ionized plasma source must have been greatly drained.

Inside now, he nonetheless felt victorious.

The space that he occupied could be described as the Monolith's foyer. Except that, without a proper entrance carved into its exterior, it was evident to Bastian that the structure was not meant to be casually inhabited. It was not so much a building as it was a tool.

Or a conduit.

Above, the interior was inaccessible. The darkness almost looked like an impermeable shadow, but so far as he could tell, it was solid. The daylight outside was largely obstructed by the giant beast, which according to Bastian's ears, was now being attacked by the vehicles.

However, a greater source of light drew his eye. A dull orange glow emanating from the bowels of the Monolith, not far from where he stood.

"You did it!" Fields called out, rightfully stealing his attention.

"Wait, Fields! Don't—"

Fields rushed inside, while just beyond the forced entrance the massive beast laid waste. It even tried stepping on Fields, but he managed to stumble inside. The infernal titan's tapered leg crushed the earth fifteen feet from the edge of the Monolith's surface. It was likely unable to go beyond that, lest it inadvertently damage the structure.

"It's not safe for you in here," Bastian hated to admit. His voice was barely audible through the helmet, with the perforations sealed; he still hadn't noticed, amid all the turmoil. "Who knows what kind of atmosphere this thing is harboring. Or what other anomalies are lurking inside."

Fields started to say something but a grimace afflicted his face. His brow furrowed, as if confused. He started to choke, his skin reddening. He staggered a few steps, like a man slowly turning to stone. He dropped his weapon, the slung arm remaining.

"Fields, I…I don't know what…"

Bastian started to approach Fields, just as unsure what was happening as he was in how to act.

Nonetheless, for starters, he moved to grab him. He had hopes of relocating him outside, but the danger of the behemoth would make that an unwise idea.

Unfortunately, with his apparent struggle to breathe, there were no other options. That risk was nonnegotiable.

He began to move him, Fields having become like a shivering statue, a permanent rictus upon to his beat-red face. And then it happened—Fields burst into flames. The spontaneous combustion covered him head to toe, a deep amber conflagration that consumed him instantly.

Bastian was safe inside the Monolith because of the Suit, but for Fields it was overwhelming. Like being in space without a pressure suit, except this was the exact opposite. The violent fire rendered Flynn Fields in a fit of screaming pain.

"Goddammit!" Bastian exclaimed, spittle spraying the inside of his visor and dribbling down his rubescent face. Even as he moved Fields towards the entrance, the flames raged.

With a guttural bellow, no words, tears streaking Bastian's cheeks simultaneously, he gripped Fields' screaming face and jerked it to the side, breaking his neck. Terminating his suffering. Fields dropped in a heap, the flame continuing to eat away. Bastian cursed under his breath and then did his best to move Fields' body outside, for whatever it was worth. The enormous beast was still there, being engaged by the three distant vehicles, from machinegun volleys to tank rounds, but its presence was impassable.

Occasionally a tank projectile would miss the beast and hit the Monolith. From inside, Bastian could hardly tell—there was no shaking or crumbling, just a loud resonance.

More irate than he had been since T's death, and once again corroded by grief, Bastian hastily moved toward that dull orange glow. Below the solid interior shaft of the towering Monolith, he didn't have much space to navigate. It was all impregnably dark, and while the light from outside seemed like it should have been more illuminating, even with the obstruction of the giant, it wasn't. And the glow he moved toward, which appeared to come from directly below where he had been standing earlier, neither did it provide additional lighting.

The inside of the Monolith was truly pitch black, save for that godforsaken glow.

Bastian reached its center and found himself teetering at the edge of a hole in the earth. There, below the Monolith, the ground had opened up into a vast cavern, at least thirty feet across, and spanning this gap were several narrow bridges of red, pulsing...*flesh*. Like the meat composing a robust Baron or a dozen Crawlers' viscera.

It was only when he took his eyes off the seemingly-bottomless cavern itself, which emanated a featurelessly orange glow, that he noticed the most obvious feature of all. A narrow, vertical pipe of sorts—for lack of a better word—protruding from the abyss above Bastian, and descending into the cavern's orange-tinted depths.

Into the earth itself.

This pipe was about a foot wide and cylindrical, black as obsidian but helically ribbed with a pulsing red light. Like the 'vein' on the outside of the Monolith.

*"Caution,"* his Suit announced to him, speaking for the first time since he last programmed the emergency warnings with his peers. The automated feminine voice startled him, and from thereon it nauseated him for the obvious reasons that it narrated. *"Caution. Excessive heat and air pressurization. Decompression imminent. Seek clean atmosphere."*

Bastian gulped and glanced back at the entrance he had made into the side of the Monolith. Then he gawked down yet again, peering into the pit below him. Into which the pipe vanished, surrounded by bridges of otherworldly flesh.

In the back of Bastian's mind, he now pulled to

the front, his wildest theories. While their importance always seemed to wax and wane in the past, especially in the face of more pressing matters, now they felt most critical.

Believing in them, too, ferried Bastian into a cesspool of rugged emotion. Raw and undivided. His morals were not just brought into question, but the weight of the mortal world.

Bastian recalled Z and Adhira, the Marines from Miramar, the Bandits and the rest of Avery's men, and the Master Sergeant himself.

He was also not without the pressing memories of those who *hadn't* survived up to this moment. From his beloved, irreplaceable Maggie and Eliza to T, Sam and Carla and their company, to Abby and alas, Fields.

*And me.*

Not unlike an anchor without a rope or chain attached, Bastian stepped off the ledge—and dropped. He had nonetheless aimed for one of the fleshy bridges, where it was broadest.

His feet made contact with one. It produced a disgustingly wet sound before it broke under his weight, and he fell through. Onto the next, at its narrowest point, unfortunately, and it snapped, too, like a soaked rope. He grunted and found himself tumbling into the depths, where the red light pulsing around the pipe fused with the orange glow unfathomably deeper...and deeper.

*What's down there? Hell itself?*

*Or just a version of it?*

Bastian's feet would never find stable purchase on one of these infirm bridges of flesh. He accepted this.

So he reached out and seized the pipe itself, which to his awe not only didn't vibrate but didn't shake, either. It showed no sign of motion from his grabbing onto it, not even when he slammed his entire body weight into it. Gripping it like a pole up which he would shimmy, arms and legs wrapped around, his armor scraped loudly until he stopped.

*"Caution. Decompression imminent. Seek—"*

"Aw, shut the hell up," Bastian said, and almost nonchalantly, though not without great force, slammed the brow of his helmet into the pipe. The integrated voice cut off. Desperately, he continued head-butting the pipe, trying to get some kind of reaction from the unknown material. Any sign that the pipe could be broken into.

Nothing, still.

Remaining on it like a koala clinging to a tree, he freed his left hand and armed the Exoblade. He struck it and there was a loud *clang*, but still no other effect. He tried stabbing it but it was too thin and he didn't have the right angle. So he changed arms and revved the chainsaw. When the teeth collided with it, sparks flew and the chainsaw sparked. Then it caught fire and he immediately slammed his gauntlet against the pipe, wrenching the attachment free, at the cost of twisted metal.

Into the depths below him, it tumbled.

He cursed under his breath and looked up.

Irascibly, he began shimmying in that direction, until he reached a particularly thick bridge of flesh. He leaned back onto it, sitting on it but keeping his ankles latched around the pipe, thus not giving the bridge his full weight.

This freed his hands, at least.

He proceeded to saw against the pipe with his Exoblade, starting slow at first. Gradually, he increased the speed and strength of the action, which was additionally enhanced by the Suit's power.

Sparks began to fly, but unlike the chainsaw, the serrated tungsten Exoblade was larger, sturdier, and solely powered by the Suit's entire arm. Which Bastian had complete control over.

He knew that the Suit was on its last threads so to speak. But the ionized plasma cell stored by his nape would not go down without a fight. And it would only go out…with a bang.

Bastian's aforementioned theories now surged through his mind. A storm of coherency, for once.

*The Monolith has bored into the Earth, and is either extracting from its core or* corrupting *it somehow. With whatever* Evil *that is stored in here. From somewhere else. Another planet, or another…*

His thoughts garbled after that.

Scowling, he strained harder. Sawing. Pressing. Exerting with all his might, and the Suit's. He started to feel the heat seep inside, and the air he breathed was no longer clean. His throat started to burn and tighten.

*"Ohh, that's smart,"* Eliza's voice echoed through the abysses of his mind. Recalling from earlier, when he was in the truck with them, driving to CHERI.

*"Daddy's a smart man, sweetie,"* Maggie had said. *"Aren't you, dear?"*

"Sometimes," Bastian recalled out loud.

*"Then be smart, Sebastian,"* she now said, a fresh iteration of her voice. Not a memory. *"Come home to us. Let the world be blessed with your memory. Let us be blessed with more than that."*

"I miss you so much," Bastian sobbed as he sawed against the pipe. Something metallic made a worse grinding sound than before, and a tiny split occurred between tungsten and pipe. One of the glowing red barbs shuddered, as if the light source was interrupted.

*"We love you no matter what,"* Maggie whispered. *"Don't we, sweetheart?"*

Eliza giggled.

Through a distorted expression of sadness and a torrent of tears, Bastian Thurgood smiled.

"I love you so fucking much," he started to laugh.

In the same motion that his shoulders shrugged from the laughter, he reached back and unclasped the plasma cell from its compartment. He wedged it against the lesion in the pipe, and from the perforated compartment, the ionized plasma cell glowed a soft, light blue.

Bastian cranked his left arm back and his sobbing laughter grew louder.

He struck the Exoblade against the contained cell, wedged against the cut pipe, like a hammer to a nail. The explosion was almost blinding. For Sebastian Thurgood, it was *the* White Light.

Azure flame enveloped the pipe, rising up it, and from there it combusted from the inside. A greater eruption of flame that could have been described as black fire with a deep blue heart, consumed the Monolith's interior. The previously impermeable shadow swathing the upper reaches of the structure's innards now melted. Blackness *dripped* and caught fire. Blue flame mixed with the bright red vehemence from the Monolith's intravenous system, and the pipe bored into the earth began to disintegrate from the depths.

This process climbed up.

The fleshy bridges snapped before melting, almost in the same instant. The earth shook something fierce, the sound of thunder tenfold.

Outside the shuddering structure, the abominable titan howled and its motions slowed like molasses. Though wounded by machineguns and cannon slugs, it was not mortally injured, yet still its massive features began to disintegrate. Large embers danced into the air in its place, leaving behind heaps of ash that were caught by a breeze and from there were spread into nothingness.

Inside the Monolith, explosions rocked it from peak to base.

Ultimately it crumbled, imploding, its once impenetrable shell now falling like black glass. The red beam at its center flickered before submitting to darkness.

A darkness that even its Evil could not navigate or survive.

In the wake of this collapse, the Monolith diminished to no such structure, just a dispersion of ash and embers. Like an inactive volcano crushed beneath the foot of God.

The bored cavern that its violation had formed now sealed up, the earth collapsing inwardly, like a wound coagulating.

Several hundred feet away, a group of Marines celebrated and fired their weapons into the air.

The mourning would eventually hit them like an asteroid.

# 20

Around the world, sightings of the unnamed creatures from the Monolithic Phenomenon were reported en masse. But they were not frightened eyewitness accounts. What was first a collective bewilderment quickly transitioned into one of celebration.

A *global* victory, sightings of sinkholes sealing from North America to Asia. From Africa to the Pacific Islands. Everywhere there were people, there once had been this unprecedented terror. It lasted much shorter than it did closer to the Epicenter in Calipatria, and the southwest United States.

But the entire world was affected.

With the destruction of the Monolith, came the annihilation of the enemy en masse. Sightings not just of sinkholes closing up but also creatures suddenly losing the ability to move, and then disintegrating into embers and ash.

From a dozen in the first hour to a hundred in the next. By the fifth hour, their extinction was assumed. By the next day, it was confirmed.

Months later, and search parties were still on the hunt for stragglers. They became more about partying than hunting, though, as no such sign of anomalous survivors could be found.

The reconstruction and rehabilitation of the world, especially the southwest United States, became the focus of governments and civilians around the globe.

Less than three months after the fall of the Monolith, since reduced to a much less remarkable name, the Structure, an oasis began to burgeon at the site.

In the middle of the south Californian desert. Just outside Calipatria. A rich, flourishing oasis. Eight months after the fall of the *Structure*, and geologists were still mystified.

It quickly became a tourist site, although under careful preservation and protective guidelines.

The other focal point of the immediate region was the monument erected in front of the oasis. A ten-foot-tall pentagonal slab of marble, with a plaque of granite affixed to each facing, whereupon names of victims were carved. At the top of the monument, a large stone "ST."

Eduardo Zavala led his niece, whose hand he held, up to the monument. Through a crowd of others moseying around the site, talking quietly and taking pictures, setting candles and flowers and photographs at the base of the monument, they approached it.

Z looked up at the large letters on top of the monument and smirked.

*Sebastian Thurgood*, he mused. *Didn't like being called Sebastian, though. I bet he'd* love *this.*

Z's smile was scarred with grief, but he hid it well. He also liked how the media had noted that the ST could just as well stand for Saint. Z, imagining Bastian as a saint, brought a different glow to his smile.

The true story of Bastian's endeavors had yet been explicitly told, and the details of his equipment were kept quiet to conceal the secrecy of CHERI's projects. However, those he had met along the way, the survivors, like Z, held him close to heart and knew full well of his adamant journey. His virtues. His qualities. These were what formed the story surrounding Bastian's persistent conquest against the enemy hordes and the Structure itself.

His heroism was not an individual accomplishment. The men under Avery's command, and the surviving Marines from Miramar, received especially high accolades and recognition.

Likely against what T would wish, Z kept his face out of the spotlight.

Still, with a personal connection to Adhira following the gathering of survivors, he was invited to a private celebration at CHERI. There, he developed friendships with Avery's Marines, those from Miramar, and even peers of Bastian's.

Z knelt at the base of the monument, beside his niece, who smiled and shielded her eyes against the sunlight. She looked around, in awe of the people gathered, paying their respects and marveling at the nearby oasis.

He gently let his right hand fall down the hundreds of engraved names on this particular facing. Hundreds more on each of the five facings. Victims, both civilian and military alike. Then his fingers stopped at a particular name.

Jacob Taylor.

The engraving rubbed his fingertips like a gentle handshake from the Other Side.

Z smiled weakly while tears streaked his cheeks. He shut his eyes and bowed his head momentarily. His lips moved but no words flowed. It was a silent prayer.

When he stood, Z looked around, taking in the sight of the miraculous little oasis. His expression evolved into a soft grin.

"How is this possible?" his niece asked, tugging on Z's left hand and pointing her soft brown eyes at the oasis. Confusion painted her face. "And in such a dry place?"

"Proof, *sobrina*." He smiled warmly, gently squeezing her hand. "Proof that goodness prevails."